MW00614797

# ASCENDANT

## SONGS OF CHAOS BOOK ONE

## MICHAEL R. MILLER
### IN ASSOCIATION WITH THE BROKEN BINDING

# CONTENTS

*From The Author*     vii

The Elders Song     1
1. The Crag     3
2. A Cold Morning     9
3. Heat in the Kitchens     15
4. Silas Silverstrike     22
5. Fateless     30
6. A Moment of Madness     38
7. The Long Wait     47
8. No Going Back     53
9. The Quiet Before…     58
10. The Storm     69
11. Ash     80
12. A New Flight     87
13. A Poor Funeral     93
14. Blackened and Raw     97
15. Fathers and Friends     108
16. Cores, Bonds and Dragon Songs     114
17. The Weak Link     123
18. Fort Kennet     131
19. The Blight     139
20. To Cut Out Your Heart     148
21. Exacting Tastes     158
22. The Battle for Midbell     163
23. Abilities     177
24. His Last Will     186
25. Cleansing     196
26. Cultivation     204
27. First Flight     210
28. Reliance     217
29. Rough Edges     221
30. Son of Night     232
31. Soul-Cursed     241
32. The Bastard of Athra     248
33. The Weeping Tree     257
34. Wyrm Cloaks     265
35. Pieces of the Puzzle     276

36. The Chasm 284
37. The Storm Lord 290
38. The Emerald Flight 299
39. An Impossible Task 309
40. A Belated Birthday 320
41. The Horse and the Hounds 330
42. Flight 338
43. The Hero of Feorlen 348
44. The City of a Hundred Isles 356
45. The Last of the Agravains 363
46. Chaos 370
47. Ghosts 378
48. The Twinblades 387
49. The Great Show 397
50. An Audience with Sovereign 406
51. Lesson One 412
52. No Such Thing as Parting 419
53. Preparations 423
54. The Battle for Sidastra 438
55. Retreat 449
56. A Final Invitation 461
57. To the Death 470
58. Aftermath 480
59. Duty 488
60. Song of Chaos 499
61. Fork in the Road 507
62. Farewells 515

*Afterword* 519
*Acknowledgments* 521

# FROM THE AUTHOR

Thank you for checking out my books – wherever in the world you may be! Whilst this isn't the place to thank everyone who has helped to make this book possible, here I can thank you, the reader, upfront. Without you, there would be no series.

In the past I have asked my US readers to forgive the use of British English. This time around I ask my UK readers to forgive the use of US English. Unfortunately, Amazon only allows one edition per language to be uploaded.

In saying this, I am Scottish, and so the odd mistake may still be present in the text as I attempted to write in US English. A botched spelling perhaps or a phrase not often used across the pond. Hopefully this does not affect anyone's enjoyment of the book!

Without further ado, I hope you enjoy *Ascendant*!

P.S. To chat with me and like-minded readers, join my Discord server here: https://discord.gg/C7zEJXgFSc

P.P.S. You can grab two FREE epic fantasy novellas from my worlds by signing up to my mailing list here: https://www.michaelrmiller.co.uk/signup

Storm Pe
Reaving River
Northern Tear
Smidgar
SKARL EMPIRE
Skipta
Roaring Fjord
Groef
Claw Point
Upsar
Brekka
FORNHEIM
FJARRHAF
Bitter Bay
Sk
Spe
Vardguard
Sunset Sea
Stroef
Haldask River
Port Bolca
RISALIA
Drakburg
Red
Wismar
Azure Fl
The Crag
WITHERING WOODS
Toll Pass
Red Rush
Sidastra
Midbell
Howling Hills
Range
FEORLEN
Sable Spire
Versand River
Mort Morass
BRENIN
Ruins
Aldu
Laone
The Stretched S
SE
Scalding Sea
JADE
LAKARA

# Songs of
# Chaos

WHITE WILDERNESS

hite
atch

Dead Lands

FALLOW
FRONTIER

rost Fangs

ine

Windshear
Hold

Oak Hall

Brown Wash

COEDHEN

Bright Wash

FAE FOREST

Grim Gorge

HRA

Red Rock

Loch Awe

The Serpentine

Ruins of
Freiz

DISPUTED
LANDS

lcaer
rtress

eat Chasm

MITHRAS

Alamut

Squall
Rock

ING SANDS

Negine
Sahra

AHAR

reen Way

The Caged
Sea

ngkor

# THE ELDERS SONG

The Fire Elder poured forth his rage.
The Frost Elder used her cunning.
The Storm Elder summoned his might.
The Mystic Elder whispered arcane secrets.
The Life Elder bid it grow.
And the world forever changed.

# 1

# THE CRAG

Though he was running late, Holt spared a moment when he heard the dragons roar. Breathing hard, he halted upon the carved servants' stairs and craned his neck to look at the beasts.

The Order Hall of the Crag dominated the skyline. A spire as sharp as the jagged rocks surrounding it. And swirling around the tower, as though a flock of birds, were the dragons themselves. A flight of pleasure in anticipation for the esteemed visitor expected that afternoon from rider high command.

Holt grinned. There was a bounce in his step as he continued his journey down the steps and into the town. His coin-laden pouches jingled merrily as he made his way through the streets. Inside those pouches was more money than he had ever possessed.

Sadly, it was not for his own spending. He had duties to help prepare for the visiting dragon rider. First on his list was to make payments for the food orders. Tonight, there would be a feast, and what a feast it would be. His mouth salivated imagining it.

Whole hogs of sizzling pork and haunches of beef, caramelized brown and dripping with fat. Best of all, there would be a welcoming ceremony for the visitor. All the Order would be out for it, and Holt hoped to glimpse the legendary rider for himself. If he got through all his chores in time, that was. His father had promised as much.

These happy thoughts brought Holt to the butcher's shop door in high spirits, so much so that he almost ran into a customer. Holt stopped himself at the last moment, stumbling sideways.

He fought to steady himself and fell against the shop window. Inside, the butcher was nowhere to be seen, perhaps in the backroom.

"Watch yerself," the customer said, barging past.

"S-sorry," Holt stammered, breathless.

He saw now that his near collision had been with the town's blacksmith – a bald, thickset man with arms of corded muscle.

"Good morning, Mr. Smith," Holt said.

"A good morning?" Mr. Smith blustered. "I think not." He snorted in irritation and threw a glance back inside the butcher's shop. Thinking Mr. Smith must have suffered some wrong, Holt looked into the basket the smith held. Inside lay loosely wrapped cuts of rump beef. The portion seemed terribly small for such a large man.

Mr. Smith noticed his lingering stare. "Not much, is it?" he said. "Mr. Grocer said he might spare some cabbages but made no promises. What would you do with 'em?" he added, thrusting the basket under Holt's nose.

Holt inspected the meager cuts. "They would go further in a stew..." but he trailed off. He doubted the man had time for slow cooking. And if the grocer was running thin on supplies as well, then it would be a poor stew at that.

"Hardly living up to your name, Master *Cook*," the blacksmith remarked, biting on Holt's surname – and designated profession.

Holt backed away, and the coin pouches clinked at his waist.

The blacksmith narrowed his eyes at the money bags and shook his head. "As if it weren't enough that I have to sell my wares to riders at cost, they take a chunk of our taxes and then buy up all the food too."

"It's a special day," Holt protested.

He was looking forward to the occasion, and the last thing he wanted was some anti-rider animosity bringing him down.

"For one man," scoffed the smith.

"One man? Lord Silverstrike is a legend!"

"And will he sort out the current scourge threat singlehandedly?" The blacksmith's face reddened as though kissed by his forge. "The king and his men have been doing a fine job. Sometimes I wonder if we even need riders anymore—"

Seized by the moment, Holt puffed up his chest. "We need the riders and you know it."

The smith's face darkened. Holt's heart hammered. He rarely spoke to someone above his station unless asked a direct question, never mind shout at them. It just wasn't the done thing.

Now he'd really put his foot in it.

To Holt's great relief and confusion, the blacksmith started laughing. It was a cruel, cutting sort of laugh.

"I remember feeling that way when I was your age. The years ahead ought to knock that naivety out of you. What do you know of war and the scourge? You haven't even held one of my swords, let alone know how to swing one, pot boy."

Before any more could be said, there came a loud *thunk* of metal on wood. Holt turned to see the butcher had emerged from his backroom, still gripping the cleaver he'd sunk into his workbench.

"Come here, Holt," the butcher said. "Mr. Smith has much work to attend to, like the rest of us. Don't you, Edgar?"

Half-fuming, Holt backed away through the doorway to the butcher's side. The blacksmith narrowed his eyes further, almost to slits, and then seemed to think better of it. He left, closing the door with unnecessary force.

"Never mind him," said the butcher. "A scourge rising puts everyone on edge."

"He's a fool," Holt said, though he couldn't quite meet Mr. Butcher's eyes.

"He's vital to the kingdom's army and far above your station," the butcher said, though not unkindly. "Now, I won't hear another word on the matter. You'll be here to settle your father's purchases, and best you do before my coffers run dry. The huntsmen and farmers have charged higher for this."

Holt ferreted around in the inner pocket of his jerkin and pulled out a crumpled list written in his father's hasty hand. A pot boy in the kitchens he might be, but at least he had been taught how to read. Understanding recipes would be troublesome otherwise.

"Fifty haunches of beef comes to three gold pieces," Holt began, handing over the coins. His father and the kitchen staff would roast the beef with hot peppers and spices to please the fire dragons.

The butcher took the coins with a smile and counted this off the order by raising one finger.

Holt continued. "A dozen whole pigs comes to two gold and forty silver."

The pork would be baked with a thick crust of herbs for the emerald dragons.

"And two dozen whole sheep is eight gold and forty silver."

"Seems like a waste of good wool," said the butcher, although he happily accepted the bags of money.

"We'll make six different lamb dishes," Holt said. "And have enough of each dish just in case one's more popular on the night."

The butcher bit his lip. "Don't those... *strange* dragons ever just decide which way they like their lamb best?"

"We wish. One day they like it boiled, the next they like it pan-fried in garlic, then they'll demand it roasted. Sometimes they'll change their minds on the same day. Mystic dragons are... weird."

"Fussy is what I'd call 'em," said the butcher. "Now, there's one slight issue I'm afraid. I've come up a bit short on the order of elk. Mr. Hunter was at pains to explain that he couldn't wander too far abroad on account of the scourge. A lot of the game has been scared away. Says he can barely find a rabbit above ground."

"How much short? That meat is meant for Silas Silverstrike himself; he's from the Free City of Coedhen and they have a taste for—"

The butcher waved Holt down. "I've got a whole carcass for you – ribs, loin, steak, organs and stewing cuts, if that will suffice."

"One? We asked for two. That's not a little short – it's half!"

"And as such I'll only need half the payment. As I say, the huntsman—"

"It's fine."

Yet Holt's shoulders tensed. No one, from his father to the Flight

Commander herself, would want to disappoint Silas if they could help it.

"I'm sure old Silverstrike won't mind if his favorite food runs low," said the butcher. "He's a war hero, not some pampered ealdorman's hound."

"I'm sure you're right." Holt paid the butcher for the single elk, then inspected his list again. There was plenty more to be getting on with. "I ought to get going. Father has sent one of the maids to pay Mr. Poulter, but I'm to visit Mr. Monger to get fish for the ice dragons."

The butcher nodded. "Busy day ahead. I've got the lads out back loading the wagons and I'll send them on their way soon. Take care, Master Cook, and give my best to your father for me."

"Thank you, and I will," Holt called back, already with one foot out of the door. He had to hurry if he was to make every purchase and wash every dish before Silas arrived.

Out on the streets, he heard the distant roaring of the dragons again. Holt forced himself to stay focused on the tasks at hand and kept his gaze firmly at street level. Mr. Monger's shop was farther down the lane, closer to the southern gates in the town walls.

On his way, Holt couldn't help but notice how quiet the streets were. Market stalls sat unmanned, the air was void of the general chatter and bustle of morning life. What few folk there were kept their heads down. In places the town seemed inhabited only by the stray cats lying languidly on the warm cobblestones.

Holt's general air of optimism took a knock. He'd been very young the last time the scourge had threatened the kingdom and could barely remember it. If people here were worried – with all the riders of the realm close to hand – how must those in remote villages and hamlets feel?

Soon enough he came in sight of Mr. Monger's shop and the town gates not far beyond. A sudden call came from a soldier upon the gate-house. All the soldiers in the vicinity sprang into action.

Holt drew up level with Mr. Monger's shop but didn't enter. He had become fixated by events at the gate. His senses piqued. A primal understanding that something was terribly wrong washed over him. The soldiers moved in a panic; their voices were high.

A creaking groan heralded the opening of the tall gates, and through the opening hurried in men on horses. Blood streaked their breastplates, and many struggled to dismount. Behind them followed dozens of spearmen walking as though each step brought fresh pain.

Remaining at a safe distance outside were several wagons covered in dirtied white canvas. Their cargo would have remained concealed were it not for a bare arm protruding out of one of them.

Holt gulped. All the warmth seemed to leave his blood. All the warmth seemed to abandon the world. Wings beat heavily upon the air. Knowing what sort of magic this was, Holt looked to the sky. Sure enough, there he saw a rich blue dragon descending to join the soldiers at the southern gate. The ice dragon's aura lessened as Holt's body adjusted to its presence.

The rider got down from his dragon and looked around expectantly. His eyes locked onto Holt, who was still standing dumbstruck outside of the fishmonger's shop. The rider pointed a long finger at him.

"You, kitchen boy. Come here."

# 2

# A COLD MORNING

Still in shock from the bloodied soldiers and the wagons filled with dead, Holt didn't react to the rider calling him over. Despite the morning sun, the chill presence of the ice dragon lingered in the air.

"I said, come here, boy," the rider called.

Holt shook his head as though ridding his ears of water. His wits started to return to him. This was Mirk; Holt had known him his whole life. Well, he'd known him from afar as a servant. Mirk had just given him a command, and so he should follow. He hurried over to Mirk and inclined his head.

"What would you have of me, Honored Rider?"

Mirk looked him over imperiously. He had cold eyes – matching the color of his dragon's scales – and a hardness about his mouth. Like the soldiers nearby, Mirk had gore stains on his armor; red, black and even shades of green.

"You work in the Crag's kitchens," Mirk said.

It wasn't a question so much as an observation. Mirk recognized him but couldn't summon his name. He'd probably never been told it, and of course he'd never asked.

"I have that privilege, Honored Rider. I attend mostly to the washing up."

Mirk glanced at his dragon. "Run and fetch food for Biter. He's ravenous after the skirmish." His tone was one of irritation, as though Holt should have been awaiting their return with a basket of fish. It was a tone Holt was used to hearing. All riders came from noble stock, after all.

Holt's mind spun, formulating a calibrated reply. At length he said, "Forgive me, Honored Rider, but to run back up the hill, wait for Biter's favorite dish to be prepared and then return will take a long time. Would it not be more prudent for you to fly to the tower and thus spare the time it takes for a small boy to make the journey?"

But Mirk was no longer looking at him. The rider's gaze was fixed over Holt's shoulder.

"Ah, you there. Mr. Monger," Mirk called.

Holt turned to find that the fishmonger was standing on the steps of his shop, no doubt trying to get a sense of what all the commotion was about.

"Bring out a basket of the day's catch for Biter, would you?" Mirk instructed. "Raw fish shall serve. Biter can wait until the feast for his favorite meal."

Mr. Monger hesitated. Until recently, dragon riders could requisition virtually anything in the name of fighting the scourge. When King Leofric ascended to the throne a year ago, one of his first declarations was that the riders would now pay at least cost for all their wares. Older riders like Mirk were finding it *hard* to adjust.

Holt could sense the battle waging within Mr. Monger, whether to point this fact out or to let it slide and avoid a difficult situation with a respected rider. Mr. Monger opened his mouth, shut it quickly, opened it, then closed it again.

"Aye," Mr. Monger said at last. "I'll be right out."

"My thanks," Mirk said. He turned his back upon Holt and strode off to speak to a group of soldiers.

Believing himself to be forgotten, Holt slinked back several paces and then made for the fishmonger's shop. He entered to find the poor owner red-faced and blustering.

"A moment please if you will, Master Cook. I have your order but—"

"I know. If you're wondering what to give Biter, he'll like cod the best."

"What? Don't you require that for this evening?"

"We can substitute the cod for hake. The cod is meatier and will probably satisfy the dragon better when raw."

The fishmonger rubbed his sleeve across his sweaty brow. "You're sure the dragon won't notice the difference tonight?"

Holt smiled. "The way my father and his team prepare hake, Biter won't care."

"Very well," Mr. Monger said. With wearied resignation, he moved the cod from the prepared basket and placed it into a fresh one. Likely this choice of fish stung all the more, for it wasn't cheap.

Yet it was nowhere near as expensive as the second elk carcass would have been. Holt had an idea. He withdrew coins and placed them upon the counter.

"Here. This will cover Mirk's request." He counted out the gold owed to the fishmonger for the feast and laid that sum upon the counter as well.

Mr. Monger's eyes widened. "Where did that come from?" he said, pointing to the elk money. "Don't you need it?"

"It was spare. Don't worry, I doubt it will be missed. Father is far too busy getting things ready for tonight. And if he does ask, I'll tell him I insisted. I'm sure he'll understand. He's a working man too."

"Aye. Aye, that he is." The fishmonger licked his lips, then pocketed the money. "Thank ye, Master Cook. Your basket is there, feel free to take it." With that, Mr. Monger hurried outside with the basket of cod.

Feeling he had done some measure of good, Holt collected his basket in high spirits. Outside, soldiers streamed past him in droves. Some carried stretchers between them. Holt shivered, but that might have been due to Biter.

He saw the dragon's snout descend hungrily into the basket Mr. Monger had laid before him. Moments later, the dragon gave a throaty rumble of satisfaction. The fishmonger sagged in relief; Lord Mirk actually smiled.

In that moment, Holt had a momentary daydream; of Mr. Monger crediting Holt with the choice of fish, of Lord Mirk remembering his name this time. Perhaps the rider would be friendlier from then on and remark to his fellow riders upon Holt's quick thinking in getting Biter sustenance after a hard fight.

The daydream evaporated as the fishmonger bobbed a bow and Mirk shooed him away.

Now the situation had passed, Holt felt urgency take over him once more. He was definitely running late now and would have to make up for lost time. At speed he turned and crashed into something hard and metallic. A strong hand shoved at his shoulder, and he collapsed to the cobbles. Blunt pain coursed from his legs and rear; colors flashed across his vision.

"Watch where you're stepping, pot boy."

Laughter followed, and the group of soldiers walked on. Holt didn't recognize any of them. Soldiers rotated around the kingdom, but they would have known his station from the dirty apron he had on. None stopped or offered to help Holt to his feet. He would have resented them were it not for the fact that they were the ones who faced the scourge. Fighting those menacing bugs earned you a lot of favor.

Half-dazed, Holt searched for his basket of fish. It was just out of his reach and had been turned upside down.

"No...."

Thankfully, most of the fish were whole and could be de-scaled and cleaned. Unfortunately, a few fillets of yellow smoked haddock had fallen loose of their wrappings and were now coated in the dirt and dust of the road.

Groaning, Holt bent to pick them up. They would have to be thrown away of course, but he couldn't just leave them here. A soft mewling gave him pause.

From beneath the porch of the baker's shop, a tawny cat missing most of its tail crept out. Across the road, another of the lazy cats had found a surge of energy now a basket of fish was being so openly paraded before them. This cat was a big black brute, yet the timid baker's cat with the injured tail reached him first, sniffing anxiously at the haddock.

The baker's cat had once been rather friendly until a horse had stepped on its tail. After that it had taken to hiding. Holt felt a pang for the poor creature. He dusted the worst of the dirt off the fish, then tore it into more manageable chunks. He also stood sentinel while the small cat ate, guarding it from the large black cat belonging to the apothecary. The black cat eyed him, decidedly unimpressed by his supervision.

Once the baker's cat licked its lips and scurried off, Holt nodded to the black beast and left the remainder for him.

Walking back up the road, basket of fish in hand, the tower of the Crag dominated his view. It was a beacon on the landscape, a sign of the riders and their power. With all the dragons flying around it today, looping and circling in a rhythm of their own, the tower looked even more imposing.

Light reflected from their scales, sparkling spots of every color against the clear sky. Simply seeing them up there was enough to make him feel safe. Yet people like Mr. Smith thought of them as a burden.

Holt did not understand such sentiment. The very scene he'd witnessed today was proof that the riders were needed. Every child knew that. An old song played over in his mind: 'Chaos comes, night shall fall, King or Farmer, it takes all, armies stand but cannot shoulder, only riders can bring order.'

He started his journey back up the hill. As he drew near the servants' stairs, he heard a dragon roar from the town. It was Mirk and Biter, flying back to the Crag. Had Biter just waited a while longer, they could have requested anything they liked from the kitchens. The pressure on Mr. Monger had been needless.

Moments like this did make Holt somewhat sympathetic to Mr. Smith's grievances. The demands of the riders, their indifference to people like him. Yet were servants treated differently anywhere else? Holt imagined not.

A Cook was a cook for life. That was that. And he, the lowly pot scrubber in his father's service, shouldn't dare to dream beyond the life laid before him.

'Don't break the order of things.' Such were the words of most folk. 'Only order can defeat chaos.'

His breathing increased as he took the stairs, feeling tired before the real work of the day had even begun.

'Everyone must fulfill their role.' That's what they said.

But Holt did dream. At night, he didn't just feed those dragons, he sat astride one, riding it into battle against the minions of the scourge. At night, he was a rider. He was strong and noble and a hero. When he slept, no one called him pot boy.

He paused on his climb to catch his breath. His coarse britches itched, and his ragged shoes gave his feet little comfort. For now, he was meant to run errands for his father and wash up the mess. That was his life.

Until tonight, when he would be allowed to sleep. To dream.

# 3

# HEAT IN THE KITCHENS

The heat of the Order Hall kitchens was intense; the chopping, slicing, sizzling and shouting from the staff overwhelming. A meaty smell filled the air as food cooked for fifteen dragons and their riders.

Holt stood armed with a scrubbing brush by a great basin of water. It was so deep that it would have covered his head as a child.

Huffing and puffing, he lunged for his next target, a heavy pewter pot. He brought the brush to bear against the crust of grease, pushing against the grime as though he were a spearman cutting into scourge. Once cleaned, Holt heaved the pot out and dried it, only to have a kitchenhand near enough pounce on it, take it back to his stove and begin throwing in hunks of beef with sun-burnt peppers and yellow spices.

Holt sighed and wiped his brow. A dull ache plagued his back. For each dish he washed, it seemed two more were added. Yet, working at a frantic pace, he managed to get through the seemingly endless pile.

Another kitchenhand brought over a pan still spitting goose fat and placed it atop the stack without so much as a glance at Holt. The ache in his back flared into a throb. Groaning, Holt twisted sharply to pop his spine. Relief washed through him and, with a resigned sigh, he picked up the fat laden pan. He clung to the knowledge that soon he'd be sixteen and the formal apprentice to his father. No more pot washing then.

Just as he was about to douse the pan into the soapy water, his father approached.

"Holt? What are you up to, lad?" His father looked harassed; his black hair was wild and messy, just like Holt's. He wore a stained apron over a plump belly, but his eyes were bright and full of life. A feast always excited Jonah Cook, yet whereas Holt loved the gathering of dragons and magic, his father loved the food more.

"Washing up…"

"Good. Jolly good," said his father, as though Holt washing pots was some novelty. His father could be terribly distracted at times like this. "Listen, I need to start on that elk for Silverstrike, but I think I left the recipe book down in the larder. Can you get it for me?"

Pleased for a chance to break the cycle of cleaning, Holt hurried to comply. He dabbed his wrinkly hands on a dry cloth before heading for the cellar door by the far wall.

A flight of wooden steps led down into the cool dimness beneath the kitchens. Down here, there was only eerie lantern light. Candles flickered in the gloom as though floating in mid-air. The sheer rock walls of the Crag were cold to the touch, and, thanks to the feast, the many bare shelves only added to the cavernous feeling of the place.

It didn't take long for Holt to find the recipe book. He'd had a hunch it would be by the spices and was proven right. There it lay upon a three-legged stool underneath hanging lines of onions, garlic and ginger root.

The book itself was beautiful, bound in buttery smooth red leather with a silk tassel to mark the page. Embossed in gold upon the front was a steaming cooking pot beneath a dragon in flight.

Holt picked it up delicately. It was the most expensive item his father possessed, containing recipes to please dragons with all their peculiar tastes. Not all Cooks in the land held such a treasure tome of knowledge, and it was likely why Holt's father, grandfather and great-grandfather had worked in the Crag kitchens.

One day Holt would be given the book and he would work here too.

*At least I won't be any regular old Cook,* Holt thought proudly as he scampered up the larder stairs to the kitchens.

He found his father inspecting the elk and counting out the other ingredients. He wiped his brow, looking relieved to see Holt.

"I'll take that," Jonah said. He opened the book at the page marked by the silk tassel and ran a finger down the page as his eyes flicked from the paper to the ingredients upon the table.

Holt knew the recipe well enough, having pored over it. The cups of water and wine, the bacon, the mushrooms, cinnamon, ginger, and a small dish of precious saffron seemed to be in order.

"If that is all, father, I'll return to the dishes and make sure I get through them all before Silverstrike arrives."

"Hmm?" his father grunted.

"Remember I asked—"

"What?" Jonah said, distracted. "Oh yes, we'll see, son. We'll see." Before Holt could press the issue, his father snapped the book shut and placed it upon the worktable. "Right, let's get started on this one. It will need hours to simmer."

Holt was taken aback. "You want me to help you?"

"I want you to learn. Start by dicing the steak."

And Holt did so. Happily. Working on Silverstrike's meal was an honor. He carefully diced the meat, ensuring every cut was of equal size to cook evenly. Next, he thinly sliced the rashers of bacon as well as the mushrooms in time for his father to return and inspect his work.

"Good job," his father said approvingly. "Your knife skills have come a long way. Now bring it all here and I'll get started."

Holt searched for butter to line the pot, passed it to his father, then returned for the chopping board heaped with meat. By the time he brought the board to his father's side, the butter was already browning, releasing a nutty smell. He was about to tip the meat into the pot when a sudden silence caused him to pause.

Rarely would the busy kitchens turn still in an instant. Yet for a rider to visit in person instead of their squire was an event rare enough to make everyone stop, put down their work, and stare.

Holt was no exception. For a moment, he forgot about the butter and the meat and focused on the man who had just entered. It was Brode, one of the most experienced riders at the Crag. Brode the Bold, as he'd once been known, although nowadays most called him Brode the Brooding. Holt sympathized with that sentiment.

Brode had a dark, sunken face, as though permanently under shadow. He was old, very old – no one of Holt's station knew his age for sure – yet he appeared to be middle-aged with short gray hair and coarse stubble. Despite his age, he moved with a purpose and strength that spoke of a younger man, which Holt guessed was due to a piece of his dragon's magic still within him. And that was how Brode differed from the others.

He no longer had his dragon.

Perhaps that was why he wore simple clothes – worn boots, trousers, a cream shirt and frayed black jerkin – instead of the full regalia of the Order. Despite his modest appearance, he had the sort of intense, intelligent eyes that could command a room, eyes that now fell upon Holt's father.

"Jonah, a word, if you will."

"Right away, Honored Rider," Jonah said. First, he rounded on Holt and thrust the wooden spoon into his empty hand. "Watch over this. We want a nice sear on all sides. And back to work everyone, come along now!" And then he was off, helplessly attempting to smooth down his apron as he approached Brode.

Holt dumped the meat into the pot and stirred while watching Brode out of the corner of his eye. It was most unusual for a rider to descend into the depths of the kitchens. Even for Brode, it was quite unexpected.

Smelling the bacon crisping, Holt gave the contents of the pot another good shake, then sidled back to the worktop to gather the chopped mushrooms. He risked another glance toward Brode and his father, whose eyes widened.

"Here? Now?!" Jonah exclaimed.

Returning to the pot, Holt threw in the mushrooms but forgot to stir, straining to overhear the conversation.

"Collect yourself, Mr. Cook. I'm certain you can do it. You'll just need to work quicker."

Jonah blustered something incoherent.

Holt felt a pang run through him. This could only mean that their guest of honor had arrived early, but that would mean the kitchens would need to work harder. He, Holt, would not get away to see Silverstrike.

All thought of the elk in the pot abandoned him. Holt turned, staring at his father and Brode in open-mouthed horror. Brode clasped a hand upon his father's shoulder, then turned and began ascending the staircase to the upper levels, to the glory of the Order, to the wonder.

Jonah Cook shook his head and rubbed at his eyes before bringing his hands together in a decisive clap. A kitchenhand banged a ladle to help quieten the staff.

"Everyone, Silas Silverstrike has arrived. Commander Denna wishes the feast to begin earlier. I'm afraid we won't have time for any breaks if we are to oblige her."

A collective groan rose, but the staff returned to their tasks, albeit at a more agitated speed. Jonah was soon surrounded by scullery maids and kitchenhands gesticulating and babbling at him.

Holt didn't react at first. He stood dumbstruck. Few riders of such renown ever visited this outpost at the edge of the world. And now he was to be kept slaving in the hot kitchens, confined to the endless washing up.

"Holt, stir that, for goodness' sake!"

His father's fearful cry jolted Holt from his reverie. He smelled the problem before he saw it. The meat was starting to burn.

Holt tried to salvage it, but the bacon and venison stuck to the pot. Not good. Panicked, he grabbed the cup of water set out for the dish and poured it in. The pot hissed, spat, and billowed steam. The meat and mushrooms moved a little easier now, and Holt finished by adding the two cups of wine.

By this point his father was back on the scene, his face reddened with worry. He seized the spoon from Holt and began to stir the mixture as though for all the world it would undo whatever damage had been done. Then he lifted the pan off the hot charcoals and placed it on the cooler side of the stove.

"Of all the dishes, lad," Jonah said. "Where's your head at?"

Without meaning to, Holt's gaze drifted toward the stairs.

His father sighed. "I know you'll be... disappointed."

Holt mechanically returned to the chopping board and reached out to the bag of mushrooms to begin preparing the ingredients again.

"I'm sorry. I will make everything ready for you, then return to the basin—"

"Holt," his father said, more softly.

"I won't get in your way."

He had just picked up the knife to begin slicing when his father's hand fell on his.

"Accidents happen."

"I shouldn't have—"

"No, but you're tired. We're all tired." The grim bags under Jonah's eyes attested to this.

Holt wiped his hands upon a nearby cloth then rubbed at his own eyes. From work and worry they'd barely slept for days making everything ready, and now it was to all be rushed.

"It just doesn't seem fair," Holt said.

"No, it isn't. But who are we to make demands of the riders? If they want dinner a few hours earlier, then that's that."

Holt turned his attention to the black pot. Perhaps, at least, he could try to make his mark on the occasion.

"With your leave I could prepare the chickens for Silverstrike's dragon—"

Jonah shook his head.

"Why not?" Holt asked.

"You ruined this meal, for a start."

"I know. I'm sorry. I got distracted, but I can stuff and roast five chickens."

Jonah pinched the bridge of his nose. "We've been over this, Holt. Our instructions are to roast the birds simply with plenty of butter and thyme, nothing more—"

"But our book says that storm dragons prefer it best when—"

His father gave a harder sigh. "You're only fifteen."

"I'll be your official apprentice soon."

"Even if you were already, I couldn't let you serve unrequested food, never mind to a dragon of Clesh's caliber."

"But—"

"What do you think will happen exactly? That Silverstrike's dragon will be so impressed that you'll be summoned to the Great Hall and the Flight Commander will initiate you on the spot?"

Holt lowered his head. "Low-born have become riders before..."

He knew of the stories. Of Cedric the Common who died of his wounds after killing a scourge queen and ending that incursion into Brenin. Of Hild the Humble, a beautiful washer woman who had married a rider against everyone's wishes and bonded with her husband's dragon after he fell in battle. It wasn't impossible. It had been done.

"What's our name?" His father's tone was serious now.

"Cook."

"And what will it always be?"

"Cook."

"It's the way things are, Holt. Trying to fight it is like a mouse facing down a dragon."

Still staring at his toes, Holt fought to control a flux of rising emotions. He felt powerless. Frustrated. Afraid. An anxiety boiled up that his father was right, that his life was already charted, and this was all he would be.

Holt lost the battle for control. None of it was his father's fault, but his father was the one standing before him. Holt raised his head, looked his father directly in the eye and said, "I'd rather face that dragon than live as a mouse forever!"

And with that, he ripped off his apron, threw it down and stormed off. A legendary rider was about to arrive, and he wasn't going to miss it. After all, he would have endless time to be stuck down in the kitchens.

# 4

# SILAS SILVERSTRIKE

The front courtyard of the Crag was a crescent moon in shape and large enough to fit a small army. Gnarled, twisted posts stood at intervals on the perimeter, each one holding a dancing ball of magical power. Holt heard they changed in color depending on the mood of the dragon flight. Right now, they pulsed a cheerful yellow.

By the time Holt arrived, the riders and their squires were already martialized to greet their guest. Armor and scales alike glinted under the sun. Each rider also had a great weapon strapped on their backs. Most were swords, too big for ordinary humans to wield, and each blade's shape and color were influenced by its rider's magic. Fire riders' swords appeared to ripple like flames; ice riders' blades came to sharper points; emerald riders had thick broad blades sturdy as stone; the storm riders had jagged blades which spoke of lightning; and the mystics, well, there was no end to the variety there.

Dragons stood on their four legs by their riders, taking up the space that several horse drawn wagons would, making it hard to see beyond them. Not that Holt would have been granted a privileged view at any rate.

He skirted the crowd, behind rows of regular troops, stablehands and other servants of higher rank than himself. But Holt was younger and nimbler than most, and he knew a good spot. He'd taken it up before years ago when Princess Talia had arrived, and a similar grand welcome had been thrown.

Carved statues of ancient riders flanked the main gates of the Order Hall. Their dragons were carved in stone too, although these were much smaller than their real-life counterparts. Holt scrambled up the horned back of one now, finding a perch in the crook of its wing. It wasn't comfortable and he was far from the front, but he had an unhindered view.

Despite the times, people still risked lining the streets far below as Silverstrike passed by. It was good of him to let them see him. They would feel safer for it.

Holt couldn't make Silverstrike out at this distance, although his dragon was clearly visible, large and granite-gray like a fierce storm cloud. With any luck, Silas would demonstrate his fabled powers for them.

Up in the courtyard, none of the riders showed outward signs of excitement. There was a disciplined confidence to them which, while reassuring, always gave them a sense of being different. Of being more than merely human.

Among those closest to the front was the rider Mirk and his dragon Biter, but Holt's attention was drawn to the figure at the head of the Order. Flight Commander Denna was an exceptionally tall woman in gleaming silver plate armor, which was said to be heavier than any other rider could handle. Her weapon was different too, being a huge white war hammer with green runes. He'd heard her mystic dragon granted her increased strength. On top of that, she was of the rank of Champion and might advance to the rank of Lord soon, if rumors around the Crag were to be believed. Surprisingly, Denna's dragon, the matriarch of the Crag, was nowhere to be seen. That was strange, but Holt put it out of his mind.

Beside Denna was a much younger girl who could not have been more physically different from Denna if she'd tried. Princess Talia had a slender figure and sleek hair that fell past her shoulders. That hair was of an extraordinary color, like gold reflecting firelight. Even as

Holt watched her, Talia cast a sideways glance at the Flight Commander and straightened her back.

Talia's dragon, who was called Pyra, was also present. Holt had prepared enough spiced beef for the princess' dragon to know her type was fire, even if her purple scales were an unusual coloring. Pyra was still young, just five years old, and while large enough to ride, she was smaller than the older dragons at the Crag. She stood beside Talia with a proud, stiff neck, fixated upon their approaching guest.

As Silas drew closer, the dragons of the Crag roared in greeting. Some swooped down overhead, while others bowed their long necks out of respect. And with each step, Holt felt his heart beat faster.

He was here. Really here.

Every story Holt had heard growing up about Silas had to be true because he was real.

Silas Silverstrike took his last step and emerged into the courtyard. From this distance, it was hard to make out his finer features, although his chalk-white hair was thick and wild, and lifted as though permanently blown back by the wind. His skin had darkened from decades of flying above the clouds, and he held himself unlike anyone Holt had seen, including Commander Denna. Best of all, Holt swore he could see crackles of blue static crawl around Silas' hands as though the magic he wielded might burst forth at any moment.

The orbs of light around the courtyard changed in his presence and became miniature thunderstorms trapped within the gnarled posts.

Flight Commander Denna stepped forward to meet him. She raised a clenched fist and all the dragons fell silent. Denna greeted Silas with a firm clasp of his shoulder, which he returned, and they spoke a few private words.

Holt strained his neck in a futile attempt to hear them. He was so far back that even when Commander Denna addressed the crowd, he could barely hear what she was saying. So, it came as a great surprise, and delight, when Silverstrike drew his sword – a gray, jagged blade with lines of sparking blue power – and held it skyward.

At once, a dark cloud formed in an otherwise cloudless sky, then came a flash of forked lightning that struck Silas' sword. A boom followed, echoing around every nook and cranny of the rocky Crag.

And such was his power, Silas Silverstrike stood unharmed. If anything, he looked radiant, younger than his many years, and in his free hand, a blue-silver power gathered. When the lightning bolt ceased, Silas unleashed this new power high overhead. and these strands formed the detailed outline of a dragon in flight, its eyes alive from crackling silver energy.

The riders cheered. Dragons bellowed their approval. Servants stood in awe, their mouths agape and clapping at this masterful display of magic.

Holt clapped too, so hard he almost fell from his vantage point. That was when he noticed who was standing below him.

"Ruddy show off," Brode said. He looked up, perhaps sensing someone was about to fall on top of him. "I think that might be the first smile I've seen on your face in months, boy."

His voice was gruff but flat, neutral, as if he came from nowhere. Holt had been told that accent belonged to those who grew up near the Free City of Athra, where tongues from all the world came together and melded into one.

Embarrassed, Holt found his balance and sat back up. "Sorry, Honored Rider."

"What are you sorry for? For smiling?"

Holt said nothing. His outbursts had caused enough trouble for one day.

Brode smirked. "You're alive, aren't you? Smiling more often might do you some good."

Holt stared pointedly ahead. But Brode carried on.

"You can spar back, y'know? You should tell me that 'smiling more' is rich coming from a crinkled old grump like me."

Holt looked down this time. He gulped. "Is that an order, Honored Rider?"

"Hah," Brode barked. "That's a little better. And you can drop the 'honored' when speaking with me."

He truly wasn't like the others, not least because he wasn't wearing his sword. Conversing with a rider beyond receiving orders wasn't common. In fact, it was so uncommon that Holt found himself wary. Was this some form of a trick or trap?

"Then what shall I call you?"

"Call me my name."

"Brode the Brooding?"

The old man sniggered again. "You've got some spirit in you. Deep down." He seemed to bite on the words. "That might be unfair of me. My brothers and sisters are hardly an encouraging lot."

Holt thought on Lord Mirk's demands and scornful tone that morning. Then again, the soldiers had arguably behaved even worse. In his time, Holt had found that if the person at the top kicked down, then folk continued kicking down until those at the bottom were flattened.

"We each have our role," Holt said.

"Do we?" Brode said, although his tone did not invite an answer.

Holt ignored him and turned his attention back to the welcoming of Silverstrike, who was still engrossed in conversation with Commander Denna.

A sudden restlessness came over Holt then. The very air seemed to grow taut with a tense energy. It was such an unsettling feeling that he let out a small gasp and was thankful to hear many of the servants reacting in a similar way.

"It's Clesh," Brode said.

"Silverstrike's dragon is doing this?"

"Not on purpose… I would hope. With a core as powerful as Clesh's, some of that energy is bound to emanate."

Holt didn't fully grasp Brode's meaning – the riders often talked of cores, abilities and motes, but it made little sense to him. Whatever the case, Clesh's power was impressive. Holt had of course felt the effects of a dragon's magic before – Biter had chilled the air around him that very morning – but this was on another level.

"You'll adjust in a bit," Brode assured him. He flashed a wry smile. "But, until then—" He reached up and touched Holt's leg. A jolt surged from Brode's fingertip, so powerful there was a visible flash.

"Ouch," Holt hissed. He rubbed at the spot, though there was no harm done. "He must be as powerful as the legends say."

"The stories are right on that account at least," Brode said.

"Not even Commander Denna and the Matriarch have this effect."

"Silas is of the rank of Lord. A Storm Lord. As strong as Denna is, she is still only the rank of Champion."

"Perhaps one day Commander Denna will grow that powerful as well."

Brode gave him a curious look, then shrugged.

The riders at the front of the welcoming party split ranks then. In the new space provided, Silas stepped forth and produced a glass orb the size of an apple.

"The liberation of Athra!" he declared. His accent contained the lilt and music of the people from the Fae Forest. As all eyes turned toward Silas, the Storm Lord threw the orb to the ground. Breaking upon impact, a great deal of purple mist billowed out from it – far more than such a small object should have been able to contain. The mist collected into ghostly figures, then solidified into what was unmistakably Silas and Clesh fighting against an enormous insect. The bug had too many eyes, pincers the length of pikes, and screeched so terribly that Holt winced.

He knew what this scene must be. Silas was famed for ending the greatest scourge incursion of the last century, and that final battle had taken place at the distant eastern city of Athra. Through some magic, Silas was showing them this moment.

Silas and Clesh of course prevailed, with Silas plunging his sword down through the creature's head.

Everyone applauded again and Silas beamed, his arms spread as though to take hold of their adoration. Holt enthusiastically joined in.

"If you knew how much money he just smashed on the ground you wouldn't be cheering," Brode said.

Holt ignored him this time. If Brode wished to spread his bad mood, he could do it elsewhere.

Brode carried on regardless. "Ghost orbs cost more than your father makes in a year."

Holt choked. "What?"

"You heard," Brode said, dropping his voice as the general applause died down. "And he gets a discount, given they produce them at Falcaer."

Holt wondered why Brode was telling him this. Riders were noble, nobles were rich. He'd seen the riders here carrying orbs like that around at times but had no idea they were made at Falcaer Fortress, where the Order based its headquarters. Holt cherished that nugget of information, as he did any about the riders.

The welcoming ceremony proceeded. Riders representing each school of magic came forth one by one to present Silas with gifts. And Brode kept speaking to him.

"Knowing that... do you still admire them?"

"Of course!"

"You want to be one of them, don't you?"

"I... I..."

"It's not a crime to voice a desire."

Holt bit his lip and tightened his grip on the stone wing of the dragon. No, it wasn't a crime to say such things aloud. But it was futile. At last, he found his voice.

"Who *wouldn't* want to be a rider?"

"Wise people."

"But no one can talk down to them. Everyone respects them. They have dragons who can fly – you can go anywhere if you're a rider, do anything."

"That's a very rosy picture you're painting."

"But it's true. You're free!"

Brode raised an eyebrow. "And you're not?"

"Of course I'm not. I'll never be—"

A swirl of red caught Holt's eye. His gaze moved from Brode and fell upon Princess Talia, who was shaking Silas Silverstrike's hand and conversing with him. She'd just swished her hair back off her face and it had caught in the wind, flowing in a long trail behind her. Holt quite forgot what he had been saying.

Brode coughed loudly. "Do you think she's free?"

Holt shook his head then faced the old man again. "She's a princess *and* a rider. She's above everyone. Who can tell her what to do?"

Brode mused on this for a moment. "Only her conscience can tell her what to do in the end. Yet her burden is great. Don't be so quick to envy."

Holt's mood darkened. He'd only wanted to glimpse Silverstrike in person, perhaps see some magic and forget his dreary life for a while. Brode was goading him.

"If you have nothing kind to say to me, then please leave me alone."

"Now, now, don't get upset," Brode said. "I actually came here to look for you."

"For me?" Holt said, surprised.

"For you. I have a task that needs doing, and all the other kitchen staff are too busy. Apparently, they are one man down. You wouldn't know why, would you?"

Holt's cheeks flushed.

Brode chuckled to himself and carried on. "The Matriarch is conducting a choosing of the Order's eggs today. Bad timing, but these things don't wait – even for Storm Lords from Falcaer Fortress. Still, the Matriarch would be remiss to not greet her guests, and so she is forced to push through more than she'd normally do in one session. She'll need food brought to her."

"And does she know what she would like today?"

"She's a mystic dragon, so—"

"She doesn't know… we're used to it."

"Bring a good selection and meet me down in the hatchery," Brode said. "And bring a smile with you."

# 5

# FATELESS

It had been late in the afternoon when Holt started trialing food for the Matriarch. After many attempts to please her, legs of lamb stuffed with anchovies and olives was the latest. Holt carried the meal down to the hatchery inside a cumbersome silver dish to keep it warm.

Huffing and puffing from the effort, Holt rounded the bend of the stairwell, and Brode threw out an arm to stay him. The old rider placed a finger against his lips and pointed to the Matriarch in the center of the chamber.

The hatchery was a cavernous space under the Crag, cut into the cliff itself, as though it were the great nest of some giant stone bird. The north wall remained open to the world, allowing dragons to fly in and out as they pleased. Outside, the sun was setting, the sky a red-purple bruise over a darkening ocean. Piles of straw and feathers sat stacked in the bays where the dragons would sometimes rest, and of course it was where the eggs were laid, although Holt knew little of that matter.

The Matriarch of the Crag's dragon flight – and Commander Denna's dragon – inspected the latest batch. Ysera was her name, and her scales were a pale green flecked with white. While green would normally indicate an emerald type, Ysera was quite different. In all things, mystic dragons didn't follow the usual rules. They barely followed any rules at all.

Unlike the colorful dragons, their eggs were all the same stony gray. Ysera stared at one of the eggs with intense concentration, her four legs braced as though expecting to take flight at any moment. After a time, Ysera lowered her neck and pressed her nose carefully against the egg under scrutiny. Then, with a growl of pleasure, Ysera raised her head and moved on to the next.

"That's a good sign," Brode said quietly.

"What would be a bad sign?" Holt asked.

He found out on the very next egg.

Ysera lowered herself toward the next one slowly, her eyes narrowed. She gently touched the shell with her snout then immediately recoiled, snorting great plumes of green-tinged smoke, and backed away from the egg as though it had burned her.

"What's the matter?" Holt asked.

"Could be any number of things. I doubt she knows for sure. All she knows is that egg is malformed in some way."

"Can it be helped?"

"The egg will be thrown into the sea. Never to hatch."

"What?" Holt exclaimed.

Ysera turned her narrowed eyes upon him. A darkness seemed to touch his very heart. His spirit sapped, as did his strength, and his grip upon the dish of lamb weakened. It slipped from his now too weak fingers. Brode dove for the tray. He caught it, but the lid fell off and clanged against the stone floor.

"Was that necessary?" Brode directed at Ysera. Her glare turned upon Brode, but he withstood the effect far better than Holt had.

"More effects of a dragon's magic?" Holt asked. His fingers felt numb and he tried flexing them, but to little avail.

"An angry flare in her song," Brode said. "Normal humans have no mental guards against such things."

"Err—" Holt began stupidly. He felt like he shouldn't ask any more questions, like he may have already pushed his luck by interrupting the ceremony. Clearly there was a lot about dragons he didn't know.

Ysera still glared at Brode.

"And now she's warning me against revealing rider knowledge to a lesser being." Brode faced the Matriarch down. "Give the boy a break. Curiosity isn't a sin, and what's he going to do with a few scraps? Overthrow the whole Order?"

Ysera growled low in her throat and bared a few teeth. She sniffed, and then her growling ceased as she sniffed again. With the lid of the silver dish removed, the enticing aroma of lamb had been unleashed. She snorted another cloud of green smoke, then settled down. Holt's darkened mood lifted at once.

Brode smirked. "She says she'll forgive our insolence so long as the lamb is satisfactory." He placed the lid back on, then handed the tray to Holt. "No pressure, pot boy."

Holt took the tray, gulped, then faced down the mighty dragon. What had he boldly told his father earlier? That he'd rather face down the dragon than live as a mouse forever. Now the moment was here, he wasn't so sure.

He took a few steps forward. His hands shook. The tray rattled.

"She says, hurry up."

"Yes, Lady Ysera," Holt said. Wary of how her gaze had affected him before, he averted his eyes, staring at the talons on her right foot instead. Despite his nerves, Holt couldn't help but feel excited at approaching the Matriarch herself. He wished she would speak to him directly rather than through Brode. But dragons never spoke to lesser beings, meaning anyone who wasn't a rider.

At a respectful ten feet from Ysera, he stopped, inclined his head, set the tray down, removed the lid, stepped back another five feet, and stood with his hands clasped behind his back.

*Please like this one,* Holt thought desperately. His legs were beginning to ache from running up and down the stairwells while laden with meat.

Mercifully, Ysera descended upon the lamb and devoured it, bones and all. She licked her lips with her forked tongue. Another strange sensation swept over Holt, except this time it was pleasant. He felt bolstered, emboldened, as though he might leap into the air and take flight himself. His heart raced against his ribs.

"That's the usual effect of her magic," Brode called.

Holt twisted around and gave him a worried look. Ysera might be upset that Brode was revealing more information to him.

Brode shrugged. "Commander Denna gains great strength from her bond with Ysera. That's hardly a secret. You've had a taste of it now."

Holt blinked, barely believing his luck. Few would ever have such a privilege, and it only made him yearn more for the life of a rider. To feel like this all the time.

Then he remembered the dragon egg that had caused Ysera to reel in anger and disgust. And he recalled the terrible fate it was to have. If you could call it a fate, for it would have none.

The egg itself was nearby. While it was a lighter shade than the others, the more telling sign was the jagged white scar across its shell.

Ysera snorted and clawed at the floor with a single talon.

Holt blinked and looked up at her. She tilted her head at the empty tray. Holt understood what he was to do. He picked up the silver dish but couldn't take his gaze from the egg with the white scar.

"Move, Holt," Brode called.

Ysera turned sharply, and her tail swung in an arc behind her. Holt ducked and felt the tail pass in a whoosh of air. A tremor ran through the hatchery floor as she took off. By the time Holt took his hands off his head and looked up, she was gone. The silver lid still rang from where he had dropped it. Again.

A firm hand hauled Holt to his feet.

"Are you hurt?" Brode asked.

"I'm fine. I think. What happened?"

"She said Denna was calling. It seems Silverstrike wants a *proper welcome*." If Holt wasn't mistaken, there was a bitter tone in the way Brode talked about Silas Silverstrike.

Brode clapped him on the shoulder. "Best get back to the kitchens. I imagine there's plenty of work still to do."

"Yes," Holt said. He bent to pick up the empty silver tray, then hesitated. Brode might tell him. He could only ask.

"Something wrong, boy?"

"I just… wondered, Lord Rid—"

"Brode."

"Lord Brode," Holt went on. It still felt too strange to drop the formality completely. "What will... what will happen to that egg?"

Brode's gaze moved to the egg with the white scar. "I will move it over there with all the rejects." He indicated a pile to the right-hand side of the hatchery where a small mound of eggs already sat. Judged and discarded. There were so many.

"You said it would be thrown into the sea."

"I did. So, it seems you know what will happen."

"Can nothing be done?" It seemed terribly cruel to Holt. "Mr. Fletcher's dog lost a leg and folk said to put it down, but he went to the physicians and they helped. The dog has a limp now, but otherwise it's fine."

Holt knew he was rambling, but this didn't sit easily with him. He'd never heard of the riders doing this before. Could dragons even be sick?

He blundered on. "And Mrs. Baker's cat did stop hunting after he lost his tail but he's still friendly and finds courage to come out if you just show him a bit of kindness."

Brode gave him a pitiful look. "Do you think dragons can be compared to dogs and cats?"

"Well, no, but—"

"You must have known," Brode said, picking up the egg and returning to Holt's side, "living here your whole life. What did you think a choosing ceremony was?"

"I... I don't know," Holt said. "I suppose I assumed it was where the Matriarch decided which dragons stayed in the Order and which ones were sent back to the Wild Flights."

Brode raised an eyebrow. "Amazing how well we keep these things to ourselves. Even from those living alongside us."

Holt looked at the egg, feeling pity rise in him.

"Put it out of your mind," said Brode. "This is the way things are."

"That's all anyone ever says."

"And most people just get on with it."

"Doesn't it seem wrong to you?"

"It's not my place to say."

"You're a rider. If you won't, then who will?"

"I'm half a rider, boy." A sternness entered Brode's voice. "And that's why I get to carry out delightful tasks such as these. Do you think I like sending the eggs down into those frigid waters?"

Holt shook his head.

"And do you see me moaning about it?"

He shook his head again.

"Dragons don't accept any weakness in their race," Brode said. "They do the same thing out in the wild, so far as we know. It's their choice. Not ours."

Holt nodded, but then something else rose inside him. He bit his lip, trying to resist, but he couldn't hold it back.

"It just feels wrong."

Brode closed the gap between them.

"You say you want so badly to be a rider, but it's not all glory and valor like the minstrels sing. I've tried to warn you. It's a responsibility you don't understand. Nor do you want it." His eyes flicked from the egg to Holt. A pained crease broke across his face as though he were wrestling with some inner demon, then he handed the egg to Holt. "You destroy it."

"Me?"

"You." Brode thrust the egg into Holt's hands. "It will be hard. Perhaps the hardest thing you ever do. But being a rider is hard. Cruel at times. There are times when you must end life to save it, when you must follow your oath even if it means letting your loved ones die."

Holt grew worried. Was Brode feeling all right?

"Go on then," Brode said. "Just to the cliff edge right there. Drop it off."

"You're not serious."

"I am extremely serious. You're of an age where rebellion and dreaming can often lead one astray. Life is hard, lad. Whether you are a rider or a pot boy. But if you think you've got what it takes to be one of us, do it."

Holt stood dumbstruck. He clutched the egg close to his chest, as though for all the world that would cure its ailments. Despite being smaller than the healthy eggs, it was still the size of a watermelon.

Gulping, feeling he ought to show some courage to Brode, he

edged to the opening. Night had fallen, and the world outside mirrored his mood. As he drew near to the precipice, the full force of the sea wind greeted him, forcing him to bow his head against it. Even the crashing waves sounded dim and distant up here. The black depths of the water below made it all the more brutal.

He stopped just shy of the precipice. That was a mistake. He ought to have just carried on and thrown his burden without a second thought. Stopping made him think.

*Just a few steps. Just a few steps.*

He took another two. He stopped again.

A chill pricked his skin, the wind now as biting as it was loud.

*Just do it,* he tried to tell himself.

A bright moon and stars twinkled above. And then Holt made another mistake. He looked down at the egg. Under the faint moonlight, the white scar on the egg appeared brighter, shining in a faint silver glow.

*It's probably just a reflection off the stone,* Holt reckoned. *It's only stone. Cold, rough stone.*

A heat filled his hands, and the sudden onset of it nearly made him drop the egg there and then. But he held on, amazed, not sure whether to believe it was real or his imagination. In the cold night it was welcome, but it went as quickly as it had come, and the stone returned to its cool state.

What did that mean? He knew nothing of dragon eggs. Did the creature know he was here? Did it know what he was about to do?

Holt blinked and rallied his wits. Even if he chickened out and returned without doing the deed, Ysera would demand its destruction either way. Holt would not soon forget how intense her distaste had been in that moment when her magic had touched him.

Holt took the final step. He held the egg out before him, high over its soon to be watery grave.

A battle raged within him. Did he want to be a rider so badly that he'd do anything, take any slim chance to join them? Yet, to defy Brode and Yser, to defy the whole Order, would get him no closer to his dream.

*I can't do this,* Holt thought miserably.

He stepped back from the precipice and drew the egg in tight to his body. Heat flared again from it, as though the fledging creature could sense what he had done and gave him thanks.

*Well, that's that. I failed Brode. I'll never be a rider.*

Clearly, he didn't have the guts for it.

Holt traipsed back to the center of the hatchery.

Brode picked at his teeth. His blank face was unreadable.

"I thought as much, Holt. Give it here. I'll do it."

Holt fought to keep his hands steady as he handed the egg over. Brode took the egg and tucked it under one arm. Then he ruffled Holt's hair and gave him a playful shove.

"It's not a life for everyone, understand?"

Holt was just about to say he did understand when a change came over Brode. The old rider winced. His gaze turned milky and his eyelids fluttered. Brode emerged from this seizure a moment later with a groan.

"It seems my old pal Silverstrike demands I join him for a *proper reunion.*" Brode pinched the bridge of his nose to ward against some lingering pain and then rallied. "Right, we're done here, pot boy."

He placed the egg back on the rejected pile, presumably to return and complete the grim task later. Next, he grabbed Holt by the scruff of the neck and dragged him from the hatchery.

# 6

# A MOMENT OF MADNESS

Brode only released Holt once they were clear of the hatchery. The old rider barked an order and the guard locked the door.

Holt rubbed at his sore neck and trudged back to the kitchens. He thought he could still feel the heat from the dragon egg in his hands. What a horrible business.

*Everyone has their role,* he thought. *Only order can defeat chaos...*

Not even the dragons could escape it. If you weren't fit to fight the scourge, you weren't fit at all.

With his head still reeling, he mechanically made his way over to his basin. Someone was already there, using his brush and washing his dishes. He blinked. Then his mind refocused, and he heard someone calling him.

"Holt?" his father said. "Where have you been all this time?"

"Helping Lord Brode."

"I know that," his father said, exasperated. Poor Jonah Cook looked exhausted. If there was any lingering frustration over their argument earlier, neither had the energy to revisit it. "But it's past nightfall already. And you're so pale – are you feeling well?"

"I'm a little lightheaded—"

"And, oh blazes, Holt, where's the serving dish you took?"

"What?"

His mind caught up. The silver serving dish – the expensive silver serving dish. He'd left it in the hatchery.

"I left it. Sorry, father, I—"

"Well, run and fetch it."

"But the washing up—"

"Somebody else will handle it. Someone else has picked up after you all afternoon."

Holt heard it clearly, that edge of annoyance and disappointment in his father's voice.

"I'll go then." And he left the kitchens.

He made his way back to the hatchery. It meant climbing the kitchen stairs, making his way through the servants' courtyard, entering the Crag's tower through a servant's door, then descending again, deep into the heart of the rock. With everyone so preoccupied with the feast and Silverstrike, Holt felt like he had the run of the place. There was, of course, still the same guard at the hatchery door.

The guard's eyes lingered upon Holt's apron.

"You lost? Feast is upstairs."

Servants really were invisible to them. He'd only just come out of the hatchery, and the guard had even seen him do it.

"I left something inside. A silver serving dish."

"That so? I'm not to let anyone in without Lord Brode's permission."

"I was just here. He won't mind."

"Go and get him then."

Holt did not wish to do this. Aside from the hassle, he didn't feel like being in the presence of that sour old berk if he could help it. Brode the Brooding indeed.

"No one will know," Holt said. "I'll be quick. In and out."

The guard was unmoved.

"I don't think Lord Brode will thank you for making him leave the feast to come all the way back down here," Holt added, thinking on his feet. "You know he's a close friend of Silas Silverstrike, don't you?"

Brode's icy tone had suggested the friendship was no longer

cordial; indeed, Brode may well like an excuse to leave the feast, but Holt bet the guard wouldn't know that.

"He is?"

"Oh yes," Holt said. "Lord Brode wouldn't stop talking about his friend Silverstrike and how they fought side by side at the battle of – oh what was it – the battle that ended the last great incursion?"

"The Battle of Athra."

"That's the one. I forget these things so easily," Holt lied. "We servants often do."

The guard inclined his head sagely. "Fear not, young master. There will always be a role for those with slower minds."

"Indeed," Holt said, straining not to bite upon the word. "But you'll agree that to pull Lord Brode away at this hour would be quite—"

"Yes, most unsatisfactory for their lordships." The guard tensed at the thought of it. "Very well, I'll let you in, but make sure you're quick about it."

He opened the door. Holt bowed his head and thanked him profusely before entering.

The night air and crashing anger of the sea greeted him. The serving tray was easy to spot, for it glinted under the cold starlight. He ran over and bent to pick it up. That was when he saw it.

The doomed dragon egg.

It was on the edge of the condemned pile, just where Brode had placed it before leaving. Even compared to the other eggs on this pile, it stood out, its white scar thick and prominent.

And perhaps it was his frustration at playing dumb to the guard outside, Brode's insistence that he wouldn't be a rider, or the strange warmth he'd felt in his hands while holding the egg, but Holt was struck with a mad idea.

He would save it.

Yes, he admired the riders; he thanked them daily for keeping them safe from the horrors of the scourge. Only order defeats chaos, as it had done for hundreds of years. But he didn't see why *this* Order had to be cruel.

He hadn't had the guts to throw the egg off the cliff, but he would save it.

In that mad moment, Holt threw a glance over his shoulder to check on the guard. He wasn't paying attention, so Holt lunged for the egg, picked it up, placed it inside the silver serving dish, and covered it with the lid.

He let out a breath he wasn't aware he'd been holding, and his heart thundered.

"You found it yet?" the guard called from the doorway.

"Y-yes," Holt called back.

Fighting to keep his hands from shaking, Holt stood, grunted from the weight of the egg, then made his way out of the hatchery. The guard closed the door without a second look.

"Now, you weren't here, understand?" the guard said.

"Perfectly."

And with that, Holt had stolen a dragon egg.

Although what he would do now was the more pertinent question. He had no answer. In the meantime, he walked in something of a trance, back through the Order Hall and toward the servants' court-yard as though heading for the kitchens. Staff were running hither and thither as they attended to the riders up in the tower.

Now the deed was done, he couldn't very well retrace his steps and put the egg back. That only left one option. Hide the egg. But where?

Thankfully, the solution to this dilemma came in haste.

First, he continued to the kitchens but made for the back entrance, the one riders and squires would never take. In this dark alcove, hidden away under a canopy of rock, was where waste from the kitchens collected. Barrels and crates full to bursting with fish heads, animal bones, sinew, eggshells, vegetable stalks and cores. Tonight's refuse was still fresh, so it did not yet smell foul, although Holt was well used to such odors.

As it was, part of his duties included taking crates of waste down to the Muckers' hut. If this was going to work, he'd have to move quickly. Empty crates here and there signaled that kitchenhands were already moving it.

Holt searched for a crate of the right size that was not yet full.

Finding one, he placed the silver tray inside it. It struck him that the silver lid would draw attention to anyone he might meet on the journey.

*Maybe I should take the egg out first?*

Before he could conclude on the problem, the yard door opened, and a kitchenhand came out with a bucket. Holt sprang up in alarm, leaping to block the silver dish from view.

"Evening," Holt said much too loudly.

The girl started and put a hand to her chest. "Oh, Master Cook, you gave me the frights – jumping out the shadows like that." She tutted. "Your da is lookin' for you, y'know."

"I must have missed him," said Holt. "Thought I'd get started on taking some of this down. I'll take that." He gestured toward her bucket.

*Please no entrails,* he thought as she handed it over. To his great relief, it was only carrot peelings and onion skins.

"Ta," she said, turning back without a second glance. When the door closed, Holt breathed easy again.

What was he doing? Too late now.

He dumped the bucket of peelings over the top of the silver dish. A sliver of metal remained visible in places, but it would do. With a grunt, he picked up his load. He groaned from the weight but marched on, worried with each step that something would give him away.

Yet Holt needn't have worried. A cook he would be one day. A pot boy he was currently. Few people give a pot boy much attention, let alone stop and look closely at what he is doing. Or what he is carrying. And seeing a pot boy carrying a waste crate was hardly conspicuous.

Just like that, as easily as he'd taken the egg, he made it to the servants' stairs, the roughhewn, narrow, switch-back flight that led to the poorer part of town. It was this area where he and his father lived in their squat little house.

He passed some kitchenhands on their way back from the Muckers' hut, carrying empty crates or barrels of their own. He nodded and smiled, fearing his thumping heart would be audible through his ribs.

Nearing his destination, he saw the Muckers' hut at the end of the winding street, casting soft light, whereas other homes were darkened or had their windows closed. He could just make out the Muckers readying their horse and wagon for the night's work. Then they set off.

Not wishing to be asked to offload his crate, Holt ducked into a darkened alley by the Fuller's house and waited as hooves clopped up the hard dirt street. The elder Mucker had begun his route. He stopped at each house, picking up smaller buckets of waste and upending them onto the back of his wagon, muttering to his horse all the while.

Once Mr. Mucker was well past, Holt poked out his head to check that the younger Mucker was not in the street. Seeing the road was clear, Holt emerged from the alley and carried on.

Across from the Muckers' hut was an old storehouse that stood rotting against the rock of the Crag. Once, the Muckers had used it as an extra midden, but the practice of storing such quantities of waste inside the town had long been outlawed. Yet given its location, previous use, and proximity to the ripeness of the Muckers' working hut, no one had found a new use for it.

Holt threw a final glance around, then dashed inside. Entering did not bring any relief from the night. The roof was in such need of repair that he still felt half outside. Not even the destitute would camp here. There was a thick smell of mildew, the straw either sodden or brown and withered. A rat scurried past. It was a good sign. Not even Mr. Catcher ventured here.

There was nothing left for it. He got to work. Eventually he'd have to figure out a way to get the egg past the town guards, perhaps taking it out to the woods somewhere. But that was a problem for another night.

For now, he rummaged for all the dry straw he could find and made a pile of it under the most intact section of the roof. Then he brushed off the peelings, took the lid off the dish and brought out the egg.

Holt shivered, though whether this was from nerves or the chill air he couldn't say. Then he felt it again; the egg sent out a wave of heat.

"Thank you," he said quietly.

He rested the egg on the straw, then stood back to observe his work. Deciding there wasn't much more he could do regarding the egg's comfort – if the egg even cared for such things – he raked his mind through the chances of someone finding it.

Not too likely, he concluded. Few people would come to this dead end of town, other than the Muckers and the odd kitchenhand. Everyone else placed their waste outside their homes for collection. This area was poor, and who else would wish to venture down to the Muckers' hut? Not only because of the smell, but because people feared the insects said to be drawn to rotting things. Vethrax.

Those bugs were hated almost as much as the scourge, although Holt had never actually seen one. Probably because the Muckers and Sweeps did such a good job of keeping the streets clean.

Fearing his absence would be noted again, Holt crouched and, not entirely sure why he was doing this, patted the top of the egg.

"I need to go," he said stupidly.

No heat came from the egg this time. Disappointed, Holt realized he'd been hoping it could hear him. Maybe dragon eggs became warm at random and he'd given it more meaning than it held.

He got up, returned to the crate of food waste and the silver dish, and then realized his issue. If he covered the dish to sneak it back up and was spotted, it would look strange to be returning waste to the kitchens. Carrying the dish on its own was out of the question. He could leave it here, but his father had asked him to go get it in the first place. Someone might look for it tomorrow, and then there would be questions.

He had no choice. With luck, he wouldn't run into anyone. Covering it back over with the peelings as best he could, he picked up the crate with the dish concealed inside it and started back up the road. At least it wasn't so heavy now, but even a light weight would become a burden when climbing.

Halfway back up the winding servants' stairs, breathing hard and legs burning from the effort, he heard voices coming from around the corner above.

"Stop frettin'," a woman said. "We'll just be cooped up for a bit while the riders go off and do their business."

"Nowhere's completely safe," came a male voice.

Holt thought fast. He put the crate down, leaned against the rock and placed a hand to his stomach. Two kitchenhands came around the corner, neither mercifully the girl he had run into earlier.

"You arite, Holt?"

"Just catching my breath," Holt said, which was true enough. "Embarrassed to say I got a stitch on the way down."

"It's been a long day," the man said knowingly.

"Yer father's dismissed us for the night," said the woman. "We were just headin' home, but if you want a hand with that—"

"No, no," Holt said. "You two go on. I'll manage."

"Right you are, Master Cook."

They both continued down.

Holt didn't waste a second more than he had to. Taking the stairs as quick as his body allowed, he went to the refuse yard, removed the dish, and placed the crate down with the others. After a feast, no one would think twice that not everything had been emptied yet. Wiping his hands on his apron as best he could, he retrieved the dish and entered the kitchens through the back door.

He hung back, peeking around the corner until he saw his father descend into the larder for a stock check. With a window of opportunity to avoid immediate questions, he ducked in, made for his washbasin, and began cleaning the silver tray. He scrubbed a little too hard, as though he could scrub the evidence of his crime away.

The kitchens were quiet now. Most of the staff had left for the night, and when Holt dried and replaced the silver dish there wasn't a utensil out of place nor a workspace that wasn't clean.

The larder trap door opened, and Jonah Cook emerged with a wearied groan.

"There you are," he said. He raised a hand to dissuade any excuses for Holt's tardiness. "We'll talk in the morning. Let's go home."

They made that journey in silence, and Holt stripped to his small clothes and got into bed with nothing more than a sullen, "Good night." He wasn't sure whether his father was angry with him or just exhausted from the day. For his part, Holt was too anxious to dare utter a word, fearing his voice would give away his secret.

Lying in bed, a fresh wave of guilt washed over him for abandoning the kitchens earlier. If he hadn't stormed out, he may never have been asked to go to the hatchery and would never have learned the terrible truth behind the choosing ceremony. He shivered, although this time it was definitely not from the cold, but he pulled his sheets tighter around himself all the same.

Sleep eluded Holt, even long after his father's snoring filled their little house.

*What have I done?*

# 7

# THE LONG WAIT

When Holt woke the next morning, he enjoyed a pleasant moment in which events of the day before were forgotten. Then it all came flooding back. The confrontation with Mr. Smith, dealing with Lord Mirk, half-burning Silas Silverstrike's meal, the argument with his father, and then Brode's impossible task. Oh, and the dragon egg he'd taken.

He blinked against the cold morning light and heard his father bustling around in his morning routine. Dreading an awkward breakfast, Holt rolled out of bed, found fresh small clothes, and put on yesterday's shirt and trousers. The chore of household laundry fell to him, and as he washed pots all day, he didn't relish having to wash more at night; so, he tended to wear the same clothes until his father made him get on with it.

As Holt clambered down the ladder from his loft space, his father offered an uncharacteristically gruff, "Morning."

"Morning, Father." He reached ground level and turned to find his father sitting at their squat table by the hearth. A quarter wheel of cheese, a small loaf of dark rye bread and a dish of butter had been laid out. The kettle was already heating.

"Food's ready," Jonah said. He shoved another chunk of bread and cheese into his mouth, perhaps as a way of avoiding further discussion.

While the tension was palpable, Holt didn't feel like breaking it himself, so he quietly joined his father and began to butter some bread. For a while there was only the sound of chewing and cutlery scraping on plates. The kettle soon whistled. Jonah made to get up, but Holt jumped up first to attend to it, hoping to redeem himself by being helpful. He poured some tea into a pair of mugs and handed one to his father. Jonah's expression softened.

"The feast went well," he said.

"I'm glad." Holt hesitated to ask but felt he ought to. "Did Silverstrike like his meal?"

"He did. I'm told he said it was the perfect reminder of home. Elk was a good choice."

Holt nodded, then, unsure what to say next, returned to his bread and cheese.

"Did you enjoy working with Lord Brode yesterday? You were gone for hours."

Holt nearly choked on his food. Coughing and spluttering, he beat his chest and managed to gasp out, "… nothing."

Jonah raised an eyebrow.

"Nothing exciting," Holt said. "Just feeding Lady Ysera."

"Since when did anything rider-related not excite you?"

Stumped, Holt shoved more food into his mouth and sipped on his mug of tea.

Jonah tapped a finger on his own mug. "I'm sorry we argued yesterday. I was worried about the feast. And I let my temper get the better of me."

Holt opened his mouth to say something, but his father barrelled on.

"I know I don't always give you enough of my time. I know you want to stretch your wings, learn more from me. I'm aware washing up isn't inspiring work. It's been… well, I've been stretched thin since your mother—"

"I know," Holt cut in. He didn't like to bring the topic up any more than his father did. "I'm sorry, too."

"Hmm," Jonah mused. He took a swig of tea. "I can understand you wanting more. But being the Cook of an Order Hall kitchen isn't a bad life. You'll be warm in the winter and you'll never go hungry. And you and your family will be safe whenever the scourge threatens the land."

Holt offered a soft smile. "That's true."

"Good," Jonah said. "Then we'll leave the matter there for now. Besides, soon you'll be sixteen, and I'll have you so busy you'll wish you were back to washing dishes." He laughed. "Now eat up and let's go. Wouldn't want to anger the riders with a late breakfast."

"No," Holt laughed nervously. His thoughts jumped to the egg in the storehouse ruins. He'd have to get it outside of town as soon as possible.

Yet luck was not on his side.

Later that very day, word began to spread that King Leofric had ordered the Summons. On his way from the distant Falcaer Fortress, Silas had visited Sidastra, the capital city of Feorlen. While there, he had witnessed the Summons go out and so now informed the riders of Feorlen ahead of the king's official messengers. The migration of citizens would begin, shepherding people toward the capital and so draw the forces of the scourge to that one place for a final confrontation.

The people of the Crag were exempt from making the long journey to Sidastra. Distance was one factor, but the presence of the riders kept the threat of the scourge well at bay. And the town's modest population wouldn't swing the balance of the realm greatly enough to affect the pull of the swarm toward the capital.

Yet Holt felt a change in the air. A year of skirmishes and rising worry was starting to come to a head.

As the only Order Hall in Feorlen, the riders of the Crag would be expected to handle the swarm by themselves. A small Order Hall for a small kingdom. Silas had been sent from headquarters to aid Commander Denna's efforts, although other branches in other kingdoms could be called upon for aid in an emergency. Those in the kingdoms of Brenin and Risalia were closest, and while Feorlen had been at war with Risalia only a year ago, the riders took no part. If Commander Denna called for their aid, they would come.

However, while the civilians at the Crag enjoyed the luxury of remaining in their own homes during a rising, the gates were still to be shut. No one was to leave or enter the town without the say of Commander Denna until the incursion was dealt with.

Holt's stomach knotted painfully when he heard the news and nearly vomited into his washbasin. He and his dragon egg would be trapped. His reaction went unnoticed, for everyone became on edge during times like these.

Silverstrike's arrival had proved to be perfectly timed. The riders increased their patrols, reconnaissance flights and skirmishes with scourge forces, which was good for Holt as fewer riders at the Crag meant a lower chance of him being caught. Yet it did mean a scourge incursion was fully in effect now, which wasn't so good. But here, so far from the fighting and the horrors, Holt felt numb to it. His own situation was far more pressing to him.

The following week passed in a mixture of painfully slow days and rushed evenings. Holt offered to make more deliveries than usual to the Muckers, just to reduce the risk that others might stumble upon his secret. After his father fell asleep, he snuck down to check on the egg, and he sat rocking on the damp floor as he considered how he might remove it from town. No ideas came to him, and to his horror the egg grew larger each day, making his mission even harder. By the fourth day, it had nearly doubled in size.

This made him all the more nervous. If the egg was growing, then the dragon inside must surely be growing too. And if it hatched, well, he'd be lucky if Ysera didn't squash them both flat.

Each night he slept less. Each day he got through less work. People commented on the dark bags under his eyes, but most assumed he was just worried about the scourge. First incursion jitters, they claimed, and slapped him on the back, telling him not to fret – the riders would smash the bugs against the walls of Sidastra as they had done time and time again. Holt nodded and smiled and agreed he was being foolish. Of course, he still worried.

One week later, and Holt was starting to panic. The dragon egg had grown so large he could barely move it. How close was it to hatching? He tried to subtly ask about dragon eggs around the Crag, but the servants knew little more than he did, and he reckoned asking Brode would raise immediate suspicion.

He became stuck in a sort of waking nightmare. Unable to act. Unable to do anything other than wait for the inevitable.

That moment came on the eighth day.

Holt was in the kitchens, his arms elbow deep in the basin of water as he wrestled with the day's washing up. He'd just drawn up a freshly scrubbed plate dripping in soap when a squire entered the kitchens. Squires were initiates of the Order, young nobles waiting for a dragon to bond with them and assisting older riders in the meantime. Holt paid him little mind. But then the squire made an announcement.

"Hatchings! The hatchings have begun!"

"Now?" Jonah said, sounding harassed. "It's almost dark."

The squire carried on as though he had not heard. "Mr. Cook, prepare a selection of soft meats for the hatchlings."

At once the kitchen staff were chatting about the new dragons. It was always a time of great excitement, yet it would also mean significantly more work for them.

To Holt, the news was crushing. A lump formed in his throat, then plummeted through his stomach toward his legs which now seemed frozen in place. A crash cut above the noise of the chatter. Holt blinked. Then he noticed everyone was staring at him. Looking down, he realized that he'd dropped the plate he'd been holding. Pieces of ceramic lay scattered on the ground. A fine plate of the Order Hall smashed due to him. Well, that was the least of his concerns.

He suddenly found it hard to breathe. Hard to think. The room seemed to spin, and he was altogether too hot. Too hot in the stuffy kitchens. And why was everyone staring at him?

"Son?" his father said. He was by Holt's side in a flash. "Are you okay?"

"Uhm..." Holt tried to say something, but words failed him.

His father placed a hand on his brow. "You're rather hot. Do you feel sick?"

*Sick?* Yes. Sick. He could work with that.

"My… my stomach," Holt said, placing a hand on his belly. "Oh, the plate, Father I'm so sorry."

"Never mind that, it's done. I was going to have you join me in visiting the hatchlings. Do you feel up to it?"

Holt fiercely shook his head.

"You must be ill to turn down a chance to see the dragons," Jonah said. A flicker of the worst fear crossed Jonah Cook's face; sickness at these times could mean the blight. Jonah gulped, and Holt saw that fear visibly shrink from his father as he processed it. No bugs had made it close enough to the Crag; no one else had been infected. Just a stomach pain or a cold, that was all. "Go home. Now. Take some food with you. Boil water and drink lots of it. I'll call the healers in the morning if you aren't better."

"Food. Yes," Holt said mechanically.

Jonah gave him a hug which Holt gladly returned. His father had just given him a lifeline. At least for this evening.

As the bustle of the kitchens returned to normal, Holt went about gathering food for himself. He grabbed a little extra when no one was looking, stuffing a few chicken legs and a cut of pork into his knapsack. Once out of the servants' courtyard and away from prying eyes, he bolted down the narrow steps into town, raced through the streets, dodged the Muckers setting off on their evening round, and arrived at the crumbling old storehouse.

He stood for a while at its threshold, doubled over and breathing hard from his run. Fear of what he'd find inside also kept him rooted. If he didn't go in, it wouldn't become real. Eventually, he gave himself a slap. It was about to get nightmarishly real whether he stepped inside or not. So, screwing up his courage, Holt entered the Crag's newest hatchery.

# 8

# NO GOING BACK

The dragon egg shook.

Holt approached warily, at a loss as to what he should do. Rats scurried away from the egg, squealing shrilly to one another. The white scar across the shell had stretched tight and seemed close to bursting. A rattling sounded as the dragon inside rustled around, trying to break free.

And then it did.

There was a small pop, a crack, and then a segment of the outer shell fell away. A slimy substance oozed out like raw egg white, and a tiny talon poked its way through. It flexed, as a baby might flex a little finger at the world.

Holt stood in awe, transfixed as the baby dragon began to demolish the egg, smashing the shell to pieces. Within seconds it was there before him. A new dragon to fight the terror of the scourge. But something was wrong.

He couldn't say what caused this feeling, but it was something in the way the baby moved. Its head was turned away from him, looking at the rotting wood of the storehouse wall. Holt had never been to an actual hatching before, but he'd delivered food to young dragons in his time. They were always inquisitive, intelligent creatures, interested in everything around them. This dragon seemed confused.

Its color was unusual too, paler than snow so that even its scales were hard to discern. Two white stumps protruded where its wings would later grow. Holt had never seen a white dragon, nor heard of one. He wasn't sure what magic type it was. Definitely not fire, nor emerald. Perhaps it was linked to ice or storm? But such a unique coloring could make it a mystic dragon.

The baby gargled as it took in its surroundings. Then it began to thrash, and its cry became higher and more panicked.

Worried the noise would draw unwanted attention, Holt crouched down and made hushing sounds.

"Shhhh," Holt hissed as he rummaged in the knapsack for a chicken leg. Most likely the baby was looking for food. "It's okay. Over here." He felt a bit silly talking this way to a dragon, as though it were a puppy on the street.

The baby pivoted ungracefully in the remnants of its shell, but even once it turned around, it still had a hard time focusing on Holt. Now he could see its face better, he thought he understood why. The dragon's eyes were startlingly blue, like a clear sky on a crisp winter's day. Yet its whites were milky, and it wasn't looking directly at Holt. Rather, the dragon focused on a point just past his elbow.

*Can it see me?*

Holt called softly to the baby again. The dragon moved its head from side to side, evidently struggling to pinpoint the source of his voice.

*It's blind.*

The realization struck Holt like a hammer blow. What had Brode said? Ysera had detected weakness in the egg, and that was why the dragons wouldn't want it to hatch. Was this the weakness? Blindness. Could this be linked to why the dragon was white as well?

*Well, if it can't see me, I should go to it.*

Still crouched, he shuffled his right leg forward. Immediately the dragon squawked again, wailing in its high, strained tone. It stumbled, slipped on the slime from its own egg, collapsed in a heap and squirmed in distress.

"I'm sorry," Holt said desperately.

What was he to do? This was his fault. Guilt clawed at him, and his heart sank. Well, it was done now, and the baby would need to be fed one way or another.

Clearly moving toward the dragon was no good as it couldn't see him and was terrified by a larger creature moving in the dark around it. Holt could hardly blame it. So, he brought out the chicken leg from the sack and tore a small chunk free from the bone, hoping to attract the dragon over to him.

The baby ceased crying to sniff at the air instead. With the promise of food nearby it rallied, scrambling back up and smelling its way forward. The poor thing slipped again on its way to Holt, tumbling in a roly-poly toward him and landing spread-eagled upon its four short legs. But this time it was determined and got back up, sniffing for the chicken.

Very carefully, Holt edged his outstretched hand farther, holding the meat between his thumb and forefinger. The dragon stepped up, sniffed at the food, then at Holt's fingers, and then back at the chicken. Then, in one quick motion, the dragon took a bite and began chomping away. It chirruped happily and took another bite.

Holt tore a few more pieces from the chicken and fed them to the dragon. It seemed to really like the poultry, which made him think it might be a storm dragon – like Clesh – but it was too soon to say for sure. All dragons liked meat in general. They just got fussier and found their preference as they matured. Once the first chicken leg was gone, Holt decided to try the pork.

The baby leaped at this new delight. It attacked the meat so eagerly that it nipped Holt's finger.

"Ouch!" Holt whipped his hand back and sucked on the wound. He tasted blood.

The dragon squawked and stumbled back. It was looking directly at him now, though its eyes were still off-focus, and it yelped little wails of worry. *As if…* Holt thought, *as if it knows it did something wrong.*

"It's okay," he told the baby. "I'm fine."

It tilted its head at him but continued cooing lowly. Holt began to feel sensations that weren't his own, much like when Ysera's anger had hit him, although these were far lighter, like hearing your name called out from a great distance. He felt lost, confused, and frightened, but he, Holt, didn't feel those things per se. He knew they were coming from the baby. The poor thing was so distressed that its fledgling core – if that's what it was – was actually affecting him.

Another wave of guilt crashed into Holt. Maybe the Matriarch had had a point? The other dragons wouldn't like this. How could it fight the scourge if it couldn't see? And how could it survive in the wild alone?

"It will be all right," Holt said. He extended his hand again to the baby. "Come here. Follow my voice. It will be all right."

Holt thought the dragon would be shy and back away. It didn't back away, but it didn't come closer either. Holt persisted.

"Come here. Come on. It's okay."

He spoke gently, encouragingly, and after a bit of coaxing, the dragon took a tentative step closer. Once it reached Holt's hand, he stroked the dragon down its neck with one finger. The baby shuddered, unsure at first about this new sensation, but it then eased into it. Its wails died down to sounds of comfort, and Holt began petting it with his whole hand. Just like a cat. He stroked the dragon just like a cat.

*What the hell am I doing?*

Crouching was causing his legs to seize up, so he sat on the ground cross-legged. The dragon edged in even closer to him. Holt fed the baby the rest of the chicken and pork, and once all the meat was gone, it curled up into the crook of his arm and fell asleep.

Holt felt a warmth gather deep inside him, like the feeling of drinking hot tea but constant, and somehow deeper than his bones. It gathered just below his sternum, light and unobtrusive, and he couldn't reach out to it or even understand it. And then that nugget of warmth began to beat inside him.

Was this the dragon's magic again? Was this normal?

All Holt knew for sure was that he would not be parted from the dragon now it was here. If they took the dragon, they'd have to take him. It wasn't a rational thought, but nor was the strange rhythm beating inside his chest.

Holt was sure of one other thing. He was in the worst trouble of his entire life.

# 9

# THE QUIET BEFORE…

Holt left the dragon asleep, covering it with the sack he'd brought from the kitchens. If he didn't leave for home his father would return before he did, and then there would be serious questions. He resolved to come back early in the morning, with proper blankets and more food before his father woke. But what he would do after that, he did not know. Nor did he much want to think about it.

He managed to make it home just before his father arrived.

"You're even warmer than before," Jonah said with a worried frown. "How are you feeling?"

Holt considered this. He didn't feel hot, other than the strange beating deep inside him, although it had grown fainter since he'd left the dragon. At this point, however, the ruse of sickness might do more harm than good. Alarm over his health would draw too much unwanted attention.

"I feel fine."

"Hmm," Jonah intoned. "Get some sleep and we'll see how you are in the morning."

Once again, Holt tried to sleep, but it eluded him. He tossed and turned for hours until the palest light of pre-dawn shimmered through his window. Quiet as he could, he got up, pulled out his spare blanket and swiped three cured sausages before hurrying off.

Mercifully, the dragon was still fast asleep when he arrived. It seemed to sense his arrival, waking the moment he approached, opening its dazzlingly blue eyes wide. The beat inside Holt quickened and a powerful hunger gripped him, although it did not feel wholly his own.

"I have some more food for you."

The baby cooed softly, then got up, stretched its neck and wobbled over to Holt. He fed the first sausage to the dragon, and at once the feeling of hunger within himself died down, replaced with a sort of primal happiness. It was the most peculiar thing to observe these sensations within himself. When Ysera had affected him he'd been consumed completely, whereas these emotions coming from the baby sat alongside his own.

Lost in thought, Holt didn't reach for the second sausage. The baby squeaked and pressed its nose into his hand as though accusing Holt of holding back on it.

"Hey, shhh," Holt said. He tapped the baby on the nose. When it quietened down, he fed it another piece of sausage. "Now stay quiet." The dragon did and he fed it another bite. "Good, boy," he said, giving the baby a stroke along its neck.

Now he considered it, he wasn't sure whether the dragon was a boy or not. And you couldn't check dragons in the usual way. He listened to the beating inside him and decided it was a boy. He couldn't say why. It was just the way it felt, and he could barely comprehend what was happening to him at any rate.

The remainder of the second sausage vanished in one great mouthful, and between the broken rafters the sunrise was now in full flow.

"I have to go again," he told the baby.

It opened its mouth, then seemed to remember that it was supposed to remain quiet and closed it again. How it could understand him already was incredible. Maybe it sensed his intentions and tone more so than his words. Rather than voice its sadness, the dragon pressed forward, fumbling in trying to find Holt's torso. Once it did, it tried to curl up beside him.

"I'm sorry," Holt said. He scooped the dragon up and put it back down on the straw, feeling a lump form in his throat. "I'll come back tonight. The very moment I can."

The baby tilted its head at him, its gaze focusing somewhere over his shoulder.

Holt felt like a terrible person. He was going to leave this poor blind baby here all day on its own. But what other choice did he have? Maybe there was a way to let it know he was still nearby, some way to give it comfort?

Holt closed his eyes and concentrated with all his might on feeling the rhythmic beat. He strained, clenching his fists as he did so, and willed the dragon to understand that he wasn't going far and that he would return. A great deal of energy seemed to leave his body. He swayed and rubbed at his eyes.

Just as he worried it hadn't worked, the knot of warmth flared inside him. For a moment it was as though he were warming his hands by the fire and the beating rang loud and true. Holt took that for an affirmative.

He opened his eyes and looked at the dragon. It seemed calm and settled. Perhaps Holt's experiment had worked after all?

The baby yawned. Holt laid down the spare blankets he'd taken from his house and moved the dragon to them. It began padding around in an awkward circle, treading out a spot where it would sleep. He placed the third sausage by its nest in case it woke up again.

And with that, he left, off back home for breakfast, trying to pretend like this was just any other day.

As if life hadn't become uncertain enough, things got worse the very next day. A mounted messenger came from Fort Kennet, bearing fresh news from the capital.

The king was dead.

Holt was in the middle of collecting dishes from the midday meal when he overheard some squires talking about it.

"I recall him from banquets I attended in Sidastra; he rarely danced."

"Stomach plagued him, or so they say. He didn't join the war either."

"I heard he wanted to ride but King Godric forbade it."

"Just as well he didn't, I suppose. Not that it's helped him in the end."

"Bad timing, though."

"Is it? Hear me out, will you? Tragic though this is, his uncle will make for a better leader in the battles ahead. I recall last year—"

One of the squires slapped the table in mock astonishment. "What's this, Edmund?" Did you fight under Osric and Ealdor Harroway in the war? Gracious, you should have mentioned it before!"

"Very funny. But seriously, Osric Agravain is something else. Every soldier stood straighter in his mere presence. I've not seen respect like that other than for the riders. He's traveled everywhere, fought on every front. With him in charge—"

The group noticed Holt lingering nearby then. They shot him dark looks and hurried off, leaving their mess for him to clean up. He groaned, added their plates to his tottering pile and made to leave the Great Hall. No sooner had he stepped out into the corridor than someone collided with him in a swirl of red.

Knocked backward, Holt lost control of the plates. They crashed to the floor with a piercing, echoing ring.

"Hey, watch—" He caught himself at the last second, but the disrespect had already been done. Everyone inside the Order Hall would be far above his station.

When he saw who it was, he dropped to his knees.

Princess Talia. Only she didn't look like herself. Her face and eyes were puffy, her cheeks flushed as red as her hair. She opened her mouth, choked back a breath, then closed it. A fresh tear rolled down her cheek. Then she turned and ran, her sobs audible as she sprinted for the front courtyard of the Crag where Pyra, her purple dragon, waited for her.

Holt's own dragon seemed distraught by the incident. A feeling of worry washed across the strange connection they held. Holt tried to convey that he was fine, and after a while the dragon settled back down. When the beating returned to a deep slow gong, he guessed the baby had gone back to sleep.

That evening was a quiet one in the Crag. King Leofric's death and his uncle's regency was the talk of the Crag for days to come. The riders sequestered themselves in long meetings, demanding additional provisions well after dark. Exhausted and worn, each night Holt and his father walked with sore feet back home. Each evening, when his father fell asleep, Holt snuck back out and down the now familiar route to the abandoned store house by the Muckers' hut.

He fed and played with the dragon and was surprised to find that it had already grown. He couldn't be certain, for he was half-delirious from tiredness and worry, but he reckoned it had. It was now comparable to the largest cats he'd ever seen, but that meant it wasn't beyond curling up with him, which it seemed to want to do the most.

As he sat there one night, with the rhythmic beat thumping alongside his own heartbeat, Holt nodded off.

He awoke in the morning light. Dawn was long past. His head ached from lying on stone, and the baby dragon lay sprawled across his chest.

Voices reached him. A horse whinnied.

"Calm, girl, what's got into you?"

"Been like that for days, she has."

Holt gritted his teeth. The Muckers were already at their hut. His father might already be awake and wondering where he was.

Groaning, Holt pushed himself up and caught the dragon as it slid off him. It remained steadfastly asleep as he put it down on the blankets, its little tail swishing from some dream.

The horse snorted and whinnied again. As the Muckers fought to control her, Holt took his chance and darted out, rushing home as fast as he could. Had the horse sensed or smelled the dragon nearby? How long until another dragon realized what was going on?

*I can't keep this up for long.*

He knew he'd have to try and think of a way to get the dragon out of town. At the least, he needed to learn more about dragon hatchlings in case he was in for a nasty surprise.

Yet a full week passed, and Holt was none the wiser.

One day, Silas Silverstrike gathered the senior riders and left the Crag. Word spread that Silas, Commander Denna, and the eldest, most experienced riders were heading to the capital of Sidastra to prepare the defenses. Of those riders at Champion rank, only Mirk remained as temporary head of the Crag.

Their departure reduced the number of riders at the Crag to ten, with only nine dragons as old Brode did not have one. Except for the hatchlings, of course, and Holt's own dragon, although he still had not thought of a name – if it was even his place to choose a name. The remaining riders were still Novices in training or were at the middling rank of Ascendant like Princess Talia. They would be summoned later. The upcoming battle with the swarm would be their first great test.

Holt had never seen one of the monstrous insects for himself. There were enough vivid descriptions in stories told to children, and great murals and paintings within the Order Hall depicted the creatures too – clashing in battle with the riders upon grim battlefields of ages past.

Now the Crag had fewer riders, Holt lingered in the front hall to look at the largest painting, balancing a pile of dishes stacked between his hands. Portrayed were great horn-headed bugs, larger than war horses; tall, wiry insects with blade-like arms; oversized, deformed skeletons towering over the smaller foot soldiers of the scourge – the part-human, part-insectoid ghouls. Giant wasp-like creatures blotted the skyline.

Yet at the heart of the swarm, the worst of the monsters reigned. It stood upright on four great legs beneath a pinched waist and a torso of hardened carapace. A giant set of dark wings folded around the bug like a traveling cloak. Holt's mistaking the wings for a cloak could be forgiven, for the face of the creature – if it had one – was obscured beneath a hood of shell, as though the bug thought to garb itself like a thief. Under that cowl of carapace there was only darkness; darkness and eyes like bleeding stars.

The queen of the swarm.

*Thump. Thump. Thump.*

His bond with the baby dragon quickened as he looked upon the painting, as though some inherent fear was shared between them. Holt understood little of things beyond the Crag and its town, but he hoped dearly that the kingdom was ready for such an attack. Holt had to agree with the squires' assessment of the situation. Osric Agravain was a hero from the war against Risalia the previous year. He'd won the Toll Pass in a fierce battle, although he had arrived too late to save Talia's father. That aside, Osric was a renowned warrior and adventurer in his own right. The kingdom was surely in more capable hands now than it had been with Talia's sickly brother.

"Shouldn't you be washing those?"

Holt turned to find Brode. He had a bright red apple in his gnarled hand and took a bite as he approached.

"I should, Lord Brode. Forgive my tardiness." He was about to leave when something about the painting caught his eye. A dragon, a deep red-scaled dragon, was bleeding out and surrounded by enemies. Its face was one of sheer terror. He hadn't thought of the riders as capable of fear, never mind the dragons themselves. A fresh pang of worry for the baby rose in him, met with a sympathetic pulse across their bond.

The question left his lips before he'd really thought it through.

"Must all dragons fight the scourge?"

Brode sniffed, considered Holt, then took another bite from his apple. He swallowed and then finally answered, "No."

Holt gulped, fearful he'd given something away. If it had been anyone other than Brode standing before him, he wouldn't risk taking up their time.

"There are dragons out in the wild, aren't there?" Holt asked. "Dragons not part of the order?"

"There are Wild Flights, yes."

"And they do not fight?"

"They'll defend themselves if it comes to it, but must they fight? No. They could fly away and let others deal with it. In the past, they have. Such was The Pact. The riders were formed to repel the scourge, and both the humans and dragons who commit to that cause must do so willingly." Brode's gaze fell upon the painting. "Or else how could anyone accept that as their fate?" His focus snapped back to Holt. "Why do you ask, pot boy?"

"I'm sorry to ask such trifling questions, Lord Brode. I should not be concerned. Especially with Silas Silverstrike fighting with us. They say he's worth ten Champions."

Brode's eyes rolled again at the mention of Silverstrike. "You believe every story you hear, don't you?"

Holt only just realized his lack of tact. Brode was one of the eldest riders at the Crag, yet he had been left behind.

"Is it as awful as folk say?" Holt asked. "To face the scourge?"

Brode's face darkened. "Words cannot convey how terrible it is, Holt. These paintings you admire make it too pretty."

"Do you think the kingdom is prepared?" Holt asked.

Brode shrugged, returning to his apple.

"I suppose if Princess Talia became queen," Holt began, "then the Order would be able to direct our armies even better."

Brode spat out a pip. Holt watched it sail to the floor and spared a thought for the servant who would clean it up.

"For someone who listens to every tale he hears, you understand little. Talia can never become queen."

"Why?"

"Because rider neutrality is sacrosanct. Or at least it was. The fact that Talia is a rider at all is controversial, something you might know if you'd traveled more than a day beyond the town walls." Brode checked himself and cleared his throat. "Look," he said in a hurried voice, "people like the riders when the scourge threatens them, but when there is peace and calm, they grumble about paying taxes for our upkeep. And they worry we might start to overreach, as they see it. Nobles and merchants might have armies and castles, but we have dragons. If the riders wanted to, they could seize power, and there are some who would even support it. So, the nobles fear us, as much as they depend on us."

"But all riders are noble," Holt said. This was confusing for him. Riders were above all in station, equal to royalty in some eyes. "How can the nobles both fear the riders and also form their ranks?"

"Ah, you've discovered the only thing the nobles fear more than the riders taking power. And that's giving their lessers more." He waved a hand over Holt to indicate such a person. "At least if the noble families make up the riders, then family love and ties will hinder bloodshed. Or so it goes in theory. There are also the sworn oaths of the Order: to stay neutral; to never marry and have children; to keep our attention always on the dangers of the scourge. If Talia became queen, it would break not only her own vows but the delicate relationship of the Order with each nation from the Skarl Empire to the Free City of Mithra. They would see it as the riders taking the reins of power. Of course, some believe the royal line should remain intact no matter what... She should never have joined us," he added as a final dark thought.

By the sounds of it, Holt thought Brode had a point. Then again, he, Holt, had recently made a decision that broke all the rules, so he could hardly judge Talia himself.

"They should have taken you with them," Holt said. "Commander Denna and the others. It doesn't seem right."

"I'll be making a little trip soon," Brode growled. "Not that it is your place to talk ill of our Flight Commander, pot boy."

"No, Lord Brode. Of course, I forgot myself. I shall leave you now."

He scurried off, but Brode called out after him.

"As payment for our chat, I'll take two boiled eggs with runny yolks. And thick *dark* bread, mind, none of that fluffy white slop. Now, if you please."

Holt trotted off, thinking it odd that Brode requested brown bread. Riders, being noble, tended to eat the more expensive, sweeter white loaves when they could, which was virtually all the time. Brode really was an oddity.

When Holt reached the kitchens, he fulfilled Brode's order and then tended to the dishes. Scrubbing every cup, plate and piece of cutlery, he kept his mind on the night ahead with the dragon.

For night was their time.

When the world slept.

When, moreover, his father slept.

One night, Holt thought it best to let the baby find its way to him just from the sound of his voice. It would need to get used to doing such things. He stood a few feet away, and then he moved farther back. Each time the dragon found him, he stroked its neck, fed it some food, and then stepped back again. Eventually, the dragon could move from one side of the storehouse to the other without falling over or bumping into anything, albeit slowly.

"You're quite clever, aren't you?"

It nipped playfully at his finger without leaving a mark.

Holt walked back to where its nest of blankets lay. He called to the dragon, and after a few attempts it turned and began making its way to him. The beating deep inside his chest grew louder and louder. And then Holt heard a voice in his mind. It was not his own.

"*Boy...*"

The voice was high and young; it echoed lightly and sounded half-formed, as though the person was struggling with the word.

No, not a person. The dragon.

Holt stared bug-eyed at the baby. Was it talking to him? Older dragons could do that, as Ysera had spoken to Brode in the hatchery. But dragons seldom spoke to anyone but their rider or someone of equal standing.

"*Boy...*" the voice called again. The dragon moved gingerly, sniffing the air.

"I'm here," Holt said.

The dragon drew closer. "*Boy...*"

"Come to me. You can do it."

"*Boy!*" The voice in Holt's head rang clear and true as the dragon found him and nuzzled into his palm.

Holt understood then that he was truly stuck. The idea of parting with the dragon would be like parting with one of his limbs. Ripping a piece of his heart away would be easier.

Whatever happened now, they'd have to be together. For better or worse.

"My name is Holt," he told the baby.

"*Hhhooww—*" the dragon attempted, its squeaky tone unable to wrap around the word. "*Hoowwooo... howot.*"

Holt grinned and rubbed the dragon's back. "We can work on that."

"*Food,*" the dragon said.

Holt gave it the last of the smoked fish he'd snuck out of the kitchens that evening. Now the dragon was beginning to speak to him – sort of – he might find out which meat it liked the best. That would help narrow down its magic type. For now, it was happy to guzzle down anything.

*Him,* Holt reminded himself. *I should come up with a name.*

It might not be the way things were usually done, but nothing about this situation was the way things were usually done.

Despite himself, Holt fell asleep again that night with the dragon.

Waking up early this time, he trudged back up the road to his home, skirting the edge of the backstreets and alleys to avoid detection. Despite his worries, there was something tranquil about the world at this time of day that Holt enjoyed.

Soft smoke rose from the Muckers' mounds outside of town, unmoving in the still air. Only the waves could be heard. The air smelled fresher somehow, as though the whole world slept at night and awoke rested in the morning.

This day was different, however, as the distinct sound of beating wings cut through the skies. With his nerves heightened at the thought of being caught, Holt ducked down beside a water barrel as though that would conceal him from a patrolling rider. Feeling foolish, he glanced up and saw a purple dragon flying east away from the Crag.

Only Princess Talia's dragon was of that color. Where was she going? Sidastra was to the southeast, and he doubted she would have been summoned there alone ahead of the other Ascendants. He thought he could see more than one person upon the dragon's back, but it was so hard to tell and the distance between him and Talia grew with each second. Fleeing the Crag would be breaking her oath, but maybe she didn't care anymore with the deaths of her father and brother coming so close together.

Whatever she was doing, it wasn't his business.

Holt had enough on his mind.

# 10

# THE STORM

A few days after Talia's departure, the baby dragon had grown to the size of a hunting hound. Holt could no longer sneak enough food away to keep it satiated for long. Small hillocks of meat were being prepared in the kitchens and sent off to the hatchery, and Holt could only look at the quantity in horror.

Still, he persisted. Until one night, after he had carefully got out of bed, got dressed, grabbed his sack of pilfered food, and climbed down from his loft, bells began to ring.

Rapid, high-pitched bells, with bellowing voices alongside them. Holt had only heard similar alarms for fires, but this was much worse.

Some instinct sent a shiver up his spine.

This wasn't right.

His father awoke with a start. "What's going on?" He looked to Holt, perplexed as to why his son was awake, dressed, and carrying a laden sack.

Still barefoot, Holt hastened for the door and stepped out into the street.

People stumbled from their homes, some half-asleep and annoyed, others with panicked expressions. Out here, Holt heard the town criers call, "Attack! We're under attack!"

Holt's heart skipped a beat. His thoughts immediately turned to his dragon. Judging by the pace of the beat across the bond, the baby was still asleep, although the noise would surely wake it.

A pained roar cut over the bells and drew everyone's attention. Seemingly appearing from the night, Ysera beat her wings and hovered high over the center of town. The Matriarch of the Crag called to the tower. Distant roars answered her. The riders were being summoned.

At first, Holt's heart leaped. If the Flight Commander had returned with Silverstrike, then they would be saved from whatever attacked them. Yet something wasn't right with her either. Another shiver ran up Holt's spine. He noticed it a moment later in the way Ysera favored one side. Gouges had been torn in the sinew of her right wing, and there was another wound above the dragon's front leg. Blood seeped from it, running down her pale green scales toward her belly.

"Put your shoes and cloak on," Jonah said in a wavering voice. "Now, son. Quick!"

At that very moment, the baby woke up. Distressed by the bells, its panic reached Holt across the bond and mixed sourly with his own worry.

He had to fetch the dragon. He couldn't leave him.

"Holt?" His father pulled him back inside. "Come on. I know it's frightening, but we've got to go!"

Holt dropped the sack of meat and mechanically found his shoes and traveling cloak, his fingers fumbling with the fastenings at his neck. He'd barely got it on when his father grabbed his arm and hauled him outside.

The situation had deteriorated. People were running in terror up the street toward the center of town where they might make for the grand stairs to the Order's tower. Women screamed, children wailed, men roared orders to their families or else cried in terror themselves. And farther off in the distance, coming from the eastern town wall, was a sound more chilling than winter's frost. A shrill, rattling cry like the braying of a dying horse mixed with cattle groans.

Before Holt could even think, his father, still holding his arm, yanked him into the rush of people surging up the dirt street.

Despite everything that was happening, all Holt could think about was the baby and how he would get to him. What would happen even if he managed to? How could a blind dragon flee alongside them all?

The beat over their bond became a flutter of short pulses, as though the baby was breathing hard. Guilt filled Holt, and he would have turned around right there but for the fact his father would notice and haul him back. He'd have every reason to do so. Turning back now would seem like insanity to everyone else, but if he didn't go back, then the dragon would surely die.

Guards barred the stairs to the tower, and others ushered the townsfolk down the road toward the western gate instead, yelling all the while,

"Scourge!"

"The scourge have come!"

"Flee to the west gate!"

Holt had barely registered the meaning of this when a buzzing arose from the east. Creatures with jagged wings glided over the town wall. Unresisted, they dove into the streets below.

More roaring sounded, this time from behind, and a second later two of the Crag's dragon riders soared to meet the winged menaces with fire and ice.

There had only been eight riders left at the Crag, nine now that Commander Denna had returned. Yet she was injured, and the riders scrambling to meet the enemy were the younger ones. Would they be enough? The fact that Commander Denna had ordered an evacuation suggested not.

Why was this happening? They said the scourge never dared come so close to the Order. This was an outright assault.

His mind numb, Holt was swept up along with the crowd and carried some distance before he realized his father was no longer at his side. He whipped around.

"Dad? Dad!"

He spotted his father some way back, struggling to keep up. Jonah was bent over double, his chest heaving. Life as a Cook had ill-prepared him for such a run.

They were all unprepared for this.

Holt darted back through the throng of people and wrapped his father's arm around his own shoulder.

"No," Jonah protested. "You go on. Run as fast as you can."

"Not without you."

Fleeing without the dragon was torture enough. He wasn't going to leave his father too. As though the baby could sense his thoughts, that pitiful high voice entered his mind once more.

*"Boy?"*

Tears welled in Holt's eyes. He had to go back. Somehow, he had to.

By the time they'd made it to the west gate, priority coaches and wagons were filling up. Mothers with young children, the old and the injured huddled in fear, rammed into any available spaces on board.

Jonah pushed Holt toward the closest wagon.

"You get on," he said, still breathing hard. A soldier grabbed Holt's arm and pulled him up onto the back of the wagon before he could say or do anything in protest. Even as Holt turned around, the soldier raised the back board of the cart and slammed a bolt in place to secure it.

Holt gripped the edge of the wagon. "No. Wait!"

He attempted to jump off, but the soldier shoved him back in.

"I'll find you again," Jonah said. "I lost your mother. I won't lose you."

Before anything more could be said, a soldier called out to the wagon driver, the reins came down, and the wagon moved. Holt lurched forward, almost tumbling out over the side of the cart. Steadying himself, he froze in horror as he was taken away from his father. How would he get out?

Holt reached out a hand, and choked, "Dad—"

His words were silenced by another blood-curdling shriek and intense buzzing. Shadows passed overhead, and then the winged scourge creatures descended in the space between them.

It was Holt's first close look at the monsters from all the stories, the whole reason the dragon riders existed. Seeing them now, the very warmth of his blood abandoned him. Brode had spoken true; the paintings made it all too pretty.

These creatures were the giant wasps twisted nightmarishly wrong, with black wings and two long antennae which swung like swords. Their mandible mouths frothed, their six legs were muscled and powerful, their bodies were armored in a dark-green carapace, and their heavy stingers scored lines across the ground.

Soldiers rushed to meet them but were knocked aside like rag dolls. A spearman managed to strike one, but the blow didn't stop the creature. Its frothing maw clamped down on the weapon's shaft, gripped, then yanked the spearhead out. With a sweep of its leg, it brought the soldier in close before crushing him.

Amidst the chaos, Holt could just make out a group of soldiers defending his father and the other civilians trapped on the wrong side of the scourge stingers. Then a new shadow loomed, and a green dragon landed to engage the enemy.

Holt was certain this emerald dragon's magic manifested in control of the air, and sure enough, the stingers found themselves buffeted by conjured gales. Their wings crumpled, and they could not move.

Wielding a lime-colored blade already shining with dark blood, the rider slid down from his dragon's back to engage the enemy.

Holt had almost forgotten he'd been trying to escape from the wagon when panic enthralled him again. Across the bond, the baby's terror was all-consuming. For the briefest instant, he heard what the dragon could hear, felt what it could feel. When the moment passed, it called out to him again.

"Boy?"

The west gate drew closer; soon he would be out beyond the town walls. Holt gripped the side of the wagon again and jumped.

People called out to him, but Holt ignored them. He hit the ground, and the shock of the impact thrummed up his body before he dove into an ungraceful roll. Gasping from the pain of it, he darted into the nearest alley so no one would stop him and tried to weave his way back toward the base of the Crag.

He knew the town well, and the western side was largely clear with the attack coming from the east, but he sensed the fight was not going well. With every minute, the roars of the dragons sounded weaker while the scourge cries only grew. The unmistakable smell of smoke reached him, and the dragon bond thrummed madly, thumping with every step upon the cobbled streets.

At one turning, he skidded to a halt to avoid a skirmish between beleaguered soldiers and dead-looking men with chitinous hides.

Holt's world turned inward as he ran until he could only feel the aches in his legs, the burn in his chest, the acrid taste in the air. A street away from the storehouse, the pulse of the bond dropped to an echo.

"No!" Holt screamed, driving his legs harder than ever. He'd rather have bloody stumps than lose the dragon.

He reached the storehouse and flew inside, braced for the worst.

*"Boy! Boy!"*

The knot of warmth that was the bond blazed into a fire in Holt's chest. It pulsed painfully and grew within him – the kernel swelling to a walnut. The dragon burst out of a corner, running haphazardly. Holt met it halfway and crouched to embrace it.

"I'm here. I'm here."

It licked him and yapped happily.

"We have to go."

But just how they'd make it, he wasn't sure. The baby had been getting better at following his voice, but there was a world of difference between a peaceful night and a hellscape.

The dragon sensed his concerns. The bond flared, and Holt glimpsed how it sensed the world right now. It was darkness. It was more noise than Holt could comprehend. It was smoke and blood and death. There was no way it could follow him by his voice alone. Likely it only knew he was here because of their bond.

"I'll carry you," Holt said. He picked the dragon up, although its size didn't make this easy.

Back on the street, Holt felt quite alone and quite defeated. Flames were spreading fast, jumping from thatch roof to thatch roof as the whole town burned. He glanced to the sky in the hopes of finding a rider to save them, but he only spotted four still up there, and they were too far away to have a hope of hearing or seeing him.

His only choice was to run again, but his legs were failing. His empty stomach twisted, his head pounded, his breath came harder as smoke gathered. The fires were so fierce that his way back to the western wall was completely blocked. As was the way toward the base of the grand stairs.

But not the servants' stairway.

Holt took to it, knowing he might be trapped up in the Crag, but what choice did he have? The riders would deal with the scourge or fall back to the higher defensive ground to hold out. If he couldn't flee the town, then the tower was the safest place he could go.

Yet he didn't have the strength left to make the ascent while carrying the dragon. Just as he left the smoke behind, his legs turned to jelly and gave out.

"I don't think I can make it," he told the dragon.

Its blue eyes tried to meet his but were, as ever, a little off.

Holt's mouth turned bone dry. "I... don't think I can..."

The dragon blinked then scrambled to get out of his grasp.

*"Down."*

Holt understood its meaning. He let go. The dragon landed on the step beside him and placed a determined foot forward.

"Are you sure?"

*"Yes."*

"If you can't keep up, just tell me."

Together they set off, the baby sticking close to his leg, but somehow it managed the climb. It was the bond. Holt knew it. Yet he could feel the dragon's energy wane as it strained to blindly find its way.

When they reached the servants' courtyard, Holt paused to draw much-needed breath. When he got ahold of himself, he saw what was in the courtyard and nearly vomited.

Bodies. Everywhere. Dead servants, guards along with ghouls and great bugs. The ground was thick with green, black, and red blood.

The tower had already come under attack. Nowhere was safe.

Holt wasn't sure what to do.

Up here, the carnage below sounded distant and light.

Then thunder boomed.

A fork of blue-silver light flashed across the sky.

"Silas," Holt gasped. He bent to pull the dragon into a hug of relief. "Silverstrike has come to save us!" But the baby didn't share his joy.

It yelped into his ear and tried to pull out of his embrace. Holt turned, expecting to find a stinger swooping down at them. What he found was a confusing sight.

Commander Denna, bent low over Ysera, hovered over the front courtyard of the Crag, just at the top of the grand stairs. She and her dragon faced another pair. Holt recognized Silas' dragon Clesh, his dark gray scales almost black against the night.

Holt's own dragon kept tugging at the leg of his trousers, trying to pull him back. It could sense something that Holt could not.

What could be wrong? Silas Silverstrike was one of the greatest heroes who had fought the scourge. Why was he just hovering there with Denna and not fighting?

It was then that Commander Denna raised her war hammer, the steel glinting red from the fires across the town she had failed. With a pained roar and a jolt forward, Ysera surged through the air toward Silverstrike.

Silas didn't move. A swirling nimbus formed over his head and lightning struck down to meet his blade, just as Holt had seen him do before. Only this time, the power he unleashed was directed at the Flight Commander. Clesh opened his jaws and crackling blue energy zapped forth to join Silas' own attack.

Commander Denna and Ysera were consumed by the magic. For a moment they hung suspended in mid-air, the dragon's wings and limbs bent at crooked angles. Then they fell. Denna's smoking body parted from her dragon as they plummeted down.

Denna had been strong, a powerful rider at the limit of Champion rank. But Silas was already a Lord, and he may as well have swatted an untrained squire.

Holt's world might have ended there. He was in such shock that he didn't move a muscle, not even as scourge stingers flanked Silas Silverstrike, moving to take the tower of the Crag. And where were Mirk and his dragon Biter? They should have been at Denna's side. Perhaps they were dead too.

Down at his knees, the dragon still tugged at his clothes.

*"Boy. Come. Hide."*

A painful throb across the bond jolted Holt back to his senses. If the scourge had overrun the Crag, then nowhere would be safe. Nowhere above ground at any rate.

"The larder," Holt thought aloud before sprinting across the courtyard, leaping over bodies of the fallen with the dragon close behind him.

At the bottom of the stairwell to the kitchens, the dragon lost its footing and tumbled head over tail, slid across the floor and slammed against an upturned table. Holt ran to its side, but it seemed unharmed. The hatchling was sturdier than it looked.

The kitchens were a total mess. Pots, pans and knives lay strewn across the floor. Perhaps the few servants who had been here had tried to fight their way out. One of the great worktables had been upturned, and its location made Holt's heart sink.

The table blocked the trap door to the larder.

Holt groaned. This wasn't fair. He couldn't move that on his own. Yet he had no choice but to try.

His first attempts were laughable. He could barely get a grip on the enormous table, never mind move it. Again and again he tried to push, pull or lift it, but his feeble limbs and exhausted body didn't have the power.

The dragon started roaring squeakily. Panting, Holt looked over to the stairwell where the baby paced like a guard dog.

*"They come. They come."*

The fight in Holt died. He flopped down, defeated. He couldn't move this hunk of wood on his own, and soon the scourge would finish him off.

"Boy," the dragon bounded over to him. *"Hide."*

"I can't move it," Holt wheezed. It felt painful just to speak. "It's too heavy. We're stuck."

*"Help you,"* the dragon said. It took a second to get its bearings, then approached the upturned table at speed only to smack its head off the wood. Undeterred, the dragon shook off the pain, then stood on its hind legs and started pressing against the table with its front claws. It hardly helped, but Holt felt shamed by the baby.

If it wouldn't give up, then neither would he.

He got up and joined the dragon in pushing again. He cried out from the effort, but still the table barely budged.

A clanking echoed from the staircase.

"Come on!" Holt yelled. The dragon roared as mightily as it could too, and Holt felt the beat of their bond begin to pound. More than that, there seemed to be another sound behind the beating – a sort of... music.

Holt had never heard such music before, if indeed that's what it was. It was light, haunting and powerful all at once. He caught only a few notes of it, but in that moment his body changed.

His exhaustion vanished. His head cleared. His muscles grew taut with newfound strength.

Feet braced, Holt pushed at the table again. This time it moved. In fact, it did more than move. Holt sent it skidding across the kitchens to crash into the wall, snapping off one of its legs.

As quickly as the strength had filled him, it left. Holt could no longer hear the music across the dragon bond, but it didn't matter. He pulled up the trap door to the larder and ushered the dragon to his side. He'd already put one foot down the steps when something caught his eye.

Upon the ground by the great hearth, laid open and with a torn page, was his family's recipe book. Despite the clanking from the stairs and knowing he had only moments, Holt dashed for it, picked it up, bolted back, and pulled the dragon down to the larder.

The trap door wouldn't lock from this side, but he didn't think those creatures would think to open it or know how.

Down here, he would be safe.

A cold blackness enveloped him. There were no candles lit this time. Now both he and his dragon were blind.

Holt staggered until he found a shelf to slump against, then slid to the floor. He put the recipe book beside him. Padding feet followed, and then the dragon pressed into him. Holt fumbled in the dark to give it an awkward hug.

Heavy footsteps trod across the kitchen and echoed through the stone. Holt drew in shallow breaths until the footsteps moved on. Once they were gone, he let out a shuddering sigh of relief.

"*Tired,*" the dragon told him.

"You can rest now. You did so well."

"*No. You're tired,*" the dragon insisted. Its voice wasn't quite so high now, its words better formed, as though a toddler had matured to a young child in the blink of an eye.

Holt could only nod.

"*Sleep, Holt,*" the dragon said. "*I will listen for them.*"

"Thank you," Holt said wearily.

Closing his eyes meant little in this darkness, but Holt fell asleep the very moment he did.

# 11

# ASH

Banging and long scratching screeches ran through the walls. Holt awoke, or thought he did. In the total dark it was hard to tell. He fell asleep, woke again, slept then woke. Cold sweat gathered on his skin. As his mind raced for some comfort, a small song came to him, a song his mother sang to him when he was very young.

*Far beyond the Sunset Sea, Where even dragons cannot fly, I know there is a place, Where the living do not die.*

Its words tumbled in him, repeating over and over, a mixture of his own voice, a hundred singers, his mother, his father.

*Far beyond the endless blue, Where every harvest overflows, Where the blight cannot take hold, Far beyond the sea.*

He woke again, trembling. Yet something warm nestled up tighter against him, and a second heartbeat thumped in his soul. That settled him. His eyelids fluttered and closed, and this time the drift to sleep was easier.

*Yonder cross the Sunset Sea, Where winter cannot bite, I know, I know there is a place, Where dreams may come to light, Out there, far beyond the sea...*

. . .

Holt awoke with a start in the darkness. Fully awake this time, his heart beating as though he had been running. He had not slept well. Recent events rushed in a blur before him: the bells, the monsters, fire, smoke, blood, and the look on his father's face as the wagon trundled away. It had been a look of relief; he believed Holt was going to be safe.

Reality couldn't have been further from the truth.

Holt forced thoughts of his father to one side for now. He had to have faith that his father had made it out of town and was fleeing with the others. Maybe a rider or two from the Crag would be there to protect them.

Yet the worst memory of the attack drifted back to him then. Silas Silverstrike had betrayed them all. He'd struck down Flight Commander Denna and seemed to be on the same side as the scourge. The implications of this were... well, they were too huge for Holt to comprehend.

Not on an empty stomach, at any rate.

He also noticed the dragon had left his side, or at least it wasn't in arms' reach as he grasped in the dark.

"Where are you?"

He'd really have to name the dragon now that they would live or die together.

*"Eating,"* the dragon said happily. *"I'll bring you some."*

"Okay," Holt said into the blackness. He felt rather stupid and useless just slumped here.

*I'm as blind as the dragon. Although he at least seems to have managed to move around.*

The dragon's talons clacked off the stone floor as it moved. Something else tapped rhythmically too, though it was out of sync with the dragon's footsteps.

"Can you find me?" Holt said. "Follow my voice like we've practiced."

And then he realized, foolishly, that the dragon must have been moving around while he was still asleep. The out-of-sync tapping between the dragon's footsteps continued.

*He's whacking his tail off the floor,* Holt thought. *That's odd.*

"Why are you hitting your tail like that?"

*"To make noise. Sound changes depending on what's around me."*

While the concept was new to the dragon, it of course made perfect sense to Holt. Realization dawned, and he understood the dragon tapping its tail in a new light. Hollow objects would sound different from solid ones. Noise would ring and echo in hard environments like the kitchens, compared to soft surroundings such as a bed and pillows. Yet never had he stopped to consider the matter in any detail. He had never had to. For the dragon, learning the distinctions would be crucial in building up a mental picture of the world.

A moment later, there came a thud, then the distinct shattering of clay. A *glug, glug, glug* followed as oil spilled from a broken jar. So, the dragon was not yet a master of its movements. Then again, it was doing far better than Holt could do in the pitch black.

"You okay?" Holt asked.

*"Yes, boy. I thought that was part of the wall. It sounded solid to me."*

"I suppose the jar must have *sounded* solid," Holt said. "I think it was full of oil."

Their bond flared as the dragon reached him.

*"I can tell where things are, just not always what they are. Not yet. I'm still learning."*

"Well I'm very impressed," Holt said. He reached out a hand for the dragon's snout to pat him but felt a coarse sack in his way. This must contain the promised food the dragon was bringing. "You found food well enough then?"

The dragon dropped the bundle into Holt's lap. He was pleased it didn't feel wet or cold. Nothing raw then.

*"I could smell it."*

*Of course*, Holt thought. He had heard of blind people having greater strength in their other senses. Perhaps the dragon benefitted from this as well, maybe doubly so because it was a magical creature.

"What's easier for you to 'see' by?" Holt asked. "Sound or smell?"

*"Not everything has a smell. I need sound for some things, but both is best."*

"I can still call out for you when you need to find me, if it helps?"

*"You're easy to find, boy. I know your smell, and I can hear a beating from inside you."*

"You can hear my heartbeat?"

*"I hear it more and more each day. I hear and smell more things each day."* The dragon nudged at Holt's hand and then at the sack it had brought him. *"Go on, eat. It's good."*

Gingerly, Holt reached for the sack and wormed his hand inside. It felt like meat, dried out and tough. Placing a strip in his mouth, he soon discovered it was beef jerky, salty and chewy, but in his current state it tasted exquisite. Holt began shoveling the stuff into his mouth.

*"More?"* the dragon asked.

"Have you had enough?" Holt said thickly.

*"For now. I should get more for when we leave."*

"Uh, yes… that's a good idea."

The dragon padded off again, tapping its tail off the stone as it went, seemingly unaware it had left Holt in no small measure of shock.

Just how quickly did dragons mature? A week ago, it could barely speak, and now it was formulating plans about their ration supply? Not only that but its ability to comprehend the world was improving rapidly. Just how powerful would its remaining senses become?

Holt decided not to dwell on the matter. The more capable the dragon was, the better for them both. It returned, dragging something behind it. From the sound of cloth scraping along stone, it had grabbed another bundle of jerky. When its wet nose nuzzled into Holt, he almost jumped from surprise, and he vowed never to take his own sight for granted again.

"I wonder if the scourge have gone?"

*"They have."*

"You're sure?"

*"I can't hear anything moving above."*

Unable to hear anything beyond his own breathing down here, Holt decided to take the dragon at its word.

"They might still be in the town or up in the main tower."

The dragon didn't have an answer for him. Holt ate a few more pieces of jerky as he contemplated their options. They would have to venture back up at some point. So long as the dragon could pick up on movement from further away than he could, they could always retreat and try again later.

"We don't even know whether it's day or night," Holt lamented. He couldn't be sure how long he'd slept for.

"*It's daytime.*" The dragon spoke with some authority on the matter.

"How can you possibly know that?"

"*I just do… I feel stronger at night.*"

"Stronger? How?"

"*I don't know. But night is when you're with me.*"

Holt was touched. Maybe their bond worked both ways.

"Does this have something to do with how I moved that table covering the trap door? Did you… make me stronger?"

"*I don't know.*"

Holt supposed that was fair. He didn't exactly know how his own body worked, never mind having magic involved too.

"Well, if you're sure it's daytime, I suppose we should head up. Carefully."

He was about to get up but remembered his father's recipe book. He tapped around on his left side and found the smooth leather cover. With the book in one hand, he would need his other hand free to open the trap door.

"Can you grab the food, please?"

A rustle and bite of teeth told him the dragon had obliged.

"Okay. Here goes."

Slowly, he felt his way back along the shelves, knocking a few jars to the floor. Well, more broken things hardly mattered now. Holt had to help the dragon negotiate the steep, ladder-like steps, but they emerged into the kitchens without incident.

"Do you hear anything?"

When the dragon shook its head, they moved on. Nothing gave them pause reaching the servants' courtyard either. The dragon had been correct; it was daytime, although what time of day was a mystery. Holt couldn't see the sun. Clouds blackened the sky as far as he could see. There was hardly a breeze at all, the waves were barely audible. It was as if the whole world had turned grim and lifeless.

Fire had ruined everything. Charred bodies and burned remains of buildings made up the servants' courtyard. Dreading what else he would find, Holt turned and had his fears confirmed. The tower of the Crag had burned too, and what stone remained was now scorched. Sections were still burning from unnatural black fires that neither spread nor grew but lingered like dark wounds on a corpse.

As though in a trance, Holt made his way around to the front courtyard where similar scenes of battle met him. Lying in a crumpled, broken heap at the top of the grand stairs was the pale body of Ysera. And covering the battlefield at the tower's base was a thick layer of ash. Some still trickled down from the highest reaches of the once tall tower.

Everything and everyone Holt had known was gone.

The dragon put down the bundle of food and began walking to the middle of the courtyard, its feet making imprints on the ash as if it were freshly fallen snow. Surrounded by white and gray, the dragon blended in. Hard as it was to believe, Holt's dragon, the one he was supposed to have destroyed, was now the last dragon at the Crag.

Sorrow for the other hatchlings filled Holt, a pain amplified by the dragon's own sense of loss. Sadness washed across their bond and the dragon wailed. It twisted its neck this way and that, as though searching for an answer that would never come. When it finished, it turned around and looked straight at Holt.

*"I sense them still, crying out…"*

Their bond drummed, and Holt caught a glimmer of what the dragon could sense with its magic. Unlike the night before, when he'd heard that beautiful music, the notes he heard now were broken and stricken, like a songbird uttering its dying breaths.

Holt gulped, then fell to his knees. "I'm sorry. I'm so sorry."

The dragon remained where it was. Suddenly it braced its feet as though it was about to pounce, craned its neck skyward, and roared, as loud as a grown drake, and the ground cracked through some unseen force.

Neither of them moved a muscle. Holt simply stared at the dragon as it grieved. Dirty white cinders landed on the dragon's back, almost blending in with its scales.

"Ash..." Holt rolled the name around in his mind. He found it suiting. "I'm going to call you, Ash."

The baby cocked its head.

"Do you like that?"

"*I do,*" the dragon said, and then its voice turned suddenly harsh and older. Holt could feel the dragon's conviction through the bond. "*I will avenge this.*"

As quickly as the change had come over the dragon, it ceased. Ash's stance relaxed and he lowered his head, sniffing to pinpoint Holt, his eyes wide like two sapphires.

"I'm right ahead of you," Holt said.

Ash yapped and bounded to his side.

"You okay? You went a bit... strange."

"*I'm not sure,*" Ash said, though his voice was far younger again, less assured. "*But I know we have to find the ones who did this.*"

"Easier said than done."

Still on his knees, Holt looked out across the smoking town. Where would he go? What would he do?

Another distant roar reached Holt's ears.

Ash twisted his neck around in search of the noise.

"What is it?" Holt asked.

"*Another dragon.*"

Holt's stomach plummeted. Probably Silas Silverstrike coming back to ensure the job was complete. He heard the cry of the dragon again, much clearer this time. The dragon and its rider were surely near.

"We need to run back to the larder."

"*Wait. It's not an elder male's call.*"

"What then?"

"*Younger. Female.*"

"Ash, I don't know if we should risk it—" But he cut himself short. To the north he saw a dragon drop down below the clouds. A dragon with purple scales. And there was only one dragon he knew of that color. Pyra.

Princess Talia had returned.

# 12

# A NEW FLIGHT

Despite his relief in seeing Talia and Pyra, Holt worried over how they would react to Ash. He led Ash into the entrance of the ruined tower and convinced him to stay put until called. When Talia drew closer, Holt ran out into the courtyard and began jumping up and down, waving his arms and yelling to ensure they saw him.

Pyra roared mournfully when she reached the courtyard. She hovered over the remains of the Matriarch, then turned her baleful yellows eyes upon Holt. Swiftly she descended, sending up clouds of cinders when she touched down. It was then Holt noticed there was a second rider on Pyra's back.

Lord Brode.

Then it hit him. Brode had said he was going on a trip, and Talia had flown away a few days ago. Holt only now realized that he hadn't seen Brode around the Crag since then.

The old rider slid down from Pyra first, and the dragon sagged in relief. She was still a young dragon herself, and carrying two people must have taken its toll on her.

"What are you still doing here?" Brode asked him. He approached Holt cautiously, one hand gripping the hilt of his sword, ready to draw it at a moment's notice.

Holt was taken aback. Of all the reactions, he hadn't expected this. Brode was treating him like a threat.

"I hid."

"Civilians would have been evacuated," Brode said. "No one else remains. Just you."

"You can't think I was involved?"

"Where's your father?"

Holt gulped. "I... I don't know. I think he got away."

*I hope he got away.*

Talia slid down from Pyra then and unsheathed her own sword, a flowing crimson blade, blazing as though freshly drawn from a smith's forge.

"Master Brode," she called, her voice stiff from suppressed grief. "Pyra and I sense another core nearby—"

Brode spun and threw out an arm. "Stay back, Talia. And get back on your dragon. If this turns out to be a trap—"

"But you know me," Holt interjected. "What trap could I possibly—"

"Silence," Brode said, rounding on him. "I don't know what to think. The scourge have magic of their own. This could be some illusion."

"Then how can I prove to you I'm me?"

Brode considered him evenly, then met his eye and spoke firmly. "What task did I give you?"

Holt's stomach squirmed. Well, it had to come out at some point.

"You gave me a dragon egg to destroy."

Brode relaxed his grip on his sword.

"Another core nearby..." he muttered, stepping closer to Holt. "An egg to destroy... and did you do something incredibly stupid?"

His gaze left Holt, roving the courtyard instead and then the entrance to the Crag itself.

"I..." Holt hesitated. What would happen to Ash?

Brode towered over him and shook him roughly. "Did you?"

Holt nodded, his eyes fixed on the ground.

"Where is it?"

"Do you promise not to hurt him?"

"Where is it, pot boy?"

Heart and bond thumping, Holt turned to face the Crag. "Ash? Come on out. Come to my voice."

Ash stepped slowly out from behind the Order Hall doorway. The moment he did so, Pyra growled and pivoted so fast she nearly knocked Talia over. She let loose a low, rumbling roar, and the full disapproval of her amber eyes was trained on Ash. He wasn't able to see the threatening look Pyra gave him, but her tone was unmistakable. Poor Ash bowed his head in fright and picked up his pace, running to Holt to take refuge behind him.

Talia ran over to them, ignoring Brode's orders. "Pyra says he is the reason the scourge came."

"That's crazy," Holt said.

Talia acted like Holt wasn't there.

"She says his weakness has brought ruin upon the flight." Her voice went wooden, her eyes glazed over, and she raised her sword. "She says he should never have hatched. He's an insult to *our* race."

Holt looked at her drawn sword with newfound alarm. He placed himself between Talia and Ash.

"Leave him alone," he said. Then, with the family recipe book still in hand, he threw his weight behind it and shoved Talia with all his might.

Several things happened at once. Talia's eyes returned to normal, a horrified look broke across her face, and she dropped her sword, wringing her hand as though it had burned her. Across the courtyard, Pyra roared with fury and began bounding toward the group. And Brode snatched at the back of Holt's neck, pulled him away from Talia, and threw out a hand toward Pyra.

"Enough!" Brode yelled. Pyra skidded to a stop, a little too close for Holt's comfort. "No one is going to hurt anyone. There's been enough death already."

"Pyra says—" Talia began.

"I know damn well what she'll be saying. No, the dragon shouldn't have hatched, but it's happened now. It's done."

Pyra snorted smoke, beat a claw against the ground, then lowered her head and turned away from Brode.

"And you, Princess," Brode carried on, "do not allow your dragon's emotions to dominate you so easily. Resist. Your mind is your own."

"Yes, Master Brode." She picked up her sword and sheathed it, her cheeks turning as bright as her hair.

Holt squirmed but Brode had him in an iron grip. For an old man, he was very strong.

"You let me down," Brode said darkly. "Don't disobey me again, if you want to live." He let Holt go, throwing him back toward Ash. "What's wrong with him?" Brode barked as an afterthought.

"He's blind," Holt said.

"Poor thing," Talia said.

"But he's capable," Holt said. He knelt to Ash's level and was about to stroke his head and neck when Talia snatched his hand away.

"Don't do that, you fool. Hatchlings aren't careful with humans."

"What are you talking about? Ash wouldn't hurt me."

"Ash?" Talia said in disbelief. "You named it?"

Holt looked to Brode for help.

"That's a nice name, Holt. But it's not our place to name dragons. They're not pets."

"His name is Ash," Holt said with more determination than he felt.

Brode frowned.

Feeling he wouldn't be interrupted again, Holt returned to scratching Ash down his neck. The bond warmed him gently from within. And then he experienced a new sensation, akin to the feeling of being watched, but it came from inside of him. A gentle touch at his soul followed, light as a feather and gone just as quick.

"He has a bond," Talia said. "Of low Novice rank to be sure, and the dragon's core is barely a heartbeat – no wonder nobody picked up on it while the Order was here – but it's... solid for what it is."

Brode came over and crouched beside them. His face softened, and he looked more his age than ever, exhausted and sad. "What happened here?"

Holt told them the whole sorry tale, from the moment he heard the bells to the moment he had closed his eyes to escape the waking nightmare.

Talia let out a choked whisper. "Silas Silverstrike would never betray us. You must be mistaken."

Holt met Talia's eyes then, the first time he'd truly met them. They were dark green and full of sorrow. He didn't need a dragon bond with her to know they shared the same feeling. Silas had been as much a hero to her as to himself, probably more so given she was a rider.

"I'm not mistaken." Holt's voice cracked in admitting it. "I saw it happen."

Ash growled to signal his agreement.

Across the courtyard, Pyra rumbled low in her throat. She stood at the site of Ysera's and Commander Denna's demise, her head bowed almost to the ground.

All the fight seemed to drain from the princess. Her shoulders slumped and she sighed heavily. "Pyra says she can sense an echo of the storm magic. It's true."

Brode grunted. He dropped to one knee by Ash. "No obvious type, and he's looking a little thin."

"I tried my best to feed him," Holt said.

"Couldn't sneak enough food away, I imagine," Brode said, without taking his eyes from Ash.

"I think he might be a mystic dragon."

"Could be," Brode said. He reached out a hand to Ash, who sniffed at it, then allowed Brode to run a finger down his snout. "I take it he has spoken with you?"

"He's getting better," Holt said. "Say something to Brode, boy."

"*I cannot reach his mind,*" Ash said.

Holt opened his mouth in confusion but Brode laughed it off. "It's not as easy as that, especially for one as young as him. Nor are hatchlings so comfortable around humans to allow them close like this. Your bond must be strong. Fascinating."

"Well," Talia said with a swish of her red hair, "whatever he's done to this dragon can be dealt with by a senior rider from Falcaer Fortress. You can look after the pot boy, Master Brode, and I'll go to Sidastra and—"

Brode jumped to his feet and caught Talia by the arm as she attempted to leave. "You'll do no such thing."

Talia scowled. "I have a duty to the realm. I must go to warn my uncle, ready the army and lead the defense."

"You'll do no such *thing*."

Talia closed her eyes.

Brode groaned. "Don't you—"

Talia reopened her eyes, and now they shone like bright emeralds. Tendrils of thin flames burst from her arm where Brode's hand gripped her. Brode cursed and loosened his grip enough for her to throw him off and start running for Pyra faster than Holt thought possible.

Brode wrung his hand and called after her. "You're a rider first. You swore the oath!"

"Riders fight the scourge. That's what I'm doing."

"What happens at court isn't your concern."

"It's my family!" Talia screamed back. "I won't turn my back again. I won't!" She climbed onto Pyra's back, but the dragon didn't take off. "Come on," Talia wailed. "Come on, girl. Go!"

"The Crag's flight might be decimated, but we're still here. I am still here. Pyra knows her duty."

Talia's strength faded with every plea she made. "Pyra, go, please, please, for me. Go."

Pyra's amber eyes, so recently full of hate, were now wells of pity. She looked to Brode, and her expression hardened. Pyra may not have liked following the order, but she would obey a senior rider.

A moment later, all the fight went out of the princess. She collapsed sobbing onto her dragon's back and wrapped her arms around Pyra's neck.

Now it was clear Talia wouldn't be going anywhere, Brode relaxed.

Holt too let out a breath he hadn't been aware of holding.

Ash nudged his head into Holt's knee. *"What will we do?"*

"We'll stick with Brode," Holt whispered. "He'll look after us."

Although what one young rider, an old dragonless rider, a hatchling and a Cook's son would achieve when all else had fallen, Holt hadn't the faintest idea.

# 13

# A POOR FUNERAL

In a silent comradery and remembrance for the dead, the unlikely party picked their way through the ashes of the Crag, gathering what supplies they could. Little was left, so little that Brode commented a dark magic must have helped to fuel the spread of the flames. Not even a spare bedroll or set of clothes could be found for Holt. But Brode offered the use of his own bedding and wouldn't hear a word against it.

They climbed the tower slowly. On the fourth level, shards of glass lay strewn in the doorway of the library.

"Our ghost orbs," Talia said. "All that knowledge, memories of the Order here. Gone."

The armory had survived better than most rooms, though the contents had been pillaged.

"They've taken my armor," Talia bemoaned. She kicked at a charred helmet, then sucked in a sharp breath from the pain of it, though she didn't let it show on her face with Holt looking.

"The scourge did this?" Holt asked. He didn't rate those monsters as thinking creatures.

"Their risen dead – the ghouls – can wield weapons and wear armor," Talia said. "Even if they don't make it themselves."

Holt's throat went dry again. He was sorry he'd asked.

They did retrieve some weaponry from the debris: a thick steel dagger for each of them and a plain longsword. Talia had no use for the sword, given she still had her own unique rider blade, as did Brode. Holt reached out a hand expectantly for it, but Brode laughed and kept a firm grip on the scabbard. Servants were forbidden from bearing a sword.

Surely that did not matter now?

"Shouldn't I have a weapon?" Holt asked.

Brode wrestled with the notion. Holt could see it play out upon his face. Before Holt could say more, the old rider thrust the sheath of a dagger into his hand.

"Carry this for now," Brode said. "You have some skill with knives already, I dare say."

Holt strapped it to a belt around his waist, unwilling to press the issue for now. Brode took the spare sword with them, suggesting there was some hope of training in his future.

Holt led them to the kitchens and the larder next. This time they managed to find a few candles to see by and scavenged every provision and utensil they could reasonably carry. The fresher vegetables would be welcome, and the red meat would keep for a while on the road, though they salted it all the same. More important were dried goods: mushrooms, fish, and meat, all sorts of spices, pickled onions and carrots, and hard cheese. Jars of jam and loaves of the darkest bread filled out the rest of the sacks. A good haul, all things considered, and it made the immediate days ahead seem marginally less terrible.

Meat for Pyra was the most difficult consideration. Dragons had quite the appetite and Pyra would demand beef, as Talia constantly reminded them. There were several cattle carcasses in the deep storage. Brode and Talia went off in search of further supplies while Holt butchered the meat for the road.

All experienced Cooks knew butchery as well as any trained Butcher. Holt did not consider himself a master of the techniques yet, but he knew enough, and these cuts hardly needed to be neat or clean. That done, he found the sack of meat too heavy to lift and resorted to dragging it back through the larder. The others found him struggling to heave it up the stairs to the kitchens. Without a word, Talia took his burden from him, lifting the bloody sack as though it weighed no more than a feather.

The dragons had waited for them outside, although judging by Pyra's aloofness and Ash's wandering on the other side of the court-yard, there had been little interaction. Pyra snorted another plume of smoke when it was announced they would strap much of the supplies to her back. She growled, stamped her claws, and flexed her talons menacingly.

Holt thought Brode would have a word with her, but it was the princess who threw down the sack of meat and berated her own dragon. Pyra relented after that and agreed she would carry her own food.

When at last they were ready to leave, Brode called them over to the top of the grand staircase.

"The walk through town will feel endless," he said solemnly. "Keep your heads up, and don't dwell on what's around you. Pyra, use your fire and burn any remaining bodies – all of them. The last thing we need is a scourge-risen dragon following us." He jerked his head to indicate she should start with the bodies of Ysera and Denna. Then he walked on.

"Wait," Talia called. "Master Brode, should we not say a few words... or something."

Brode stood for a moment facing the smoking town before turning. "If it will help you."

Without missing a beat, he continued down the stairs.

Talia looked appalled. She also seemed lost for the very words she considered so important.

Feeling awkward and that he should say something, Holt asked, "Did you know her well?"

Talia rolled her eyes. "Well, no. Those of Novice rank and even fresh Ascendants aren't trained by the Flight Commander herself. Not that you'd know—" She caught herself before saying anything further.

Ash nudged into Holt's leg, and he gave the dragon a scratch on his head.

*"She is sad. She does not intend her anger."*

"I know," Holt said. He thought about walking on with Brode all the same. He hardly had anything to say about the death of the Flight Commander.

Just then, Talia knelt, brushed her hair behind her ears, and placed a hand on the Commander's great breastplate. "I should have been here. I'm... I'm sorry."

Holt thought this a strange thing to say. "What good would that have done? At least you're alive."

Talia gave him a dark look. "I'm never where I should be."

Holt felt like he'd put his foot in it somehow. This talk of death made him uncomfortable, but words from his father surfaced in his mind.

"If you love with your eyes, death is forever. If you love with your heart, there is no such thing as parting."

Talia sniffed. "Where did you learn that, pot boy?" Her tone was kindly enough.

"My father said that to me after... after my mother died."

"It's a beautiful thought." She gave him a weak smile. A single tear rolled down her cheek as she stood up. "I can't say I loved Commander Denna but... I did love this place. Thank you—" She struggled for half a moment before remembering, "—Holt. I guess you aren't just a pot boy anymore."

Ash cooed his agreement, craning his neck to the sky. Holt was about to answer when Brode called from behind, "Move it, you two."

Holt turned away as Pyra began bathing Ysera and Denna in her fiery breath. He stayed several steps behind Talia out of ingrained habit, but he had Ash by his side for company.

As they neared the western gate, Holt cast around, looking for his father. He couldn't inspect each body, nor did he wish to get too close, but when he saw no sign of his father's cloak, his spirits lifted. It gave him hope to hold onto.

# 14

# BLACKENED AND RAW

After marching south for hours, and when the gray sky finally turned to a starless black, Brode called a halt. Holt slumped to the ground. He'd never walked so long in all his life and his feet ached. Ash, on the other hand, seemed fine. In fact, he looked more energetic if anything, bounding around Holt in a circle.

"Hardly the time to rest," Brode said. "We'll need firewood. There are some trees off to our left. Go see what you can find."

Groaning, Holt got back to his feet. He noted with interest that Talia wasn't joining him. *I'm still the servant then,* he thought.

Ash followed along, although he wasn't of much help.

*"There are so many new smells here,"* he said, excited. *"What's this? Food? Why won't it stay still?"* A brief sound of chewing preceded a disgusted spit. *"That was not tasty! Too many legs."*

Holt chuckled. "I don't imagine bugs taste good no matter how hungry you are." He started picking up what fallen branches he could find but before long his own stomach began to wail from hunger again. Shaking fresh life into his limbs, he picked up a final fallen branch and returned to camp. Brode helped him stack the firewood, and then at last Talia stirred.

She sat cross-legged; her rider's blade lay on the ground next to her, as she'd be unable to sit with it still strapped to her back. Slowly, she brought her hands together as though holding an invisible ball. Next her eyes flared bright, and in the empty space between her palms, a sphere of fire swirled into existence, blue at its center and trailing red on its outer edges. Talia parted her hands, and the ball of flame remained floating above her right palm. She focused on it, seeming to move it with her mind down to the tip of her finger before lowering it to the base of the stacked firewood. It caught, and the wood ignited into a blooming fire quicker than flint and tinder would achieve.

"Wow," Holt gasped.

Pyra made a throaty rumble laced with derision.

"She says you are easily impressed," Talia said.

He looked at his own hands rather stupidly, then to Ash, hoping for some new power to surface in himself.

Ash cocked his head and licked his lips. *"I'm hungry."*

*Well,* Holt thought, *perhaps in time we'll have magic too?*

"Easy does it, Talia," Brode warned. "You're exhausted as it is. Save drawing on Pyra's core until we need it. You can Cleanse and Forge after dinner. Now, let's eat."

Talia yawned. "Good thing we have a Cook with us."

Holt couldn't be sure whether she was joking or not, and due to his own state of exhaustion, hunger and anxiety, his sense of propriety abandoned him.

"I already got the firewood. Am I to make your dinner too? What was calling me a dragon rider earlier all about if you didn't mean it?"

Talia looked at him, astonished. Holt felt a strong pang of horror as a lifetime of ingrained manners and etiquette tried to force him to take it back, to apologize. But he held his own.

At length Talia responded, slowly. "I didn't call you a rider. I said you weren't a pot boy, but honestly, I'm not sure what you are now. Perhaps my squire?"

Holt puffed up his chest. "I have a dragon."

"A blind dragon," Talia reminded him. "You're only going to hold us back. It will be up to me—"

"Enough," Brode said. He didn't raise his voice, but they both stopped and faced him. "Empty stomachs are the root of most arguments. Eat first, and you'll find your moods improve. Stick to the bread and cheese tonight. That way no one has to cook other than some meat for the dragons, and you can each provide for your own."

"Thank you, Brode," Holt said, feeling like he'd come out the victor.

Brode scowled. "I won't tolerate whining. You two start while I cut some beef for the dragons."

Feeling quite put in his place, Holt quietly searched the sacks of food; retrieving a loaf of bread and wedges of cheese, he passed Talia her share.

The first bite Holt took sent a pang through his jaw as the muscles awoke. A few mouthfuls later and he was already feeling better but continued to chew in silence, as did Talia.

Brode cut a large steak for Ash and a veritable slab for Pyra. He speared the beef onto the ends of metal skewers they had brought from the kitchens and set them near the fire.

Once Holt had had his fill, he raised Ash's steak over the campfire, turning it every fifteen seconds to sear each side well without overdoing the middle, a trick he'd picked up from his father without even realizing. A beefy smell filled the air. Ash perked up. He crept closer to the fire and near enough fell over Holt in an effort to get closer to the sizzling meat. Once the steak was ready, Holt shimmied the skewer until it fell onto the grass. Ash pounced on it. A warm satisfied glow rippled over their bond.

Ash made no attempt to eat quietly – gnashing, chewing, and swallowing loudly. Out of the darkness, Pyra snorted again but Holt ignored her.

By now Talia had finished eating and crept closer to the campfire herself, clearly working up to the task at hand. She lifted the much larger cut of meat over the fire and began turning it as Holt had, although her timing was erratic, and she wasn't holding it evenly over the flames.

"Erm, princess," Holt began, "you might want to try—"

"I can manage," Talia said. Pyra growled in agreement. Her yellow eyes, like fireflies in the night, trained onto Holt with a new intensity.

And then he heard a new voice in his mind. It was female, deep and haughty.

*"Talia is of noble birth and lineage. She does not require the aid of a kitchen rat."*

Holt's heart skipped a beat, and he found he could not hold Pyra's gaze. He bowed his head and looked away. Ash actually stopped eating.

*"Boy, are you okay?"*

"I'm fine," he croaked and gave Ash a scratch down his neck. "Go back to your steak."

"Did she speak to you?" Brode asked. His face had become a series of dancing shadows.

"She did," Holt said, trying to pretend like it was nothing.

Brode cut another chunk of cheese and thumbed it into his mouth. "She's got a nasty tongue at times," he said thickly. "Don't let her get to you."

Pyra turned on Brode and snorted more smoke.

Brode shrugged and continued with his meal.

Despite the rudeness from Pyra, Holt couldn't help but smirk. She may claim to not think much of him, but dragons rarely spoke to humans, if ever, save for riders. It was a recognition of sorts.

"It's done," Talia suddenly announced, taking the beef to Pyra.

From the burnt smell of it, Holt had to agree it was 'done'. Far too well-done.

Pyra seemed to agree. A few bites in, and the dragon spat the food out and groaned weakly.

"What do you mean?" Talia asked. "I gave it plenty of heat."

Holt risked a glance in the direction of the fallen beef. Talia had managed to burn the outside while still leaving the meat raw at the center. An impressive feat in its own way.

Pyra rumbled again, looking reproachfully at her rider.

"What? No, I didn't spice it," Talia said. "I'm sorry, Pyra, but I'm sure it's fine. I'll put it back on."

"Pampered beast," Brode scoffed. "Back in my day, dragons still hunted for their meals. None of this cooking to preference with personal orders."

Ash wandered over to the discarded beef, sniffing at it.

*"The grumpy one does not want it?"*

Before Holt could answer, Pyra sniffed snootily and turned away from the camp.

"Pyra," Talia wailed, but Brode cut her off with a wave of his hand.

"Let her sulk. She'll come around when she's hungry enough. Look, the hatchling doesn't mind it." Even as Brode spoke, Ash tore a bloody chunk off the ill-cooked slab and chewed happily. "See, all dragons can eat any meat in any form if needed. Ours have become fussy."

Talia sat down in a huff, then buried her face into her hands.

Holt eyed Ash with some annoyance. *So, you'll just eat any old rubbish, will you? Why do I bother?* He would have been better off making Pyra's food after all.

A notion came to him then, and he pulled out his father's recipe book, flicking through to the section on fire dragons. He found the recipe he had in mind soon enough, then considered whether to follow through.

Pyra had been nothing but mean and stuck up this whole time; she'd even called him a rat. But they were stuck together, and they'd be better off getting along.

Holt recalled the occasion about a year ago when a new kitchen-hand came into his father's service. The older hands had hated her at first because she didn't know how things were done and she caused more trouble than assistance in those first weeks. But then one night she stayed and worked through until dawn, leaving the others with so little to do the next day it had been like a holiday for them. She'd done far more than her fair share to appease the others. After that, they'd all got along like old friends.

This situation wasn't quite the same, but Holt figured he ought to try.

"Master Brode," he said boldly, "if you'll cut some more beef, I'd like to try something."

Brode raised his eyebrows but did not protest. As he played the butcher, Holt opened the bag of utensils and felt around until he found a skillet. Next, he opened each bag of spices and herbs he'd taken from the larder, smelling the contents until he found the two he needed. That done, he moved everything to the fireside.

"How's this?" Brode asked. He presented a roughly hewn fillet which was uneven and much too thick at one end. But Holt knew how to fix it.

He drew out the dagger he had received earlier that day. It was harder to handle than a cook's knife, but he carefully sliced into the thickest end to butterfly the cut. Then he picked up the pan. It was black iron and heavy on his wrist, but he held it with a new confidence. The beef was likely to stick without oil, and he would have to hold the pan over the fire for a long time to heat properly – an open fire being far colder than hot coals – but he'd make do.

Eventually, the meat was sizzling, filling the air with its beefy scent as the fat rendered down. Out of the corner of his eye, he saw Pyra shift in the darkness, edging back closer to the fire, but he paid her no mind. He was focused on his task now.

"The recipe is for a quick beef dish while on the move," Holt told them. "The spices are simple. Ground kracker pepper from the Searing Sands and a small pinch of a tangy spice from the Jade Jungle."

He added these ingredients now, judging how much to add given the size of the cut he was dealing with. At once, a peppery blast filled his nostrils. Even Ash looked up from his devouring of the charred meat.

Holt turned Pyra's dinner over a few more times, checking the coloring was even before deciding it was ready. He whipped the skillet away from the fire, approached Pyra until he was about ten paces away, and placed the new dish onto the grass for her.

Pyra rushed at the beef with such speed Holt had to leap back in alarm. She devoured her meal in two great bites and started emanating a hearty rumble in her throat.

"*Thank you,*" she said. It was far from an apology, but nonetheless, Holt was pleased.

Talia perked up too and smiled. "Is that better, girl?" She rubbed Pyra's chest. Holt wondered whether Pyra feeling better made Talia feel better too. Given what he had felt over his bond, he wouldn't be surprised, and her bond with Pyra was surely far stronger than his with Ash.

The party enjoyed a short silence after this, which felt less tense than before, but there were still many unanswered questions and uncertainties.

It was Talia who broke the silence, bringing her hands together in a decisive clap.

"Master Brode," she said impatiently, as though the old man were ignoring her, "what is our plan?"

"If I had a firm idea, I'd tell you. I'm still considering."

Holt's thoughts returned to his father and where he might be. "The civilians were being escorted away, but we've seen no sign of them. Where will they have gone?"

"They'll have been taken to Fort Kennet," Brode said. "It's some way to the south. There they will stay as long as supplies allow. Assuming it's still standing and the whole countryside is not yet overrun."

"Are we safe in the open like this?" Holt asked.

"Yes," Talia said, with all the enthusiasm of a student who knows the answer. "The scourge are drawn toward areas with the highest population. It's like they want to add to their numbers in the most efficient way possible. A small group like ours won't attract them."

"So, we're safe?"

"We'll never be truly safe," Brode said. "Out here, we're exposed, and even behind thick walls, well, you saw what can happen."

Holt bit his lip and lowered his head.

"Try not to dwell on your father," Brode said. "I didn't notice the bodies of Mirk or Biter in the ruins of the town. Might be they got away to take the people to the fort. If so, they will have had some protection on the road. We'll know soon enough when we reach the fort."

"You shouldn't think about your father at all," Talia said.

"Is that so, princess?" Brode said, giving her a knowing look. Holt found it a strange thing for her to say as well; he'd seen her weeping over the news of her brother's death.

"If he is to join the Order, yes," Talia said. "We all must forget our pasts."

Brode grunted. "Well, he hasn't joined yet."

Holt jumped at once to his feet. "I shall take the oath now!"

But Brode shook his head. "Even if I wanted to witness your oath, I could not. It requires a rider at the rank of Champion to induct Novices. Neither Talia nor I fit that requirement."

"You were a Champion once, Master Brode," Talia said.

"Without my dragon, I am nothing."

"But I want to be a rider." Holt didn't understand why the pair of them made it seem so sour. "I know there's danger. I've seen it now. As a Cook I felt useless; worse than useless. I want to help fight the scourge, and so does Ash."

Ash stood, stretched his neck high and growled.

"Joining the Order is not done rashly," Brode said. "I warned you before about the consequences of such a life. These would have been explained fully to you, given the proper process. You'll have duties and responsibilities far greater than you can comprehend, and you'll be swapping one form of servitude for another. But," he said, biting on the word, "I see no other path for you."

All well and good so far as Holt was concerned. What else was he supposed to do with Ash? Go roaming the world together, a blind dragon and an untrained rider hunting in the woods forever?

"Is this why you took Ash's egg?" Talia asked. "So Commander Denna would be forced to induct you?"

Holt was taken aback. "No…"

"Then what were you thinking?" Before Holt could answer, she plowed on. "Something like this would be covered by breach of rank in Sidastra. You'd be stripped of your name, your role. Banished. Didn't you think of that?"

Holt bit his lip. What had been going through his mind? It was hard to recall.

"It just… felt like the right thing at the time…"

Talia folded her arms. "I don't believe you."

"You're giving the boy too much credit, Talia," Brode said. "Or too little."

Ash cocked his head, and Holt agreed with the sentiment. He couldn't discern Brode's meaning either.

"I didn't take Ash's egg *just* to join the Order, if that's what you mean. That never even crossed my mind. I just wanted to... to save it."

Brode cut another slice of cheese. "Thinking with your heart over your mind can be a dangerous thing."

Ash padded over, and Holt ran a hand down the dragon's back. The bond thumped with pleasure. Holt's stomach whirred with the same tangled guilt and stress it had for the past weeks. Brode and Talia made it seem like he had done something wrong, and maybe they were right. He wouldn't be feeling like this if nothing were amiss. The one question that had plagued him these past weeks had to be asked. He had to know.

"If we had been caught, what would have happened to Ash?"

Brode and Talia looked at each other. Brode chewed, swallowed, then answered.

"At Falcaer, he'd have been killed for sure. At the Crag... rules are looser. Aren't they Talia?"

The princess curled up into a tighter ball. "They are, Master Brode. I don't think Commander Denna would have had him killed, although it would have been Lady Ysera's decision. As for Holt, the commander wouldn't want a rogue rider on her record, so he would have been sworn in, I think. But your father—"

"What about him?"

"He may have been found in breach of rank in your stead," Talia said.

"Why?" Holt said. "I did it. Maybe I didn't think it through, but I'd have accepted any punishment. It's not my father's fault."

"Someone would have to be—"

"Why him though?"

"Because we can't have any commoner with light fingers thinking they can get away with stealing dragon eggs," Talia said. "What happens then? Chaos, Holt, not order."

"That's not fair—"

"Life's not fair," Brode barked. "Haven't I mentioned that already?"

Holt slumped back onto the grass. Ash pressed in closer to him, sending soothing waves across the bond.

"I just did what I thought was right."

"Aye," Brode said. "You did at that. What's done is done. Question is, what do you do now? I have no authority over you. You're as free as you'll ever be."

"I have to find my father, whether he is alive or... dead. So, if you're heading for Fort Kennet, then I should come with you."

"Very well," Brode said. "And I promise that, while you are in my company, I shall train you as best I can. I feel this is partly my fault."

Talia narrowed her eyes but said nothing.

"Thank you," Holt said. "When the time comes to take the oath, I hope I am ready."

Talia cleared her throat. "If you're both heading to the Fort, perhaps I should fly on to the capital after all."

"I'll hear no more on the matter, Talia," Brode said. "Silas is still out there. He's too dangerous, and you're too valuable. Chaos infects every limb of Feorlen at present." He raised a hand to silence Talia before she interrupted. "And yet, we will have to make for the capital in the end. The summons was made. So, we will go, in our own time. From there we can alert Falcaer and other Order Halls to the threat and call for aid. Although whether we risk journeying off-road or move between the garrisons for speed will be a decision I make after we reach Fort Kennet and learn more."

Holt nodded, feeling reassured by Brode's calm manner. Yet visions of those terrible stingers and shambling ghouls with diseased skin and dead eyes sent fresh shivers up his spine.

"Do you think this attack is like those from the old tales?" Holt asked. "A true incursion to threaten the world? Or might it be a smaller rising and be over soon?"

A dark look passed over Brode's face. "I cannot say. It is too soon. Yet Silas' involvement suggests something far more sinister. His betrayal troubles me more than a thousand ghouls."

"You fought alongside him during the last incursion, didn't you?" Talia asked.

"I did, but I shall not speak of it now. It's been a terrible day already, and we won't solve all our problems in one night. Now, Talia," he said with an air of finality, "you should Cleanse and Forge before taking rest."

She inclined her head and immediately took up a cross-legged position. She rested her hands upon her knees, closed her eyes and began breathing very slowly. Pyra made her way closer to their campfire and crouched low to the ground before spreading her wings wide and bending them as if to envelope the flames.

Unsure what was going on, Holt looked to Talia again, but her eyes remained firmly shut. Her breath suddenly croaked, rattled, and then a trail of flames leaped from her shoulders, disappearing as quickly as they'd come.

"What's she doing?" Holt asked of Brode. "Should I be doing that?"

"In time, yes. Sleep for now, Holt. Tomorrow we'll continue to Fort Kennet and pray Silas and his swarm do not find us along the way."

## 15

# FATHERS AND FRIENDS

The journey south was slower than Holt anticipated. He'd always supposed being on an adventure as a rider would be swift and daring; instead they plodded along one foot after another, hugging the coast-line of the Sunset Sea.

Pyra and Talia took the lead, knowing the country as well as Brode. Ash's presence seemed to irritate Pyra, so he and Holt straddled the middle ground between them and Brode, who took up the rear.

*My new mentor,* Holt thought. Although, so far, he'd barely spoken a word to Holt that morning, and it was almost noon. They stopped only once to fill their waterskins in a cool stream. Then, on they trudged. He was painfully aware that this delay was down to himself and Ash. Until his dragon could fly, they were grounded.

Yet Holt hoped that wouldn't be long now. Ash had grown again. Budding stumps of bone and muscle also showed his wings developing.

"Do they hurt?" Holt asked as Ash walked by his side.

*"No. I can feel they are there, but I cannot move them."*

"That must feel strange. I can't imagine having a limb I could not use."

*"One day I will, and on that day I shall fly!"* Ash said with glee. Then

his mood seemed to darken. He bowed his head, and the beat of the bond mellowed. Before Holt could ask more, Ash came to a sudden halt.

"What's wrong? Don't you want to fly?"

*"More than anything. Only I... I... can't see it."*

The ball of guilt in Holt throbbed painfully.

"You don't see flying. You experience it! Perhaps Pyra might—" But he cut himself short there. Pyra was unlikely to offer words of kindness or explanation.

*"I can't see the sky,"* Ash said. *"I want to be high in it, higher than clouds, but I do not know them."*

"What's the matter here?" Brode asked. "There isn't time to stop."

"Ash is saddened by something," Holt said. He felt a painful pulse through the bond, a deep longing like missing a friend who has moved far away. "He speaks of flying and the sky and clouds, only how can he know of them?"

Now Holt considered the matter, he wondered how Ash knew language at all. Could it all be down to a dragon's magic?

"You feel the echoing verses of your lineage," Brode told Ash.

Ash opened his mouth, showing rows of ever-sharpening teeth, although he currently looked confused rather than intimidating.

"What does that mean?" Holt asked.

"Dragons do not learn like humans do, starting from a point of no experience. Rather, dragons seem to re-learn all that was once learned by their ancestors. It would be akin to having many compartments of knowledge already within your mind and finding the keys to unlock them."

"And that happens naturally?"

"For the most part it comes with age, yes," Brode said. "Although direct experience will accelerate things. I suspect our young friend will be forced to learn quicker than a hatchling is expected to. That could be why he is growing so fast."

Ash perked up at that.

"Hatchlings tend to grow quickly," Holt said.

"Not like this," Brode intoned. "Nor would they speak so soon, nor would their wings develop for a matter of months at best. I suspect the trials the pair of you have faced have triggered some deep survival instinct in Ash – to grow and gain flight to escape the danger – though I do not think it will be without cost."

Ash yawned deeply as if to emphasize the burden of his rapid growth.

"Are you sure of this, Master Brode, or are you guessing?"

"A mixture of both, boy. You've gone ahead and put us in unknown territory. What I am sure of is there is always a counterbalance to these matters of magic. Keep close and look after him. He'll need you, I think, more than a dragon should."

Ash was now rooting around in the leaves and dirt on the trail of some interesting smell. Holt bit his lip, then lowered his voice in the hope that only Brode would hear him.

"Will he be able to fly like a normal dragon?"

Brode's expression was unmoving. "Only time will tell."

"We'll both have a lot to learn."

"For once you speak with some wisdom. Now let's get moving. We can't afford to stop, and I can see Talia waiting for us ahead."

Holt ran over to Ash's side to bring him along. The dragon was standing over a dark rabbit hole, his legs braced and his neck as stiff as a board.

"*It's down there,*" Ash said intensely, as though he'd tracked down a life-long nemesis.

Holt knelt beside him, imagining the rabbit within shaking from fear. "I don't think it will come up while you're standing here."

"*Hungry,*" Ash said predictably.

At least Holt had some explanation for Ash's insatiable stomach now.

"We'll get some food out of the packs for you, but we have to keep moving."

With evident effort, Ash tore himself away from the rabbit hole and walked close beside Holt as they caught up with the others. He was much quieter than before, and Holt had an inkling as to what was wrong.

"You heard everything Brode said back there, didn't you?"

"*Yes,*" Ash said flatly.

Holt couldn't help but be impressed at the dragon's hearing. "I'm sorry."

*"Why? It is not for you to know. The elder one should have told you and not held back."*

"Who? Brode? I don't think he understands this either."

*"But an elder should know."*

"This is a new situation for him," Holt said. "It would be like a rider asking my father to prepare a meal he's never cooked before and without a recipe. He'll do it, pulling pieces of knowledge and inspiration from elsewhere to do so, and he knows enough that it should be fine. But there's no guarantee the first time around."

*"Father..."* Ash rolled the word around, as though testing it. *"You speak of this thing often, but I do not know it."*

Holt was struck again by how wildly different dragons were. Scales, magic, wings and all that aside, of course. Yet not having a set family, not having a mother and a father, the way humans did, was difficult to comprehend. Just as Ash could not visualize his echoing memories, Holt found he was blind when trying to grasp at what being a dragon was like. He tried to think of a way Ash might understand it.

"My father is like... he's like an elder – my elder, I suppose."

*"So, he is ancient with a pure core, hard scales and directs your flight's song?"*

"Uh, no," Holt said. This wasn't going to be easy. He didn't fail to notice that even Ash was aware of this 'core'. He made a note to pester Brode about it later. "For humans, my father is my one elder. Only mine. He is father to no one else, unless I had a brother or sister."

*"You are from his egg?"*

Holt sighed. This wasn't getting anywhere.

"Words can be crude," Brode called from behind. He had sharp ears as well.

"What do you mean?" Holt asked.

"Sometimes more is said in a single look or movement. Sometimes more is said by silence..." Brode cleared his throat. "What I mean to say is that you have a bond with this dragon. It runs deeper than mere words. Try communicating to Ash through it. Make him *feel it*, and he'll understand."

Holt drew in a deep breath. He'd rarely actively sought the bond before and had sent vague sensations such as comfort over it, but it had been instinctual and not really on purpose.

He tried to focus while walking and found he couldn't concentrate hard enough. So, he stopped. He shut his eyes and turned all his being toward the beating bond below his sternum, his second heartbeat as he'd come to think of it. Now he focused on it solely, all other sound seemed to fade as though the world was now far away and only he and Ash remained.

Encouragement pulsed over the bond. Ash's reassurance strengthened Holt's will. Yet now he came to do it, Holt wasn't sure what he should send.

How did you convey what a parent was without words?

Holt searched for memories, delving deep into his past to when he was barely knee-high and learning his first words. He saw his father coming home at the end of the day and ran gleefully into his arms, happy to the point of childish giggling. These feelings passed over the bond.

He sat high upon his father's shoulders as they strolled through the markets and tried his first piece of strong cheese; his father had told him all about its making. Then it was years later, he was a little older now, and he was chopping his first onion. The knife slipped, cut his finger. He hadn't wanted to continue, but his father handed the knife back and told him to try again, to not give up.

He lay sweating in bed with a terrible fever and a racing heart. His father spooned warm broth into his mouth, placed a cold cloth on his head and told him gently again and again that it would be okay.

Unbidden, a darker memory came. The day his mother died. He'd pressed his face into his father's chest just to stem the sound of his own grief. He remembered the grip of that embrace, how he didn't want to let go—

"Stop," Ash said. *"That sadness is great."*

Holt opened his eyes, and reality came back in a rush.

He shook his head. "Sorry, Ash. I didn't mean to upset you."

*"I am sorry, Holt. Sorry that you have felt these things. But I think I under-stand what you mean by father now. You find all things in him, joy and love and learning. And I know now why you seek him."*

"I *have* to find him."

*"I shall help you do this. I would not want to be apart from you either. Those feelings you share are things you mean to me too, though not quite in the same way. I am not certain."*

"I reckon we're friends."

*"Friends..."* Ash said slowly, and Holt wondered if this concept was alien to him as well. Then the dragon bounced in approval. *"Friends. Yes. Closer than even flight siblings."* He turned and nipped at Holt's forearm.

"Ouch," Holt said, whipping his arm away. "Maybe refrain from the biting? I appreciate the sentiment, but I'm not a dragon with scales."

*"A squishy friend,"* Ash said, nudging Holt instead. Holt gave him a playful shove in return. He swore he heard Brode chuckle from behind, but when Holt turned the old rider was just as grim-faced as usual.

"Seems to have worked," Brode said. "You're a quick learner, pot boy. I'll give you that. Eventually you may speak with Ash using words across your bond and keep your conversations more private if you wish. But that will do for now."

"Wh – Why?" Holt yawned. A sudden tiredness had taken hold of him, and he rubbed fiercely at his eyes.

Brode was by his side then, offering him a sip of water, which he gladly took.

"Because these matters of magic always take their toll," Brode said. "Especially when you're not used to it."

Holt nodded, not wishing to push himself any further, for the moment at any rate.

"Let's pick up our pace now," Brode said. "The lack of signs of the scourge passing across the land disturb me. I fear whatever or whoever is in control of this swarm has a keen mind and may already have reached Fort Kennet ahead of us."

# 16

# CORES, BONDS AND DRAGON SONGS

Over rough land they battled, avoiding the road, fighting through tall grass and thickets, with a western wind beating into them. Brode only called a halt when dark had already fallen.

That night at camp, Talia, Brode and Holt ate first, before Holt wearily went about preparing meat for Pyra and Ash. Pyra said little, although she did ask politely for the beef to be cooked by Holt, which was nice of her.

"Hold on, I'd like a slice of that," Brode said, referring to Pyra's spiced beef. Before receiving an answer, he cut a wedge off and fed it to Ash. "Let's see how he likes that now it's spiced. Might be able to get a sense of whether he's a fire type or not."

Ash munched on it as happily as he did with any food.

"How will he know?" Holt asked.

"He'll know," Brode said.

Ash swallowed the beef. *"I don't feel any different."*

"Nothing," Holt said.

"We have some fish with us too," Brode said. "Give him some of that."

"He's surely too young, Master Brode," Talia said. "Every book and scroll on dragon lore I've read states that a dragon's magic type manifests at one year of age."

Brode smirked. "I'm sure those books also tell you that emotional communication via the bond takes months to develop. Holt here achieved it this morning while we walked."

Talia looked to Holt aghast. "You did what, pot boy?"

Holt was taken aback. "You were testing me?"

"I'll be testing you in many ways from now on, Holt. Get used to it."

"That's... that's not possible," Talia said. "It took me months before I could even sense Pyra from afar." She looked at her purple drake, as though it were Pyra's fault.

"As I've said," Brode went on, "there is much about Holt and Ash that is unusual. You felt their bond, after all."

"As strong as a Novice pairing after months of training, Forging and Cleansing," Talia said. She didn't sound happy about it. "It's solid. Like rock."

"Unusual just about covers it then," Brode said. "I'll return to my original request." He snapped his fingers. "Bring out the fish, Holt."

Holt did as instructed and threw half a smoked white fish to Ash, who wolfed it down.

*"I still don't feel anything."*

"Nothing again," said Holt.

"So, that rules out fire and ice," Brode said, checking the types off on his fingers.

"If he's even at the point of manifesting his type," Talia repeated. "Besides, being that white, he looks more like a storm dragon to me."

The image of Silas Silverstrike unleashing his powerful lightning against Commander Denna sprang to Holt's mind. That would make Ash powerful. They'd be able to defend themselves easily if that were the case.

"Storm drakes normally range from grays to blacks," Brode said.

Holt's spirits deflated a little.

"Maybe he's an unusual emerald drake," Holt suggested. "That would lead to nature magic."

Brode shrugged. "A mystic is most likely. Sadly, we lack the meat to tell."

"Is there no other way?" Holt asked. "I think I've felt some of his magic already."

He recounted his experience of moving the heavy kitchen workbench covering the larder trap door. Upon reaching the point of his story where he heard the music across Ash's bond and felt new strength in his limbs, Pyra puffed a great deal of smoke and beat her wings, Talia spat out the water she'd been about to swallow, and Brode let out a long-drawn whistle.

"Is that... bad?" Holt asked.

"Bad?" Talia said, her voice high. "Holt, it can take a Novice nearly a full year to draw from their dragon's core." She opened and closed her mouth several times in quick succession, clearly struggling to put her feelings into words.

"Still think I'm wrong to suspect his magic is close at hand?" Brode asked her.

Talia had a look of final defeat about her. She answered but looked at Holt as she did so. "No. I first drew from Pyra's core six months after we bonded, and everyone said that was exceptional."

Holt gulped. Talia had arrived at the Crag to join the Order over two years ago.

"But what does that mean?" Holt asked, feeling frustrated. The two riders were talking as if he wasn't there. "Why did I hear music? I thought they had cores or something?"

"Calm down," Brode said. "It's quite simple. Dragons are beings of magic; their power gathers and matures within their very souls. That is what we call the core. Sometimes we hear a piece of that power in the core – the dragons refer to this as their song."

"I only heard it for a few seconds," Holt said, "but it sounded light now I come to think on it." This worried him. Could Ash's blindness also affect the strength of his magical core? Would he be a cripple in more ways than one?

Brode frowned, perhaps sensing Holt's worry. "Don't worry. Ash is very young, his song will not sound mature. The physical realm should not impact on the magical one, so his blindness shouldn't affect the growth of his core."

"Right," Holt said, not entirely reassured.

"A dragon's core grows by gathering in motes of magic related to their power type," Talia said, slipping into her eager student tone again. "As a fire drake, Pyra pulls in motes of fire energy – tiny specks of magical power we cannot see with our human eyes or senses. The motes are drawn to her, as rivers are drawn to the sea."

Pyra and Talia's strange behavior the night before made more sense now.

"So that's what you were doing last night by the fire," Holt said. "Pyra was drawing in fire energy from our own campfire."

"Not so confusing, is it?" Brode said. "Yet the Order insists on veiling the process in as much mysticism as possible."

Holt ignored him. He was discovering more about the riders than he'd ever dreamed.

"And what were you doing? Princess?" he added hastily. It felt too strange not to show her deference still.

"I was Cleansing and Forging," Talia said. "It's the rider's work of the partnership. Humans aren't beings of magic. We have no core to grow and so we can only draw magic from our dragon via the bond."

"That sounds like we're leeching from them," Holt said. It didn't sound heroic at all. "Why would the dragons let us do that?"

"If you let me speak," Talia said tersely, "I'll tell you."

Holt pressed his lips shut.

Talia continued. "If we only drew on their strength then there would be no benefit to the partnership. Thankfully for us, we can help through the bond. As dragons gather motes of magic into their core, they also pull in motes of other magic types not suitable for them. Last night Pyra would have drawn in air and nature energy as well, even frost motes from the cold of night and mystic motes from our very thoughts. Pyra can't take these into her core, and so they linger in her soul as impurities. Out in the wild, dragons will passively remove these, like our own bodies dispose of waste, however it's a slow process for them. Very slow."

"Meant to live for a long time, dragons," Brode said. "Growing stronger and wiser over centuries."

Holt was beginning to piece it together. "And so, we, the rider that is, can help remove these impurities for them?"

"That's Cleansing," Talia said. "Breathing techniques allow us to accelerate the removal of impurities, creating a cleaner, purer source of power for both dragon and rider to draw from. We can also help push the correct motes of energy into our dragon's core so it gains more power. That's called Forging."

"And what of the bond?" Holt asked.

"It too can grow stronger," Brode said. He raised a hand to stop Holt's inevitable question and then began to dig two small holes in the ground. He did it with one cupped hand, scooping dirt as easily as if he were using a spade with his increased strength. Once satisfied with his work, Brode filled one hole with some water and pointed to it.

"Think of Ash's core like a well of power. Humans don't have innate magic. But through a bond with a dragon, we can draw upon some of theirs." Dexterously, Brode cut a gradual line between the holes with surgical precision. A trickle of water began running into the empty one. "This is closer to your position. With training, a Novice can draw up to one quarter of their dragon's magic before the bond frays under the stress of it. When a bond frays, it will recover, but you won't be able to draw on magic until it has healed. Strengthening your bond will allow you to draw on more magic before it frays."

"Does that mean Ash could grow more powerful, but I wouldn't, if our bond was weak?"

"Something like that," Brode said. "As Ash's core grows, you may find you can summon a little more magic as you are drawing from a larger pool. But unless you develop your bond, you'll always be limited by that weaker connection."

"What will happen to me as the bond strengthens?" Holt asked. He was keen to hear more. As scary as the future might be, there was a glimmer of something glorious awaiting him. If he could manage it.

It was Talia who cut in again. "Roughly speaking, the ranks of the

Order are dictated by your bond strength." She began counting off on her fingers. "Squires have no dragon, no bond, and thus no magic. Novices have weak bonds and can draw up to about one quarter of the dragon's core. Ascendants can draw up to half of the core before the bond frays. The bodies of Ascendants also change, increasing in strength. It's the most commonly achieved rank and what I recently became. Yet some make it to the rank of Champion and can access three-quarters of the core. Master Brode was once a Champion."

Brode grunted in acknowledgment.

"And a few exceptional riders make it to the rank of Dragon Lord," Talia said in awe.

"Like Silas Silverstrike?" Holt asked.

"Just like him," Brode said darkly.

Talia hurried on, clearly enjoying herself. "Dragon Lords have bonds so strong they never fray. They could drain the core in full if they wanted. And they become so linked to their dragon that their bodies begin to take on aspects of them – it's like the rider reaches a point of physical perfection in themselves. Their skin becomes tough like hide and takes on some property of the magic type of their dragon. There aren't many of them though."

"How come?" Holt asked.

"How come?" She seemed astonished he'd even ask such a foolish question. "Because riders die, Holt. They die defending the world. Bonds are hard to grow and take time. Experience is key to strengthening a bond. Learning together and overcoming struggles. Battle provides the greatest experience, of course. The bond is truly strengthened and tested then."

Holt thought about how the bond with Ash had felt during the attack on the Crag.

"I think I felt my bond with Ash growing already. During the attack, when I ran back for him, the bond beat so hard I thought it might burst and it burned painfully. Then it seemed to swell and has felt larger since."

"Gains come quickly at first," Talia said.

"So why don't the riders just fight each other all the time?" Holt asked. "That way they'd all grow more powerful."

"Dueling each other wouldn't work," Brode said. "You have to feel your life is on the line for it to matter. True fear like that is impossible to fake."

Talia's expression stiffened then. "The skirmishes over the last year have helped to strengthen Pyra and me, but they say that... that..."

"That true incursions separate the Paragons from the dead," Brode finished for her.

*Paragons?* Holt thought.

"There is a rank beyond Lord?" he asked.

"Not really," Talia said. "You can't get more powerful than drawing on one hundred percent of your dragon's core, but the dragon's core itself can continue to mature and gain in power. The Paragons are the most powerful of the Lords. They lead the Order at Falcaer Fortress."

Brode scoffed. "If you think I'm old and bitter, Holt, just wait until you meet them."

Holt smiled nervously. He didn't like to imagine what these ancient and mighty dragon riders would think of him and Ash.

"Do you understand better?" Talia asked. Her tone implied he very much ought to.

Holt nodded. He felt he understood things well enough in theory. If this whole matter was a recipe, the meat of the thing was the core of magic within the dragon. Everything else was there to complement it. Cleansing sounded like cutting away the gristle to leave only lean meat, while Forging was like packing in more flavor through seasoning.

"Help Ash with his core, strengthen the bond through battle. Got it."

"You're already well underway," Brode said. "Drawing on Ash's core after, what, just shy of two weeks?"

"I didn't mean to do it."

"And that only makes it all the more impressive," said Brode. "I remember the first time I heard a snippet of the song. I'd been with Erdra for a year by then."

It was the first time Holt had heard Brode speak openly of his dragon.

Brode continued, his tone no longer dour but one of excitement.

"In time you'll be able to channel that power into magical abilities based on your dragon's type. Show him again, Talia."

She obediently closed her eyes in concentration. When she opened them again, they flared as green as summer grass and a wisp of fire curled around her fingertips. The flames gathered into a ball in her palm.

"It can be hard to hold on at times," she explained in a low voice. "Especially if you're trying to do other things at the same time, like staying alive in a battle."

The fire vanished, and her eyes dimmed back to normal.

Holt rubbed at his tired eyes. Things were moving more quickly than he could keep up with. Just this morning he'd learned he would be able to communicate with Ash over their bond; now he was being told he was on the verge of having to master actual magic too. While it was exciting, thrilling even, it was a lot to take in. A daunting challenge for one used to scrubbing pots.

Sensing his doubts, Ash came to sit by his side to show support, placing his head on Holt's lap. He scratched down the dragon's neck. Their bond glowed warm, and Holt felt calmer for it.

"I'm not sure I'm ready for this," Holt said.

Brode barked a laugh. "You should have thought of that before you stole the egg. We'll discover Ash's type soon enough, and then I'll have you learn Cleansing and Forging."

There was an air of finality in Brode's words.

Talia stood up then, dusted herself off and flexed her fingers. "There is one aspect of being a rider that doesn't come through magical cores and bonds," she said, flashing Holt a dark look. "And that is skill with a blade. Shall we spar, Master Brode? It has been some time."

"Aren't you tired?" Brode asked.

"I can train for a bit," she said stiffly.

Holt jumped to his feet too. "Can I learn?"

Talia groaned, and Brode chose the diplomatic route.

"You've learned enough for one day. Besides, we lack training swords, and I'm not giving you live steel to do yourself damage with."

Holt folded his arms. "I'm used to handling knives."

But Brode just laughed again. Then the old rider stomped over to the root of the lone tree they'd camped by and hacked at a thick low hanging branch with his rider's sword. The blade cut through the wood in one clean strike and the branch fell. Brode picked it up with ease and tossed it to Holt. He caught the branch clumsily, and its weight surprised him, pulling him forward before he secured it with two hands.

"Get used to holding that in one arm as best you can," Brode said. "You'll have to start on the basics soon. Perhaps tomorrow if time allows. For now, simply watch. See if you can learn a little that way."

So, Holt did. He sat by the warmth of the fire and watched as Brode and Talia exchanged blows. He knew nothing of swordcraft, but it seemed to him that Talia's movements were far more fluid and graceful, precise without lacking in power. Her feet shuffled in as much of a blur as her hands. Of the two, she was clearly the natural. Brode's experience lent him an edge, but barely so.

*"It is hard to place them,"* Ash said. *"They move so fast and clash their metal talons so loudly."*

"Someday we'll be in a real battle and it will be far worse," Holt said. That made his stomach squirm again. Ash shared the sentiment across the bond. Holt wrapped an arm tightly around Ash, although this was getting harder almost every hour as the dragon grew.

Only now did he realize the full extent of all he'd have to master. They had so much to learn, and precious little time to do it in.

Perhaps it would be too much for a Cook. Perhaps Brode was right and he should have thought twice before he'd saved Ash's egg. He might have been with his father right now if he had. Well, Brode was right. What was done was done. And Holt would just have to work as hard as he could to make the best of it.

Thankfully, hard work was nothing new to a Cook.

# 17

# THE WEAK LINK

The next day was much the same. Brode spoke to Holt on the dragon core and the methods used to purify and strengthen it, yet they didn't have the time to stop and practice in depth.

Holt tried to take it in, but his mind kept drifting to swordcraft. That seemed the more pressing issue to him. And there was another reason. Servants and others of his status were not permitted to buy or carry weapons. To him, wielding a sword held a mystique of its own.

Sadly, given their need to keep moving, Brode could only promise training in the future and left to speak with Talia. Holt still had the heavy branch Brode had given him, and he held it aloft for as long as he could, determined to prove himself and be ready for when the time came to learn for real.

The day wore on and night gathered. Holt's feet ached and his chest felt tight, but he'd reached the point where he was numb to it, planting one foot after another in the hope Brode would call a halt.

Half in a daze from weariness, he didn't register at first that the others had stopped walking. Nor that Pyra growled and pawed at the ground. He caught up with them and gasped. Before he could go farther, Brode placed a hand on his shoulder.

"Stay back."

Ash bounded up, and he too began to growl. *"I sense the scourge here. And death."*

Before them, down at the bottom of a ditch, was the body of a dragon and a rider. Both had jagged black lines charred across their skin and scales. In the dim light, the dragon's coloring wasn't clear, although Holt thought it a rich blue. More alarming were the many rips in the dragon's wings and deep gashes in its body.

"Lord Mirk," Holt said. His mouth had gone dry.

"And Biter," Talia said sadly. "So, one of our number did make it away from the Crag... for a while."

Holt's heart leaped into his throat. "If they were protecting the civilians then... then that must mean—"

"I don't see more causalities," Brode said. He squeezed Holt's shoulder. "Talia, do you feel Silas out there?"

Talia shifted her head, as though seeking the trail with her nose. "No rider is nearby."

"I shall go investigate, then," said Brode. "But be ready, Talia. These bodies may well be bait."

Talia nodded, her grim face set. She unsheathed her huge red sword from upon her back. Pyra braced herself, her jaw loose, ready to breathe fire if needed.

Holt raised his stick and became painfully aware of how useless he looked and was. His cheeks flushed a color akin to Pyra's scales. Ash, for his part, walked to Pyra's side. He must have sensed where Pyra's head was, perhaps the pressure she pressed into the ground, for Ash did his best to imitate her. His lack of vision led to an awkward imitation, however, and his breath came out more like a pant as he tried to summon fire he did not have.

Talia gave the hatchling a sideways look of pity, then looked at Holt. He caught her looking at him, but rather than quickly averting her eyes, her frown deepened. In that moment, Holt felt a familiar and powerful feeling of being reprimanded by a superior, unable to defend himself and simply having to stand and take it.

But that wasn't true anymore, was it?

His emotions once again got the better of him, and his next words tumbled out before he could stop himself.

"You resent me, don't you?"

Talia blinked, taken aback. But the moment passed, and she settled back into a frown.

"Don't flatter yourself."

"You and Brode would have an easier time if we weren't here."

"We would," she said seriously. "We could fly then. Go with speed. We might have joined Mirk and then he wouldn't have stood alone."

"You couldn't have taken on Silverstrike."

"Oh, and you could?"

"That's not what I meant."

"I'm the only *real* rider left in Feorlen now. I may have to fight him, if help doesn't come in time."

"You'll have Brode and Ash. And me!"

"What are you going to do? Have Silas laugh himself to death as you run at him with that stick?"

Holt's cheeks flushed.

"Look," she went on, "I'm just trying to face the hard truth. You are holding us back, pot boy—"

"My name is Holt."

But she either didn't hear him or didn't care.

"—I have the fate of the kingdom to worry about. It's a lot. I can't add you to that list, especially if it comes to a fight."

"Don't then," Holt said, curtly. He'd tried to reach out and she was being cold with him. "You look after you, and I'll look out for myself and Ash. I won't slow you down any more than I can help."

"That's not... that's... I've just lost a lot recently," she said, her voice softer now.

Holt wrinkled his nose, feeling the heat of anger drain from him. "Your brother. The King. I'm sorry about that. I understand."

"You don't unders—"

"Yes, I do. I lost my mother, not that you cared to even ask about it. You can tell me all the hard truths in the world, princess, but you can't tell me how I feel."

She met his eyes again, raised her eyebrows and blinked once in shock. "If we were back at the Crag, I could strike you for insolence."

"Go ahead. Although Ash will give you a pretty nasty bite for it."

He regretted saying it immediately.

But Talia smirked. "You were never meant to be a Cook with that sort of spirit." She raised her hand, and Holt winced, thinking she was about to smack him with her rider enhanced strength. She feigned the strike and lowered her hand. "All that courage and you're still jumpy? When did you ever see me hit a servant before?"

"Not once," Holt admitted. "But it happens."

"Yes... It happens."

"But I'm not a servant anymore."

"You're not yet a rider either," Talia said. "Look, let's not be at each other's throats. Master Brode has enough to deal with as it is." She held out a hand for him to shake. Holt took it and fought back a gasp as Talia squeezed with undue strength.

"I hope the pair of you aren't conspiring to make me collect the firewood tonight," Brode said as he trudged back up the incline. "Because I'll ignore you." When neither of them answered, he carried on. "Looks like Silas's work all right. Those scorch marks weren't made by flames. More worrying are the other injuries on Biter's body. His wings were shredded badly. Even if he'd lived, I doubt he'd ever have flown again. I think he was tortured."

"I never imagined dragons could be broken like that," Holt said. He gulped and looked to Ash.

"It's not the dragon Silas was trying to break," Brode said. "It was the rider."

Talia moved to Pyra's side to place a comforting hand on her dragon. "This is horrible. Just horrible."

"You see," Brode continued, speaking to Holt, "even the thought of your dragon being in pain caused you to be afraid. Silas knows this. Biter would have endured tremendous pain, perhaps never breaking. But Mirk... I suspect feeling the pain of his dragon broke him quickly. We're not as strong as they are."

"Mirk would have known when we left the Crag," Talia said. She ran her hands down her face before placing them behind her head. "And he knew where we went," she said in sudden fear. "Master Brode, do you think—"

"I fear he did," Brode said. "Hence why Silas dispatched him."

Holt's heart thumped. "So Silas knows you and Talia are still out here?"

"I assume so," said Brode. "I've found it unsettling that we've seen no signs of the swarm on our march. No wasting of the land, nor any trail of destruction which would usually follow in their wake. Silas's efforts seem focused on removing the riders, which makes sense enough. He would have counted the dragons after the attack on the town and judged two had escaped him. Once he caught up to Mirk and Biter and found Pyra and Talia were not with him, he would want to know where they were."

"And not you?" Holt asked.

Brode sniffed. "Doubt he cares. I have no dragon. No magic. Still, if Mirk broke and told him..." he trailed off, looking at Talia in some alarm as she started pacing and biting at one nail. "Don't fret, girl. I doubt Silas would reveal himself so openly by following our footsteps. Far simpler to just wait at the Crag and catch us upon our return."

Talia ceased her pacing and nodded. "Yes, Master Brode. I should not even worry, of course."

Brode grunted an acknowledgment, then thumped the strap of his sword belt, lost in thought again.

Holt wondered what could have caused Talia such concern. Where had the two of them been? Countless questions were still unanswered. Why would Silas do this? What were they to do? What had become of his father?

"None of this makes sense," Holt said, as though in some conclusion.

Brode looked at him. The hand playing at his sword belt tightened on the leather. "A few things do, I think. If we accept that, for whatever twisted reason, Silas is able to control this swarm. How he's done this, I cannot say. Some powerful mystic dragons can influence the minds of others, but Clesh is not a mystic. Nor do any stories of mystics being able to sway the scourge come to mind – the creatures are mostly mindless drones, bar the Swarm Queens."

"Perhaps it is the other way around," Talia offered. "Silas may have been taken and corrupted by the scourge and now is under their sway."

Brode considered this. "Anything is possible. Normally anything the scourge corrupts becomes part of the swarm, incapable of independent thought. And ordinarily only the dead may rise to join their ranks. Some new, darker power might be behind it. For now, we don't know enough to say. Yet given we know he has turned to the scourge, this leaves the question of why he would hunt down the riders an obvious one. Should the riders fall, the scourge will sweep across Feorlen unchecked."

"Only the swarm is being held back from attacking everything it comes across," Talia said. "Presumably by Silverstrike."

Brode nodded. "Removing the riders in a few careful moves, and quietly, would leave the kingdom exposed. The swarm could descend upon Sidastra and take it before the rest of the riders could be made aware of the true danger. But he may have miscalculated. Holt, you said that Commander Denna was already injured when she returned to the Crag, is that right?"

"Ysera was injured."

"And the attack followed swiftly after she returned?"

"Almost at once," Holt said.

"Then I think we may safely assume a few events," Brode said. "Silverstrike claimed he was taking the Commander and company to ready Feorlen's defenses. It would have been a simple matter for him to lead the others into a trap. But with his failing and our flicker of hope, Denna managed to escape. He pursued her, likely with a smaller, swifter portion of his swarm to the Crag. There he and his limited forces faced Mirk the Champion, not enough to cause him a real threat but enough to occupy him for a time."

"That might explain why the civilians were able to get away," Talia said.

Brode nodded. "His focus would have been on the remaining riders. Once they were dead and the tower of the Crag left a smoldering ruin, he discovered two dragons were missing: Pyra and Biter. He renewed his pursuit and came upon Mirk and Biter. At this point, things become less clear. He may have returned to the Crag to lie in wait for Talia and me, or he may have pursued the civilians. I can't imagine he's pleased so many got away. Any word of his betrayal or his swarm's strange behavior might ruin his plans."

"Do you think the people made it to the fort?" Holt asked. This was one point he needed reassurance on.

"My gut feeling is they have," Brode said. "We've yet to see evidence that he caught them. Mirk and Biter may have turned to face Silas and distract him for long enough to allow the refugees to reach Fort Kennet."

"Is such a thing possible?" Talia asked. "Mirk was strong but only a Champion and not really as mighty as Denna. Silas is a Lord."

"Even Lords can run their supply of magic low," Brode said. "He fought Denna and the officers somewhere in the wild. He fought again at the Crag. Mirk may well have been able to give him a real fight by then."

"And withstand his questioning afterward," Talia said. "Enough time to allow the people to make it to Fort Kennet."

"Could the fort hold out against him?" Holt asked.

Brode shrugged. "With sufficient warning, I'd say so. Clesh's power would be all but spent by then, and a prepared fort would be a hard thing for him to besiege with his small forces. Warnings may even now be racing to every corner of the kingdom."

"That might just make him accelerate his plans," Talia said. "The Summons was already sent. If he means to take the kingdom, he'll have to face the full might of Feorlen upon the walls of Sidastra."

"Will he?" Brode said ominously. "If he has control of the swarm – and I'll assume the worst – then he could easily change tactics and pick off smaller towns. Attacking the weakest points will draw your uncle Osric and the army out into the open. Away from the capital's defenses, the scourge have the advantage. Of course, his priority will be to hunt us. If he catches us, then he'll prevent word reaching other Order Halls."

Holt looked to the darkening sky then, as though he might see Silverstrike as a black outline of doom, hunting them in the wild. He lowered his head and moved to give Ash a hug, wrapping his arms around the dragon's ever-growing neck.

*"Do not fear. If your father made it to the fort, then he will be safe."*

The bond hummed, and for a moment all anxiety left Holt.

Talia's next words brought it all back. "Even if Silas's plans haven't gone perfectly, it still seems to me like he's winning. If spreading word about him is so vital, then let me fly with Pyra. If we can make it to Sidastra, then I can warn my uncle and we'll ride west with every soldier we have before he can gather the full swarm. Already the army will be assembling."

But Brode only shook his head again. "The skies will be watched, more so than the ground. Clesh is too powerful a storm dragon; Pyra can't outfly him. And something still does not feel right to me."

"Why would he do this?" Talia asked, sounding more desperate than Holt had ever heard her. "What possible reason – what does he have to gain by it?"

"I don't know," Brode said darkly.

"You fought beside him," she said. "If anyone would know, it's you."

"We're missing some piece of the puzzle," said Brode. "Something vital. Something terrible. Until we know, we must stick together."

Talia seemed spent. She nodded, and her shoulders slumped.

"Once we reach Fort Kennet, things may become clearer," Brode said with an air of finality. "For now, we should get as far away from here as we can and try to get some rest. Pyra, make sure to burn these bodies."

Pyra growled in agreement and took to the air, her purple scales blending with the twilight sky.

By the time they stopped to rest that night, the bonfire that was Mirk and Biter was but a candle flame in the distance behind them.

# 18

# FORT KENNET

The final night of their journey was a restless one. Partly because the discovery of Mirk and Biter made the danger they faced deadly clear, and partly because today Holt would discover the fate of his father. While on the road he'd been able to fend off his fears and anxieties, pushing them into the unknown future. Yet soon he'd have to face reality, whether it be good or ill.

And he wasn't sure what he would do in either case.

If his father hadn't survived, that would make things simple, if unbearably painful. He would be free to join Brode and Talia in their quest without hesitation. Yet if his father was still alive, what then? Could he just abandon Brode and Talia? The princess would prefer that. Not having a hatchling and an untrained rider in tow would give them the best shot at countering the scourge. But he and Ash would be bereft of training – easy prey for Silas Silverstrike. And, if Silas was hunting riders, then Holt would put his father in danger by staying with him.

No path seemed easy.

Thus, Holt was wide awake when Brode stirred in the gray dawn light. Ash took some cajoling to wake. He seemed to have grown again overnight; his wings were developing rapidly, if still too small to allow him to take off. He also devoured the very last of their meat after Pyra had her portion. Holt hoped the fort was still standing just so they wouldn't have to worry about supplies. The three humans ate a simple breakfast of the remaining bread, jams and cheese, then shouldered their packs and began marching again.

It was not a pleasant day. The sky darkened and broke in a drizzling rain long before they came within sight of the walls of Fort Kennet. Underfoot the ground became slippery, and the air enveloped them in a muggy embrace. Holt still had his heavy branch and now used it as a walking stick to help negotiate the terrain.

Around mid-morning, they arrived at the fort. Holt had imagined it to be some great stone behemoth he'd heard tales of in distant lands, unyielding to time or assault. Perhaps it was another check on his fantasies, or perhaps it was his weariness, fears or the dreary day, but Fort Kennet looked so... ordinary.

The walls were no larger than the town walls of the Crag and were made of wood, not stone, but they were stout and studded with numerous crenellations and canopies so that archers could take shelter. Behind was a higher inner wall, with ballistae sitting atop tall towers. One tower was half a ruin, its platform collapsed and useless. The whole fort stood upon a raised mound of earth, not quite a hill, but high enough to command the surrounding land.

Before the walls, however, was something quite unexpected. Dirtied tents, dozens of cooking fires ringed with huddled figures in tattered cloaks.

"Could they be from the Crag?" Holt asked.

"Could be," Brode said. "At least the fort is standing, and that is a positive sign. Although I see there has been some attack. We'll soon find out."

They approached the fort, negotiating the muddy slope to the gates with care, and drawing the eyes of every man, woman and child they passed. Many shouted praise and gave thanks that dragon riders had come, although a few asked bitterly where they had been.

Holt became aware of their stares, feeling their worry and their disappointment as they took him in. Just a scrawny boy with a stick and a little dragon. What good was he to them?

Still, he tried to get a good look at everyone they passed, hoping to find his father in the crowd. He didn't see him. Nor did he recognize any of their faces. None of them were from home.

As the party drew close, the gates of Fort Kennet opened. Out came a small retinue of the most armored men Holt had ever seen. Their entire bodies were encased in plate armor, with shields upon their backs and longswords at their sides.

*"They rattle and scratch when they move,"* Ash said.

The man at the head of the retinue was clean-shaven and had a single bloodstained bandage wrapped over one ear.

"Honored Rider, your arrival lifts my heart." He enunciated his words perfectly, sounding more like Princess Talia than anyone Holt had ever met. He looked to Brode expectantly. "You're just in time!"

"In time for what, exactly?" Brode asked.

"To join us in our sortie against the scourge. That fire dragon of yours will be their bane."

Pyra ruffled at the insinuation of belonging to Brode. Talia patted her gently, then moved to stand before the armored giant. She had to tilt her head back to speak to him.

"Pyra is my dragon, Sir Knight. Master Brode here is our mentor and guide."

Holt couldn't help but let out an awed breath. "A real knight..."

He'd never met one at the Crag. The riders commanded the soldiers there, so there was no need for them. These were brave men, riding into the fiercest battles without dragons by their side or magic at their command. Holt looked again at his branch and quickly tried to hide the embarrassing piece of wood behind his back.

"Apologies, Lady," the knight said, inclining his head to Talia. "My name is Alexander Knight, captain of this fort. At your service."

"Talia Agravain, at yours," she said.

"Agravain?" Alexander said, shock breaking across his face. He fell to one knee, as did his companions. "Your Royal Highness, I am sorry if I offended—"

"Please stand," Talia said. "I am a dragon rider and swore the oaths. My uncle Osric currently holds the position as regent, although you may call me princess, as many find it easier to do."

Alexander stood. "As you will, princess. May I offer my condolences on the death of your late brother? I also fought for a time under your father during the war against Risalia. They were both good men."

Talia nodded. It seemed like she wanted to say more but hesitated.

Brode stepped in for her. "Captain, what happened here?"

"We came under attack the night before last, only hours after refugees from the Crag arrived seeking shelter. We had enough time to prepare the walls and man the ballistae, and that might have saved us. Another of your Order, Lord Mirk, stood with us that night and was of great service. He took off the morning after the assault in search of the swarm. He may have passed you on the road."

"Unfortunately, we did pass him," said Brode. "We found him dead last night. Killed by the scourge." He gave Holt a sharp, piercing look, and Holt understood he was to be silent on the matter of Silverstrike. "Do you know why Lord Mirk chose to abandon the fort?"

"It seemed a scourge risen drake or some other winged creature was among them. It scorched one of our towers but backed off when we turned the other siege equipment its way. I believe he went to investigate."

*Or draw Silas away from the fort,* Holt thought. Lord Mirk rose in his estimation.

Brode nodded along as the knight confirmed many of his theories of the night before. "Did you get a sense of the size and strength of the swarm?"

"Hard to say, given they struck at night and with such a gathering of storm clouds along with them. It can't have been a true swarm, for their forces lacked juggernauts and abominations, else I fear the gates would not have held."

Holt was anxious for them to get onto the topic of the refugees. People from the Crag had arrived, but where were they now?

"You did well, Knight Captain," Brode said. "Do not waste that good action now and abandon the safety of your walls to meet the scourge in the field."

"We have no choice," Alexander said. "The swarm moved southeast toward the town of Midbell. The town was already suffering, according to the reports we received a week ago. With fresh enemy forces, they may not last."

"Is the garrison even strong enough?" Talia said. "Half your men will have marched for the capital. My brother sent the Summons before he died."

"We were preparing to march, but the Master of War sent revised orders. The western garrisons are not to march to Sidastra but must remain at our posts."

Talia's face was a picture of confusion. Even Brode was surprised.

"That's unorthodox," Brode said.

Alexander inclined his head again. "I agree, but respectfully, Honored Rider, those are my orders. It is breaking them enough to ride to the aid of Midbell, but what are we to do? Allow Midbell to fall? A town of that size—"

"I quite agree, Knight Captain," Brode said. "I must speak to my pupils on the matter of joining your expedition. We have urgent matters of our own."

Alexander's expression stiffened, but he inclined his head without protest.

"We set out tomorrow," Alexander said. "A skeleton garrison shall remain. You may resupply as best you can before setting off, if that is your wish. Dragon riders have their oaths but so do knights, and I shall not forsake mine, whatever the cost."

Alexander took his leave.

Holt couldn't restrain himself anymore. He started forward, the words spilling out of him. "What happened to the people from the Crag?"

The Knight Captain turned. He eyed Holt curiously, taking in his ragged clothes and his evident lack of a nobleman's voice.

"Many left after the attack, heading east toward Fort Carrick and from there onto Sidastra. The summons to gather in the capital did go out after all. Only the troops in the west are to remain."

"Did my father go with them?" Holt asked in his haste and worry, knowing immediately such a question was foolish. The knight would hardly know. "His name is Jonah Cook."

"A Cook?" Alexander's eyes widened further as he took in Holt's scraggy appearance once more, then looked to Ash standing by his side.

"Ash has bonded with me," Holt said.

"*If he dares insult you, he will be sorry,*" Ash declared. Although such threats, coming over their bond alone, lacked real bite.

"Has he indeed, Honored Rider?" Alexander said in a curious tone. "These are strange times indeed. As for your inquiry, I'm afraid I have no knowledge of your father. Perhaps those camped outside our walls will know. He may still be here himself. Alas, I cannot spare the men to search for him. We must make ready."

Holt nodded and clenched his jaw. It wasn't bad news, but it wasn't good news either.

"The lad understands," Brode said. "That will be all, Sir Knight."

"Very well," Alexander said. "Princess," he added with a bow before sweeping off.

Brode, Holt and Talia closed into a huddle, or as close as they could with two dragons also vying for space.

"I can't believe you, Brode," Talia hissed.

"Master Brode," he reminded her.

"To question going? What is the point of the Order if not to help those in need such as at Midbell?"

"The point of our Order, princess, is to defeat the scourge. For the good of the whole world. Not just for one town. Not even for an entire kingdom. It's why royals are generally forbidden from joining."

"Why? Because we care about our own people?"

"Precisely. Sacrifices must sometimes be made. You've done well not to let your heart lead you thus far, do not let it now."

"Are you going to order me not to help these men?" she asked through gritted teeth.

"On this occasion, no."

Talia blinked in confusion.

Holt too felt taken aback, as did Ash.

"*The elder one speaks often in riddles.*"

"I don't like the idea of being in the thick of things. It could bring Silas down upon us," Brode said. "But, should Midbell fall, the western regions will be overrun with risen ghouls. The swarm will grow out of control, and whether we make it to Sidastra in one piece or not won't matter. I don't like it, but the garrison will march with or without us. Better they have a fire drake with them."

Talia opened her mouth, closed it, then opened it again.

"I think it's the right idea," Holt chimed in. "We should help those people if we can."

Brode rounded on him. "You would say that. Your heart leads you along at a hundred miles an hour. In any case, it is decided. We'll help relieve Midbell. But if there should be consequences of revealing ourselves, may it be a lesson to both of you."

"Thank you, Master Brode," Talia said. "I won't let you down." Then she dropped her voice, almost to a whisper. "There's something I don't understand. Why would orders be sent to the western garrisons not to march to Sidastra? There's no way my uncle would do that. He's too experienced a general, and this will cut his army down by almost a quarter."

"Did your mother say who the new Master of War is?" Brode asked.

Holt wondered when Talia had last spoken to the queen, well the queen mother, well... now he wasn't sure what she was anymore. Perhaps she'd sent a private letter to Talia.

"The curia appointed Lord Harroway," Talia said. "I find it hard to believe he'd do this either. He was my uncle's closest advisor during the war with Risalia. They won the Toll Pass together."

Brode frowned. His face gave little away, but Holt thought he saw worry in the old rider's eyes.

"Nothing is happening as it's supposed to," Brode said. "Order beats chaos, but we're in the midst of chaos, and if we're not careful it will consume us."

He looked at Holt as though it were all his fault. And perhaps it was. Perhaps Pyra had been right. By stealing an egg and bonding with a dragon, Holt had imbalanced all worldly sense. Perhaps he should have stayed in his place.

The moment passed, and Brode carried on. "For now, Talia, go and see if you can find armor that fits and get a sense of the strength of the garrison. I'll take young Holt here into the camps and see if we can find a trace of his father."

While glad Brode was taking the issue of his father seriously, Holt rankled at being called 'young'.

"I'm not much younger than Talia," he said.

"And yet still the youngest here, setting the hatchling aside. Now, we have much to do and must still take what rest we can. By this time tomorrow, we'll be on the road again."

# 19

# THE BLIGHT

Talia jumped onto Pyra's back and the pair took flight, soaring over the walls of Fort Kennet before descending below the lip of the defenses and out of sight.

A part of Holt couldn't help but look on in excitement. One day he might be able to do that with Ash, if the dragon's blindness didn't impede him. Currently, Ash had his nose pressed close to the ground, sniffing some smell or other.

Brode stretched, arching his back and pushing his arms high into the air.

"Well then, Master Cook, let's try and find your father."

"You don't sound very hopeful," Holt said. He fell in line beside Brode, and Ash trailed behind them. They made an odd trio, heading back down the mound toward the camps.

"I try not to lean on hope," Brode said, "nor give room to despair. Take each event as it comes."

"That sounds both hard and joyless."

"I *had* hoped that I was past the days of being asked constant and irritating questions," Brode said, though not unkindly. "Alas, here I am."

They reached the border of the first camp without incident. An unclean smell mixed with smoke in the heavy air. Now Holt was closer to the campfires, he saw many only had a simple spit set up, yet with nothing cooking on them. What few black pots there were showed signs of rust; not the thicker, high-quality metal Holt was used to working with in the Order Hall kitchens.

"All of this has happened in just a week or two?" Holt asked aloud.

"Things unravel quickly in chaos," Brode said. "I take it you see no sign of your father?"

"Not yet."

As they picked their way across the sprawling campsite, Holt felt like they were being watched. Many of the men had grim expressions and watched them pass in uncomfortable silence.

"Stick close, Holt."

"*I sense great fear from them,*" Ash said. "*Fear and anger.*" He drew closer to Holt in turn.

"Don't worry," Holt said. "They won't hurt you."

"*I do not fear for me. I'm keeping you safe.*" Ash bared a few teeth, his head low to the ground like a hound.

As Holt tightened his grip on his stick, he thought Ash had a point. The looks they were receiving were unsettling. He still had his dagger if he needed it, and his fingers fidgeted at its hilt. But that was worrying needlessly. No one would dare attack riders.

Brode seemed to sense his anxiety. "It will be fine." Yet there was an edge to his voice all the same. Brode still had a measure of his old rider strength and agility, but that was all. Without a dragon and magic, he was little better than a man and could hardly take on a whole crowd alone.

As they came upon a fresh section of the camp, Holt started to pick out the odd face from the crowd. He said as much to Brode.

"I'm starting to recognize a few myself," Brode said. "There's Felix Hunter with his bow – I wonder if the garrison asked him to stay to help with the defense. And there's old Annie Weaver, and Master Tailor—"

"And Mr. Smith," Holt said. A bald head made the blacksmith easy to spot. In his surprise, Holt had spoken loudly.

This drew the attention of the Crag onlookers, especially Edgar

Smith. He spoke softly to a small girl by his side, then got to his feet and rolled back his great shoulders. His dark eyes, blackened further with tiredness, homed in on Holt before flitting first to Brode, then to Ash, then back to Brode. The blacksmith narrowed his eyes but moved to meet the trio all the same. A few others gathered in.

"Edgar," Brode began, "it's a relief to see so many of you alive."

The blacksmith hawked spit onto the ground between them. Given Mr. Smith's views about dragon riders, Holt reckoned it wasn't solely to clear his throat.

"Lord Brode," Edgar said, as though it pained him. "Did the riders see the scourge off? Can we go home?"

Brode eyed the spittle in the mud before giving the blacksmith a level look. "I'm afraid not. The Crag is a flaming ruin, as is much of the town. The swarm is still at large. It will be some time before it's over."

Those gathered behind the blacksmith gasped, sighed and wept in equal measure. Most of them looked to Mr. Smith. It seemed he was providing leadership.

"So where are the riders?" he asked. "It's your job to deal with these monsters."

"All riders from the Crag perished in the attack," Brode said.

"Lord Mirk was with us on the road."

"I'm afraid he too is dead."

The blacksmith spat onto the ground again. "All those years and high talk of what the riders can do… for nothing."

"It's not their fault," Holt said. "Silas Silverstrike betrayed them. They had no way of preparing for that."

Brode clasped a hand on Holt's shoulder and squeezed. "Everyone is strained and weary. I'm sure such words are not meant," he added pointedly.

Edgar gritted his teeth but managed to control himself.

"Now," Brode continued, "what happened to the rest of the townsfolk?"

"The Knight Captain implored those of us with skills useful to his troops to stay," Edgar said. "Half the soldiers with us joined the garrison here, and the rest continued with those moving on."

"Where's my father?" Holt asked.

"Heading to Sidastra with the others," Edgar said. "They were long gone even before the swarm attacked the fort." He eyed Holt then. "Your father was in some state. He thinks you're dead. Inconsolable he was. Why weren't you with him?"

Guilt – the now all too familiar guilt – crashed into Holt again.

He couldn't have left Ash, but hearing that his father was in pain because of it turned his throat dry. Holt sniffed and wiped his nose on his ruinously dirty shirt. In truth, his appearance was little better than that of those in the camps.

Ash licked at his hand. *We shall find him. It is our task.*

The blacksmith looked at Ash in astonishment. Likely he'd assumed the dragon belonged to Brode. Before he could say anything, however, a young girl pushed her way through the crowd and wrapped her arms around Mr. Smith's waist.

"Go back beside the fire," Mr. Smith said. "I'll be back soon."

"I'm cold, Daddy," she said in a sad little voice. "And my tummy hurts."

Holt was sure her name was Ceilia. She was maybe four years old at best, and despite her claim of being cold, the sweat on her brow and at the nape of her neck spoke of the opposite. If that wasn't enough, her pallor alone confirmed it. She was very ill.

"I know, sweetheart, I know," said Mr. Smith. "I'll try to get some more food for you." He looked to Brode again, this time imploringly. "Some of the soldiers in the garrison could sell us food out of their rations, if we'd been able to bring any money with us. Don't suppose you could speak with the knights and get supplies sent down to us?"

Brode's expression could have been carved from stone. "I'm afraid food won't help. Look at her arm."

Holt only noticed it now. There was a puffy streak of skin on the girl's forearm, which had a faint green tinge to it.

"It's some rash," the blacksmith said.

"It's the blight," said Brode.

In that moment, all resentment Holt felt for the blacksmith vanished.

Mr. Smith's own skin turned deathly white. "No..." he said weakly.

"Step away from her," Brode said, clearly fighting to keep his voice steady. His hand edged to the hilt of his sword. "I'm so sorry—"

"No!" Mr. Smith flung himself between Brode and his daughter. "You can't. She can't – it only affects the dead. That's what everyone says."

"It only raises the dead, yes," said Brode. "But the disease can sometimes latch onto the very old, the weak, or the young and help them on their way."

Holt swore he saw Brode's eyes water, but the old rider didn't blink once. Was he afraid that tears would fall? Did he care about presenting a strong front so badly?

"Please," Edgar wailed, "there must be something you can do?"

"Daddy?" Ceilia pulled on her father's arm, his sudden terror upsetting her.

Brode drew his sword. "Nothing can be done. To turn fully would be worse than death."

Just then – quite unexpectedly and without a word to Holt – Ash padded out past Brode, heading toward the blacksmith and his daughter.

"Keep that thing back," Mr. Smith said, waving his hands at Ash in the hope of fending off the perceived attack.

"Ash, what are you doing?" Brode asked.

*"She has the same evil in her I sensed back at our nest,"* Ash told Holt. *"And last night on the bodies we found. But it's weaker. Far weaker."*

"Brode said there's nothing to be done," Holt said, worried that the crowd might mob Ash in an effort to keep him away from the girl.

*"I can help."*

"What?" Holt said, completely at a loss.

"What's he saying?" Brode asked.

"He says he can help her."

"Impossible," said Brode.

*"The rot is weak. I can help."*

"He seems sure," Holt said. "Mr. Smith, please. I know you're scared—"

"Keep it away!" Mr. Smith grabbed his daughter and pulled her tightly to him, placing his arms protectively in front of her.

"Ash would never hurt her," Holt said. "He says he can help. Let him try." Holt looked to Brode for approval. The old rider was clearly apprehensive but gave a single nod. Holt nodded back and then said, "Go on, Ash."

*"I must connect with her."*

"Ceilia," Holt said. "Ceilia?" She was crying now, her illness and the fear of the adults around her too much to handle. She watched Ash approach like an injured lamb might watch a wolf. "He won't hurt you, I swear. But he's blind, so you have to hold out your hand for him."

Ceilia looked at Ash in a new light. "Like," she began thickly, "like I do for Mrs. Baker's cat?"

"Exactly like that," Holt said. "Ash likes a scratch on his head too."

That seemed to help, and despite Ash being considerably bigger than her, she held out her hand for him.

Ash took a final step forward and pressed his snout into her open palm.

Every onlooker held their breath.

The blacksmith's eyes bulged.

*"I can hear the magic of the scourge in her,"* Ash said. *"It is dim, weak, but scratchy and painful."*

Holt wasn't certain what to make of this. He'd ask Ash on it more later, but it sounded like the magic of the scourge had a distorted song of its own.

*"I need your help,"* Ash said.

"My help?" Holt asked. He looked to Brode for advice, but the old rider looked as perplexed by the situation as anyone.

"Younger dragons sometimes find it harder to tap into their own core," Brode said. "Focus on your bond. If you can draw on the power yourself, it may open the flow for Ash."

Holt took a deep breath and then strode forward to Ash's side. Surely proximity would only help. He placed his hand onto the top of Ash's snout and let his fingers fall to connect with Ceilia's.

*Focus on the bond,* he thought. *How? He glanced back at Brode.*

"Try the meditation techniques we discussed."

Wishing his first attempt wasn't a matter of life and death, Holt closed his eyes. He breathed slowly, trying to think only of the bond and nothing else. Everything was a distraction – people coughing, the tap of rain, Ceilia's sniveling. With every ounce of might he possessed, he pushed everything else aside. Soon not only did the world vanish but so did the feeling of the breeze against his cheek, the crackle of fires, the smell of damp earth and smoke. The beating of the bond thrummed, louder and louder as he focused on it, louder still until it was almost deafening.

Silence. And then, Holt saw it.

Ash's core.

It appeared in his mind's eye: a small, pulsing ball of light, dim as a guttering candle against a navy sky but very much there. The beat of the bond sent a strand of light his way. Holt breathed in, and the light seemed to fill him.

This time, rather than feel his muscles growing taut with strength, the magic seemed to flow down his arm to the hand helping Ash. His legs became weak, but the feeling was distant, as though he were only an observer of his own body.

A flare of heat shot through him. Through his closed eyes, he thought there was a flash of purple-white light. Then a scream, gasping voices, and he knew he had to wrench himself back to reality.

Holt opened his eyes and found he'd fallen to his knees. Mud squelched as he scrambled to his feet, although he wobbled and fell again. He was so tired. Everything ached.

Ash backpedaled away from Ceilia. She was crying, and the blacksmith's face had turned beet red with anger. Brode stepped in front of Ash to shield him.

"Let me see her," Brode said. He dropped to one knee and rolled up Ceilia's sleeve.

"That beast burned her," said Mr. Smith.

"Edgar—"

"As if it wasn't bad enough—"

"Edgar," Brode said, "the blight is gone. Look."

Holt summoned some reserve of strength and picked himself up to see. Sure enough, the skin on Ceilia's arm was no longer tinged a sickly green. There was, however, a peculiar burn where the blight had been before. Rather than bright red, the burn was a deeper purple, marbled with silver streaks as though the veins beneath had turned to precious metal.

"She's... she's cured?" Mr. Smith choked out.

"It's not possible," Brode said. "But yet... she is. Ash, do you sense any blight remaining inside her?"

Ash yapped lightly twice.

*"Tell the elder one no."*

"He says it's gone," Holt relayed.

"Thank goodness," Edgar wailed. He collapsed to his knees, holding his daughter close, as though afraid she might fly away if he let go.

"It hurts," Ceilia sobbed.

"I imagine it will," Brode said. He placed a hand on her forehead. "But your fever has already broken. Do you feel better?"

She nodded.

"I think you'll be fine," Brode said. "In fact, with Ash's magic, I think you'll live a long and healthy life."

This pleased her. She wiped her eyes and smiled. "Thank you."

"Thank you, *Honored Rider,*" her father corrected her. The black-smith of the Crag blinked back his own tears, then thanked each of them in turn. "I was wrong to doubt you. Thank you."

Holt felt dizzy now. He swayed and only remained on his feet because Ash helped to steady him.

Brode joined them and helped prop Holt up as they walked.

"I have no idea how you did that, Ash," Brode said. "But it is very promising. And clearly your magic is manifesting. With any luck, we can find new meats here at the fort and test the remaining schools."

Ash yapped happily again.

"I don't feel so good," Holt said.

A sudden pain split his chest, and the dragon bond seared as it had done back at the Crag. It was brief, but it was enough to push at its boundaries again. Through the strengthened bond, Holt heard the dragon song. It had changed. The tinny drumbeat was joined now by a lighter melodic layer, and the rhythm picked up as though the song had grown a new verse. As quickly as it came, it echoed off into noth-ingness.

Brode looked at him expectantly.

"I think... I think our bond just improved," Holt said.

"That's not surprising," Brode said. "Quite the experience I'm sure, curing the blight and saving a young girl's life."

"I thought it only improved in combat?"

"That's usually the way after the initial easy gains, but not the only one."

"I don't think I want to advance if I feel this badly each time."

"You'll get used to it, pot boy." He slapped Holt on the back. "Come on. We'll make a rider of you yet."

Though in pain, Holt held his head high as they made their way up the hill to Fort Kennet.

## 20

# TO CUT OUT YOUR HEART

The rest of the day passed in a blur. Drained from using magic, Holt perched on a barrel in the yard of Fort Kennet and watched the garrison prepare to move out. When the clouds parted, Pyra rested in the shade of one of the barracks while Ash stayed loyally by his side. The dragon seemed unaffected by the morning's events, but Holt supposed the magic was innate to Ash; his human body would have to get used to it.

At some point a soldier brought him fresh clothes, then measured him and returned with a mail shirt and tough leather armor to go over it. He was scrawny, so the mail shirt was too big despite being the smallest they had. As it didn't fit right and wasn't of the highest quality, it felt heavy, but he was assured he'd get used to that as well. He noted that nobody had brought him a sword, but he wouldn't know how to use it anyway.

A hot drink was thrust into his hand and he sipped it gratefully. This perked him up, and he realized it was nairn-root tea, both sweet and spicy. He had often brewed it for the riders when they trained but was seldom allowed to drink it himself. Nairn-root was rare. Brode also brought him a molten cake, which was a bit like a cheesy scone with a meaty center and was very filling.

By the time Holt recovered, dusk had gathered, and torches were lit along the fort's walls. Talia and Brode emerged from the Knight Captain's headquarters and strode across the yard to Holt.

The princess scrutinized him, as though trying to figure out a tough riddle.

"Master Brode told me what happened in the camps. Impressive."

Princess Talia had just called him impressive. Holt's chest swelled with pride, and he beamed back at her.

"Thank you. It just sort of... sort of happened!"

"Once you've trained properly, you and Ash will be useful."

This seemed rather curt to Holt, given that curing the blight was surely a step up from being merely 'useful'.

"I hope you've been Cleansing and Forging this afternoon," Talia said.

"I don't know how. I've been—"

"*Don't know?*" Talia repeated in shock. "Master Brode, he—"

"He will learn," Brode said, in a tone that suggested he too thought Talia was being overly critical. "Starting tomorrow. You, however, princess, do not need rest. Let us spar. No magic; I want to focus on your technique."

Talia made a grave expression and nodded.

"*I sense a tension in her,*" Ash noted. "*A deep worry for one so young.*"

Holt looked at Ash, holding back a verbal response while the others were nearby. Talia did have a lot weighing on her, not least the outcome of the upcoming fight at Midbell. Holt resolved to bear that in mind, although her constant dismissal and belittling of him was becoming grating.

Determined to prove himself, he got down from his barrel, picked up his branch and faced Brode.

"Can I start to learn swordsmanship tonight?"

"What part of 'tomorrow' did you not understand?"

"If we're heading for a battle soon, I ought to know the basics."

Brode gave him a measured look and then beckoned him over. Thinking he was about to be handed a sword, Holt eagerly stepped up only to receive a cuff around the back of the head.

"You'll not be partaking in any battle," Brode said. "So you can get that notion out of your head. You'll be a danger to yourself, and others, but certainly not to the scourge."

"I ought to know," Holt said, though not quite meeting Brode's eye.

"Let him watch," Talia said. Then she turned on the spot and strode off without waiting for an answer. Brode looked taken aback but also quietly impressed with her.

"Is she all right?" Holt asked.

"No," Brode said. "None of us are."

With that, he too stomped off across the yard. Holt called for Ash to follow, and then they hurried to catch up with Brode and Talia.

A training ground was sectioned off by low wooden posts behind one of the barracks. Despite the oncoming night and the early morning before them, many of the soldiers gathered to watch the two riders fight.

Holt and Ash were right at the front of the crowd, so he had a perfect view.

The combatants used blunted training swords. Brode would shout out guard stances for Talia to take and then he'd attack her, trying for an opening. She gave him little ground, though he did land a few hard blows. Soldiers winced and probably thought she had been injured, given the strength of Brode's swings.

But they didn't know what Holt knew. Both Brode and Talia had the bodies of ranked dragon riders – they were more than just human.

Ash sat uncannily still throughout the fighting.

Holt placed a hand on the back of his head, where scaly, hardened ridges were beginning to form. "You okay?"

*"I am tracking their movements."*

"You can even hear where a sword is moving in the air now?"

*"I hear them move, yes, but also I can feel the air rippling out like water as they cut. Right now, I think Talia is holding her sword high overhead."*

This was correct. Talia held the hilt of her sword to the side of her head at temple height, but the blade was pointed down at Brode.

*"Once they start moving it becomes difficult."*

"I don't doubt it," Holt said. "They move fast." Still, he was in awe of the dragon's progress and tried to send a bit of encouragement over the bond. Yet with all the noise around them, he found it much harder to focus. He settled for scratching Ash's neck instead.

The sooner Ash could understand movements around him, the better chance they would have of surviving in a real fight.

After another round of guards and stances for Talia, Brode called a halt.

"Very good," he said. "Now we switch."

This time Talia called out the stances for Brode to take, and she tried to get through his guard. The old rider was as slippery as a fox and twice as cunning, lulling her in at times to trip her or throw her off balance. Talia was clearly excellent, but it seemed she had something to learn still.

After one hard fall, she rounded on Brode in frustration.

"With my magic that wouldn't happen."

"Better to not need it at all," Brode said. "Save your magic for the bigger bugs."

Holt considered that. How were the riders supposed to fight the greater creatures of the scourge? He'd seen a rider engage the large scourge stingers back at the Crag, but that fight had unfolded so quickly he'd barely glimpsed it.

"Discipline," Brode went on, speaking with conviction. "Focus, precision. What is the scourge?"

"Chaos," Talia answered.

"And what defeats chaos?" Brode shouted to the crowd at large.

"Order defeats chaos," every soldier recited in perfect harmony.

Caught off guard, not being a soldier, Holt was the only one who didn't join in.

Brode's steely eyes lingered on Holt in that moment. He felt judged. He and Ash were chaos in the otherwise perfect system; well, perfect if you were born highly in it.

Did Brode think poorly of him, as Talia did? A commoner trying to fill a nobleman's shoes. Did he think Holt would never live up to it?

"And yet," Brode said at length, his eyes still fixed on Holt, "perhaps a little chaos is exactly what we need now."

There was a great murmuring amongst the troops at that. Brode might just have told them the ocean would be better off dry. Some noticed who Brode was looking at and turned to face Holt for themselves.

He raised the heavy branch that Brode had given him. He had no idea why he did this, other than it seemed people were expecting something of him. Brode certainly was.

"Will you train me?"

Brode smirked. "Come here, Master Cook."

The murmuring of the soldiers grew louder.

"A cook?" They gasped in disbelief.

Now he felt truly judged.

The whisperings grew to a buzzing speculation as Holt stepped into the arena.

*"Prove them wrong,"* Ash said, and their bond flared. It gave him courage.

Talia handed her training sword to him. Holt dropped his branch and accepted the sword reverently, as though he was being handed some ancient artifact. No one in his family had ever been handed a sword. No Cook for hundreds of years would have been allowed to learn a skill not meant for them.

He'd expected it to be heavy in his hand. It wasn't. In fact, the sword was quite light, certainly lighter than the branch.

Holt felt a fool then.

"You made me carry that branch for no good reason."

"Proper swords are no heavier than they need to be," Brode said. "And it made you feel like you were preparing yourself, did it not?"

A little laughter rang through soldiers.

*Why is he doing this in front of everyone? Is it some test?*

"You wanted the basics, yes?" Brode went on. "Then we'll start with a proper strike from above. Try it."

*Just like that?* Holt thought in alarm. He felt like he was missing some trick. Heat rose in his cheeks as he sensed the eyes of the crowd boring into him.

Brode tapped his foot. "Come on."

*Fine,* Holt thought, growing angry now. He breathed hard through his nose and lunged at Brode, bringing his sword up and down as hard as he could.

Brode flicked his own sword up, swatting Holt's attack away.

"You're far stronger than me," Holt said.

"So I am, though I won't even need that advantage if you keep swinging like that. You nearly missed me. Now, go back to the start."

Holt did so.

"Let's fix your stance," Brode said. "Left foot forward. That's it, with a slight bend in the knee. Distribute your weight evenly and square your hips. Your whole body needs to face the target. Hold the sword at shoulder height. You're right-handed, yes? Right hand higher up the hilt, and your left below. Good."

Holt followed all the instructions and felt a bit odd in his current position. Yet he did feel more in control already, and he looked much more like Talia had during her training.

"Now," Brode said, "when you step in to attack me, don't jump in like a maniac and expose your whole body. Rather step forward on your right foot, then bring your sword straight down – no wild motions. Try that."

Holt did. He performed the movements a bit slowly and stiltedly, but this time his strike was in no danger of missing. It was a big improvement. Brode let the blade hit him; given its blunt edge and his enhanced body, he probably didn't feel a thing.

"Much better," Brode said. "All those years with knives in the kitchens weren't for nothing then."

Another murmur ran through the soldiers, but Holt couldn't help but smile. Finally, he was learning swordsmanship.

*I wonder what Father would say if he could see me now.*

The training continued, but soon Brode stopped being so kind. Holt was given little time to master a movement before Brode's sword whacked into him. Frequently Holt fell over trying to maintain his guard while stepping aside from Brode's attacks. Before long, all the jubilation of minutes ago abandoned him.

Brode came at him again in a whirl of steel, and before Holt could blink, he found himself flat on his back with a pounding pain in his leg.

Laughter rose from the soldiers.

Holt grunted and fought back tears, not of pain or shame but rage.

Those men would never have dared laugh at a noble learning for the first time, never mind a rider. Everyone walked on eggshells around Talia at the Crag. But a Cook? Cooks were fair game. Washers, Furriers, Catchers and Fishers were all fair game.

He hauled himself upright, ready to go again. The laughter didn't stop. He glanced around at their faces and found Talia standing beside Ash. She wasn't laughing at him, but she wasn't telling them to stop either – she who had all the power to do so.

He wanted to shout at them, all of them, but instead he settled for just Brode.

"Won't you at least give me a chance?"

Brode raised his eyebrows. "You think I am being unfair, pot boy? You wish me to go easy on you?"

"I'm trying to learn—"

"You're trying to be a rider," Brode said. "Riders do not have easy lives. And if you thought that was hard, think again."

He moved before Holt could think, and the strength behind Brode's attack was magnitudes above what it had been before. Not just one strike, but many, and Holt crumpled to the muddy ground, quite unable to get up.

"You are a rod of iron," Brode said. "And I will beat you into steel."

Holt's head rang from the latest thrashing. He blinked as colors flashed before him.

"Lesson one," Brode continued, "as a rider you cannot save them all. We do not have the luxury of caring."

Though his head still rang, Holt managed to roll onto his back and looked into the old rider's eyes. Brode talked hard, but he cared. Deep down, he cared.

"You cared enough about the girl earlier today?"

"What?"

"Ceilia. Mr. Smith's daughter. I saw you nearly cry at the thought of killing her."

Brode's hesitation was subtle but there. Had he thought no one had noticed?

"Wouldn't the thought of it cause you pain?"

Holt groaned and pushed up, planting his feet back into the earth.

"It would for me, but you keep making it clear you don't care much for anything other than stopping the scourge. You didn't even linger over the dead at the Crag. But something about her got to you."

"Do you think me so callous?"

"No, because I saw how much it affected you. Stop avoiding the question!"

Brode's expression darkened. "You don't have the stomach to hear it."

Thinking Brode distracted, Holt stepped in for an attack, but Brode moved like a lynx. The blunt edge of Brode's training sword connected with Holt's belly, and he crumpled again, winded.

Another round of rapturous laughter and even applause rang from the soldiers.

Lying on his back again, Holt stared up at the stars. There was a bright crescent moon out. And perhaps it was the pain he felt, but somehow the rays of the stars and moon felt warm to him. In its embrace, all the sound of the arena melted away. He closed his eyes. Holt's only concern became his breath; he slowed it from a pant to coolly taking it in through his nose and out through his mouth, and the dragon bond became an anchor in an otherwise desolate landscape.

Holt seized upon it.

"*Prove them wrong,*" Ash said, and this time his voice was harsh, deeper, as though the dragon to be was clawing to get out.

Power infused Holt's limbs, his whole body. Every sense heightened so that he could smell horses away in their stables, pick out each man individually in the laughing crowd. This was stronger than before, far stronger than even earlier that day. When he gripped the hilt of his sword, he felt as though he could break stone with it.

He opened his eyes, leaped to his feet, and, in the second before he struck, saw surprise break across Brode's face. Of the two of them, Brode was now the slower.

Holt's strike knocked Brode's guard aside, then he pushed Brode over. He stood over the old rider and pressed the tip of his sword against Brode's throat.

"You think I can't handle what you have to say? Try me."

It happened so fast that some of the soldiers hadn't yet registered it. Yet they all fell silent when Ash bellowed his delight at Holt's victory. The dragon roared more fiercely than he had before, and while still nothing on Pyra's cry, it was plenty to silence the men.

Many would laugh at a pot boy.

No one dared laugh at a dragon.

Brode was delighted. He got to his feet, smiling broadly, and took Holt's shoulders in a fierce grip.

"I told you I'd beat you into steel. Learn to draw upon Ash's core at will in battle and you might just survive the coming weeks." He rounded on Talia then. "But that doesn't mean he should rely on it."

"Yes, Master Brode," Talia said. She inclined her head, but her gaze was fixed on Holt, although whether her stare was one of admiration or dislike, he couldn't say.

"We're done for the night," Brode called to the crowd. "Back to your dorms and rest. Tomorrow will be a long day." As the soldiers dispersed, he spoke more quietly so that only Holt could hear. "You want to know why that girl affected me so much?"

Holt nodded. Talia crept forward to join them, Ash padding alongside her.

"Very well," Brode said to the group. "My dragon Erdra – my heart and soul and joy – most of the Order believe she fell in battle. If only she had." His voice wavered, and his grizzled façade crumbled as he spoke. "The blight infected her. We were fighting for so long her core drained, and even her song grew faint. So many injuries. It took hold of her. I had to... I had to..." He clenched his fist. Even admitting it seemed to bring back all the pain of that moment.

Talia spoke for him. "You killed your own dragon?"

Brode didn't need to answer. It was plain. And then Talia did something Holt didn't think her capable of. She hugged Brode. And Brode hugged her in return.

"I'm so, so sorry," she said. "Doing that for Pyra would be like cutting out my own heart."

Holt went to crouch by Ash and hugged him. "Me too."

Brode parted from Talia, and his usual demeanor returned. "And the great hero Silas Silverstrike... he left us to die." Brode near enough spat the words.

Holt's stomach knotted. Weeks ago, he had revered that man. How wrong placed his admiration had been.

"Enough for one night," Brode said. He trudged off into the darkness of the fort courtyard, leaving Holt and Talia in an awkward silence and with the looming thought of tomorrow's long march ahead of them.

# 21

# EXACTING TASTES

"This doesn't make any sense," Talia said. "Are you sure you fed him lamb and not beef?"

"If there's one thing I know more about than you, it's food," Holt said.

"Give it a minute," Brode said. "We've tried the pork already, so it has to be lamb. He must be a mystic."

After days of hard marching southeast with the garrison, the party sat in the glow of a new campfire. They watched Ash eagerly as though he were a toddler attempting to take his first steps. Even Pyra drew in closer, her great eyes wide with anticipation.

Ash pressed all four claws into the earth and visibly tensed his body. Even the dragon bond changed, growing taut under Ash's efforts to summon his magic.

"Anything boy?" Holt asked.

"*No,*" Ash said miserably.

Holt shook his head for the benefit of the others.

Brode scratched his chin. Talia folded her arms and cocked an eyebrow.

"What does this mean?" Holt asked.

"It means he's strange," Talia said.

"Maybe we didn't feed him enough?" Holt said.

Ash groaned at that. *"I don't want anymore. Tasted of grass."*

"Now he's saying he didn't like it."

Talia blew hair out of her face in frustration. "Okay, now he's just defying all known dragon lore. Mystics love lamb."

Pyra snorted and let loose another rumble from deep in her throat.

"I don't think his blindness has anything to do with it," Talia said. Pyra snorted louder. "Why? Because nothing like that has ever been recorded.... yes, I know there will have been too few like him to know for sure... no, I'm sure he's not defective... because he does have magic, Pyra. And it must be strong if it cured a blight infection."

"If I may," Brode interjected. "Perhaps he's not a mystic at all."

"Impossible," Talia hastened to say. "No other dragon type could develop healing powers."

"I agree. And yet we're in a unique position where he isn't responding to the food of that power type while also displaying an otherwise undefined magic. So, either Ash himself is defying everything or, more likely, there is something about dragons we do not know. Ash and Holt are the most unique pairing I've ever seen."

Holt cleared his throat. Once again, he felt like he was getting left behind in the conversation.

"But what does all this mean for us? What should Ash and I do?"

"For now, we'll keep an eye on you, watch for more manifestations of his powers and be patient," said Brode. "It's all we can do, even if it gives Talia nightmares not knowing the answer to a question."

Talia rolled her eyes. "Hysterical. *Master Brode,*" she added apologetically.

He dismissed her with a wave of his hand and laughed. He'd softened somewhat since telling them of his past, as though a mist surrounding him had lifted. And for that glorious moment, Holt forgot that they were about to enter battle tomorrow.

Then it came back, and a gloom settled over the party.

"We should find the Knight Captain," Talia said. "He'll be awaiting your expertise, Master Brode."

Brode got to his feet. "I'll do all I can, but I no longer have a dragon. The troops will look to you on the battlefield."

Talia put on a brave face, but Holt swore he saw her gulp.

"I'm ready to fight," she said. There was a hard edge in her voice. "Pyra too."

"This will be far worse than the skirmishes you fought over the last year alongside experienced members of the Order."

"We know," she said, wrapping an arm around Pyra's neck. Pyra growled in acknowledgment.

Holt's thoughts turned to his one and only encounter with the scourge. The horrors he'd witnessed during the attack on the Crag; the monstrous stingers, the ghoulish risen bodies of men and women with bug-like carapaces instead of skin. Fear gripped him just thinking about it, but he was a dragon rider now. Brode had even given him a sword.

Plucking up his courage, Holt jumped to his feet and stood to attention like a soldier.

"What about me and Ash? What should we do?"

Talia looked sheepish and turned to Brode for the answer.

"You'll stay as far away from trouble as you can," Brode said.

"But—"

"But nothing. Stay back with the baggage train. Talia and I can't look after you in a full battle."

Holt hung his head, although he was secretly relieved.

"I just wanted to help."

To his great shock, Talia gave him a smile.

"That's cute, pot boy. Don't worry, you can risk your life too the moment you and Ash are ready."

Holt bristled, but her attention shifted to Ash. She moved to his side and crouched to his level. As Ash struggled to look directly at her, she gently cupped his head.

"You might be a weirdo, Ash, but I'm grateful you could cure that little girl. Maybe your powers can help more people in time but, even now, it's good to know that Mr. Smith doesn't hate riders anymore. The more people who see the value in our Order, the better we'll be."

Ash licked Talia's face by way of saying 'you're welcome.'

"Ugh," Talia said, wiping her face with her sleeve. "Thanks for that."

Brode cleared his throat again in a manner to signal they ought to be going. Talia got up, and she and Pyra moved off.

"Get some rest, Holt," Brode said. "I'll come find you again in the morning."

Holt tried to calm himself, but even by the time he'd laid out his bedroll, warmed his feet by the fire, and taken off his mail coat, his head was still spinning.

A battle. A real battle with soldiers and dragons and the scourge. It was every legend he'd heard of growing up coming to life. And it didn't feel glorious. It just felt terrifying.

Ash came back out of the darkness quietly. Holt's mind was so preoccupied with the next day he hadn't noticed the dragon had gone on a wander.

The dragon stopped just out of reach.

"What's the matter?" Holt asked.

*"I'm sorry I'm not yet strong enough to help. I worry for the elder one and the troubled one. Even the grumpy one."*

"You know they have names, right?"

*"I do, but their names do not reflect who they truly are."*

"And you think Pyra is only grumpy?"

*"Well, she is. And she can be mean."*

"She can, but I think she'll warm up in time."

*"Yes, she will grow warmer, for she commands fire."*

Their own bond flared, and Ash started a high oscillating growl that Holt took to be laughter. Holt laughed too, although more to be kind. The pun wasn't that funny.

Ash really was an odd creature. At times he seemed so wise, and yet his speech and behavior – like licking Talia's face – spoke of a much younger soul. Were all dragons like this? He would ask Pyra, but he might receive a burn for irritating her.

"And... the 'troubled one' – that's Talia, right?"

*"Yes."*

"So even you can feel it. It's not just me."

*"It is clear in her voice, and in her heartbeat. Both are rarely calm."*

So, not only was Ash able to hear heartbeats but he could even determine someone's emotions by them. Holt might have pondered on its uses, were he not so afraid about tomorrow.

His worry must have crossed the dragon bond, for Ash padded closer, although he had his nose close to the ground for some reason. A moment later, Holt saw he had sniffed out the leather cover of his father's recipe book and was pushing it over to him. He'd been using it to check on simple recipes for pork and lamb.

"Thanks, boy," Holt said.

He picked up the recipe book, laid down on his side and put the book under one arm. Foolish as it may be, he found comfort in holding it.

He had to believe his father was still alive. Perhaps he was already halfway to Sidastra and would soon be behind its walls. Thinking of any other outcome was too much to bear on top of everything else.

Ash came to curl up at his back. Holt could feel his coarse hide through his shirt, but he didn't mind. The pulse of the bond washed away such small discomforts.

As the pair lay side by side, Holt swore that Ash's breathing picked up a rhythm as though an echo of the song from his core rose to send them both into a dreamless sleep.

# 22

# THE BATTLE FOR MIDBELL

Holt was woken roughly.

"Time to get up," Brode said.

Bleary eyed, Holt struggled to a sitting position, feeling like he'd been yanked from a deep sleep. The world was gray again, clouds hanging low as though trying to press down upon the land.

Around him the garrison was already in motion; soldiers were geared and forming ranks, while the camp followers and those remaining to guard it were already repacking the wagons.

"Why didn't you wake me earlier?" Holt asked, his words hoarse from a parched mouth. He wondered how he had not woken up by himself with all this activity around him.

"I felt you and Ash could use the rest," Brode said. "He's grown again."

Ash yawned widely and stretched until he reached about ten feet from tail to snout. His wings had formed, although they were comically small in proportion to his body. He was still some way off flying. Yet he was large enough now that a child might ride him into battle.

Holt rubbed at his eyes. "What do you want us to do?" He stood up, swayed from the rush of blood from his head, and met resistance from Brode's hand pressing into his chest.

The old rider wore a coat of chainmail, with armored vambraces on his forearms and greaves on his legs. Not as heavily armored as a full knight; Brode clearly favored agility. His special rider's sword had cut through thick tree branches with ease, and Holt imagined Brode weaving deftly through a battle, carving through the scourge.

"Pack up," Brode said. "We're moving."

Their march was swift, taking the main road east. And it was quiet. A tense silence gripped them as they stepped ever closer to battle.

Smoke rose in a pillar farther to the southeast. High rolling hills rose behind it, and a ringing wind echoed across the land.

Ash froze, his whole body going taut.

*"The scourge are close."*

"We must be near Midbell now," Holt said. His ill-fitting chainmail coat weighed him down, but he was thankful for it.

*"I can hear their screeching,"* Ash said. He snaked his head at an angle impossible for a human and sniffed at the air. *"And I can smell their filth."*

Holt took a deep breath and let it go slowly. He had to stay calm. Brode and Talia would handle this.

"Come on, Ash. We need to keep up."

The army turned off the road, heading south.

Time passed in an odd manner for Holt. Each step seemed to take an age, and yet all too soon they arrived at the lip of the land and gazed into the plain below.

At the foot of the Howling Hills, the town of Midbell was aflame on one side. The fires were black and evil, the same wicked magic that had reduced the Crag. Yet the walls were not taken. A writhing mass of creatures assailed the town, while stingers circled overhead like poisonous vultures. The shrieks of the scourge carried, even to Holt's human ears.

Orders were called. The troops assembled into tight formations. Horns blew.

Holt watched it unravel in a haze of uncertainty. What was he supposed to do?

Brode found him. "Stay here with the baggage train. And stay safe."

Panic gripped Holt. "What if you don't come back?"

Brode didn't skip a beat. "You can't think like that."

"But—"

"Enough. Right now, Talia needs me more than you do." He left without another word.

Holt searched for a sign of Talia but could not see her. Then Pyra swooped down overhead, landing in a thunderous crash in front of the garrison. The dragon stretched her neck and roared, louder and more savage than Holt had ever heard a dragon bellow before.

A challenging call. Pyra was ready.

Upon her back, Talia steadied herself, then turned to face the men and women gathering behind her. She drew her rider's blade, and the red steel flickered even under the gray morning light.

"Soldiers of Feorlen today we... we—"

Some part of the swarm answered Pyra's roar, crying out in a pitch high enough to break glass. Talia's hesitation drew out into too long a pause.

Holt felt everyone waiting for her to roar in her own way and give them courage that a dragon rider of the Order was at hand.

When she didn't, Brode rode out to save her, with Alexander Knight by his side. He had his own green blade held high.

"Come with me and crush this swarm!"

Cheers answered him.

"Fight," Brode called. "Fight!"

More cheering, clashing metal and stamping feet. And then the army was off, marching to meet the swarm as the bugs and ghouls peeled away from the town walls to face the new threat.

Battle was now inevitable.

Holt remained where he was, doing as he was told for once but feeling useless all the same.

"There are so many of them," he said aloud. "Can they even do this?"

*"They do not need to kill them all,"* Ash said.

"What do you mean?" Holt asked, taken aback. He hadn't expected an answer.

"I have... *memories,*" Ash said, faltering a little as though it were hard for him to recall. "*Such great swarms. The land covered in their green blood. Always one we look for. The queen that controls them.*"

"You mean that one of those creatures down there is actually... in charge?"

"*I think so. If enough of the scourge are killed, the queen reveals itself. Kill the queen and you diminish the swarm.*"

"How will they know which one to kill?" At least from this distance, all the scourge creatures looked so similar. No one monster stood out.

"*The queen will come to challenge our strongest warrior.*"

"Talia is our strongest fighter."

"*Yes. She must win the day for us.*"

Holt blew out his cheeks. "No wonder she was nervous."

Not that he felt any better now. He fidgeted with his hands. He felt so useless just standing here, but without training there was little he could do.

Across the plain, the garrison prepared for the final charge. The cavalry split into two wings, one moving to either flank except for two horsemen who held back behind the main body of infantry. Judging by their armor, these two figures were the Knight Captain and Brode.

As the infantry trudged on, a division of archers held back, planting their feet into the earth and readying longbows. The front ranks of infantry began to lower spears and tighten ranks, becoming something like a hedgehog with steel-tipped spines.

It all looked seamless and well-drilled to Holt.

"Maybe I'm worrying over nothing," he thought aloud.

"*There is much knowledge on how to defeat the enemy,*" Ash said. "*And this is only a small force.*"

Holt nodded and sighed in relief. He'd let his nerves get to him. Brode wouldn't have let them partake in any adventure too perilous.

"*They come where the most people are,*" Ash said. "*And against strong walls they are crushed like wolves trapped inside a cave.*"

Holt nodded. Even commoners knew the rhymes and stories.

"Talia and Pyra will take this queen bug," Holt said. "Pyra's fire will see to it."

*"Fire is their fear,"* Ash said sagely.

Right on cue, Pyra bellowed again and leaped into the air, beating her wings furiously to take her higher. A group of stingers swooped around and made for her. High above the approaching ground forces, the first stroke of the battle fell. Pyra bathed the stingers in fire. Singed bodies dropped from the sky before Pyra clamped her jaws upon one that had avoided her breath.

On the ground, the streaming scourge forces crashed into the garrison's spear formation. The soldiers held. Archers loosed, and Holt understood why Pyra had flown so high as arrows sailed over the brunt of the fighting to hit the back ranks of the enemy.

Holt watched transfixed as the battle unfolded. He tried to keep tabs on Brode and Talia; the princess was easy to follow, but Brode vanished into the melee. Distant as it was, he heard only the faint cacophony of screams and steel, occasionally broken by Pyra's roars.

Ash could hear far more. Feel more.

Holt sensed it over the bond. Ash's very being whimpered, even if the dragon showed no outward sign of distress.

"Hey," Holt said, crouching down. "It'll be all right. Like you said, Talia will defeat the queen and—"

But Ash snorted, growled fearfully and stepped back even as Holt reached out to him.

*"So many of them. I want to fight but I... I..."*

Their bond burned, causing Holt to gasp in pain as images raced through his mind. Ash's memories of the Crag came to the fore. Memories of smoke-choked air, blistering heat, shrill cries and the smell of death. Ash's fear was far greater than Holt's own. It was a fear akin to a much younger child, and that was what Ash was in truth. Barely a month old, and yet necessity was forcing rapid growth and danger upon him.

Even though the memories were not his own, Holt found it hard to overcome them.

"Ash, it's okay. Talia and Pyra will keep us safe."

Yet Ash seemed too far gone. He whimpered for real this time and slinked off to the safety of the baggage train where physicians were already preparing for the wounded that would arrive.

Holt hesitated to follow. For once he was torn whether or not to join the dragon and stood dumbfounded in the no-man's-land between the camp and the soldiers fighting and dying in the distance.

Before he could decide, another glass-shattering shriek carried across the battlefield, and a fresh wave of the enemy emerged from a valley of the Howling Hills. This group was much smaller than the main force, yet at its center was a creature of remarkable size. Larger even than Pyra, it stood upright upon two legs with a sickly light reflected off its shell-like exoskeleton. And it moved at speed.

It looked nothing like the swarm queen depicted in the painting at the Crag. Rather it seemed to Holt to be an enormous flayer, a fast-moving bug that slashed in broad strokes with razor-sharp bladed arms. Pyra swooped down to meet the beast.

Before Holt could consider it further, the pull across the dragon bond became too much to resist. He wrested himself from observing the battle and ran for Ash, finding the dragon hiding under a weapons cart and shaking like a traumatized alley cat.

"Hey, it's okay. It's okay." Holt reached out a hand for Ash to sniff and find. Ash pressed his snout into Holt's palm, and the scattered, wild beating of the bond calmed. But not by much. Holt gulped, unsure what he could do to help. "What happened to that fierce dragon who helped me move the giant table in the kitchens?"

Ash growled but said nothing.

"And when I trained with Master Brode, you told me to prove them wrong. Where's that dragon gone?"

A fresh tremor ran down Ash's spine and through his tail.

*"I'm not ready. Not ready to fight them."*

"We won't have to fight them—"

Ash froze. His whole body went stiff.

*"Holt, the scourge are close."*

"What?"

*"They are coming fast."*

"How can you tell?"

But before Ash could say anything, the remaining soldiers guarding the baggage train called out to each other.

"Scourge approaching!"

"Ready yourselves!"

Holt ran out to see for himself. This couldn't be. The scourge were drawn to the densest collection of people – to cities and armies. Their swarms didn't think strategically.

Yet the moment Holt returned to his previous spot and looked across the battlefield before Midbell, he saw the truth for himself.

A line of shambling ghouls had broken off from the main swarm. Scores of them. They moved at speeds no human could maintain if alive. And they were heading right for Holt and the baggage train. Worse still were the stingers flying above them, survivors of Pyra's initial assault.

Holt searched desperately for the purple dragon, but Pyra and Talia were pursuing the giant flayer and had not seen the splinter force.

More scourge separated from the main host and flanked the infantry, heading for the exposed archers. No one had thought they would be endangered. The light cavalry of the garrison had committed to an attack already and couldn't disengage quickly enough.

The scourge forces – the supposedly mindless, animalistic force of nature – were outmaneuvering the garrison.

Holt's heart pounded so hard he thought his ribs would crack.

The soldiers nearby drew their swords, though they stood half-heartedly, as lost and confused as Holt. This wasn't supposed to happen. No one had trained them for a situation like this.

Civilians screamed as they realized what was coming.

Holt's body reacted before his mind did. He ran and was back at Ash's cart before he could properly think.

"We have to go!"

Ash scurried out and clung to Holt's side as they fled. Now screeches of the scourge mixed with scraping steel as they engaged the soldiers. With so few defenders, most of the ghouls sped past into the baggage train.

Holt ducked as buzzing overhead signaled the arrival of a stinger. The wasp buzzed on ahead, swooping down upon a lone soldier caught unprepared, its great sting piercing chainmail as though it were butter.

Ash wailed, his breath ragged, and his shame was palpable across the bond.

At least they would be together when the end came.

As they neared the back of the baggage train, Holt ran past the wagon containing his, Brode's and Talia's supplies. He caught himself, wheeled about, intending to fetch his father's recipe book if he could.

"Keep running," he yelled, not stopping to see if the dragon kept going or not.

Before he reached the wagon, a ghoul lumbered in front of him to block his path.

What this person had been in life, Holt could not say for sure; a man, judging by its size. A ragged tunic hung torn and limp from its bony frame. Perhaps it had been a farmer or a farmhand, for it carried a bloody sickle. Its pale, lidless eyes fixed upon Holt, and the ghoul opened its rotten mouth and screamed.

Holt came to a halt and tried to force his panicked breathing to calm. He reached for Ash's core, but it was no use in this panicked state. Drawing his sword anyway, he held it just as Brode had taught him, bracing himself with his left foot forward.

The ghoul ran at him, its arms flailing. Yelling in defiance, Holt stepped forward on his right foot and struck down hard. Steel bit deep into the exposed flesh of the ghoul's shoulder. Green blood spurted from the wound. It crumpled.

Barely registering that he'd made his first kill, Holt continued on to the wagon. Frantically he searched his sack and pulled out the recipe book. He'd only just taken hold of it when bony fingers clamped on his leg in a vise-like grip and pulled.

Holt was heaved bodily backward. His world spun. Now flat on his back, he realized he'd dropped both the recipe book and his sword. He tried reaching out for his fallen weapon, but his fingers found only grass.

"Ash..." he said, dazed.

The dragon bond seared, but then a new ghoul appeared over Holt like a slavering hound, its breath hot and foul. It pressed a knee onto his outstretched arm. Pinned like this, he doubted the strength from Ash's magic would have saved him.

Time slowed as the ghoul raised one arm that ended in a sharpened bone – it needed no other weapon.

"*Boy!*" Ash cried.

A white streak hit the ghoul in turn, cutting off its howl of triumph.

Holt gasped for air, rolled over, grabbed his sword, got to his feet. Ash raked at the ghoul with his talons, and Holt dashed over and plunged his blade into the ghoul's belly.

The creature shrieked, and Holt realized he'd not broken through the ghoul's developing chitinous hide. He struck again, as hard as he could, and his time drove the blade through the weakened gap in the ghoul's armor.

Holt stepped back and looked upon the dead woman's face. It had been a woman once, who knew how long ago. Its skin was gray now, lifeless, and tinged the same sickly green that had almost taken the blacksmith's daughter.

Ash came to Holt's side and roared, not as menacing as Pyra had been, but it was his most fearsome yet; wild bears would have bowed in his presence.

"*I will fight,*" Ash declared. "*I will fight if you will.*"

Holt glanced around. It was naught but carnage and death: soldiers fighting desperately in pairs or alone; women face down in pools of blood; ghouls biting into the necks of the fallen.

To their right, a set of wagons blew apart into splinters as a bull-size beetle with a hammer-like head stampeded through. A juggernaut.

Ghouls. Stingers. A giant flayer. And now this. Holt passed beyond mere fear. And with his blood up, he became numb to the terror.

"Talia and Brode wouldn't run. We won't either. I'll fight."

Ash roared again, and Holt felt the dragon bond flare hot in his soul, a blazing fire in the darkness. Its outer edges pushed a little farther, expanded the bond a fraction more. Holt concentrated, gained a glimpse of Ash's core and reached for it—

But another ghoul lunged at them. Ash grabbed the ghoul by the leg and felled it, allowing Holt an easy kill. Quick as it was, Holt lost his grip on Ash's core. It was like trying to grasp a greased-up doorknob at the edge of reach.

Ahead of them, a pair of soldiers disappeared into a blaze of black fire and collapsed dead in a burnt heap. A ghoul of sorts, although thinner, with longer limbs and enlarged hands cut off the spell of fire channeling from its hands. It swooped down upon the bodies of the soldiers, presumably to bite them and spread the blight.

Rage gripped Holt. These creatures must have been responsible for burning the Crag. Those flames seemed a terrible way to die. He tried to clear all of that from his mind, focusing instead upon drawing on magic from Ash's core.

The scourge caster got up from the fallen soldier and fixated on Holt. Its bloody mouth opened wide in anticipation and it began to gather dark magic between its hands.

"For life," Holt cried, as the heroes did in the songs, and charged toward the ghoul.

The black ball swirled.

Holt forced everything else from his mind. There was only the bond, there was only the bond. He no longer felt his pounding feet. His inner reach flailed once more, falling short.

He tried again.

The ghoul's magic peaked. It pulled back, ready to launch—

Holt made it. He breathed in the light of Ash's core, heard a flurry of the dragon song loud and racing. It snapped power into his limbs, sharpened his senses, cleared his head of the daze from his injury.

Yelling from the effort, Holt's feet carried him the remainder of the distance in an eye blink. He struck his enemy with such force that he cut deep through the chitinous armor on the first attack.

Momentum carried him forward, but enhanced balance kept him on his feet even as another ghoul came, then another. Life narrowed into the next second, the next threat, the next desperate move. All the while, Ash was by his side, mauling ghouls with sheer ferocity as Holt knocked them aside.

Magic flowed across the bond. All he felt was the grip of his sword; all he smelled was acrid scourge blood; his only thought was to not let any of them pass. He would stop them. Speed and power made up for his lack of training, but with every swing his arms ached more, and the light of the core dwindled.

He didn't know how long it would last, nor how long his bond would hold up. He'd only be able to draw upon less than a quarter of the core at most before it frayed.

His vision began to darken from the effort, and he knew the end was close.

A blur of brown hair and steel rushed into view. Hooves beat and dozens of horses charged past, riding down straggling ghouls.

Holt blinked and looked at the rider above him. It was none other than the Knight Captain himself. Alexander Knight raised his visor and called orders to the other cavalry around him.

"Full retreat," he cried.

"Knight Captain, sir?"

The captain didn't seem to register Holt.

"Three riders, take that juggernaut – give the civilians time."

"Knight Captain!"

Alexander looked down now. "Young rider, you should flee too."

"What about Brode and Talia?"

"They said they would cover the retreat."

"But if we kill that massive flayer, we can—"

"I know full well how to defeat a group of scourge," Alexander snapped. "But this is no ordinary swarm. We're broken. It's done."

"But—"

Holt's words died in his throat. The Knight Captain clanked his visor back into place and rode off. Streams of foot soldiers arrived from the battlefield now, half-fighting, half-running as they fled. Pockets of resistance gathered for a last stand, only to be surrounded in moments.

Dragon roars and baleful screeching drew Holt's attention south. Pyra had engaged the great flayer, and it looked like Talia was still riding on her back.

The flayer had a torso that rose up like a praying mantis, with mandibles at its mouth and scythe-like arms ending in pincers. One of these blade arms stabbed down hard enough to send up torrents of earth.

It was all Pyra could do to dodge the blows. She must have been injured or she would surely fly. With every step she gave ground – drawing closer to the baggage train – and the rest of the garrison retreated around her.

He saw no sign of Brode.

Holt knew he should run as well – he'd been doing just that minutes ago. But something kept him in place. He was a rider. Talia, Pyra and Brode were out there and needed him.

Ash's core had been growing faint before Alexander Knight had arrived and it stayed low, but it was still there. Greater strength still pulsed in Holt's veins.

*"We help them,"* Ash said, his voice deepening.

Perhaps that was why the core had dimmed; perhaps Ash had tapped into it himself? Holt could think of it in no other way, but there was an aura to the dragon now, a power radiating that made nearby scourge wary. Ash pulled back his lips, revealing sharp white teeth and a forked tongue, and was far more menacing for it. Between the gaps in his fangs, a purplish-white energy crackled. The same light that had cured Ceilia.

Brode said that extreme circumstances might hasten his development. If this battle wasn't an extreme circumstance, Holt didn't know what was.

The rout of the garrison and the ghouls chasing them made a scene of total chaos.

Holt placed a hand on Ash. "Can you find your way through?"

*"Lead the way."*

Holt drew in a deep breath, knowing this was mad, then charged toward the titanic duel between Pyra and the scourge queen. Soon Holt was close enough to feel the ground shake with every strike and stamp of the flayer. It shrieked in frustration as Pyra dodged yet again and then proceeded to bathe the flayer's leg in fire.

"Holt, get out of here!"

Brode. Brode was yelling at him.

# 23

# ABILITIES

Holt half-awoke to the pale light falling upon his face. His eyes were heavy, and he closed them again until the pain in his head became too much to ignore. Unable now to close his eyes, he sat upright and clutched at his temple, feeling as though someone had taken a mallet to it.

*Where am I? Where is Ash?*

Panicked, he reached for the dragon bond. It wasn't right. Each beat sputtered like a broken kettle. He could only catch a glimpse of Ash's core as though he were seeing it through a broken, dirtied window. The light flickered. This hardly helped his worry, but at least if it was still there, in some form, then Ash must be too.

Then – as though his senses were delayed – he realized he was on something soft. Very soft. A bed with plump pillows and the smoothest sheets Holt had ever felt in his life. The whole room was one of luxury. A polished decanter sat on a tray with bunches of grapes by the window, and a pile of folded clothes lay on a chair by the fireplace.

And sitting atop the bedside cabinet was the leather-bound recipe book. Miraculously it was intact, its gold embossed front unblemished. Holt breathed easier. Somehow, seeing it there made things okay.

He got up, swayed from the effort, then pulled on the clean new clothes: they were the sort of white shirt and tanned trousers that nobles wore. He grabbed the recipe book, stumbled to the door and carefully negotiated a staircase leading down to a stone courtyard.

Ash bounded to him and nearly knocked him over.

*"You're awake!"* His voice had returned to its lighter, happier state. *"I told them you were up! I told them!"*

"Easy, Ash," Holt said, blinking against the light reflecting off the dragon's white scales. "I don't think you know your own strength anymore. And told who?"

"Told us," Brode called.

Holt looked around and saw Brode and Talia sitting at what looked like a workbench laden with food instead of tools. The courtyard was so large that even Pyra sat comfortably inside it. Lining the space were flowerbeds blooming with red and yellow petals while brass bells and windchimes hung in bunches above.

"How do you feel?" Brode asked.

"Like I'll never have a clear head again." Holt blinked and raised a hand against the overbearing daylight.

Brode came to his side. "You're lucky to be alive. But you two seem to live by luck. Come and sit down. Eating will help."

Holt allowed Brode to navigate him over to the workbench-cum-dining table. He sat opposite Talia and began picking at a bread roll.

"What happened?" Holt asked.

"I have a suspicion," Brode began. "You were clearly drawing on Ash's core but still collapsed. Did you cut it off?"

"Ash asked me to."

"I thought as much."

Holt understood from Brode's tone that this wasn't good. Then again, he understood that well enough from his own aching head.

"Next time," Brode continued, "you have to ease it off. You can't just sever ties to the core while your body is saturated with its magic. Even if it does grant Ash more power in the moment."

He faced Ash next.

"And you, young dragon, don't go powering a single attack with the entirety of your core unless you too want to be knocked out cold."

Despite the seriousness of his words, he wasn't scorning them. Rather, Brode tossed Ash a thick slice of ham.

"What happened was an easy mistake to make at Novice rank but one you should not repeat lightly."

"Saving the day through a mistake," Talia said. She scrutinized Holt as she had back at the fort, and again Holt couldn't tell whether she admired or hated him.

"Well, Ash saved the day really," Holt said.

Ash gave a throaty, happy rumble.

"How long was I out for?"

"Almost two days," Brode said. "I would have been worried, but Ash woke up first and let us know he could feel your health returning over the bond."

"The bond doesn't feel healthy at all," Holt said. "Is this what a 'frayed' bond feels like?"

"It would have felt even worse a day ago," Brode said. "Can you see anything of Ash's core yet?"

"Sort of, but it's hard to do so and looks... blurry?"

"Then it's already recovering. A truly frayed bond makes it impossible to see or draw upon the core. Means you can't Cleanse or Forge either, which isn't helpful after a battle. It's unwise to push the limits of your bond unless absolutely necessary. Bear it in mind for the future."

"I will," Holt said. "But wait, you said Ash spoke to you? He must be getting stronger. And what was it that he... blasted at that giant flayer?"

"Some sort of light or energy," Talia said. "I've never seen nor heard of anything like it before. Neither has Master Brode."

Holt couldn't help but grin through the pain. He and Ash did have a useful power after all, and not just for healing the blight. It seemed they could do some real damage too.

A swift, sharp pain to the back of his head knocked the smile from his face. Brode had cuffed him.

"I wouldn't be so pleased with yourself," Brode said. "You almost got yourself killed. Fool. But," and he softened now, "I do thank you for being a fool in that moment."

"*I thank you too,*" Pyra said. "*I was wrong to doubt your heart. You have spirit like one of our own.*"

Holt turned to tell her she was welcome face-to-face. "You're hurt," he said instead, seeing a ragged tear in the sinew of her folded wing.

"One of the stingers managed to get a claw into her," Talia said. "It wasn't so bad, but the fight with the flayer made it worse. It's my fault."

Holt turned back around. "How is it your fault?"

"I wanted to help Midbell," Talia said.

"So did I," said Holt.

Talia looked downcast all the same. Holt recalled Brode telling her it would be a chance for her to gain experience of commanding a large force. He also remembered how her nerve gave out when addressing the troops before the battle. She needed a lift.

"You and Pyra were inspiring," Holt said. "The way you charged into that group of stingers was amazing. And you two did most of the work taking on the flayer. Ash's magic might not have been so effective if you hadn't cut a gap in its armor."

"For once, Holt speaks sense," Brode said. "Don't be too hard on yourself, girl. You did more than anyone of your rank would be expected to."

Talia smiled weakly but seemed unconvinced. She returned to picking at her food.

Feeling more words would only make things worse, Holt started on a roast chicken leg. After picking the meat down to the bone and taking a long drink of water, he began to feel human again.

A strong breeze picked up in the courtyard, whipping in from the archways behind them. The windchimes rang pleasantly.

"*Bells ring across the town,*" Ash told him.

"I take it we are in Midbell," Holt said.

"At the house of Ealdor Ebru," Brode said. "Specifically, her carriage house. The carriages have been removed to allow Pyra in."

"It seems very grand," Holt said.

"Well," said Brode, "the Ebrus, Midbell and its citizens find themselves in your debt, Holt."

"Ash said the swarm would weaken if we killed the queen but that was a flayer, unless I'm mistaken."

"A giant flayer," Talia said. "But smaller swarms like that are often led by the biggest, brutalest bug. Queens lead true swarms. The ones that level cities and kingdoms. You'll see one at Sidastra... if we make it."

Holt gulped. That flayer had been bad enough. "So, killing the flayer had a similar effect to killing a queen? The swarm dispersed?"

Brode's face darkened. "Removing the controlling bug – even a little one like that – sends the swarm into a state of confusion."

Holt swallowed his mouthful of chicken, hard. He hadn't failed to register Brode's comment that the flayer they'd just faced was a 'little one'.

"The death of the flayer spurred the last defenders of Midbell to ride out and join us," Brode continued. "But we lost many soldiers in that rout. More than I anticipated," he ended darkly.

Holt focused on his food. Talia too had nothing to say.

"Such is war," Brode told them. "Especially war against the scourge."

Brode carried on, but Holt wasn't paying attention.

So much death, so easily. Out in the open, the scourge, it seemed, had every advantage. And his father was out in the open, on the road to Sidastra, if he was even still alive. Holt placed a hand upon the recipe book for comfort, wishing then that humans could form connections like the dragon bond. If they could, then he'd at least know if his father was alive.

"Holt?" Brode was trying to get his attention. He faced the old rider. "I'd like you to try drawing on the core again."

"But my bond is still recovering."

"Just a trickle," Brode said. "I know you're still weak, but Ash's magic has matured. Show him Ash, shoot your breath skyward – not too strong now, we don't want any damage."

All turned to watch the young dragon.

Sure enough, Ash parted his lips, showing his growing teeth and forked tongue. White-purple light gathered at his mouth, then he tilted his neck up and released.

The light was otherworldly and pale. It traveled straight and true, without a flicker like fire and struck one of the bunches of bells. They rattled, suggesting the light had a force behind it. About ten feet farther the light dissipated, but the beam, such as it was, was maintained until Ash closed his jaws. The metal of the bells was left slightly singed.

"What are you?" Talia asked aloud, more to herself than the others.

"That light is close in color to Silas's magic," Holt said. "Perhaps he is a storm dragon?"

Brode shook his head. "We tried all the food. Nothing worked for him. And storm dragons deal in lightning or wind, not pure light. No, Ash is something new. Something special." Brode now had an eagerness about him Holt had rarely seen. "But as his dragon breath has awakened, your first main ability with magic will also have unlocked."

"My *ability?*"

Talia flew into an explanation. "While the core grants the rider general manipulation of magic, a few key abilities come more easily, requiring only a small amount of magic to power with practice. New abilities unlock at each rank as you're able to draw more efficiently on the magic."

She began counting off on her fingers.

"Once a Novice has matured their bond, the dragon breath will indicate their magic type. Pyra is a fire dragon, so I can cast a Fireball as my primary attack."

She tapped a second finger.

"At the rank of Ascendant, the rider can push their magical attack out in a radius around or in front of them. It's a weaker attack than focusing on a single target, but you can hit multiple enemies that way, so it can come in handy. I'm still getting the hang of my Flamewave ability, but I can send out fire about twelve feet in every direction if I really push."

Holt blinked. That seemed very powerful indeed, and not just for fighting the scourge. It was certainly a good thing the riders didn't partake in other wars. Then he thought about Silas and wondered just what other devasting abilities a rider at the rank of Lord would have at their disposal.

"What comes after the rank of Ascendant?" Holt asked.

"At Champion rank, things begin to vary rider to rider," Talia said. "Unique cores and experiences lead to unique songs – every dragon is different after all. It alters the later abilities, but they remain within your school of magic, of course."

Holt looked to Brode, who'd gone rather still as Talia spoke, as though expecting Holt would ask this of him.

"You want to know what my abilities were at Champion rank?" Brode asked.

"No," Holt said quickly. "I mean, yes. I mean, only if you—"

"It's all right," Brode said. He put down the heel of bread he'd been tearing into and picked at something stuck between his teeth. Anything to delay the answer, it seemed, but at last, he did tell them.

"Erdra was an emerald dragon, as wild as a thicket yet more beautiful than all the gardens of Coedhen. And she had an affinity for the earth. Her magic wasn't aggressive so much as it allowed me to control a battlefield. I could sink the ground beneath a juggernaut's feet, ensnare a group of ghouls in the mud. When I advanced to Champion, I found I could raise the earth to block the paths of enemies or defend our flanks."

"Wow..." Holt said. That sounded like it was extremely useful if he was supported by other riders. Perhaps it had been. Silas Silverstrike had fought beside him. And then he had left Brode and Erdra to die.

Holt could hardly believe he'd been excited to see that man not long ago.

Brode seemed to feel he'd said enough. He returned to his heel of bread but just turned it over and over in his hands.

Talia looked to Holt expectantly. "Don't you want to try yours out?"

Holt flexed his fingers. "I do," he said warily.

"Reach for the core carefully," Talia told him, "and rather than letting it wash over your whole body for strength, direct it into one hand."

Holt raised his right hand.

"Better to practice with your left," Talia said, "so you can learn to use magic while still holding your sword."

Holt quickly switched hands. He got up, stepped away from their table, and took a deep breath. He really didn't want to pass out again. Carefully, he reached for the dragon bond. In its damaged state, he saw the light of Ash's core like he might a lantern through a cracked door at the end of a distant hallway. But he *could* just see it.

A strong breeze passed through the courtyard. Bells rang and the windchimes chinked. Then an echo of music played lightly for a moment. Ash's song must have added yet more notes after the battle; there was something akin to a lute's plucked string in there.

Carefully, he pulled in a wispy strand of light from the core. Even this small piece of power wanted to flood through him, but he fought against it this time, trying with great effort to force it toward his outstretched hand. It wasn't easy, like trying to direct the tide.

His arm began to shake.

"Easy," Talia said.

Pyra snorted and raised her head, perhaps checking on whether she ought to move out of harm's way.

Holt continued to struggle, feeling a heat gather on his palm, and then the same white light of Ash's breath began to gather there. The shaking grew worse. He couldn't help it.

"Holt!" Talia began moving toward him. "Aim up!"

The heat in Holt's palm grew unbearable. He heard Talia running. He tried to move his hand, but it was numb with pain. He grabbed at his left wrist with his other hand, desperately pulling it upward.

He was too late.

Light shot from his palm, as quick as an arrow. It hurtled through the air, toward an archway. Toward the man who had just stepped into its path.

"Look out!" Talia gasped.

The man yelped. Holt's heart skipped a beat as the man dove to the ground. The light flew over his head and crashed harmlessly against a distant wall.

"You idiot," Talia said to Holt.

"I'm sorry," Holt replied. He turned to the stranger. "Sorry! Are you all right?"

"Y-yes," came the breathless reply. The man got up, brushed himself down, and tentatively edged into the courtyard. He wore fine leather riding garments, a rich wine-colored cloak and held a letter.

Talia stepped forward, her expression one of shock. "Nibo, what are you doing here?"

The man, Nibo, bowed low. "Your Royal Highness. I bear you a message from your brother."

## 24

# HIS LAST WILL

Silence fell with the messenger's words.

Talia moved and spoke as though her body were numb. "From... from my brother?"

"I last saw him weeks ago, princess. I've discovered since that he has... that he has passed." The messenger, this Nibo, seemed as choked up by it as Talia.

She seemed unable to summon more words.

Brode intervened. "Why don't you tell us your story, Nibo? How did you come here?"

"Honored Rider." Nibo bowed to Brode and then began his tale. "King Leofric summoned me one morning before dawn. He was troubled, distant, distracted. He told me I was to make for the Crag at once and to place this letter only in Talia's hands. I was to burn it rather than let anyone else read its contents. Yet such was the secrecy of my mission, and Leofric's fear, I was forbidden from taking the horse relay routes via the forts. The roads would be watched, he said. As I say, the king was distressed."

Nibo's shoulders slumped.

"I asked him to confide in me, but he said he could not. If I were his friend, I would ask him no more. And so, I left, and began the arduous journey over rough country. Six days ago, I came upon the edge of the Howling Hills and found streams of people fleeing to Midbell."

He averted his eyes now.

"Forgive me, princess, but I disobeyed your brother in making for the town myself. I know a lone traveler will not attract a swarm, but I felt myself in too much danger in the open."

"There is nothing to forgive," Talia said. "My brother would not have wished you to risk your life and your mission."

"I am relieved to hear your pardon all the same. I intended to set out as soon as the siege was over, but everyone spoke of a dragon rider who turned the battle. I thought I might get information on your whereabouts. It's my one stroke of good fortune that the rider who saved the town should turn out to be you!"

Talia glanced at Holt at this but said nothing.

Nibo presented her the letter. It was still sealed with purple wax.

Talia took it as though receiving her brother's own ashes and began to read. Nibo stepped back until he was at a servant's distance from Talia, a space Holt knew all too well.

"I'm sorry I almost hit you with magic," Holt said.

Nibo blinked. "No offense is taken, Honored Rider." He actually bowed.

Holt opened his mouth, then closed it. With the exception of the Knight Captain, the people at Fort Kennet hadn't afforded him the title and the etiquette usually given to riders. But they had known he was a Cook, and he'd still been in his commoner cloth then. Now he wore a well-pressed white shirt and had cast a magical ability. Would Nibo have acted differently if he knew the truth?

Talia turned milk pale. "I don't believe it."

Nibo eyed the letter as though it were responsible for the death of his friend. "I dread what it says. I fear Leofric suffered for it. I never saw him so distressed, even when word arrived from the Toll Pass last year."

"May I?" Brode said, walking over to Talia with his hand outstretched.

She handed him the letter without protest, her eyes fixed somewhere on the ground.

Holt could only wonder how terrible a message it was. He patted Ash's neck by way of comforting himself, feeling the bond glow warm.

*"Your magic felt strong,"* Ash remarked.

"The bolt of light?" Holt said quietly. "I'll need to practice."

Now he thought on it, he'd also need to name his ability, as Talia had. Her first ability was Fireball – so what was his? 'Light Beam' didn't seem right. Too wordy, and it wasn't so much a beam, as Ash's breath was, but more of a blast. A shock.

"I'll call it Shock for now," he told Ash.

The dragon hummed in agreement.

At that point, Brode had finished scanning the letter and lowered it. "Grave news indeed."

"What is it?" Holt asked.

Brode looked to Talia, who nodded, and then Holt was handed the letter. He began to read.

*Dearest Sister,*

*I write to you out of desperation. I need your help.*

*Evidence has reached me of a conspiracy so terrible it is hard to fathom. Yet it is undeniable to those in our family. A rot which has burrowed to the very heart of our kingdom. Given how deep it runs I dare not move without you by my side. As powerful as our opponents are, they cannot hope to stand against a dragon rider when the time comes.*

*I have told no one else. I cannot. I know even my conversations with Mother are overheard by prying ears in the palace, and I have long suspected that my letters to councilors are opened and read before they arrive.*

*Even as I write, there is a rider staying in the palace on his way to the Crag – the legendary Silas Silverstrike. He has been kind to me and offered me tonics from your Order to aid my aching belly. Were it that I could give him this note, but then it would doubtless find its way into the hands of your Commander Denna.*

*I know your oaths prevent you from action, but I beg that you come all the same. If the Order cannot accept that justice needs to be served, then perhaps their detractors are right to call them a burden after all.*

*Should something happen to me, you can find what you need where even the scourge cannot reach.*

*Love, your brother,*
   *Leofric*

Holt read it quickly once more to ensure he'd taken everything in. It was a lot. The accusations and implications in this letter, though vague, were enormous.

Struggling for something to say, Holt said, "The king must have had great faith in you, Nibo."

Nibo smiled weakly. "I am a Coterie by birth and by chance grew up with His Majesty. It was an honor to be his servant and friend."

A Coterie. That made sense. The highest-ranking servants whose families had attended the royals for generations. Just as Holt's own family had cooked for generations.

Talia's anxiety transformed into rage. Flames gathered around her fists.

"My brother was murdered. I'll see whoever did this pays a thousand times over."

Pyra stood, stretched her long neck and tail, and roared in agreement. Buffeted by the dragon's bellow, the bells and windchimes answered her call, ringing as though to summon vengeance.

"Calm yourself," Brode warned. He eyed the windows of Ealdor Ebru's estate. Given the news, Holt understood his concern. Suddenly those high walls felt imprisoning; those windows perfect for a spy to overhear them.

First Silas Silverstrike and now a conspiracy within the court.

Who could they still trust?

With great effort, it seemed, Talia did calm herself. The fires around her fists went out, and she straightened herself.

"The three of us must discuss our next move in private, Nibo. Please leave us, but don't stray far from the estate as I may have need of you."

"Princess." Nibo bowed and left the courtyard.

Once he was out of sight and earshot, Talia and Brode entered a furious discussion in hushed tones.

"Don't think about doing anything stupid," Brode said.

"And my brother's murder doesn't change that?"

"Technically you don't have a brother, Ascendant."

Talia growled, but Brode spoke over her.

"We don't know exactly what happened to Leofric—" Though even Brode caught himself on these words. Holt thought the implications plain enough. King Leofric was known to have been ill, but the timing of that letter and his death seemed too coincidental.

'If it smells like rot, then it's rot,' his father would tell him when inspecting meat in the larder.

"Did you read it?" Talia chided. "Snakes at court. We knew the anti-rider cabal was bitter, but this?"

"Might the finger not point at Silas?" said Brode. "Your brother as good as tells us he was poisoned by him."

"He died after Silas arrived at the Crag—"

"As if poison cannot be a slow death."

Talia's eyes popped as she grasped for answers. "Why would Silas do this?"

"We know Silas has every reason to sow discord and chaos," said Brode. "Think, girl, what earthly reason would these nobles have to work with a rogue rider actively endangering the kingdom? It would be no good holding a coup only to all be dead a week later."

"Maybe they didn't know his true intentions," Talia said.

"You're letting your resentment of this faction cloud your judgment."

"Oh, and you're clear-headed when it comes to Silas?"

They glared at each other.

Holt found his voice. "You may both be right." Both Brode and Talia turned their narrowed eyes upon him now. "Well," Holt continued, "Talia seems sure there is a group working against her family. The letter speaks of a rot at the heart of the kingdom. That can't refer to Silas. Yet we know Silas was there, and he would want to wreak havoc as Master Brode says."

"What are you saying?" Talia asked. "That Silas just happened to kill my brother right as he uncovered another plot at court?"

Holt clenched his jaw. He agreed with Talia that the coincidence sounded far-fetched. On the other hand, he also agreed with Brode. It made no sense for this cabal of nobles to actively endanger the kingdom with an incursion on the rise. Of the two theories, he thought Brode's held more water, weak as it was.

He resorted to shrugging. "I don't think we know enough to say for sure either way."

"Once again, the pot boy has a point," said Brode. "Talia, we're basing all of this off one letter. We need more information."

"My uncle is still in danger," Talia said, as though she had not heard them. She jumped on Pyra's back, but Pyra did not move. Talia's face was a picture of frustration, and then her gaze turned upon Pyra's injured wing. She ran her hands through her golden-red hair, suppressed a cry of frustration, then leaped down to land in front of Brode.

"You didn't let us go when we could still fly," she said, pointing an accusatory finger at his chest.

"As well I did, for I may have spared you walking blindly into a viper's nest."

"If Osric dies, the crown and kingdom will fall into chaos right in the middle of an incursion, unless I—"

"Impossible. You swore an oath."

"I know—"

"And even were it possible, you would not be ready for it."

"I know!" Talia shouted these final words before slumping her shoulders and burying her face in her hands. Pyra got up and padded over to Talia, softly nudging her snout into her rider and wrapping a wing around the princess.

Holt realized he was still holding the letter from the king and gingerly approached Talia. She emerged from behind her hands, her eyes red but not tearful. She took the letter and carefully folded it away.

"Now we've got that out of our systems," Brode said, "we need a plan. Come closer. Ash, feel free to make a bit of noise."

Ash needed no encouraging and began bounding around the yard with all the energy of a vastly oversized toddler.

Holt moved closer as instructed so that he, Talia and Brode formed a tight group.

"This faction at court," Brode began, "your mother spoke about it to you, yes?"

"Ealdor Harroway," Talia said, and she shook with anger at the very thought of the man.

"And she didn't seem suspicious of foul play?" Brode asked.

"No..." Talia said, her anger subsiding a little. "Nothing more than the usual."

"Wait," Holt said, feeling left behind as ever. "When did you speak with Queen Felice?" He called Talia's mother that as that was how he'd known of her his whole life while King Godric, Talia's father, was still alive.

"That's where we were when the Crag came under attack," Brode said. "A journey to Beordan, a northern estate for the royals to hunker down during a scourge rising. Although from the size of her entourage, it seemed like she'd taken half of Sidastra with her."

"Oh please," Talia said.

"But you said you were going on a mission," Holt said, recalling the conversation with Brode in the Great Hall of the Crag.

Brode raised his eyebrows. "You have a mind for details. I may have embellished."

"But riders can't see their families," Holt said. "Not once they've sworn the oath." This was the very thing Talia had insisted herself.

Talia at least had the grace to look ashamed. "Given half a chance, anyone would go after years apart. Commander Denna said it was out of compassion," she added hastily, as though trying to convince herself as much as Holt. "My brother had just died."

"Commander Denna let you go for the same reason she let you join in the first place," Brode said. "To buy goodwill with your family."

Talia's expression hardened.

A prickle ran up the back of Holt's neck. How cold and calculating could the riders be?

"So, if Talia hadn't been a former princess, she wouldn't have been allowed to leave to mourn the death of her brother?"

Brode shook his head. "Compassion? Denna? The riders? Even with the Commander's desire known, the vote only passed by one to let Talia go."

"And I'm sure you happily voted against it, Master Brode."

Brode's cheek twitched and he bit back a reply before speaking as though Talia had said nothing untoward. "My point being, your mother did not believe Leofric had been murdered."

"No," Talia said. "She didn't. Just said his illness became severe. Feverish and rambling before the end, she said..." She stared off into the semi-distance, her thoughts now far away.

Holt didn't think this solid evidence of anything. "Leofric said in his letter that his conversations with your mother were overheard. He must have been afraid to confide in her."

Talia's eyes flared with fire again, though she contained herself. "I don't know what to think."

"We lack information," Brode said again. "Either Silas killed your brother coincidentally, or Harroway's faction has indeed acted rashly and killed the king in the middle of an incursion. I find the latter unlikely, but perhaps Harroway thinks it easier to take such drastic steps when people are pre-occupied. The fact that your uncle remained and took up the regency leads me to think Silas was responsible. Harroway would gain little by killing the king only for another Agravain to take the throne."

Talia frowned. "I wish I could agree. Harroway fought beside my uncle in the war. They're close. He's a good soldier, but then why did he give orders for the western garrisons not to be summoned?"

Harroway. The name at last clicked into place in Holt's mind. Ealdor Harroway was the new Master of War. Alexander Knight had told them that Harroway had sent revised orders not to march to Sidastra's aid.

"He must be up to something," Talia said. "The western regions have always had a good relationship with the Order, given where the Crag is. Maybe he wanted those troops kept well away from the city so he could make his move unhindered once the incursion ends?"

Brode barked a laugh. "If so, the fool will regret that when the swarm arrives on his doorstep."

"Maybe," said Talia. "It does seem like a strange gamble."

"All the more reason why he and Silas must be acting separately," Brode said. "Harroway couldn't have anticipated the riders being wiped out. I bet he counted on our aid in the battle while plotting to undermine us the moment it was over. Politics," he said with a venom as potent as the blight. He tapped his feet then began pacing. "Everything falling apart at once seems too much to be pure chance. None of it adds up. There is something we're missing."

The sound of breaking clay made them all turn. Whether on purpose or because of his blindness, Ash had knocked over some potted plants as he bounced around the courtyard. Pyra blew smoke at him, but it seemed playful.

The trio turned back to face each other.

"Well," Holt began slowly, "whatever his involvement with your brother's death, it seems to me like this Harroway needs to be confronted. He's in the capital, and that's where we were heading. And I still need to find my father there. Nothing has changed, really. Other than your uncle may need saving as much as everyone else."

"One thing has changed," Talia said as fire curled around her fists. "I'll make sure Harroway and anyone involved in his scheming is brought to justice."

Brode cleared his throat pointedly.

"Not personally, of course," Talia corrected. "That would not be proper. Though, I feel that should the evidence that Leofric gathered be placed into the right hands... well, I hope they take *all* necessary action."

Holt recalled the last line of the letter. "What did your brother mean by '*where even the scourge cannot reach*'?"

"I'll tell you later," she said, and, like Brode, she looked warily up to the open windows above them. "But I'm sure I know."

"Very well," Brode said. "Sidastra is still our destination, but much will have to change, Holt, namely our road. The garrisons and roads are no longer safe to us, if Harroway's treachery is true. Nor is open country much better, with Silas and his swarm out there. If he returned to the Crag, he'll have discovered an echo of Pyra's song from the bodies she burned, and news of Midbell won't be far behind. But what I wouldn't give for one fair fight with him," he added darkly.

Holt bit his lip. "So nowhere is safe."

"Now you're getting it," Brode said. "Not even the skies, even if Pyra wasn't injured and Ash could fly. No road bodes well, so we'll take the least dangerous option. The Withering Woods."

An instinctual shiver ran up Holt's spine at the name. Nothing good was said of the Withering Woods.

"But that forest has blight in it?" Holt said. "What if the scourge are there?"

Both Brode and Talia gave him confused looks.

"Scourge are everywhere right now," Brode said.

"Did you think you'd had your last encounter with them?" Talia asked.

"Well, no..." he trailed off, not knowing what he had thought. When he'd taken Ash's egg, he had certainly not considered this. His life was to fight the scourge now.

"It still seems like a risk," Talia said.

"Activity in the woods should be low," Brode said. "The swarm seeks people out, and the woods are barren of people. Once there, the tree cover will help shield us from eyes both above and on the ground. We can't fully hide from Silas detecting your bonds and the cores of the dragons, but even a Lord cannot cast their net so wide. Soldiers don't patrol there, and the forest's eastern borders run close to Sidastra. If we make it through, we'll be in striking distance of the city."

"*If,*" Talia said sharply. "*If* we make it through."

Pyra growled haughtily.

"Do you have a better idea?" Brode asked.

It seemed she didn't.

Ash stopped leaping around the yard and padded over to Holt's side. He seemed to sense a finality to their discussion.

"*I'm not afraid.*" Judging by how the others faced Ash, it seemed he had spoken to the group at large, broadcasting his speech out like Pyra sometimes did.

"Well I wouldn't want to go there without you, boy," Holt said.

"So, it's settled," Brode said. "We make for the Withering Woods."

# 25

# CLEANSING

Their plan, their terrifying plan, was made.

First, they had to ensure Nibo would remain safe. He could not return to Sidastra, nor travel to the royal estate at Beordan to warn Talia's mother. Although he didn't know the contents of the letter, if Harroway's faction took him, they might discover Leofric had reached out to Talia and would then be forewarned of her arrival. They might be scared into accelerating whatever plans they had. So, Talia urged Nibo to stay with Alexander Knight and offer what service he could in the meantime. He agreed.

Brode cautioned against a hasty departure from Midbell as Holt needed his bond to recover in relative safety, and it would be better for them to slip away under cover of darkness. He also wanted to spend some time dropping hints as to a false plan, telling everyone from Lady Ebru herself to other ranking members of the town that the three dragon riders would make for the capital by the rough country to the south, when in fact they would be heading north. He even lied to Alexander Knight, who had given them no cause to doubt him, but the less he knew the safer he and they would be.

The hope was that anyone sent to tail them would be thrown off and any information sent to Harroway would be false. Silverstrike might not be welcomed in Midbell or at Fort Kennet anymore, but there were plenty of other outposts he could visit where his treachery was not known. If he did, then he too would receive the wrong information.

After another day's rest, Holt felt that his bond had recovered enough to get moving. Its beating had not yet returned to a smooth second heartbeat, but it felt whole again, and he could see Ash's core clearly. Resupplied and refreshed, Holt felt physically well too. Were it not for the gnawing worries over the colossal tasks before the three of them, he might have been cheerful.

When they'd left the Crag, just surviving had seemed hard enough. Now a Novice, an Ascendant, and their old dragonless tutor had to not only outrun a Storm Lord but also a mounting scourge incursion and most of the royal army. And all this before arriving at the capital, somehow confronting a group of treacherous nobles, and readying the city for the inevitable siege.

Holt hoped that word of his involvement wouldn't make it to Sidastra. Few knew who he really was, and so his father – if his father had made it there – should be safe from Harroway's reach.

Given how personal this had become, Holt thought Talia must feel even worse than he did, but she hid it well. She spent almost every waking moment quietly Cleansing and Forging to keep Pyra's core in peak condition, and perhaps to avoid facing what lay before her. Holt watched her carefully, knowing he would have to master those techniques soon.

On the third night after the Battle of Midbell, Holt, Brode, Talia, Pyra and Ash left the town in the dead of night. The gatekeepers would report their departure but not until the morning, and by then they'd be well away. Anyone hoping to tail them would have a difficult time of it. Brode took the extra precaution of leading them off-road the moment the glow of the town vanished behind them. He spurred them on to cover as much distance as they could, walking through the dawn and day. When at last they stopped, the moon was shining, and the Withering Wood was still days away.

Yet it hardly meant a chance to rest.

"You'll train and meditate every night," Brode said.

Groaning, Holt got back to his feet. It had been so nice to sit by the fire and dine even on their modest meal of salt pork and barley bread. A lot could be said for having a full stomach. But long hours on the road or not, he was a rider and was expected to cope.

"You wanted this, remember," Brode said.

"I don't have the extra strength yet like you."

"Then think how easy it will all feel once you do."

Brode trained Holt further in swordsmanship while Talia meditated. Puffs of fire burst from her body as she purified Pyra's core.

After what seemed an eon of being battered, Brode called a halt.

"Enough for tonight," he said. "I still need you to walk."

Holt let his sword arm drop, panting. He wasn't sure whether he was getting any better.

"Now, meditation," Brode said. "Come, sit. You'll enjoy that."

Lacking even the energy to scowl, Holt sheathed his sword and sat down. He glanced at Talia, who was sat cross-legged, and so he imitated her. Brode placed his green rider's blade on the ground and then took up a space on the grass opposite Holt.

"When starting any session, you should always begin by slowing your breath and clearing your mind."

Holt tried this. Steadying his breath was easy enough, though it took a while given his recent exertions. Clearing his mind was never as easy as thoughts flicked in and out, and then he'd just think about how he wasn't able to empty his mind. A vicious cycle if he got caught in it.

"Once calm," Brode continued, "you begin by reaching for the dragon bond. Do so gently, not yet drawing on any power from the core."

Holt did so. Once he was so focused on his inner mind, reaching for the core was relatively simple. Perhaps it got easier as the bond grew. This time, as he reached for it and looked to Ash's core, a brilliant flash of light made him wince. He opened his eyes with a start.

"What happened?" Brode asked.

"It was so bright."

"Hmm. Ash has likely been pulling in motes of his magic type, perhaps more rapidly given his growth spurt. A good thing we're going to start tidying that up." He frowned. "You say it was bright. In what way?"

"A bit like looking directly at the sun," Holt said. "Only paler. Much paler."

"Fascinating," said Brode.

"His core is a sort of pulsing ball of light."

"As is his breath and your Shock ability," said Brode. "Light then. Although I find it hard to believe a power like this has never manifested before."

"Do cores from other types look… different?" Holt asked, not sure if that was the right way to phrase it.

Brode nodded. "They tend to reflect the type in some way. Erdra's was a rock formation that grew to a mountain as she gained power. Pyra's core began as a candle, I believe."

"It's a bonfire now," Talia muttered, still with her eyes closed.

"It's magic, Holt," Brode said in answer to Holt's confused expression. "Just as we sometimes hear the core as a song, we view it as well as our human senses can understand. Now, assuming you aren't blinded again, have another look at Ash's core, but don't draw any power in."

Holt closed his eyes and refocused. This time he was ready, and while the light was still bright, he squinted, so to speak, and allowed himself to get accustomed to it. Ash's bond was still comprised of the same smoky, pale light as before. It swirled around some central point with tendrils peeling off here and there, but it seemed hazier than before, as though fogged by a mist.

"It's grown," Holt said, keeping his eyes closed. "But it's not clear. Like looking through a dirty window."

"That will be the motes of magic which are not Ash's type," Brode said. "You won't be able to tell what they are, unfortunately. If we could, we would have been able to detect additional power types before now."

"How do I remove them?"

"You take in a little power, then remove the impurities, and put it back."

"A bit like sieving a consommé," Holt said. "Only you skim the scum off the top rather than drain the soup to a different pot and then return it but—"

"You get the idea then," said Brode. "Now, drawing on the magic to Cleanse it requires more subtle control than using it for battle. You want to take in just enough so that the power sits inside your soul and doesn't actually enter your body."

"My soul?" Holt asked. "That's a real thing then?" He'd considered that was where the dragon bond sat within him, as he had no other way of conceiving it.

"Soul, spirit, however you wish to name it," said Brode. "I won't pretend to understand it. Never did when my tutors tried explaining it to me. Doubt they understood it either. Now, draw on the magic carefully I say, not fully into yourself, but keeping it tethered in the space between you and Ash. When you manage it, you'll feel it."

Holt nodded and tried. His first attempt was much too forceful, drawing power into his body so that he felt lithe and strong. He shook his head, steadied his breath, and tried again. This time went better; less magic flowed into him, but he lost his tentative grip on it and it drained away. Thankfully Brode stayed quiet while he fumbled, trying to learn. It was something Holt had to learn alone, and he was determined. At last, after what felt like scores of attempts, he got it just right.

A sudden weight pressed upon his chest, right where the bond sat inside him. It wasn't painful, but breathing suddenly felt difficult, as though he was deep underwater but able to draw the faintest of breaths. Unprepared for this, Holt lost control. The magic slithered away; Ash's core vanished.

Gasping, he opened his eyes.

Brode smiled. "There you go. Now I'll tell you the next step."

"That was hard enough," Holt spluttered.

"Remind me who said this was easy? Now, once the magic is sitting in your soul, you must take in as deep a breath as you can manage, hold it for a few seconds, then push it out faster. Don't blast it out, mind, maintain control at all times, but it must be faster than drawing the breath in."

Holt blinked. "Okay..." he said, very unsure how this was supposed to work.

"As you breathe out," Brode continued, "that magic in your soul will vibrate and motes of magic not suitable to Ash – and therefore you – will feel rough. They show up as rattles or crackles in our breath as we breathe out. Let's start by having you find one."

Once again, Holt underwent the process of gathering some magic into his soul, keeping it just outside his body. It didn't take so many attempts to understand how the breathing technique worked. On his third attempt, after only a few seconds of breathing out, he felt an unmistakable rattle in his own throat. His breath crackled and he faltered, losing his concentration and his position in the breathing cycle.

"It will be easy to begin with," said Brode. "Ash will have many impurities around his core. Over time you'll have to empty your lungs to find those crackling spots, but it's necessary work."

"What do I do next?"

"Once you find a crackle, breathe in again, nice and controlled. You want to return to the spot just before the troubled energy, ready to push on it again on your breath out. Try, I'll talk you through it."

Holt repeated the process, getting all the way to pushing his breath out until he felt and heard the crackle. He was so happy to have found it again that he almost forgot the next step and breathed in too hastily. Still, he felt a slight rattle as he did so, indicating he had passed the impurity on his way back up.

"That's it," Brode said. "And out again."

Holt pushed his breath out, faster than before, and he felt the crackle *shift*. It felt to him as though it had moved up, higher in his chest, and when he next breathed in, he had to do so for longer until he felt the impurity again.

*This is so delicate*, Holt thought. He had considered at first that it might be like using a rolling pin to flatten out dough, constantly rolling over the same spot. If only. Using a pin was quick and easy work – Cleansing felt as though the dough were playing hide and seek with him.

"The reason for breathing out faster," Brode continued, "is that this shifts the impurity up and away from the rest of the magic."

Struggling but determined, Holt kept the process up.

"Slowly, step by step, we keep raising it until—"

Holt nearly choked. He'd felt the crackle move substantially, as though it were now sitting at the back of his throat.

"—a final effort dispels the impurity," Brode said.

Holt strained. The feeling in his throat was like a blockage, but he breathed out as hard as he could, and the impurity shifted. It was much like clearing his throat of a bad cough. A light flashed from somewhere. He saw it through his eyelids and blinked them open, not realizing quite how forcefully he'd had them closed this whole time.

"What was that?" he asked.

"That was the energy being expelled from your body," Brode said. "It was a flash of the same white light you and Ash produce."

Now the irregular streaks of fire that peeled away from Talia as she Cleansed made sense. Holt also understood why the riders spent hours at this. It seemed laborious, and it required immense amounts of concentration just to get started, never mind purifying for hours on end.

"How long should I do this for each day?"

"Ideally until you hear no more crackles in the magic and Ash's core appears crystal clear to you, although it's something of a never-ending task."

"What about Forging?" Holt asked. "Shouldn't I know that too?"

"One thing at a time," Brode said. "Cleanse first, Forge second. Work on this technique and we'll tackle Forging later."

Holt nodded. He stood up, stretched, and heard his back crack and pop.

"You'll need to sit with better posture too," Brode growled.

Holt sighed, ran his hands through his hair several times, then looked for Ash. The dragon was dozing happily by the fire.

"Is there anything Ash should be doing?"

"If dragons could actively Forge motes into their own cores, they wouldn't need us. Their natural process of doing so takes them a lifetime to achieve what we can in years."

Ash yawned. *"You are doing very well."*

"Thanks," Holt said bitterly. He was jealous of Ash's leisure, but the moment passed quickly. This was the least Holt could do for dragging Ash into the world, and it was his side of the partnership. In return, he got to use magic. To be a rider.

After warming his hands by the fire and giving Ash a scratch down his neck, Holt sat himself down to Cleanse, intending to do so until he collapsed from exhaustion. Or until Brode ordered him to bed.

# 26

# CULTIVATION

Time melded into one long procession of marching, swordcraft and Cleansing until, one evening, they came to the woodland's edge. Under twilight, the gnarled branches cast long eerie shadows, woven into a frenzied dance upon the ground. The air grew heavy, smelling sweet but sickly, and reminded Holt of the refuse piles outside the Crag's kitchens.

In the gloom of those trees, Brode called for them to make camp. The old rider's mood seemed to brighten now they had made it to what he deemed relative safety, but his bite remained in his training sessions.

Despite the beating Holt took when learning the sword, he preferred that pain to the difficulty of Cleansing. That night, he made the mistake of stretching his tired limbs during his meditation.

"Don't fidget," Brode called over to him. "You're still breathing in too fast as well. I can see the rise and fall in your chest."

Holt overcompensated on his next breath in, going too slowly this time, and lost the delicate connection. He huffed in frustration and buried his face in his hands for a moment. Ash rumbled sympathetically beside him.

A tiredness threatened to take Holt then. The allure of the campfire warmth nearly took over. It had been hard going the past few days, but he felt good about making progress – it felt like he was at least doing something now. He stifled a yawn and said, "Sorry, Master Brode. It's proving much harder to search for impurities. I'll keep trying."

Brode raised his eyebrows. "It's a hard thing to perfect. Takes years, a lifetime even."

Holt quietly returned to Cleansing. Brode hadn't suggested he'd take a break and Holt would rather push himself anyway. He and Ash had a lot of catching up to do if they were to be of any use in the fights ahead.

"If you've Cleansed the worst of the excess away," Brode went on, "perhaps it's time to learn the basics of Forging."

Holt opened his eyes, met Brode's and simply nodded.

"I presume Ash's core is clearer to you now?"

Holt checked. Ash's core shone like a chandelier in a dark hall. The mist of ill-suited magic had mostly cleared, and now he could discern individual specks of light orbiting the core. These must be motes of light energy Ash had yet to absorb, something Holt could help him with through Forging.

"Most consider it an easier process once you get the hang of it," Brode said. "The difficulty is maintaining the rhythm once you find it. For this requires you to slow or increase your own heart rate to match the beat of the dragon bond."

"More breathing techniques?" Holt asked.

"Afraid so. As I say, the aim is to match your heart to the beat of the bond. Deeper, infrequent breaths will slow your heart down; shallow, faster ones will raise it. In doing this, you will press loose motes of energy toward Ash's core. Keep up the pressure and you'll beat the motes into the core – like a smith striking steel."

"And this adds to Ash's pool of magic?" Holt asked.

"Yes and no," Brode said. "Motes of magic in their raw form, like you can see orbiting the core, are still magic; they're just weak. Should a core run empty, a dragon or rider can pull on the raw motes, but the effects would barely register compared to core forged magic."

Holt was unsure on this. "What is it about the core that makes the magic so strong?"

"The density of it," Brode said. "That's the best way I can describe it. Or perhaps you might consider it like the effectiveness of a lone soldier as opposed to a seasoned battalion. The latter can achieve so much more than the former. Within the core, the motes are compact and pressed against each other, increasing the strength of each one many times over. Aside from that, the core acts as a store of energy. You need not be near a raw source of your magic type so long as there is power within the core."

"Raw motes," Holt muttered, trying to figure these things out in his own terms. Brode's use of the word 'raw' got him thinking of raw food. One didn't eat food raw, though it is technically still food. Cooking releases water, intensifying flavor. Forging motes into a dragon's core was akin to adding ingredients to a stewing pot, inside of which the flavors could deepen and enrich into something truly wonderful.

He just had one question.

"I understand that motes must be Forged into a dragon's core to make it strong, but, just how much weaker is the magic when raw? Fire still burns, does it not?"

Talia – who had been Cleansing and Forging herself this whole time – stirred at this. Evidently, she had also been listening in. "I can demonstrate for you."

Pyra had her wings over the fire like two great nets. She withdrew them at Talia's word and looked at Holt expectantly. This made him nervous. How exactly were they going to demonstrate this for him?

Talia got up and came to sit closer to him. She held her palm out before her and conjured fire. The heat was so intense that its center was a rich blue, while its outer edges were razor sharp and almost solid.

Holt gasped, drew up an arm to shield himself and scrambled back a bit on the grass.

"This is core-forged fire," Talia said. "This will burn clean through the shell of a flayer or stinger, or indeed most armor." She clenched her fist and let the fire wink out. "Now, this is drawing on raw motes."

She reopened her hand, and a redder set of flames appeared. These rippled and shook even in the light breeze, and tendrils curled up and away into nothingness like any common fire. "You could pass your hand through it and be fine," Talia said.

Taking her words as a challenge, Holt quickly passed his hand through the top of the flames. Just as passing a finger through a candle flame would do no damage, so too was Holt's hand completely unharmed.

"I see what you mean," Holt said. "Though if you're desperate, it would be better than nothing. It's still fire. I wouldn't want to hold my hand in it."

"Maybe," Talia said. "But that would be desperate. This wouldn't help much in a fight, and remember Pyra would have to be close to a source of fire to have an abundance of raw fire motes to even make this work. Without the campfire I doubt I could do even this." She dissipated the weak flames in her hand. "And drawing raw motes across a bond will strain it like drawing on the core, just not so severely."

"If our little demonstration is over," Brode began, "I'd like Pyra to return to shielding the flames from any searching eyes in the night."

Pyra stretched out her wings, then returned to enveloping the fire, dulling most of its light.

Brode turned to Holt. "Do you understand better now?"

Holt nodded. "I'd like to see the difference in our own magic, if I may – I won't let the light travel," he hastened to add. He hardly wished to attract attention either.

Brode grunted. "Carefully."

Still sitting cross-legged, Holt raised his left palm and aimed down at the grass nearby. He formed a Shock and released it, feeling the kick up his arm as it left his body. The Shock hit the earth with a satisfying thud, throwing up grass, dirt and small stones buried beneath its surface.

Next, he tried pulling on the raw motes. They lay in the ethereal space between Holt's bond and Ash's core, so he could pull on them. What he hadn't expected was for it to be more difficult. He tried breathing them into himself, but the swirling motes only vaguely moved toward him before dancing off again. The bright, dense light of the core was far easier to take hold of. It was solid. Holt felt as though he could reach out and touch the light of the core, but these raw motes were elusive.

After several attempts he managed it, channeling the magic down his left arm. The light produced this time was watery and without force. Instead of a concentrated beam, it spread out almost lazily, only just creating enough light to see by before it fizzled and died without him even cutting it off.

"Take some well-worn advice," Brode said. "Stick to the core."

Holt drew a deep breath. More challenges were being piled upon him and Ash daily. He hadn't expected being a rider would require as much work, perhaps even more work, than any servant dealt with.

"I understand, Master Brode," he said. "I'm prepared to work."

Brode went over the basic techniques of Forging again before telling Holt to make his first attempt. As with Cleansing, it took many false starts before he got even close. The first time he managed to match his heart rate to the bond it was only brief, and the music that suddenly rose in his head caused him to break the rhythm.

"Am I supposed to hear the dragon song?"

"It's one of the more pleasurable aspects of Forging," said Brode. "It will rise and fall, but pay attention. You can learn a lot about the state of your dragon from it."

Holt opened one eye. Brode smirked.

"Baby steps, pot boy."

Holt's first Forging session passed slowly. Every single mote that he pressed into Ash's core was an uphill struggle, but each one gave Holt a jolt of accomplishment and spurred him on. After what must have been an hour, he swore the core had grown, but he may have just been hopeful.

Only once more that night did he hear the dragon song. It rose suddenly, and this time Holt held the connection to hear it. Ash's song still had a light, tinny quality to it – probably due to his age. However, there was a swell of power too, like a ringing chorus, and something else, something sad, as if a lone flute played in a desolate land. It passed quickly, but it left an impression on Holt. Heat prickled at the corners of his eyes.

Was Ash in pain? Was he wrestling with some inner struggle?

He blinked and was grateful no tears fell but noticed something else. Ash had come close. His snout was almost touching Holt's nose. Had he felt something over the bond?

*"Holt, I'm bored."*

Holt stifled a laugh and pushed playfully on Ash's snout. "You should practice using your breath, as Master Brode said."

Ash took a step back and turned his head in a guilty manner.

*"I have been. But it's hard to know if I'm getting any better at aiming without targets to hit."*

Holt thought this fair. Brode had told Ash to keep his beams of light low to the ground so that they would hit the earth quickly and not give away their position.

"Once we're in the woods I'm sure we can do more. And you'll get better in no time. You already took out that flayer!"

*"That was a very big target. Hard to miss."*

"True."

Ash tilted his head the other way. A quiver of excitement ran down his spine, not unlike a cat ready to pounce. The dragon leaped backward, then braced his four claws into the earth, head low and tail high.

*"My wings have grown."*

Ash raised and extended them, and Holt was impressed at their size now. He hadn't noticed how much the wings had developed while they were tucked in. Now they were fully extended, it looked like two white sails had been hoisted on either side of Ash.

*"I want to fly."*

## 27

# FIRST FLIGHT

Ash wanted to fly. Holt's heart leaped at the idea. All thoughts of continuing the laborious process of Cleansing and Forging fled.

"But," he said cautiously, recalling Ash's concerns over his blindness, "won't it be hard for you?"

*"We have to try."*

Although Ash's eyes didn't quite meet Holt's own, they were so big and ice blue that it was hard to say no. They could only try, after all.

He got up. "Master Brode?"

Brode and Talia paused in their sparring.

"Shouldn't you be Forging?" Brode said.

"Ash thinks he is ready to try flying."

"Does he now?"

Ash walked proudly forward, wings out like a peacock displaying its feathers.

"Well, they look grown enough," Brode said. "What do you think, Pyra?"

Pyra lazily looked upon Ash and blinked her big amber eyes.

"She thinks he's ready to try," Talia told them. "Although she thinks he'll crash straight away."

"We won't go too high," Holt said.

He'd only taken a step toward Ash when Brode called, "And what do you think you're doing?"

"Getting on my dragon?"

"Do you even know how to ride a horse?" Brode asked.

"Well, no," Holt admitted, "but—"

"But what?" Brode chided. "You've never sat astride a horse and you think you can hop up onto a dragon's back, just like that?"

Pyra rumbled at that.

*"Dragons are not to be ridden like a common nag,"* she said, projecting her thoughts for all to hear now. *"We do not need a rider to tell us where to go."*

"Dammit, you're right," Brode said, his voice dripping with sarcasm. "I'd forgotten that dragons and horses were different creatures. Thank goodness you're here, Pyra, to set me straight."

Pyra snorted, turned her head and raised her wing higher to cover her snout.

"Was that needed?" Talia asked.

Brode rolled his eyes. "Sometimes, I wonder which of the pair of you is the *real* princess. The point is, we do not know how Ash's condition will affect him. He'll likely need Holt's aid to direct him in some way, but before we get close to trying that out, he needs to be comfortable on his own before hauling someone around." He cleared his throat. "The older dragons usually help the hatchlings at this stage. Pyra?"

Pyra flicked her tail.

*"Just do it,"* she said. *"Experience is the true teacher."*

Holt opened his mouth to plead on his dragon's behalf when Ash nudged him again.

*"It's okay,"* Ash said. *"The grumpy one is right. I feel like I know what to do."*

With that, Ash began to beat his wings. He lifted a little off the ground, then a little more, until with a great jump he took off, wings flapping madly, climbing, climbing, climbing. Only to fall. He crashed and rolled, coming to rest like a tripped puppy.

Pyra emerged from behind her wing and gave a throaty rumble of laughter. Holt was almost about to snap at her and her haughtiness when the purple dragon got up.

Before she could do anything, Ash attempted flight again. He climbed higher this time before returning ungracefully to earth. Pyra stalked to Ash's side and nipped at him to get his attention. Silent words passed between them. On Ash's third attempt, he managed to glide himself back down but didn't land well.

Holt dashed over to his dragon. "Are you all right?"

*"I'm fine,"* Ash grumbled.

Holt looked to Brode and Talia for some reassurance that struggling to fly was normal for a young dragon. Their faces spoke otherwise.

"You've got this," Holt told Ash. He patted the dragon's neck, but Ash shrugged him away sourly. He took off again. And again. And again.

"That's enough," Brode said. "You'll hurt yourself, Ash."

Ash lowered his head. He was actually panting.

*"I can't see."*

"I know," Holt said sadly.

*"The wind roars in my ears once I descend. Hard to build a picture of the world like that."*

Pity welled in Holt. His thoughts turned to the sad note in Ash's song and his own guilt, and how this was all his fault. Then that pity he felt turned into another burst of madness. He threw his arm around Ash's neck, hoisted himself onto the dragon's back, and settled between two ridges of bone, all before the others could stop him.

"Holt," Brode barked, running over. "Get down, now!"

"I'll be your eyes," Holt said into Ash's ear. The dragon's scales were smooth enough, but as Holt shifted his weight they dug in hard as stone.

"Get down!" It was Talia shouting now. Pyra stomped her front claws in protest as well. "If you can't speak to Ash telepathically, you're not ready."

"He needs to be able to fly," Holt said. There was a waver in his voice, but he held firm.

Ash had only come into the world because he, Holt, had taken his egg. Ash wouldn't have had to suffer through with damaged eyes were it not for him. Wouldn't have had to handle Pyra's scorn. What would other dragons think of him?

Holt would make this right.

He looked Talia in the eye, hoping she would understand where Brode might not.

"He needs to fly," Holt said again. This time he couldn't help choking on the words.

"You think too much with your heart, Master Cook. Go on."

Beaming, Holt leaned down and gripped onto Ash as best he could. "Fly, boy."

"*Hold on!*" Ash said, excited. Then he kicked off the ground.

Holt's stomach lurched as they took off. A moment of panic consumed him as he wondered what on earth he'd done. What if he fell?

"*Guide me,*" Ash said.

Only then did Holt realize he had closed his eyes in his terror. Opening them again, he struggled to cope with the cold wind beating against his face. He narrowed his eyes against the elements. Perhaps an Ascendant's body could handle these pressures better than a Novice?

The night was dark, but moonlight did glint through small gaps in the clouds, enough to see by now his eyes had adjusted away from their campfire. His first thought was how strange the world looked from up high, entirely colored in shades of nightly black and blue. Stretching out to the east was the Withering Wood. Silhouetted canopies wrinkled to the horizon like so many leagues of tossed soil.

As for their training, Holt thought that trying to simply change direction would be a good start.

"Let's turn right," Holt said. Nothing happened. Even with Ash's prodigious hearing, Holt would not be heard over the wind unless he shouted. Feeling a fool, Holt called out the instruction again, hoping this time his voice would be heard.

Ash moved this time, veering right and then leveling out so they now faced south and away from the forest.

"*You see,*" Ash said triumphantly, "*we can do this.*"

"Let's turn back then," Holt called. Ash did turn back, but fully around, one hundred and eighty degrees so that he faced due north. Holt groaned. What he had meant was for them to return to their previous course. Ash had interpreted Holt's instruction differently. Shouting instructions had its flaws. He would have to be crystal clear and yet still brief enough to allow for quick movements. In a battle, this would be difficult. Not to mention that in stormier weather, his voice might be drowned out entirely. He understood then why telepathic communication was needed for this.

Experience truly was the greatest teacher.

As they glided through the night, Holt considered the matter. Perhaps if they agreed upon some choice phrases then Holt's meaning would be clearer; their own private set of commands, much as captains called to their troops. It would take time and practice, but it might work. And if he incorporated touch with his verbal commands, then they might create any number of combinations and meanings.

Holt may have never ridden a horse, but he'd seen people on them who appeared to pull on the reins and use their legs and feet to guide their steed. The reins he lacked, but Holt still had his feet.

He tried to tap his right foot on Ash's side and regretted lifting his leg at once. He was not yet steady enough on the dragon's back to feel comfortable shifting around. Frightened of the fall, Holt bent low and wrapped his arms as far around Ash's neck as he could. Feeling somewhat more secure, he then lifted his right leg and rapped his foot off Ash's side.

"*Boy?*" Ash asked with some concern. "*What are you doing?*"

Holt grunted and carefully sat upright. Touch would require a lot of work too. Even if he found a way to do it well, the slightest wrong pressure or placement of his foot or hand might create a miscommunication.

Worry crept up that this might be impossible. Holt pushed the anxiety back down.

He'd keep trying. He would find a way. He had to.

Ash must have sensed his woes. "*Don't worry,*" Ash said. Then he began to climb higher.

*Don't worry?* Holt thought. That was easier said than done. Yet as Ash continued to ascend, the wind dropped to a cool breeze. Without that to contend with, Holt opened his eyes fully and felt more relaxed. There was something so free, Holt thought, as they climbed into the night, higher and higher as though seeking the stars.

The clouds parted, and a brilliant half-moon gleamed white, bathing them in moonlight. Ash's scales glistened; his wings seemed to trail a pale light and he grew warm. Heat passed over the dragon bond too. Holt checked on the core and found it was near blinding again.

Before he could think on the meaning of this, Ash announced, *"Going down is the most fun. Ready?"*

Holt braced himself. This would be the true test.

"Ready—"

He'd barely gotten the word out when Ash broke into a steep dive. For a second, Holt cried out in terror as they dropped, scrambling to hold onto Ash with all his might. The bond drummed. Joy and pleasure passed over from Ash, and then Holt too began to enjoy himself.

The sensation was unlike anything Holt had experienced in all his life.

This was wondrous. This was joy. How could any rider feel burdened when they could do this? His heart pounded, and his veins coursed from the thrill of it as the ground rushed to meet them.

"Pull up," he yelled gleefully, and Ash did. He swooped upward, twisted to the east once more, and then they were gliding over the treetops of the Withering Woods.

The dragon bond warmed Holt from the inside out. He'd never felt closer to Ash, not even when the dragon had slept in the nook of his arm. All Holt wanted was for them to fly on forever, far away from all their troubles.

It was a moment that passed.

"We should head back," Holt said. It took several goes until Ash heard him.

*"Will we fly tomorrow?"* Ash asked.

Holt patted the dragon. "If Brode lets us."

They turned. Holt called to Ash when they were heading the right way. They were still high enough that a glimmer of a campfire could be seen, despite Pyra shielding most of it with her body. That thought brought little comfort. Holt would have to tell Brode about it, and then they would be sleeping in the pitch dark, with no heat in the night.

Ash dipped in his flight so that his talons scraped the top of the tallest trees.

"Careful," Holt said, and even as he said this a flock of birds burst from the treetops, a scattering of black shapes against the starlight. Ash roared and rolled from side to side as he tried to shake them off.

Holt clung on for dear life again. Ash climbed in the air as he shook to get rid of the annoying birds.

"Calm down!" Holt cried. Yet Ash tilted near vertical now as he swatted and writhed in mid-air, and Holt slipped. His hand scrambled at rough hide. And then he was falling.

This descent was not wondrous. His heart and bond thundered again, only this time from panic. Holt did the only thing he could think of and screamed for Ash, screamed so loud his lungs would burst but at least Ash might hear him – find him.

Ash twisted in mid-air, unable to pinpoint him.

*"Ash!"* Holt called. Only this time, he had not spoken the words. He'd sent the cry for help telepathically to Ash without meaning to. Whether he'd managed it due to a clarity brought on by impending death, Holt did not know, but the dragon bond flared like never before. It burned so hot Holt was sure he was on fire, beat so hard he thought his ribs would break.

And then his eyes widened, taking in more than a human ought to. More stars appeared in the expanse of night, and he could pick out every scale on Ash's body.

Ash pivoted in the air and seemed to lock onto his location. The dragon dove, wings pressed tight into his sides. He enveloped Holt just before they both hit the top branches of the tree beneath them. Though shielded by Ash's body, Holt felt every smash and thump as they crashed their way down to earth.

# 28

# RELIANCE

Holt groaned. Pain flared across his body but not too sharply in one place. Nothing broken then.

His head lay on wet soil and he tasted damp leaves. Ash's wing still enveloped him. Lifting the leathery flesh, he crawled out to meet darkness and humid air. Holt sniffed and almost choked on the smell. It was so sickly sweet. Brode wanted them to walk through this?

Getting up, he tried to get a grip on their immediate surroundings. What little light shone from the moon and stars was lost down here. Every way he looked, he saw nothing but creeping shadows. Only Ash's white body stood out to him, nestled it seemed on a bed of broken branches. He was just about to check on Ash when the dragon stirred.

"Are you okay?" Holt asked.

Ash got up, extended and flexed his wings, and twisted his long neck this way and that.

*"I feel dazed, but I'm not hurt."*

Holt marveled again at the toughness of dragons.

*"More importantly, are you okay?"*

"I'm fine," Holt said, though he patted his body down absentmindedly to make sure. "What happened back there?"

*"I saw through your eyes."*

"You... what?"

*"I saw through your eyes. For a moment we were one and I saw myself above you. That's how I was able to catch you."*

Holt had no words.

After a while, he rallied. "Are you still seeing through my eyes?"

*"No..."* And Ash sounded a little sad. *"But I shall treasure that image of the moon and stars so bright."*

For a moment, Holt wondered how Ash knew what the moon and stars were. Then he remembered the impressions and memories inherited from his ancestors.

He gave the dragon a hug. "If it happened once it might happen again." He tried then and there to focus on the bond with a similar intensity, but nothing quite so dramatic happened. However, he did notice that the bond had grown again – the edges of it still burned, but the connection felt more robust than before.

Brode said battle was the best way to develop a bond because of the true danger and fear. Holt falling appeared to have simulated that, although, as with dueling other riders, they couldn't just repeat it over and over again. If Holt knew he would be caught, the danger wouldn't be real enough to affect the bond.

He explained this to Ash.

*"Well at least something good came out of it,"* Ash said.

Holt grinned. "We were still flying! With practice I'm sure we'll get there. Now, use that hearing of yours. Find the way back."

Ash raised his head, and a few of the scaled ridges at the back of his head lifted as though pricking his ears. The dragon's enhanced hearing might not work so well in the air where there was nothing for sound to bounce off, but back on the ground it was like a magical ability all of its own.

*"This way,"* Ash said, turning. *"I can hear them coming to look for us."*

It didn't take long until they came to the edge of the woods and found Brode, Talia and Pyra. After Holt explained what had happened, Brode looked intrigued while Talia frowned.

Holt had the distinct impression she was using her magical sense to inspect the strength of his bond again. Sure enough, he felt the tell-tale gentle touch upon his soul.

"You're progressing to the edge of Novice already," Talia said.

"This is the quickest bond to develop I've ever known," said Brode.

"Thank you, Master Brode," Holt said. He was just relieved Brode wasn't angry about their botched flight. Yet, as he inclined his head out of respect, he received one of Brode's signature cuffs.

"But a part of me wished it hadn't gone this way," Brode said. "I don't want to encourage you to seek near-death experiences to jump-start your progression." He huffed, then went on. "You say Ash saw through your eyes?"

"Yes, and I think it somehow improved my own sight," Holt said.

"Sense-sharing," Brode said slowly. "I hadn't considered it. Usually the bond must be much stronger before it's possible, and it rarely if ever has any benefit, but for you two... yes. Perhaps mastery of this will let you fly after all."

Ash swished his tail and happily stamped his feet.

"It will strain your bond when doing it," Talia said. "You'll want to do such a thing sparingly."

"It's better than nothing," said Holt. "And at least Ash and I will be able to help you against scourge stingers and the like."

"Indeed, and very soon you'll rank up to Champion and you'll be teaching me things." Her tone could have cut glass. "I'm tired," she announced. "Come, Pyra. Let's get some sleep."

Holt made to go after her but Brode held him back.

"Leave her be. You'll only make it worse."

Holt sighed. He hadn't done anything wrong.

"I don't mean for stuff like this to happen."

"Oh, I'm well aware of that," Brode said. "If you were halfway competent, you'd be the most dangerous rider alive with your luck." He focused on Ash next. "How are you doing after such a strong connection?... I'm glad to hear it... Oh flying, yes, it's wonderful. I miss it dearly."

Guessing what had passed between the two, Holt said, "When we're more experienced, Ash and I could take you on flights with us."

A hint of a smile played at the corners of Brode's lips. "Thank you. I'd like that."

Ash roared in delight again until Brode cut him off.

"Calm, Ash. We don't want to draw any attention beyond what your escapades may already have done."

Holt wanted to roar in triumph himself. The idea of Ash being held back and unable to live like other dragons had been a weight on his heart. Assuming Brode was right and they could train with this 'sense-sharing' then that wouldn't be the case at all. Ash would be able to see – well, see as well as he could hope for – and their biggest hurdle would be overcome.

Except, one last nagging thought came to him.

"Would that mean Ash will be reliant on me to fly?" Holt asked.

"It would appear so."

Holt lowered his head. His shoulders slumped as his breath left him; all trace of the high from the moment before gone. Ash would still be different than the others then.

The dragon nudged into him and licked his face.

*"I'd rather fly with you than on my own anyway."*

Holt smiled. "I look forward to it."

# 29

# ROUGH EDGES

They re-entered the woods in the morning and headed east. It wasn't an easy road. Pyra was so large that she couldn't fit between close-growing trunks, meaning they had to often double back and seek alternative routes. Her wing was still injured, not that Brode would let her fly by day even if she was fighting fit.

At least in the light of day the trees did not seem so menacing. Most looked normal, save for the odd shrunken trunk with hollowed, rotting centers and sagging branches. Holt wrinkled his nose as the foul smell grew heavier in the already thick air. He noticed that a bile-green bark grew upon the sick trees, reminding him of the skin of the blacksmith's daughter.

He lingered too long looking at a sick tree before noticing he had fallen behind. He quickened his pace to catch up but was sure Talia had noticed him lagging.

"What do you know of these woods?" she asked.

"Nothing much," Holt said. "Only that most folk avoid them. Mr. Hunter always said he'd rather come back with no kill than have to set foot in here."

"The Foresters and Jacks have a hard life working here."

Holt had never met a Forester and knew little of them. He knew that Jacks worked in lumber mills, but he'd never been to one of those either.

"It's the blight, isn't it?"

Talia nodded. "The Forest of Feorlen used to span from the mountains of the Red Range in the east to the borders of the Crag's territory. Yet the blight took hold – likely during an incursion centuries ago. The rot spread. Sections were cleared and burned, but a trace of that dark poison always survived. It might all rot, and the scourge will win even if the last bug is slain."

She spoke as if the scourge had already won.

"Since my grandfather's time it's been called the Withering Woods instead."

"Well," Holt began, attempting to brighten the mood, "maybe if the last bug is defeated the blight will end with it."

She gave him a sideways glance. "You're quite a hopeful person, aren't you?"

Holt considered his response. He'd never thought of himself as optimistic. In fact he'd often lamented how his life was charted for him with little room for him to make his own bearings. And he worried about Ash's future and the fate of his father constantly. But compared to Talia's current dejection, he supposed he was a burst of sunshine.

"We don't know tomorrow, so it may always be brighter."

"Another piece of wisdom from your father?"

"From my mother," Holt said. It was one of the few memories of her he still held intact. "I was very young and very sick, and somehow I'd broken my favorite toy dragon."

"Oh, I'd have thought the world was ending too," Talia said.

Holt took it for a joke and laughed softly. "Yes, well I certainly did. Anyway, she said that, and the next morning I found a new toy waiting for me on the kitchen table."

"That's a sweet memory, Holt."

Then, quick as a flash, she jumped high over a fallen tree that was in their way. That was fine for her and her Ascendant body. Holt didn't want to draw on magic for trivial reasons, so he stepped around the obstacle instead.

He found Talia staring back at the fallen tree as though it had personally done her harm.

"My brother wanted to clear the forest of the remaining blight." She spoke in a hurry as though the words were breaking from a dam. "A concerted effort. He said he'd fix the woods and then have acorns planted to expand it. It was something we both urged Father to do, but he was too obsessed with his war. And Leofric never even got a chance."

Holt stepped closer. "Ash's magic removed the blight from Mr. Smith's daughter. Maybe he can help the trees too." He lifted one hand, intending to place it on her shoulder as a gesture of comfort – something any friend might do – but he faltered and lowered it awkwardly.

She was the princess. He was the servant. Her subject, whatever technicalities of oaths might say. Despite the change in circumstance, some habits are too ingrained.

Talia had the grace to say nothing of his fumble. Perhaps she found it as strange to be conversing so casually with one so low of station as he found it surreal to be speaking to her.

She smiled weakly. "Well, that would be something." Then she took her leave, running to catch up with Pyra.

Holt didn't feel like running after her. She didn't seem to want to talk about her father or brother. She rarely did.

That night, as he and Talia were collecting wood for the fire, Brode announced he would go hunt for their meal. As fallen branches weren't hard to come by here, they gathered the firewood in record time, leaving Holt and Talia alone with the dragons.

She was content to quietly sit on the far side of the fire with Pyra. Her rider blade lay beside her, huge, red and deadly. Despite his weariness, Holt felt restless. He tried to meditate but couldn't.

He needed some activity. Usually he just trained with Brode, but he'd never trained with Talia. Maybe the interaction would help break down the barriers between them.

Deciding it couldn't hurt to ask, he got up, picked up the blunted training swords, and moved to the other side of the fire. Talia watched him approach with her arms folded.

"Come on," Holt said, "let's spar."

"Master Brode should be the one who trains you—"

"I mean a real spar."

*That should get her attention,* he thought.

Talia smirked. When he remained serious, she looked at him as though he were ill.

"Really? You want to fight me?"

"Why not?" He looked at her defiantly. She would of course outmaneuver him completely. The odds were as equally matched as a cat against a three-legged mouse.

Pyra rumbled a laugh and nudged Talia. The princess shrugged and got up.

"It's you who'll be sore," she said.

Holt passed her one of the swords. They moved to as open a space as they could find amongst the leaves, moss and roots, and the dragons followed them silently. He'd barely taken his ready position when Talia came at him in a whirl of red hair and steel. She struck and left his side stinging.

Holt gasped and clutched at his side. "I wasn't even ready."

"I'm an Ascendant. Do you want me to slow down for you?"

Holt grumbled. What had compelled him to do this again?

"No," he said. "Come on."

Each turn of blows went predictably badly for him. At last he stepped back too hastily, tripped on the root of a tree, and collapsed onto his backside. Talia didn't even come to help him up.

*"At least she didn't hit you that time,"* Ash said by way of encouragement.

Holt cleared his throat and got up. This seemed to be some test of will, one he wouldn't lose. He wouldn't ask her to go easy on him.

A few more rounds passed.

"You sure you don't want me to ease off?"

Holt gritted his teeth. "I'm sure."

She did anyway. She absolutely moved slower than she was capable of in their next bout. Holt was able to step in close this time, although he lost his footing on the damp, leafy earth and missed his attack. She slapped the back of his calf with the flat of her blade, although far softer than her earlier blows had been.

"I said don't go easy on me."

"I don't want to hurt you," she said in a level voice.

"Really? You hardly held back before. I'm aching." He clenched his jaw after that, frustrated that he'd let slip he was suffering.

"You're not a natural at swordcraft," she said, still in that measured tone.

"What do you mean?"

"I mean you lack innate talent."

"I'm still learning!"

"Your footwork. It's not the best. It's not even good. That's why you're losing balance. I could just let you fall over and win that way."

"I'll get better."

"Some people never do."

Holt's frustration boiled over. "Do you really dislike me so much? Are Ash and I still such a burden to you on this journey? We saved your life at Midbell, remember? Or was I just a servant doing my job?"

She gave him a cool look. "If I really wanted to hurt you, I wouldn't have pulled my hits. Master Brode and I could break your bones like twigs if we didn't hold back. So no, I'm not trying to hurt you, Holt."

His cheeks flushed with embarrassment. Of course, she had been holding back the entire time. She had to for his own sake.

"I'm sorry," he grumbled.

"Didn't hear that."

"I'm sorry," he said clearly.

"That's all right." She twirled her sword in her hand, a flourish Holt had yet to perfect, but Brode told him it was useless in combat anyway. Once again, she stared at him intently.

"You do that a lot," he said.

She raised an eyebrow.

"Look at me like... that." He gesticulated by way of clarification. It seemed to clarify nothing for her. "That sour look. Like you want to punch me or something."

She blinked and looked quite taken aback.

"I feel like you're the one who doesn't like me."

"Me?" Holt said, confused. He didn't dislike Talia. He found it irksome that she wanted to keep her distance despite what they were going through. She could help him learn but kept to herself instead. Rather than congratulate him on his progress, she would roll her eyes and make a smarmy remark, as if anyone expected Ash and him to take on the incursion alone. He didn't have a clue what she was talking about.

"I think you need to take that chip off your shoulder," she said.

She wasn't angry, nor was she stern. In fact, she was exasperatingly cool, which made Holt feel all the more confused and frustrated that he was the one getting worked up.

"Chip off my—"

"Yes, you seem to think I have it in for you. Is it because you think I look down on everyone else? Trample the servants under my boot?"

"No—" Holt tried to start.

"Because not all of us are like that." Her façade started to break down. "All the nobles and riders, I mean. Some are. But way less than you think and certainly not me. If you're thinking about what I said as we left the Crag—"

"That Ash and I should try 'not to slow you down'."

"I was just telling the truth." She stomped toward him, her eyes reflecting the campfire. Or was that her magic flaring? "The two of you were useless. We were in a horrible position – as if we're hardly better off now. And how was I supposed to know you'd advance this fast and have, what, anti-blight magic?"

"Which seems like a good thing to me. But instead of trying to help or even just be encouraging, you just scowl at me."

Talia balled her fists and screwed up her face before the words burst from her.

"I've been jealous. There. Are you happy?"

Holt wasn't sure what he'd been expecting, but it hadn't been this. Princess Talia. *Princess* Talia was jealous of him.

"W-what?"

She sighed and ran her hands down her face. "It's incredible what you and Ash have achieved so quickly. Really it is. And that's only a good thing. But... oh, I don't know... it just feels... unfair, I suppose. I spent my whole life fighting to become a rider. Mother and I had to pull out every trick to get my father, the court, and the riders themselves to allow it. Deliberately screwing up or insulting every marriage candidate I was forced to meet. Hoping I could make a real difference by defending Feorlen from the scourge while my brother handled the rest. *That* was how things were supposed to go."

She paced now, waving her arms at every word. That dam of emotion inside her had well and truly burst.

"And then I make it to the Order. And they finally let me in. And I train every day and read every scroll, and everyone is impressed that I advance to Ascendant so quickly. But I wasn't happy. I wanted more. Needed more to feel like I'd earned my place and show them it was the right thing to let me in. And then you just show up and do it all in about three weeks."

"I've not exactly done it on purpose," Holt said sheepishly.

"Exactly!" Talia preached to the heavens. "You don't even mean it to happen and the advancements come in leaps and bounds. Your bond with Ash is rock solid already. You *stole* a dragon egg and got away with it!"

Her shoulders slumped then.

"So yes, I've been jealous of you. Is that so hard to understand?"

Holt still felt stunned. Scrambling for words, he said, "It just always seemed to me like you had everything. And, well, many of higher rank treat those beneath them poorly."

She nodded slowly, and the smallest of smiles tugged at the corner of her lips. "So you decided I was the same?"

"I didn't think much on it, if I'm honest."

"No, you didn't. Hence the chip."

Most of the fight went out of her then, and she took a seat right there on the leaves.

"You broke all the rules," she continued. "You still break the rules, or what we thought were the rules. You and Ash—" Something stopped her. She seemed to want to say more but couldn't.

Holt had frozen, unsure what to do. Then it seemed Talia was fighting back tears.

Pyra puffed up, raising her great body off the earth and headed their way.

"It's okay, girl," Talia sniffed.

Right there, surrounded by broken leaves and with mud on her clothes, Talia wasn't a princess. She wasn't even a rider. She was just a girl, a person, and barely older than Holt when it came down to it. All that Brode had said to Holt made sense to him now.

He gulped and moved to kneel beside her, all ingrained propriety forgotten.

He took her hand.

"I'm sorry. I knew what you were going through, but I never really understood it."

"I'm sorry too. I could have handled it better. I just wonder whether, if I had advanced like you have… if Pyra and I had… well, it's too late now."

Holt had an inkling as to what she meant. "We can still save the kingdom."

"Not that," she said. "I mean, yes, but I meant it's too late for my brother or father. I could have saved them both, if I had been with them. But I wasn't. I'm never where I *should* be. It's my fault."

Holt was stunned. "You can't blame yourself for that."

A regal presence entered his mind. *"But she does anyway, little one,"* Pyra said. *"Only time will help, if it can."*

Talia hadn't shed a tear. Strong to the end, she spoke with a sort of pride. "I'd give it all up, Holt. Every right, all my powers, every jewel and palace – right now, if I could get them back."

Holt's mind turned to that memory of his mother giving him the toy. Of the look of joy on his father's face when he thought Holt was being taken to safety.

"I know you would."

Talia seemed to wake up as if from a dream. She looked down, saw her hand in his, and looked him in the eye.

"Your hands are *really* rough," she said.

"So are yours."

"I'm a dragon rider."

Holt shrugged. "I'm a pot boy."

She smirked. "Good one." Then she punched him on the shoulder. His shoulder sang in pain, his breath left him in a shocked wheeze, and he went sprawling to the earth. She clearly had forgotten to pull that *particular* punch.

"Oh, I'm sorry. I'm sorry," Talia said, swooping down on him.

Holt spat out some moss and wheezed as she turned him over. Before their talk he would have been mad or resentful – now he just laughed. Looking relieved, Talia sunk onto her knees, more relaxed than he'd ever seen her before.

Well, at least he could counter her strength one way.

He looked inward to the bond and to Ash's bright core. As a trickle of magic filled his body, he grinned and got up, raising a fist of his own. A light must have glowed in his eyes to indicate his use of magic, for Talia scrambled up and stepped back.

"Don't you dare," she said, half-laughing.

He decided he would dare. He broke the rules, after all.

And he was just about to leap at her when a disapproving cough cut over everything.

Brode had returned. A dead deer lay at his feet.

Ash got up at once, stretched his neck and tail, and moved to sniff at the carcass.

"Having fun, are we?" Brode asked. Before either Holt or Talia could say anything, Brode continued. "Good," he barked. "The pair of you are so serious all the time."

Holt thought that rather rich coming from Brode the Brooding. Yet before either he or Talia could so much as share a shocked glance between them, Brode waved them over.

"Come, give me a hand with this beast, Master Cook. Talia, you can probably make the fire larger tonight. Under this canopy I think we can risk some more light. The heat won't go amiss either."

Holt helped Brode in dressing the deer, although the old rider clearly knew what he was doing.

"I didn't know they trained riders to do this?" Holt said.

"Long ago, they used to train all riders how to do this," Brode said happily. Speaking of days gone by always brightened his mood. "Made sure to learn it myself. Silas never bothered." He carried on for a while, contented in his grumbling until he glanced at Talia and Holt, shook his head and concluded, "Soft."

Holt ignored him.

He had a haunch of venison to contend with. The weight of it would have been hard to manage, but he drew a pinch of strength from Ash's core and skewered the great slab of meat onto a stake for the fire. That would do for one of the dragons. He cut smaller steaks for the human members of the party.

It wasn't like Pyra needed it spiced and no one else would mind too much about the taste, so he reckoned a simple fry would do. They still had some oil from Midbell and there might be some mushrooms nearby that were good enough to eat. He left Talia in charge of turning the spit with strict instructions to keep the flames at an even heat across the meat. This would be a trifle for her. *A fire rider's skills would be invaluable in a kitchen*, he thought. That done, he set off in search of edible fungi.

Ash as ever was fidgety around the food, unable to contain his eagerness for a feed. An echo of Ash's anticipation flitted across the bond, and Holt's own mouth salivated. This escalated as the air filled with the sweet roasting juices of the venison. By the time Holt returned from his mushroom hunt, the meat on the spit was ready.

He'd barely gotten the haunch off the wooden stake when Ash pounced on it.

*"This is the best thing you've ever made,"* Ash crooned. His delight was so intense that for a moment the bond glowed white-hot again, and Holt really could taste the meat as Ash did.

The most perfectly balanced piece of meat – salted and caramelized on the outside, melt in your mouth texture – he'd ever tasted. Every hit of the sweet juices was like honeyed wine.

Holt eyed Ash, thinking this reaction a bit over the top. It was only a lump of meat charred over the fire, after all.

"I think you're just hungry," Holt said.

Then it hit him again. A wave of power across the bond; it burned and beat like many trumpeters calling for battle. He looked across the bond and saw a sea of those motes of light swirling around the core.

Holt realized what this meant and grinned. "Master Brode, I think we've found Ash's meat preference."

# 30

# SON OF NIGHT

Holt raised his hands, feeling the power inside him twitch. Heat and white light flecked with purple began to gather around his palms. But it was Ash who struggled to contain the energy.

The dragon tossed his head, fighting to control the gathering power. Ash clamped his jaw but only held it for a moment before the magic forced his mouth wide. Holt looked across their bond and saw the countless new motes racing toward Ash's core, crashing into one another and shaking like frothing rapids on a river.

"Easy does it," Brode said. He approached Ash as he might a rabid dog. "The swell in motes can be hard to manage the first time. Just don't—"

Too late. Ash twisted, faced away from them all and blasted his beam-like breath into the night. The beam had enough power behind it to cause Ash to stagger backward.

Holt found that strange. Raw motes alone should not have had that effect.

The beam of light illuminated the forest briefly before slamming into a tree, breaking the trunk clean through with a terrible crack. Then all went dark. And quiet. And just as Holt thought it was over, creaking rose like a rusted door being thrown open. Leaves rustled, breaking branches filled the night, and finally came a thundering crash as the tree collapsed into the undergrowth.

"Wow," Holt said. He struggled for his next breath. Tentatively, he checked upon Ash's core. The sudden swell of motes seemed to have entirely dissipated. Ash's core blinked dimly, seeming to be half full compared to a moment ago. So, the beam had not been entirely comprised of raw magic then. In his struggle to control the power, Ash had pulled upon magic from his core, or perhaps it had overflowed.

Ash swayed upon his four legs but remained standing.

"Steady," Brode said, placing a firm hand on Ash's side. "You'll get used to handling spikes in power like that."

Holt went to his dragon's side too. "How you feeling?"

Ash swayed again, then all at once he seemed to regain his composure and swept his tail excitedly through the leaves on the forest floor.

*"We shall become mighty!"* Ash said gleefully.

A spark of warmth passed between them over the bond. Holt was delighted Ash had found his meat preference. But it was venison. An unknown preference. What did it mean?

"I know I'm not a rider nor in the Order," Holt said, "but this must confirm Ash is a new magic type rather than a mystic."

Both Talia and Brode nodded, though neither had anything more to add. They were as lost as he was.

"Venison..." Holt said aloud. Something twigged in his mind. He and his father rarely prepared the meat, but they had when Silas Silverstrike visited the Crag. They had made it because Silas came from the Free City of Coedhen in the Fae Forest and Commander Denna had wanted to serve him a dish from his homeland. And the recipe for that dish...

With haste he made for his pack and pulled out the recipe book. The gold embossed dragon flying over a steaming pot was luminous in the firelight.

Holt had opened the book to study the recipe so much that he found the venison stew quickly. Grimacing at the thought of revering Silas, he began flicking back toward the main title page covering this part of the book.

Each meat had its own section, with lamb having the largest, given the varied needs of the mystics. This section on venison was small indeed. Only a handful of recipes were here, and all of them were simple. Once he reached the title page, he found the heading 'Deer' in bold flowing script with an inked silhouette of stag horns beside it. He smiled briefly at the skill of his ancestors, even if the paragraph below was written in scratchy handwriting. He scanned the text eagerly for some clue or insight.

*While deer meat is the preference of no dragon type, a few recipes are worth knowing in case other meats are in short supply. Even mystics will eat it in a pinch, which is especially useful at times.*

Underneath this were lines written by another hand. This writing was much neater and easier to understand.

*Deer is a growing delicacy in the Free City of Coedhen and the surrounding territories. Despite large herds living in the Fae Forest, it is considered a rare dish. A merchant from Coedhen explained how the deer in that forest are craftier than elsewhere, moving at night as the moon waxes and wanes. During the full moon, huntsmen state that the deer travel solely at night, and the quality of meat is reputed to be superior if a beast is felled at this time.*

Holt lowered the book and looked to the sky as though his answer would be written in the stars. Only a dirty gray light greeted him, all that could penetrate the dense canopy of the Withering Wood.

Feeling Brode and Talia watching him, he said, "It's the moon."

"The moon?" Talia said.

"Ash's powers are linked to the moon."

"And you got that from your cookbook?"

He glanced down to the barely filled page again. "There's something here about deer being affected by the moon. Not many recipes though..." He trailed off, thinking of the lack of knowledge and the blank pages that could be filled now Ash was in the world.

It just felt right. Moonlight and starlight were types of light, after all. And Ash was always the most animated of the group after sundown.

*"I do like nighttime,"* Ash said.

Holt put the recipe book away and went to the dragon's side. He thought about scratching Ash under the chin, but the dragon's size made that prospect seem rather silly now. He settled for patting his neck instead.

"A lunar drake," Holt said. "Guess I should call Shock, Lunar Shock instead. I wonder what my next abilities will be?" The thought excited him. Maybe he would be able to melt the scourge in a huge beam of moonlight. Although why a lunar drake would have abilities to counter the blight was still a mystery.

He said as much to the others.

"I don't think they have a direct weakness to moon or starlight," Brode said. "The bugs are perfectly happy to move and strike at night. If anything, they prefer the night."

"And yet Ash's breath was able to sear a hole through a massive flayer."

"With its armor cracked open," Brode said. "And using all of his core in one attack. But yes, he hit hard. Far harder than a fire drake at his age could hope to."

"Fire being effective against the scourge at least makes sense," Talia said. "If the blight is a disease and fire cleanses."

Pyra widened her eyes at that, and the campfire blossomed. Doubtless she was absorbing many extra fire motes, giving Talia ample Forging work. Then Holt was struck by how much sense the brightness of Ash's core made. He had only been Cleansing at night, given they were moving by day, but this would be exactly when more lunar motes would pass through the orbit of Ash's core.

"If I'm right," he announced, "there is surely an easy way to test it. Pyra sits by the fire to absorb extra fire motes. If Ash sat under direct moonlight, and more motes enter the orbit of his core, we'll know for sure." He looked up to the dense leaves that sheltered them. "We need to climb above the trees."

"*We should fly!*" Ash said, bouncing merrily around the fire.

Talia nodded. "It would be the quickest way to test it."

Brode grumbled. "And if you alert the whole forest to our presence?"

Ash came to a halt and drooped his head.

"What if Ash just climbed a tree and poked his head through the leaves?" Holt said. He twisted this way and that, looking for a big enough trunk for Ash to leap upon.

"He's a dragon, not a squirrel," said Brode. "Come here. You might as well start getting used to sense-sharing if this is how you will fly."

Holt smiled but inwardly groaned. Another thing he had to master? It was becoming a lot to take in.

"I'm not even sure how we did it before," Holt said. "It just sort of happened."

"You just happened to pull on Ash's core the first time too," Brode said. "Now you can do that near enough at will, can't you?"

Holt nodded.

Brode smirked. "Lucky for you, this process can be aided by a simple set of words. You do not *need* to say the words for the connection to take hold, although it helps to trigger the sense-sharing that much easier. In time, you may not need to rely upon the words at all." He gestured for the pair of them to come closer. "Now be aware, the sensation will feel disconcerting at first. I only ever tried it a handful of times with Erdra and found it bizarre to say the least."

"Why?" Holt said, approaching Brode alongside Ash.

"Blending senses is a messy business," said Brode. "The rider's increase a little but the dragon's decrease in sensitivity as they even out. Its only practical value is when the rider is in need of a boost to their hearing or eyesight while at a distance from their dragon, though it is a rare thing for a rider and dragon to be so far apart, let alone for a rider to be doing delicate espionage work."

"As long as we can fly, what's the problem?"

"The issue is that it does put a strain on the bond – it's only possible because of your connection, after all. Now while you're close together, as close as you are when flying, for instance, it should be negligible. But it will add up over prolonged use. You won't be able to fly indefinitely without rests, and should you stray too far from each other while sense-sharing, the bond will be placed under great strain to maintain the connection."

Holt nodded, eager to get on with it. Nothing Brode said gave him pause. So they had to stop and take rests, fine. A small price to pay so that they could fly. And he did not foresee a time when they would sense-share other than for flying.

"I understand, Master Brode. What is this technique?"

Rather than tell them, Brode drew his broad green blade and drove it into the earth near their campfire. "The words," he said, "are only an aid, remember. What you must ensure above all is the deliberate melding of your senses to one. Try to focus on the same things around you. The smell of smoke from our fire, focus on that."

Holt did. After a moment or two of really concentrating on smelling the burning wood, other smells seemed to fade away. It was much like when he pushed all things aside to Forge or Cleanse. Ash must have succeeded too, for a whiff of that smoke traveled across their bond, only deeper. Holt could really smell the wood and the earth trapped within the smoke when he tapped into Ash's sense of it.

"I think it's working," Holt said quietly.

"Good," Brode said, just as softly. "Now, try focusing other senses. I'm not sure if sight will work for you, although Ash can see in his own way." He tapped the hilt of his rider's blade that he had planted into the earth. Holt heard the soft touch in his own ears but, as if on a slight delay, he heard an echo of it over the bond too. To Ash, that soft touch sounded loud, as though Brode had slapped the metal.

Ash gently padded to stand before the blade and pressed his snout against it.

"Clever thing," Brode said. "Now step back, and both of you, look upon the blade as you can."

Holt gazed upon Brode's green sword while still trying to hold onto the smell of smoke alone. He held it for so long and so intently that in his own mind's eye he thought he began to 'see' the sword in the ground as Ash did. A solid, ringing surface standing amidst open nothingness and the softer, taller person right beside it.

Truly it was a strange sensation.

Brode allowed them time to adjust to this, then spoke again, almost in a whisper so as not to break their concentration. "And now the words. Speak these as you begin to focus. And both rider and dragon must say their part. Either one of you may start it by saying 'my eyes for your eyes'."

Holt spoke the first line. "My eyes for your eyes."

At once he felt the connection with Ash strengthen. For a moment, he heard distant sounds as though they were nearby, and then they were gone.

Brode continued. "Your skin for my skin – an actual touch will go a long way if you can manage."

*"Your skin for my skin,"* Ash said, lifting a wing and wrapping it around Holt's shoulder. Without taking his gaze from Brode's sword, Holt raised a hand and touched the tough, warm hide of Ash's chest.

"And then together," Brode said. "My world for your world."

"My world for your world," Holt and Ash said together.

The effect was immediate and powerful. Holt's senses expanded; distant snapping branches cracked loudly, smoke bloomed inside his nose, the heat of the campfire baked one cheek while the other cheek caught the chill of the cold night air. Feeling it was safe to look at something other than the green blade now, Holt lifted his eyes to look upon Brode's face. Every small line appeared like a crevice on his old face, and for the first time he saw the true depths of his sad eyes.

*"The elder one is different to how I imagined him,"* Ash said. He rumbled low in his throat.

"What's wrong?" Holt asked.

*"I wish I could see you this way."*

Holt's stomach knotted and he gave Ash a hug. "Nothing a mirror can't solve one day."

"I take it it's working then?" Brode asked. "How does the bond feel?"

Holt considered it. "Taut. As though we're both pulling on the end of a rope."

"Mm," Brode growled. "As I say, just be mindful of how long you hold the connection for. Now, up you go. Let's see if your theory is right, Master Cook."

Holt climbed onto Ash, settling between two of the ever-growing ridges on the dragon's back.

*"Look up for me,"* Ash said.

"Oh right," Holt said, feeling foolish. Currently he was looking straight ahead into the darkness between the trees. And what he saw,

Ash saw. This would take some getting used to if flying were to become a reality.

"Be quick about it," Brode said. "No lingering."

Holt craned his neck, showing Ash a lighter parting in the canopy. The dragon took off, breaking branches as they broke free into the night. At first, nothing happened. Holt's heart sank, thinking he had got it all wrong about the deer and the lunar drake. And then the wispy strands of cloud passed and the moon shone down upon them.

Ash's core glowed.

Holt watched as fresh lunar motes flew in like shooting stars into the navy nothingness in which the core floated. Some motes stayed; some flew past altogether without being brought into the core's orbit. Most importantly, Holt's theory was correct.

Ash was a lunar dragon.

*"It's beautiful,"* Ash said.

*"It really is."* He said it telepathically without considering it. He tried to do it again consciously but found it much harder, forcing out each word. *"Can you sense any scourge out there? Are we in danger?"*

*"No more so than on the ground. Their stink is all over, their presence a constant low burn. And yet there is something or somethings out there... bursts of power in a flat land... gone as quick as they come."*

It appeared only senses of the physical world were shared via this connection, for Holt did not gain an impression of these things. He cast out his own fledgling magical senses. Only the heat of Pyra and Talia below stood out to him. Beyond, all else was desolate to him. Dragons must have a wider read than riders.

Just then, Pyra's unmistakable presence entered his mind. *"Be careful of how you reach out to others, little one. A gentle touch is more polite. Master Brode also says to return at once."*

Holt gulped. So did Ash. He was glad to have Pyra on their side, that was for sure.

They descended as best they could, only whacking themselves a few times on their way to the ground. Brode and Talia were deep in conversation by the fireside.

As ever, letting go of the strong connection to Ash was easier than creating it. He did so, and his world returned to normal.

"He's a lunar dragon for sure," he said, getting down from Ash's back.

Brode gave him a weak smile and beckoned him closer.

Holt cast a look around their clearing as though expecting scourge to leap out from between the trees. "What's the matter? Ash said he felt something—"

"Pyra felt it too," Talia said. "As did I. Something is out there, only we can't get a grip on it."

"Likely some strong bugs," Brode said. "We can't expect to go unmolested. Sit and Forge, Holt. We'll need every drop of that lunar magic you can cultivate for us. Talia and Pyra will keep watch for the enemy."

Holt began at once, though it took him a long time to truly concentrate on the task at hand. He wanted to fight, to do his bit against the scourge, but he was becoming more and more aware of how frail he and Ash were. What if they were attacked tonight or tomorrow? Every mote Forged would count at this point.

They had to get stronger. Faster than anyone had before them.

Brode had given them all the tools. Now it was down to Holt.

They had to ascend.

# 31

# SOUL-CURSED

From far across the forest, Rake observed them.

Cresting out to the edge of his significant reach, he evaluated the newcomers. Two cores. They might have blended amidst the numerous dragons he was charged with safeguarding, only these had bonds to go with them. Riders then. Young ones. And another with them, one with a scarred soul.

Rake knew the feeling of those scars well.

He judged they could pass. This trio were no threat to the wild emeralds he had been charged with protecting. Wild dragons were not like to venture close to riders in any case. And yet, Rake found the small band intriguing. Why come to the woods? Did they know of the threat at its heart? Unlikely. Lords of the Order would investigate that. And something about the weakest of the party drew his inner eye – what notes he faintly discerned were none that he recognized.

Well, he might steal a moment here and there to observe them along their journey. He had other business this night.

From his cross-legged position, Rake stood with one fluid movement, using his tail to maintain his balance. He tightened his grip upon his polearm and drank in the dark woods with his draconic eyes.

Sickness ran deep here. The emeralds had made little headway against it despite a valiant effort, although he would refrain from complimenting the West Warden so. That dragon would get no such satisfaction from him.

Rake started running, channeling arcane energies to his feet to muffle the sound as he returned to the closest group of emeralds. Four of them – their green scales washed out in the night – had gathered around a blighted oak. Snouts held high, they swayed rhythmically together.

Synchronizing songs was delicate work, but it granted them the power to halt the blight, even cure it if enough chimed in. They'd been at this tree for an hour already, and Rake didn't wish to break their concentration now.

He reached out to the surrounding area, conducting a more intensive search than his light sweep of the wider forest, but found nothing of note. Nothing to worry about, at least. Perhaps the Life Elder had just wanted to be rid of him after all. There was no danger here worthy of Rake's attention.

And why should there be? The kingdom of Feorlen was small, out of the way and largely forgotten in the great histories. It was said to be an unwanted land. The Skarl Empire had discovered it by accident. Centuries later, an army of the long-lost Aldunei Republic conquered it by accident. In time, Feorlen became a kingdom of its own, but only because neither republic nor empire felt it worth bloodying themselves over. A spit of land at the edge of the former world and a distant afterthought of the latter. What great threats could be here?

The rumblings of the emeralds seemed to reach a crescendo and drew Rake's attention. Before his eyes, the green-gray bark on the sick tree started to recede. Progress. Always nice to see. Lucky for those who could still experience it.

Mystic motes emanated in abundance from the minds of the emeralds, so keenly focused on their task. He'd Cleanse and Forge his core beside such a group once he'd checked up on the others.

An acrid odor brushed his sensitive, reptilian nostrils. He licked the air out of an instinct very much non-human and one he had not fully adjusted to despite his long years in this form.

A squeaky cry croaked from down by his taloned foot. Rake squatted. A badger cub crawled along the forest floor. Patches of its fur had fallen away, and a slick trail of puss-flecked blood dribbled in its wake. Its cry sent a shiver to long-dormant places inside Rake.

A pained beat thumped from his soul. Rake placed his free hand over his chest, grunting a sigh as his curse plagued him.

*I know*, he thought. *But the emeralds will wish to try saving it first.*

The pain grew. Rake gripped his polearm so tight he chaffed the scales on his palm.

His dragon, Elya, was insistent. Rake never knew if talking to himself got through to her, but he did it all the same. Helped stave off the madness if nothing else. He also understood her intent.

This badger cub was doomed.

It was only one small creature. It shouldn't matter. Shouldn't stir him so much.

He lowered his hand flat on the ground, palm side up, and let the poor thing climb on. Following his nose and the trail of blood, he found its sett. He lowered and sniffed again. It didn't take an emerald dragon to know death lay down there.

His soul grew tight.

*I'm sorry you have to see this*, he thought. *With luck the emeralds will give up soon, and we can leave this wretched forest.*

He hadn't decided what to do about the badger when he realized it had grown silent. It had died right there in his hand. Sighing deeply, Rake placed the poor creature back down by the entrance to its sett. With a delicacy unthinkable for one his size, he dug his hand into the soil and dragged it over the baby and its family buried below.

Fire would have been best. They may as well have set the whole forest on fire for all the good burning one sett would do—

A snap cracked through the clearing. Rake stood, gripping his polearm in two hands, and rounded on the source of the noise. He found a flayer flanked by ghouls. He stepped coolly back – the scourge advanced – and he swung his polearm in a clean, strong arc, cutting the scourge down in a single strike. Only the flayer wiggled some more upon the ground. Rake placed his foot upon its head and pressed hard. That was the end of it.

There had been dozens of small groups like these, cut off and lost from the main swarm. Purging the woods of them was trivial work for Rake, but at least it was something to show for his time here. Although he had wondered why the riders stationed at the Crag had allowed this recent infestation to run so wild.

He put such matters aside. What the Order did or didn't do was no concern of his. They had made that clear long ago. For now, he returned to the group of emeralds. Their tree-patient looked healthy now. Another small something to show for their time here, he supposed. At least they were *trying* to do something about it, unlike the other Wild Flights. For that at least, Rake respected the Life Elder more than he did the others.

Rake moved on, checking in on other groups of emeralds and covering vast tracks of the western forest before the sun rose.

Over the next days, tracking his emerald charges and the trio of riders became harder. The emeralds continued to spread around the woods, searching for the freshest patches of infection. The young riders kept to the distant southern edge of the forest.

They wouldn't know they benefitted from his industrious scrubbing of the scourge in those parts before their arrival. An old part of him, the part that still remembered being a rider, wished them well.

One day, they passed beyond even Rake's impressive sight.

As did two of his emeralds, although they had been firmly within it only moments before.

Rake ran – a blur through the Withering Woods – until he came to where he had last sensed them. No trace of them remained, nor any sign of a struggle. He reached out for the West Warden, but the great emerald was too far away for communication.

He scanned outward again, throwing his sixth sense as far as he could, pulling on great quantities of mystic magic from his core. Still no sign of them.

Perhaps they had flown away, or the Warden had sent them home and neglected to inform Rake. That seemed like something he would do. Anything to avoid conversing with Rake the soul-cursed.

He had just resolved to find the Warden and inform him of the missing emeralds when a roar echoed to the south. Rake reeled his magical senses back in, homing in on the distant core flaring as only a core will flare in combat.

Rake ran. The core of the emerald flickered and died in his mind's eye.

An hour later, he found the body of the drake sprawled on the forest floor. Its eyes were still wide in horror, its forked tongue lolling out as it had breathed its last. A single bloody stroke ran across its neck. An execution. No dragon could make such a precise cut. The cultists that hunted dragons used pikes and arrows. Such a smooth incision could only have been made by a blade. And only a rider's blade, forged at Falcaer, wielded by a rider with immense strength, could part dragon hide so easily.

Lifting the wing of the fallen emerald, Rake found scorch marks. Not from fire. Such a fire would have burned the nearby grass or leaves. He listened to the motes, hoping to hear an echoing note. Power rumbled in the area. Storm magic.

A storm rider. A Champion at the very least, and likely pushing at the boundaries of Lord. He hoped for the latter, as the former would prove about as challenging as ghouls.

The question of why a rider had attacked wild dragons didn't trouble him at present. He could find out once he caught the rogue pair. More troubling was that the Life Elder's fears had merit. Someone was indeed hunting wild dragons. A rogue rider was nothing revolutionary to Rake, but killing wild dragons seemed senseless.

"*Rake,*" the West Warden called to him. "*What has happened?*"

The pompous dragon had edged just into telepathy range, and only because Rake's vast mystic core made it possible to answer over such a distance.

"*I am handling it, honored Warden. Fear not a dark scale on your head.*"

"*Your task, soul-curse—*"

"*Is my top priority. It is in my interest, after all. Recall your dragons to your side. I'll head south and aid wayward members of your flight. I did encourage them not to pass beyond my sight.*"

The Warden said no more.

Rake blew out his cheeks, then got to running again. South, he went. South and east. Before nightfall, he had traveled far enough to sense the young riders on their own meandering journey. He wondered now whether their presence was not so peaceful after all; perhaps they were here in a supporting role to the storm rider.

As Rake drew closer to his quarry, he sensed that their power was great. Like a lighthouse sending out its beacon. Yet he or she could fly, and Rake, fast as he was, could only run. The storm rider approached a cluster of emerald drakes that had flown too far south. They stopped but did not start fighting. Rake powered his mighty limbs, leaping in such strides as to almost take off from the ground himself.

Closer now, Rake discerned the rider was nothing less than a Storm Lord. An *extremely* powerful Storm Lord. Finally, something worth his time.

Rake muffled his feet again and crept toward the gathering. Sneaking around as a seven-foot half-dragon came easier than appearance might suggest. His present condition was, well, not exactly natural, but it came with the advantage of leaving his core almost impossible to detect in the usual way. As a result, the Storm Lord did not react as he stepped between the trees, though Rake wondered warily why the Lord had not engaged the group of emeralds. Even together, they would not be a match for his power. Suddenly, a dragon burst from the trees overhead, taking flight to the northeast. One emerald had left while the others remained. And the Storm Lord remained with them.

Intriguing.

When Rake at last drew close enough to spy the group with his own eyes, he found the Storm Lord's dark gray dragon and the emeralds deep in conversation. Rake could sense the mystic energy transmitting between them, though he couldn't tap into their thoughts. Would that he could, he would have had a great deal more fun in his life.

Whatever was being said, the storm drake had grown weary. It pulled its jaw wide and lightning began to charge. Negotiations had broken down.

Rake gathered his own power and hefted his polearm. It had his old rider's sword welded onto the end of the shaft. He ran a talon-like finger along the blade, the metal clear like orange glass. It had been years since he'd had a good fight.

A pang reverberated from his soul, although whether Elya was afraid or imploring him not to harm the storm drake and rider, he couldn't say.

*I don't think this pair deserves your sympathy,* Rake thought. *We do this, earn the Elder's favor, and we get our wish. Not long now.*

The emeralds roared in fear now and tried to back away, gathering breaths of their own. A great wind started to swirl and beat down, preventing them from taking flight. That was fine by Rake. Rake couldn't fly.

Grinning, he sprang out from behind his cover and charged the Storm Lord.

# 32

# THE BASTARD OF ATHRA

Progress through the woods was slow, but Holt thought his progress with Ash was going well. As well as it could. Every spare moment he Cleansed. And when that was done, he Forged.

Holt was getting the hang of Cleansing now. Pushing his breath out at a controlled pace, breathing in more slowly than out, all the while waiting to hear those crackles in his soul. Getting rid of them was the trouble. Sometimes the impurities would push up easily. Other times it would take minutes of shallow breathing, and it was all he could do not to draw a massive breath in as his lungs begged for air.

Hard work. Holt couldn't call it anything other than tedious. But he could already feel results. Each day Ash's core became that bit clearer. And each night Brode allowed them a brief expedition above the trees to take in lunar motes to Forge. Ash's core grew larger, brighter, denser – its smoky tendrils grasping further out into its navy void.

Each day his well of magic grew.

Their bond felt more robust too, having settled after the turmoil of battle and their first flight together. Its beating was now second nature to Holt, as much a part of him as breathing.

Ash too worked hard, training to gather his breath quicker and practiced weaving between the trunks, thickets and fallen trees that barred their passage through the forest. Each day he stumbled and crashed less.

There was swordcraft also, which Holt still found difficult. Brode drilled him in the mornings while Talia packed up their camp. Evenings were too valuable a time for him not to Cleanse and Forge.

Strangely their journey was unhindered, as they came across only a handful of ghouls. Brode seemed disappointed by this, muttering that Holt and Talia needed some proper combat, and he seemed to be made more on edge by their lack of trouble.

"It's not right," he said. "Not during an incursion."

"Perhaps the bulk of the swarm has already moved toward Sidas-tra," Talia offered.

Brode only grunted and told them to keep close.

They did have difficulty in hunting. Brode had been unable to find more game. The one deer they came across was dead already, the blight forming a bug-like shell on its skin. Pyra burned the poor beast to stop it from rising.

One morning, Holt struck what he considered gold. A clump of healthy pigweed, which he picked to add to their dinner that evening. Some greens would be a welcome addition to their traveler's diet. Later that same day, Ash started sniffing and darted eagerly after the smell.

*"Something sweet,"* he declared over a bush.

Holt caught up and discovered wild strawberries. Their sweetness would be another relief from the relentless salty meat, hard cheese and oatcakes. Those hard-packed, crumbly biscuits were the one thing they had an abundance of from Midbell.

That night he flicked through his recipe book, hoping for a stroke of inspiration on how to combine the fruits of his foraging. Nothing sprang out at him. The book was designed for rider halls with all their amenities and scale, not a quick campfire dinner.

He had the pigweed laid out before him on top of an empty sack, staring at it as though the leaves and stems might speak to him.

"Might I use some water for these?" Holt asked.

"Is it necessary?" said Brode.

"I need to wilt them somehow," Holt said. "Wish I'd found some garlic as well."

"I meant must we have—" Brode leaned closer, "—whatever that is?"

"It's pigweed."

"What?" Talia said, sounding thoroughly unimpressed.

It took Holt a moment to understand why she was so put off before realizing.

"Pigweed is what the herbalists and apothecarists call it, but it's essentially wild spinach."

"I see," Talia said, still sounding unsure. "And the stems are fine to eat, are they?"

"The whole plant is," Holt said. "But I'll need some water."

Brode checked their canisters, shaking each one gently. "Just a small amount, Master Cook." He tossed one over. Holt reached out, but the canister slipped between his fingers and whacked into his nose.

Holt winced and rubbed at his face, longing for the moment he would become an Ascendant and gain better reflexes.

He got to work, wilting the pigweed in his ration of water along with a little salt. He cooked Pyra's beef with kracker pepper and tangy spices he still had from the Crag, and he sliced off a strip of their dwindling venison supply for Ash. One stroke of inspiration came to him, and he mashed the wild strawberries down on top of Ash's meat as a sweetener. Venison worked well with some fruit, though strawberries would be an unorthodox combination to his knowledge.

"D'you like that?" he asked Ash.

Ash licked some of the strawberry paste from his lips. *"It could be better."*

Brode barked a laugh. "Becoming fussier, is he? That's what happens."

"I'll try new things when I can," Holt said, giving Ash a scratch on his head. While Ash was sitting down, this was still possible, but he was still growing. The firelight danced off his white scales, and he was now large enough that it was like having a second hearth there to light the night.

He caught Talia's squeamish expression as she picked at the spinach he'd offered up and felt embarrassed. Still, she ate it.

Once again, Holt marveled at where he was and what he was doing. He was a thousand leagues removed from his routine life in the Crag kitchens, and he would never return to it. That sent a pang through him, which he had not expected. His father had been right; it wasn't a terrible life. The smells of the kitchen, the satisfaction of hearing compliments from the riders, the joy in following one's instincts to try something new and for it to work.

When he'd taken Ash's egg, he really had not thought it through. Yet he wondered now whether a part of him, a small devious part of him, had hoped for this. As Talia had said, what had he expected the result to be? That there would be no consequences? Surely he was smarter than that. Once the madness had left him, he had expected punishment. Now there was the chance for the Order to reluctantly induct him, where he would be frowned upon for his actions.

What a choice he had made. Only to end up with no choice at all.

But Brode and Talia had had a choice.

"What made you both wish to join the Order?" Holt asked.

Brode sniffed, took a bite of his oatcake, and gave Talia a look to say, 'you first.'

"If I'd been the direct heir, it would have been out of the question," Talia said. "But as the spare? Well, my role as the spare would be to marry someone important and use my influence to aid that realm and Feorlen from afar. My mother had other ideas. She wanted me to join the Order."

"Why? She must have known how difficult that would be."

"Her closest friend joined the Order in Brenin, though she died in battle long ago. And despite that, I think mother always wanted to join herself but couldn't – destined to marry my father from birth. She's fought against Harroway and his ilk for years to keep the tithes that fund the Order in place. Father left her to it; kept his hands clean of it to appear supportive of all his ealdors. I think Mother and Denna believed that if I joined, not paying the tithes might be seen as an insult to the monarchy. A political fog no one would wish to venture into. Master Brode is right," she added with a nod to the old rider. "No one else would have been allowed to leave for bereavement. I've had special treatment."

Brode picked at his teeth and said nothing.

"So, you did it for your mother?" Holt asked.

"If it weren't for her, it would never have happened," Talia said. "She made it possible. But I threw myself on this path just as eagerly." She sighed. "Everyone has the same role in the end, don't we? Stop the scourge. Keep the living... alive. Better to fight them directly, I thought. Leofric was always better with his words. If our positions had been switched... well, it doesn't matter now."

Holt didn't want to push her any further.

"I had a brother," Brode said suddenly. Everyone, even the dragons, sat up a little straighter. "A half-brother. Big lad, strong, a good fighter – better than me. Wanted to join the Order himself, I'm told."

"Why didn't he?" Holt asked.

Brode flicked his head toward Talia. "I was the spare. A bastard." There was no bitterness in his words. "Had to be carted off as soon as could be. A senator of the Free City of Athra can't have a little brat running around. Mother was a kitchenhand, as a matter of fact." He gave Holt a wry smile. "My brother died defending the city during the last great incursion. But that was a long time ago now."

"I never thought to ask," Talia said thickly. "Did they not let you go to his funeral? Master Brode, I'm sorry if I ever—"

"Settle, girl. Never liked my brother. Carlo would beat me senseless, and our tutor didn't stop him. Silver spoon shoved so far up his ass you could see it shining at the back of his throat. Wouldn't have gone back for him even if I could."

Talia gave him a weak smile. "I understand now."

But Holt wasn't sure that she did. Brode hadn't met her eye, had kept his tone painfully low, not giving an ounce away, and Holt knew he wasn't as cold as he pretended to be.

"You voted to let Talia go," Holt said.

Brode's face changed in an instant. He might have been a hawk about to swoop on Holt.

"Did you?" Talia gasped.

Brode gritted his teeth.

"It passed by one," Holt said, recalling their argument in the court-yard back in Midbell.

"It's not like I had the deciding vote," Brode said. "That was Denna."

"Master Brode," Talia said, "I... I don't know what to say."

"Say nothing."

"But why?" she asked. "You're not afraid to make it clear how you feel about me being in the Order."

"You're still human, aren't you?" Brode snapped, perhaps more harshly than he intended. "*We're* still human, aren't we? Rules and rules and rules. Well, they didn't let the rules stop you from joining, why not let you go see your grieving mother? Damage was done already. You loved your brother too, that much was plain. Think I'd have liked the chance if it were me."

Talia got up and moved to hug the old rider.

"Thank you, Brode."

Pyra rumbled approvingly and beat her wings for want of a true roar of gratitude. Plumes of fire swirled up from the campfire, twirling into the night.

"Don't fuss," Brode said, and they parted.

"Why didn't you tell me?"

He took her rather seriously by the shoulders then. "Because I didn't think you needed any more encouragement."

"What about your mother?" Holt asked.

Brode made a sound somewhere between a scoff and disgust. "She was worse than my loving brother. Think my father suffered embarrassment for my birth? Well, she suffered worse. Already married too. Her husband didn't like me either. Didn't treat me or her well after it, and she took it out on me. As though her mistake was my fault. No, everyone was happy to pack me off to Falcaer."

"And that's where you trained with Silas?" Holt asked.

"Trained? I was his squire, Holt... his loyal squire for many years. They may never have let me become a real rider had he not vouched for me." Brode's fist clenched, and the oatcake still within his grasp crumbled.

"Master Brode," Talia said, as though speaking by his sickbed.

At last, Brode seemed to succumb. "Erdra was my only real family. And I had to burn her body and bury the ashes on some forsaken hill along the road east of Athra... because Silas left us to die. I won't leave her there forever. When my time comes, I'll make my last journey and rest by her side."

Sorrow passed over the bond from Ash. The white dragon padded gently over to Brode's side and nuzzled him as he would Holt. Brode cleared his throat and patted Ash.

Holt didn't know what to say. What could he say? Brode had suffered, really suffered; all of Holt's grievances seemed so small now. So trivial. He had a loving family, a father who wanted nothing but the best for him. A fresh vigor to save Jonah Cook swelled within him; the need to seek forgiveness for the danger he had put them both in.

That vigor turned into raw hatred for Silas Silverstrike, the man who had betrayed them all – left Brode for dead despite all Brode had done for him.

"Why?" Holt said at last. "Why did Silas leave you? Why has he done this?"

"There was a village. They were slow to answer the summons to Athra... so a swarm nearby was drawn there. Silas reckoned we should leave them. I felt we shouldn't feed the swarm more ghouls so readily if we could help it."

"Lesson one," Talia said.

"Lesson one?" Holt said, feeling he had heard them mention this before.

"It's the first thing they tell you when you take the oath," Talia said. "Lesson one: you can't save them all."

"There's a difference between that and not trying," said Brode. "And there's—"

A silver-blue light streaked above the tree line.

Brode tensed at once and looked up. Holt joined him. The thunder rolled in eventually, distant and faint.

"Twenty seconds," Brode said. "Four miles away. Quiet now," he added in a hushed tone, but there was no need for it. The whole party had turned silent as the grave. When nothing came, he said, "Talia, check above."

Talia launched herself high, grabbing onto a thick branch, then continuing up until she disappeared in a flurry of leaves.

Holt guessed Brode wanted to check for a distant storm. But Holt didn't think there would be one. The air was thick enough, but it was always thick in these woods and hadn't grown any worse. The colors in the sky hadn't been entirely natural either, but then again it had been very quick, and—

Another flash of silver-blue light. Holt counted this time too. When the thunder finally reached them, he made it twenty-three seconds.

"Farther away," Brode confirmed.

Talia dropped down and landed in a crouch. "Clear skies everywhere."

Now it was undeniable.

"Silverstrike is here," Holt said, panicked. All his recent advancements with Ash now seemed naïve and hopeless.

"We're not doomed yet," Brode said. "Something or someone is keeping him busy if he's unleashing power like that."

"Maybe his scourge forces have turned on him," Holt said.

"Maybe."

"But how did he even pick up our trail?" Talia said.

"Our measures to cover our tracks weren't foolproof," Brode said. "Even if he searched the woods by chance, he could sense us if he happened to come close enough."

Pyra braced herself and stretched her wings as far as injury would allow. *"Let him come,"* her voice rang inside Holt's mind. *"He and Clesh must answer for their crimes. I will not run. Let him exhaust himself in his search so we may burn his husk."*

She glared at Ash as if to make him join her declaration. Ash braced himself and stretched his own white wings.

*"She can be very scary,"* Ash said covertly to Holt.

"Don't let your fire get the better of you," Brode said. "You're strong, Pyra, but Clesh will leave you a smoking ruin with a single thought. Remember what happened to Mirk and Biter."

"And Commander Denna," Talia said.

"I know it's not what dragons like to do, but we will run and hide from them until there is no other choice."

Pyra snorted thick smoke and clawed at the earth.

"Pack now," Brode said. "We go deeper into the woods. Background distortion from the blight might be enough to mask us."

"And if it isn't?" Holt asked.

"Pray it is," Brode said. He jumped to his feet and began packing at speed.

Holt rubbed at his eyes but got up as well, helping in his own, slower way.

Even as they took their first steps deeper into the forest, the sky lit again with the power of the Storm Lord, and thunder boomed.

# 33

# THE WEEPING TREE

They journeyed deeper into the Withering Woods. Brode didn't risk them stopping for long, even at night. The only sleep Holt got was quick naps here and there. Nor did Brode allow them to fly above the canopy to gather lunar motes anymore.

Going deeper into the woods also meant a longer journey to Sidastra, and they had already been pressed for time when they'd entered. Holt's lack of an enhanced Ascendant's body once again slowed the group down, although Talia no longer gave him any sour looks.

On the contrary, she fell in beside him, matching his pace, and never overtaking. Her comradery gave him spirit. And that kept him going. Even when his eyes became raw from lack of sleep, even when his feet and legs protested at every step, he kept going.

As the sun set on the third day of their flight – at least, Holt thought it was the third day – Brode mercifully called a halt.

"There's been no thunder for half a day," he said.

"That doesn't mean Silas has gone," Talia said.

"No, but it does mean we've gone deep enough into the woods to merit a proper rest. Even our enhanced bodies cannot go on forever like this, and poor Holt looks pale as soap."

Holt swayed a little. "I'm fine. Really."

"Rest," Brode said.

"I'll handle the fire," Talia said, and gave Holt a look that he wasn't to try and help. He didn't have the energy to argue the point even if he'd wanted to. So, Holt took a seat on the least mossy patch of earth.

Ash collapsed dramatically beside him. *"I'm soooo hungry. Can I get some of the tasty stuff?"*

Holt mechanically reached into the bag with their remaining venison.

"I'm not sure how it's keeping."

Inside the cloth bundle the meat looked in decent condition, if a little dark. That could be deceptive. Rot in venison came in shades of red to purple; it wouldn't go brown or gray like other meats. One cut looked extremely dark on the edges, but his nose told him for sure it wasn't any good.

Holt tossed the offending piece of meat to the ground. "Don't think you can have that one."

Ash groaned.

"This should be fine," Holt said, holding up a bright steak. "Once Talia gets the fire going—"

*"Just give me it,"* Ash pleaded.

Holt tossed Ash the steak, and the dragon caught it in his mouth and swallowed it whole. A spark of light ignited in the dragon bond but just as quickly went out. Clearly eating the meat raw didn't lead to the same power spikes.

He made a mental note to write this down in his recipe book. If he ever got the chance.

Ash started sniffing, his snout edging closer to where the rotting piece of venison had fallen.

"Bet it stinks," Holt said.

*"Yes, but there are other things there. Scuttling."*

It took Holt's tired mind a moment longer to figure out Ash's meaning. When it did click into place, he scrambled back at once.

*"What's wrong?"* Ash asked. The presence of the insects didn't seem to bother him at all. Maybe that was because he couldn't see them. But Holt could.

Their bodies were like ants crossed with roaches. Each had three pairs of legs, the front pair modified for grasping, and each had long-reaching antennae. They were roughly the size of Holt's thumb and shelled in green-brown carapaces. They approached at a frightening speed but slowed down as they drew closer to the meat as though sizing it up.

"Something wrong, Holt?" Brode asked. He stomped over. "Not afraid, are you? These bugs are only little."

"What are they?"

"Look like vethrax to me," Brode said casually.

"V-vethrax?" Holt said. "Here?" He backed farther away. Vethrax were said to be omens of death, and wherever they came, the scourge would not be far behind.

"Nothing to worry about," Brode said. "You still have a boot on that foot, don't you? Just step on them if they get too close."

Holt cleared his throat and got a hold of himself. "I know... I was just taken aback is all." He refrained from admitting that the way they moved unnerved him, or that the thought of one crawling on his skin made him nauseous. "They're an ill omen."

"Nonsense." Brode inspected the creatures more closely. "I've rarely seen them in Feorlen. Rarely see them at all in truth. They don't like the light, tend to stick to dark, damp places, which I suppose the forest is."

"*I'll see to them,*" Ash said. He stalked forward, head low to the ground as he sniffed the bugs out. Yet the second Ash was within spitting distance of the vethrax, they turned and scurried into the undergrowth. Ash growled lowly after them.

"*Scared them,*" he said happily. The victory seemed to have injected fresh energy into the dragon.

"The campfire should ward them off once it gets going," Brode said. "But don't throw any more aging meat to the ground. They like rotting things to eat, and who knows what else you might attract besides."

"Won't they bring the scourge on us?" Holt asked.

"The vethrax aren't the scourge. Folk mix them together because they come for dead animals. Still, I wouldn't like to have them swarming around just in case. Any more meat that's going off can be burned instead."

Talia returned shortly later, with little wood for the fire and a pained look on her face. "It's so hard to breathe this deep in the forest. And I'm afraid most of the fallen wood is wet or rotten. The blight is in every other tree."

Holt became aware of just how dense the trees were this deep into the woods and how sickly they were. Half were infected, and the air was twice as foul compared to the edge of the forest. No birds called. Nothing rustled in the bushes or treetops. It was a dead or dying place.

Given Talia's hopes that the forest could be cleansed one day, seeing it this infected must have been hard on her. *A distant dream indeed,* Holt thought. The levity of their first evening in these woods seemed a long time ago now. Talia's mood had darkened further, that much was clear, even if she no longer took it out on him.

But if the blight caused this, then could he and Ash not do something about it?

The foolish decision to take Ash's egg had to mean something. He'd risked not just his own life but his father's and Ash's as well. A sense of injustice had boiled over and pushed him to a mad choice. Something had to come of it to make it all right.

And he wanted to help Talia feel some hope again, even if just a little.

As Brode and Talia set about preparing their fire, Holt warily got to his feet. Every breath now seemed like a fight, but whether that was the putrid air or his human fatigue from the toil he didn't know.

He went to the most infected old oak he could find with piles of gray-black leaves at its base. Gnarled bark withered into rotting voids so that the trunk resembled a wizened face wailing in agony. A sheen of disease reflected the red of the dying sun as though the wood wept blood.

Holt strained to reach out to Ash telepathically. It wasn't so easy when his life wasn't on the line.

*"Come help me."*

Ash answered with a warm pulse across the bond, and the dragon padded over.

"*Just like before,*" Holt said. "*When you cured Mr. Smith's daughter.*"

"*I remember,*" Ash said.

"Holt," Brode said, "what do you think you're doing?"

"*Probably we'll need a lot more power than last time. This tree is… well, it's a lot bigger.*"

"*And the sickness runs deeper,*" Ash said.

"This isn't the time for experiments," Brode said.

Holt faced him. "I can do this," he said, sounding more confident than he felt.

"What if it hurts you, hmm? What if the magic alerts Silas to us?"

"Let him try, please," Talia insisted. The look on her face made Holt all the more determined.

Brode looked between the two of them, then fixed his scowl upon Holt.

"Letting your heart lead the way again?"

Holt's cheeks flushed. Then, hoping to deflect some of Brode's ire, he said, "What's the point of all of this if I can't help?"

"Stand down, Holt. That's an or—" He snorted out his frustration. He couldn't give Holt a direct command because he wasn't in the Order. "We're all tired, and hungry, and stretched thin. Let's not make any rash decisions."

"Let him try," Talia said again. Her voice was so soft it seemed to break something in the old man.

"Fine, but I'm stepping in if I have to."

Holt nodded. Gulped. And turned to face the rotting tree again. "Here goes."

Then he reached for Ash's core.

He didn't really know what he was doing, as the only ability he could readily form with magic was his Lunar Shock. Blasting the tree didn't make much sense, but all Ash had done before was push a bit of his magic into Ceilia Smith.

So, he guided the magic down to his left palm, letting the heat form but not so quickly as a blast. White light flecked with purple began to shine. Controlling it was tough. Power flowed smoothly down his now practiced arm, but it pushed painfully at the edges of other pathways yet unopened.

A sudden kick to the back of the head made him alert and wide awake. The dragon song rang between his ears, but he kept the light swirling around his hand, not letting it go.

Ash gathered the same at the tip of his snout.

It had all taken just a few seconds.

"Now, Holt," Talia called, and the edge of worry to her voice urged him on.

Holt pressed his palm against the slick, rotting bark. Immediately the wood dried, and the bark grew hard and coarse against his skin. That was good. It was working, yet every fiber of his body wanted to blast the light out of him. He resisted. With painful restraint, he pushed it gently from him instead as a Cook might push frosting through a piping bag: he pushed the power into the tree itself.

"It's working!" Talia said.

Ash pressed his nose against the tree to help.

Most of the lunar-empowered light was taken in by the tree, but now it began to glow from that power. White veins wove around the tree, so many that it became a beacon. The tree sizzled and a rancid smell arose but without smoke.

With a gasp, Holt let go of the magic. The pulsing light of Ash's core flickered but remained bright, a testament to the hard work of Holt's meditation. The bond remained strong, nowhere close to its fraying point. Yet the departure of the power brought the harsh reality of his weariness crashing back. His vision blurred, and his hungering stomach squirmed nauseously.

Once the immediate danger of fainting had passed, Holt looked upon the tree, and his heart sank.

"It didn't work?"

The weeping tree, so stricken with the blight, stood virtually untouched. Only the immediate area where Holt had pressed his palm against it appeared better for his efforts, a visible handprint etched upon the bark.

"I don't understand," Holt said breathily.

Talia gave him a look of deepest sympathy, bravely smiling where

Holt knew she was disappointed, and it only made him feel ten times worse.

"No," he said, as though if he said it with enough conviction, he could fix it. "No," he said again, twisting this way and that to find another tree. He found another oak, one still more brown than gray. He made for it.

"That's enough," Brode said, intercepting and grabbing him.

But Holt pulled on Ash's core and threw Brode off with a wild burst of strength.

"I have to try," he said, as Brode collapsed to the wet leaves.

And before either Brode or Talia could stop him, Holt gathered white light at his palm and slammed it into the trunk of the oak. Once more he pushed his power into the tree rather than blasting it out in Shock. Once again white veins spanned the trunk, bright and pulsing. Poisoned wood sizzled as the lunar energy did its work.

"I said, that's enough," Brode called.

Holt struggled through the effort of maintaining a grip on his powers. "Just... a little... more."

A strong hand clamped down on his shoulder and heaved him back. This time it was Talia, her strength prodigious and impossible to resist. He staggered, almost fell, but as he righted himself, he heard Talia gasp and knew what that meant.

The tree was cured.

He punched at the air. "We did it!"

"Fool," Brode said, shoving past Holt to place a hand on the tree as though he were trying to take its pulse.

Ash began bounding around the tree in celebration. Holt considered joining him, but Talia's expression was reward enough. She looked more delighted than he had ever seen her.

"You really did it."

Holt struggled for breath. The only thing keeping him upright was the gentle burn of magic. "I'm not sure how many I could do in a row."

"It's a start," Talia said.

"Maybe once we reach a higher rank—" Holt cut himself off, his mood changing at once. Trepidation had spiked across the bond with

Ash. He checked on Ash and found the dragon had stopped moving; his body was pressed low to the ground, his ears pricked.

"What's wrong?" Holt asked.

*"Something is out there."*

"Ash can hear something."

"Scourge?" Brode asked.

When Ash next spoke, Holt felt the bond pulse harder. The dragon was speaking to them all, and it seemed to take him some magical strength to do so.

*"Heartbeats,"* Ash said.

"Heartbeats?" Holt said. "You can hear heartbeats out there?"

Talia reached behind her back and lightly touched the hilt of her sword. "Probably just animals."

*"I hear and smell beasts all the time. I know the difference between their hearts and a human's."*

Ash's hearing was becoming potent indeed.

Brode drew his blade, the dark green steel nearly camouflaged against the foliage. "How many, Ash?"

Ash's head shifted from side to side as he concentrated.

"How many?" Brode was insistent now.

*"A score, maybe more."*

Pyra stomped and growled. The trees restrained her physically but not her temper. *"If they are enemies, they shall regret their decision."*

"It can't be Silas and Clesh," Talia said in relief.

"Their allies or Harroway's are still a concern," said Brode.

"They might just be Hunters and Jacks," Talia said.

"This deep into the Withering Woods?" Brode said.

"Harroway can't have sent men in to look for us this quickly. Besides, if they're just a group of humans, why are we worried? Not unless you think—"

*"They're carrying weapons,"* Ash said.

"How can you hear that?" Holt asked, part in awe and part in disbelief.

*"Because they are almost upon us."*

# 34

# WYRM CLOAKS

Hungry, weary from travel, and having just spent a good portion of Ash's core, Holt couldn't imagine a worse time for a fight. He reached for his sword and fumbled taking a grip of the hilt.

"Which direction are they coming from?" Brode asked.

*"North. From deeper in the wood."*

"Everyone back," Brode said. "Ash, stay alert in case they try to flank us."

Pyra gouged deep lines into a tree. *"We should not cower before sheep."*

Talia held her tongue, but it seemed like she agreed with her dragon. Holt wasn't so sure. Brode wouldn't be worried without reason, but Holt couldn't fathom what a group of regular humans could do against dragon riders. Maybe if they were ambushed, but Ash had ensured that wouldn't happen. Just Talia and Brode alone could handle twenty men, and they had Pyra with them to boot.

"Holt," Brode hissed, "draw your damned sword."

Holt did so, fighting to steady his breathing and maintain a control over his bond. He pressed up against Ash for comfort.

*"You ready?"* Holt asked.

*"We've survived worse,"* Ash said, this time just to him. Then his

neck went taut and he spoke to the whole group again. *"They are here. Straight ahead."*

Figures emerged from the gloom of the forest, beyond which the last rays of the setting sun could not penetrate. At first Holt thought some carried spears, but then he noticed the elongated, pointed axe heads at the top of the shafts. These weapons were halberds, not axes, and they looked much longer and more vicious than any he had seen before. Apart from the halberds, others among their number bore great crossbows. Beyond their weaponry it was hard to distinguish between the figures, for each wore a cloak with the cowl drawn to conceal their face.

The cloaks were made of a material Holt didn't recognize. No two were the exact same color either, ranging from black and grays through to reds, blues, and greens, although all were dulled as if by a lingering shadow.

"Wyrm Cloaks," Talia said, fear entering her voice now. "You were right, Master Brode."

This meant nothing to Holt. "Who are they?"

"Members of a cult that worship dragons. But they hate the Order."

*"Vile filth,"* Pyra informed him.

"I've never heard of—"

"Later," Brode growled.

The cultists seemed to be weighing up the situation, making hand signals to one another, and fanning out to cover more ground.

"Pyra," Brode continued, "you mustn't roar once it starts. We can't afford any more attention."

Pyra fought for control. The plant life around her talons started to singe, and the already humid air became uncomfortably hot. Despite her gathering power, she wouldn't be able to unleash her full force. Nor would Talia. Setting half the wood ablaze and drawing Silverstrike to them was the very last thing they needed. They'd have to rely on their physical abilities.

Yet Pyra couldn't fly with her injury, and she was hampered greatly on the ground by the trees. Brode had no magic, and Holt felt exhausted. Ash was in a better condition, but he'd never fought in such a confined space before. Would so much noise ricocheting off trees and people make it harder for him to form a picture in his mind or just the opposite?

Brode continued issuing hurried instructions. "Pyra, Ash, keep your wings firmly folded against your back. They'll try to tear them with special arrows if you expose them."

Holt wiped his brow, keeping watch on the cultists as they readied themselves. He counted eighteen in total, a little less than Ash had estimated. Well, that was something at least.

The cultists stepped forward as one, methodical and careful. Nine carried the huge halberds; eight carried the great crossbows. The final member wore a charcoal-gray cloak without any visible weapons and stepped forward from the group.

"Riders, what are you doing so far from your tower?" The voice was clearly a man's, though it was high and tart as lemon. "I thought you had all been dealt with."

*Dealt with?* Holt thought. It sounded like the cultists were aware the Crag had come under attack.

"That will be all, cultist," Brode said with a contempt he usually reserved for Silas alone. "Be gone and we'll spare your lives this time."

The cultist cocked his head, his face still dark beneath his hood. Then he began to laugh, a skin-crawling tittering laugh.

*"Elder Brode does not frighten them,"* Ash said, unsure.

A shiver snaked up Holt's spine. To dismiss a threat made by a dragon rider seemed wild enough. But this man was *laughing.*

The cultist faced Pyra, dropped to one knee and lowered his hood. Holt didn't know what he'd been expecting the man to look like, but certainly not a face so plain. So... normal. A sharp nose and chin were the man's only distinguishing features, if they could be called remark-able at all.

"Noble fire drake, mightiest of your race, I rejoice in your survival. There is yet a chance for your glory to be saved. Let us free you of these insolent oafs so you may take your place at Sovereign's side."

While the cultist prattled on, Talia spoke low so that only Brode and Holt could hear. "We should attack now."

Brode raised his hand just enough to stay her and whispered, "Is that them all, Ash?"

"*I think so.*"

"On my signal then," Brode said. "Holt, take the crossbowmen on the right. Talia, take the left. I'll go for the halberdiers. Speed is everything."

Talia nodded.

Holt nodded too. Sweat gathered on his brow. He'd been given a proper order this time. Brode expected him to contribute.

"Their cloaks are strong," Brode said. "Strike at their heads or between the opening at their front."

His heart pounded worse than before the battle at Midbell. There he hadn't been expected to fight, he'd been surrounded by a friendly army, and Pyra and Talia had had free reign. Now they were outnumbered and confined by the forest. But they had magic. That alone should be enough for an easy victory, shouldn't it?

Holt tensed. What was Brode waiting for?

The cultist still droned on. "Any of these supplicants would gladly give themselves to satisfy your hunger. The Shroud," the lead cultist stood again and raised his cowl, "are at your service."

Pyra growled dangerously. "*I refuse. Go now and do not insult me with such offers again.*"

The leader didn't miss a beat. "Mighty drake, if you cannot speak freely with your jailor beside you, let us take their head. The red-headed one is yours, yes?"

Pyra snorted plumes of smoke.

"Pyra," Brode said warily, "you must stay cal—"

Pyra stomped forward, crushing roots beneath her. The force of her next words could have laid armies low, could have shamed the most arrogant of kings.

"*No one threatens my human. Your bones will be ash.*"

And before Brode could say anything, Pyra opened her jaws and gathered fire. At the same time, a halberd-wielding cultist in a blood-red cloak dropped his weapon and ran forward.

Brode spun, seized Holt by the shoulder and pointed at the red-cloaked cultist.

"Blast him!"

At once Holt started gathering light in his palm, but under the pressure he faltered and had to restart. While he charged his Lunar Shock, Pyra unleashed a jet of fire toward the lead cultist. Pyra's fire never made it to him. The red-cloaked cultist ran into its path, raising his cloak as though it was no more than rain, and absorbed the brunt of the attack. As the fire subsided, the cultist stood unphased with only smoke rising from him.

A beam of white light narrowly missed him next.

*"Did I hit him?"* Ash asked.

No one answered. It was all happening so fast and Holt was stunned.

The lead cultist seemed unconcerned at the whole affair. He sighed loudly. "You have succumbed, noble one. Better death than a life of servitude."

Each cultist bowed their head and chanted, "Sovereign mourns this loss."

Several things then happened at once.

The lead cultist drew a vial from his cloak and downed its contents. All the cultists snapped out of their chant, lowered halberds or raised crossbows, and moved in as one.

Talia darted left.

Holt's Lunar Shock was ready, so he raised his palm to strike when Brode stopped him.

"Focus on the crossbows," he said. "I'll take the leader."

As Brode charged off, movement flashed in Holt's peripheral vision. The closest green-cloaked cultist at the edge of the group had turned to aim at him. Holt dropped to the ground and heard the bolt whoosh overheard. From the earth he aimed his charged attack at the cultist. Even using his left hand, it was hard to miss at this range. And laying on the ground, he aimed for the softer, exposed foot of his target. His Lunar Shock had such force behind it that the cultist's foot snapped backward with a sickening crunch.

Holt scrambled up and drove his sword through the opening of the man's cloak, just like Brode had said. The man's howl of pain ceased in a wet gurgle.

Something twisted inside Holt then. Not guilt this time. Not fear. Something he could not describe nor had any wish to linger on. He'd killed someone. Not a bug, but a person. This was not a rider's duty. But his blood was hot, his life was on the line, and another of the crossbowmen was taking aim at him.

Holt was too far away to close the gap even with magic fueling his legs. A Lunar Shock would take too long to build.

The cultist changed aim at the last second and released. Ash shrieked in pain. The bolt had lodged above the dragon's right leg.

"No," Holt cried, but was he relieved to see Ash still charging the cultist. The bolt must not have penetrated his scaly hide too deep.

Holt followed. As Ash tore the crossbow from the man's grip, Holt stepped forward and brought his blade down in the most basic of overhead strikes. The steel struck at the base of the man's neck, but the sword's edge met heavy resistance from the cloak. It felt like trying to hack against stone.

Ash was on the cultist then, crushing him into the ground, biting his shoulder and tearing with his talons. The cloak didn't last long under such strain, but the fact it did at all was beyond impressive.

Two more cultists remained on Holt and Ash's side of the fray. He glanced to check on the others.

Brode fought both the leader and the crimson-cloaked cultist. They were giving the old rider with a Champion's body a hard time, which should have been impossible. What had that cultist drunk?

Holt understood now why Brode had been afraid.

Talia had carved her way through two crossbowmen as well, but the remaining pair on her side were running to join the halberdiers closing in on Pyra. She was faring worst of all. Five bolts pierced her purple scales, and her movements were sluggish. A tail swipe might have taken the halberdiers out, but she didn't have the space to make such a maneuver. She swatted clumsily at the advancing halberdiers, knocking a few aside while the others drove their pike-like weapons into her. Only one managed enough force to break her scales and then make little more than a papercut, but they had the dragon hard pressed.

Before Holt could help, he had to finish his task.

His remaining two targets trained on Ash as the main threat. They released their bolts at the dragon. One shot missed, the other grazed Ash's neck.

Across the bond, Holt felt the dragon's pain. It was all Ash could do not to roar from it. In response, Ash's eyes flashed pure white and he fired a powerful beam back at their foes. He missed again, but it separated the two cultists. One stumbled back, reloading a bolt. The other dove forward and came close enough to Holt that they dropped their crossbow and drew a sword instead.

That was bad. Holt wasn't prepared for a real sword fight, not without his magic. Quickly, he pulled on light from Ash's core. The dragon bond burned in his chest, its beating as fast as the fight he was in. He had to be careful. If he drew on too much magic then the bond would fray, and he'd be left useless.

Worse still, the cultist approaching him was clearly trained.

Holt fell for his opponent's feint and only evaded because of his temporarily heightened agility. With the cultist exposed, Holt sliced across the man's waist, but the cloak blocked the cut as though it were made of plate armor. Now too close to make an effective maneuver, the cultist rammed into Holt, pushing him to the ground. The man placed his weight down on Holt's left side so he couldn't raise his free palm for a Lunar Shock.

"Ash!" Holt called, unable to focus enough for a telepathic command. But Ash of all of them would hear him.

Two more beams of light flashed, followed by a shrill cry. Ash must have hit the last crossbowman.

*"I got one!"*

"Wrong... one," Holt choked out, struggling now as the cultist weighed upon him. "Here..." He tried to raise his sword, but the cultist pinned his elbow with one knee and readied to drive a blade through Holt's belly.

Holt let his sword go and pushed magic to his right palm. Too quickly. But he had no time. His palm burned and the Shock was only half-formed when he let it go, but it drove the cultist from him.

Holt staggered up, leaving his sword behind, and started forming another Lunar Shock. Ash took the cultist down for him.

Holt gasped with relief. He checked his side. All their enemies were lying down, dead or dying. He could not see the face of the farthest one, a blue-cloaked cultist, but they lay unmoving. That must have been the one that Ash hit.

Thinking his side clear, Holt checked on the fight at large.

The red-cloaked man was down.

Brode still exchanged blows with the leader.

Three halberdiers thwarted Talia's attempt to reach the remaining crossbowmen. Each had a scarlet cloak of their own to counter her magic and seemed to match her speed. They must have drunk the same substance that their leader had.

Pyra struggled to remain upright. Nine bolts were in her now. A bolder cultist stepped in and lunged, planting the axe head of his halberd into the thinner hide of her back. She had enough lucidity left to snap her head around and clamp the man between her jaws.

One halberdier's body lay blasted off far from the melee, as if hit by the concussive lunar magic. But that meant—

A thwack and wet thud drew Holt's attention. Ash clawed at the ground, growling a suppressed roar of pain. A fresh bolt protruded from his side. The blue-cloaked cultist had risen to a crouch, not dead as Holt had presumed. Ash had not hit him with his beam; he'd accidentally hit one of the halberdiers instead. And it was no man wrapped in the blue cloak. Her hood had fallen.

She had blond hair pulled back off her face – such a normal face. Who were these people? Why were they doing this?

She began to reload her crossbow. Holt howled in rage. Person or no, she had tried to kill his dragon. They all had. And they would pay for that mistake. His palm burned, his new Lunar Shock fully charged. In his fury, Holt gathered extra power in his untrained right palm, searing that whole arm as magic flowed through it. He brought both his hands together for a greater Shock than he had harnessed before. For a moment it was as though a star's worth of light gathered between his hands.

The cultist raised her cloak like a shield, perhaps thinking he wielded ice magic. Holt's attack blew a clean hole through the material, hit the cultist in the chest and sent her hurtling back. She landed in a crunching sprawl.

His bond with Ash strained dangerously. He could barely see through to Ash's core now and could not afford it to fray. Carefully, he let the connection drop. Holt gasped from the sudden plunge back into base humanity, feeling the acute ache of his muscles again. But there was more to do.

First, he checked on Ash. The dragon was back on his feet, though he wobbled. Blood trickled from his wounds and dripped from his teeth and talons, stark red against the white of his scales. That seemed wrong to Holt, like seeing a kind dog going savage.

*"I don't feel well,"* Ash said. He stumbled forward as though learning how to walk for the first time.

*Poison,* Holt thought. *Those bolts are tipped with some sort of poison.*

A clever tactic from the cultists. Kill the dragon first and the rider's magic dies with them.

And Pyra had nine bolts lodged in her.

"Still good to fight?" Holt asked.

Ash shook his head as though to clear it. *"Yes, boy."* Then he sniffed out Holt's sword, picked it up and brought it to him. Holt had all but forgotten it.

"Thank you."

*"Can you still fight?"*

"Magic or no, I'm not quitting."

Ash growled his approval, and they headed to help the others together.

Brode still fought the leader. The cultist was on the defensive now; the effects of his potion seemed to be wearing off.

Pyra had lost more ground to the cultists. Her eyes drooped, but she seemed to have accepted her lot and made the best of it. As the spike of a halberd sank into her, she bit down on the shaft of the weapon, pulled it free, and then dragged the cultist wielding it in closer to finish him off.

Talia had managed to kill one of the three fire-proof halberdiers defending the crossbowmen, but she was now pinned between the remaining two. At some distance from them, she poured fire at both halberdiers at once – a jet from her hand and a jet from the tip of her blade. Sweat poured down her face from the effort. This slowed her opponents but each advanced doggedly. Their scarlet and crimson cloaks were artfully raised to shield their whole bodies, and the fire burst off the material without harm. Their weapons were lowered and poised to strike should Talia give pause for just a moment.

The remaining crossbowmen had free reign to shoot either Talia or Pyra, and with Pyra nearly poisoned to a standstill, they seemed to think a stationary Talia was the better target. Both turned to take aim at her.

Words would have taken too long, so Holt passed a wordless communication to Ash – a sense of the danger to Talia and the intent to take the crossbowmen down.

Ash broke off to take the one on the left, Holt focused on the right. These cloaks would deflect his sword and his magic was all but spent. He did all his worn mind could think to do and jumped onto the back of his target, wrapped his arms around the man's neck, and pulled to one side.

The cultist yelled in shock. His shot went wild. They collapsed to the ground.

Holt rolled in the mud, tussling with the cultist in a wild scrap of flailing limbs. Somehow, he managed to bring the pommel of his sword down upon the man's head. Protected by his cowl, the cultist's skull did not crack, but the man gasped as though all the wind had been knocked from him. Dazed by the blow, the cultist ceased moving. Holt seized his chance. He scrambled upright, found the opening at the front of the cloak and stabbed down.

Exhausted, feeling as though his arms would fall off, Holt got back up and found Ash had finished off the very last crossbowman.

Talia, however, was in trouble. Her pair of attackers had crept close enough to strike with their weapons.

"Come on," Holt called. Then, with the last of his strength, he ran toward the exposed back of the closest halberdier. He and Ash took that cultist down together, just in time.

In the same instant, Talia's second foe lowered his crimson cloak and thrust his halberd forward; a one-handed strike, so fast, so hard, it would have run a wild boar through.

As strong as the potion had made him, Talia was still quicker. She extinguished her flames and swerved the attack by mere inches, then advanced and pinned the shaft of the halberd against her body. The cultist heaved but it was no good. Talia clove the shaft in two with her rider's blade.

Her enemy did the only sensible thing. He tried to run. Talia stamped hard at the back of his cloak. It caught and pulled him down. As he tumbled backward, Holt saw a glimpse of mail armor even beneath the powerful protection of the cloak. Not protection enough for a rider's blade though, as Talia found her opening.

Holt stood, panting.

Talia whirled around in a blur of golden-red hair. "I had that under control." She wiped the sweat from her brow. "Thank you, though," she said before running off at an Ascendant's pace to relieve Pyra.

Holt took a few steps, meaning to follow, but dropped to the ground. Concern from Ash flowed over the bond, and Holt sent reassurance back.

"Go on," Holt gasped.

Only three of the eighteen Wyrm Cloaks remained now. The leader broke away from his duel with Brode, running to his two comrades facing Pyra.

"Time to retreat," he called. "Sovereign will take them in the end." He downed yet another vial of the unknown substance. His fellows dropped their halberds at once and downed fresh vials of their own.

With that, they scattered in three separate directions. The leader went east, one south, and the other west. Just like that, the fight was over.

# 35

# PIECES OF THE PUZZLE

Holt remained kneeling on the dirt and damp of the forest floor. He'd felt weak enough even before the exertions of the battle. Now he fought to stay conscious. Thankfully, a faint beat let him know the bond had not frayed. But if they got into another fight now and he drew on any more magic, it would fray for sure. Then he'd be useless. Still, the bond had burned hot during the skirmish, meaning its strength must have developed due to the battle. Time would tell.

"Is anybody hurt?" Brode called.

Groaning, Holt struggled to his feet. "I'm okay…"

He trailed off as he took in the aftermath of their battle for the first time. Bodies. Men and women. Torn cloaks. And blood. Everywhere blood. He'd had the fortune to pass out at Midbell. At the Crag, they'd been burning or covered in ash.

Holt had killed some of these people.

He retched. Bile coated his mouth and he coughed and spat, desperate to be rid of the taste. Bent double, he gasped only to suck in the sticky air of the Withering Woods.

Brode was by his side then. "You're all right," he said, heaving Holt upright and pulling him into a rare embrace. "You're all right."

Holt sobbed. Tears rolled before he could stop himself, and he pressed his face hard into Brode's shoulder.

"I'm sorry," he choked.

"You're all right," Brode said again, patting Holt's back. "You did well. Very well."

Holt gulped, trying to control himself.

"They wanted to kill you," Brode said. "They weren't nice people. They wanted to kill you and skin Ash. You're all right."

Holt's heart began to subside. His breathing settled.

After what seemed a long time, he righted himself and pulled back from Brode.

"Ash got hit," he said, still half-dazed.

He searched for the dragon and quickly found him closer to Pyra and Talia. By the time they caught up, Pyra's legs finally gave up supporting her weight. She sank to the ground with a heavy thud.

"There are so many," Talia said as she yanked out another bolt lodged in Pyra. She inspected the arrowhead, then tilted it to show Brode. "Looks specially hardened."

Brode picked up one of the crossbows. "Heavier poundage than I've seen before. Mechanical crank. Superior to a standard military issue."

Pyra groaned and slowly blinked her big amber eyes.

"Is it poison?" Holt asked.

"A numbing agent," said Brode. "A potent one and extremely difficult to acquire. A lot of time and money is spent by these zealots preparing for just one attack."

"Only they couldn't have been preparing for us specifically," Holt said.

"No... not for us," Brode said. Whatever he was brooding on, he seemed to push it to one side for now. "I'll take the bolts out of Ash."

"He's my dragon," Holt said. "I'll do it."

"That poison can affect a dragon the size of Pyra," Brode said. "Do you want to find out what it will do to your unenhanced body if you accidentally cut yourself?"

Holt's next words died in his throat. He'd rather not find out. Plus,

Talia seemed to be heaving with a great effort with a bolt stuck fast in Pyra's haunch. If they were hard to remove, Holt certainly didn't have the strength. He knew when to back down.

"Fine," he said, but he stood by Ash's side anyway. "For moral support."

Brode knelt to inspect the two wounds on the dragon. "This will hurt." He grasped the first bolt and pulled hard. Ash yowled and dug his talons into the earth.

"There's no need to apologize," Brode said. Holt blinked in confusion, then realized Ash must be speaking to him privately. "We made it through... don't worry... you'll get better with practice."

On his last words, Brode pulled the second bolt free. Ash growled, and his neck drooped from relief. Nearby, Pyra stifled a cry of pain. Talia had removed the final shaft.

"Everyone catch their breath," Brode said, "while I decide what to do. Keep those ears peeled, Ash."

As Brode moved off to inspect the body of the red-cloaked cultist, Holt rubbed Ash's neck. The dragon stretched out his limbs as though waking from a deep sleep.

"Is that better?"

*"So much better."*

"What was that between you and Brode?"

*"I wanted to say sorry for missing my first shot."*

Holt was taken aback. "Why apologize for that?"

Ash groaned, a deep rumble in his gullet. *"I want to say sorry to you too."*

"For what?" The answer sprang to him; the moment in the fight when he'd been flat on his back, the cultist poised to stab him – Ash had missed with his lunar beams. "Don't worry about that."

*"You nearly died."*

"But I didn't."

He pulled Ash in for a one-armed hug, but the dragon shrugged him off.

*"And if I'd managed to hit Brode's target, Pyra's fire would have killed the one with the screechy voice."*

"I fumbled gathering my own Shock. I wasn't much help either."

Ash was not placated.

*"I didn't hit anything I meant to."*

"It's not your fault. You're bli—" Holt didn't know why he cut himself off. Admitting it felt somewhat harsh, even if it was the truth. Admitting it always felt like a stone dropping through his gut.

*"A dragon should overcome challenges,"* Ash said, more fiercely than usual. *"To fail is shameful."*

Holt grabbed Ash's head and pulled him down to look him directly in the eye. Those milky, ice-blue eyes. Perhaps he was wrong to try and avoid the subject. If he tiptoed around the issue then Ash might too, and whatever inherited memories he had were making him feel bad enough already. Holt decided not to dance around it anymore, to face it head-on, both the good and the bad. For there was definite good in it as well.

"Ash, we'd likely have all been caught off-guard and killed if you hadn't heard them coming. You saved us."

Ash growled, but the sound was lighter than before.

"And like Brode said, you can practice hitting a target. You'll get better. But you could never have trained to have hearing like yours."

Ash's growl turned to a hearty rumble. He gently pressed his snout forward toward Holt's face, just like they'd done when he was a new hatchling. Holt pressed his forehead against Ash's snout, feeling the vibrations rumble from his throat. Warmth, joy, and an unspoken thanks passed through the bond.

*"I will think on your words."*

"Excuse me for interrupting," Brode called, "but I think we should move on."

Holt parted from Ash to find Brode squatting by a blue-cloaked halberdier. He'd pulled the cloak aside to reveal the man wore plate armor. That was even more unusual than wearing chain mail. Only distinguished soldiers had access to plate armor: specialized shock troops trained from birth, heavy cavalry, high-born commanders, knights, or the riders themselves.

"Are these cultists noblemen?" Holt asked.

"Some of them may be," Brode said. "A fanatic can come from anywhere. But they all have it, the front-line fighters I mean."

"I didn't realize Wyrm Cloaks were so well equipped," Talia said. She was still close to Pyra, her arm wrapped over the base of the dragon's neck.

"Aside from their cloaks, they rarely are," Brode said.

Holt went to the closest dead halberdier and bent to inspect the cloak. The name Talia and Brode used for the cultists strongly suggested what they were made of, but he wanted to confirm it for himself. He ran a hand over the cloak and found it rough as stone, as rough in fact as Ash's scales.

"Dragon hide," Holt said. Whatever the cultists did to make these cloaks, it made the hide about as light as leather without losing its toughness. He reached inside and found a couple of vials he'd seen the cultists take out during the fight. Taking one out, he found its contents to be a red so dark it was almost black.

"That's dragon blood," Talia said, sounding as disgusted as Holt felt.

"And they drink this?" Holt asked.

"It's how they can keep up with us," Brode said. "For a time."

Holt dropped the vial, though holding it had left a bad taste in his mouth. "I don't understand. You said they worshipped dragons? Why would they kill them and skin them and—"

Just the thought of drinking that blood made him want to vomit again.

"They call themselves the Shroud," Brode said. "But we call them Wyrm Cloaks – keeps their crimes clear. You saw firsthand what effective protection their cloaks grant."

"Even against magic," Holt said.

"Dragon hide repels magic well enough," Brode said, "but it almost entirely negates magic of its own type."

"That's why those with the red cloaks came for me," Talia said. "Too well coordinated by half."

Holt was disgusted. "So, they go around killing dragons for their scales?"

"What they want, Holt, is for dragons to rule over humans."

"But... what? Why?"

Brode shrugged. "Broadly, there is a feeling that this would end all human suffering – squabbles between kingdoms would end because there would be no kingdoms. Humanity would be united under dragon rulership. The scourge would be destroyed by the might of the flights."

"But dragon riders fight the scourge," Holt said. "If they worship dragons, why kill them too? It makes no sense."

"I didn't say their logic was sound," said Brode. "In their eyes, we weak humans don't revere dragons enough, and that's why the Wild Flights keep to themselves. They hope that in destroying the Order, the Wild Flights will emerge and take their rightful place as our overlords."

"They're insane," Talia said.

Holt bit his lip. The cultists – the Wyrm Cloaks – probably were insane, but they seemed to be a real threat. Given the fact they all had dragonhide cloaks, it must mean they had killed plenty of dragons.

"So why were they here if they are all about hunting riders?"

"That's what I'd like to find out," Brode said. "A group this size, this well-equipped, deep inside a decaying forest in a small kingdom at the edge of the world where riders aren't likely to come by—"

"We shouldn't get distracted," Talia said. "We have a mission already."

Brode nodded in the direction the cultists had come from. "Their camp must be close. They arrived quickly after Holt's display with the trees."

"What if there are reinforcements?" Talia asked.

"Their leader ran east," Brode said. "They came from the north. If there was hope of help back there for him, I think he'd have retreated that way instead."

"Southeast is where we should be going," Talia said. "To Sidastra. To deal with Harroway, if we must, and save my uncle... the kingdom, I mean."

"Good catch," Brode said. "But you just said it. *Harroway.*" He picked up one of the halberds and made a show of examining it.

"These are fine weapons, not of a standard make either. At the level of craftsmanship of the Feorlen military, wouldn't you say?"

Talia picked one up too and tested it. She nodded.

"And how easy would it be for anyone other than a soldier to acquire such weaponry?" Brode asked rhetorically. "Harder than it was for Master Cook here to take even a dragon egg, I'd wager."

Holt frowned but he sensed where this was going. Even if the cultists – whoever they were – had the funds to buy such weapons and armor from a smith, they would draw the immediate attention of the local authorities. A baker, a weaver, a wick, a brewer; all would raise suspicion. The smiths would likely be too suspicious to sell them anything in the first place, unless the cultists could imitate a knight.

"They could have stolen them," Talia suggested.

"So many at once? Without raising a single alarm from Sidastra to the Crag?"

"They might have their own smiths," she said.

"One or two of their chapters may have a smith," Brode said. "But generally, they pillage materials. Their equipment is often patchy at best."

Talia opened her mouth again then closed it. Brode's theory was too neat to be easily dismissed. As Master of War, Lord Harroway would have been able to supply the Wyrm Cloaks. Yet direct evidence of his involvement, if any, surely would not be so easy to uncover.

Talia apparently thought the same. "Harroway is a careful man."

"That doesn't mean all his underlings are as vigilant," said Brode.

"He was only recently made Master of War," Talia said. "You know I'd be the last person to defend him, Master Brode, but it seems too quick."

"Perhaps these Wyrm Cloaks came from outside of Feorlen?" Holt said.

"It's possible," Brode said. "Even more reason to know what they were doing here. If we don't find the camp soon, we'll carry on. But I feel this could lead us to a link between Silas, the cultists, Harroway and his cabal, and everything else that's gone wrong. Plus, a well-supplied camp means food."

Ash predictably perked up at that.

Holt still felt like there was some intrigue raised by the cultists he wanted to ask about, something the leader had said to Pyra. It was on the tip of his tongue, just out of reach of his tired mind.

Before he could recall it, Talia nodded her assent to Brode's plan, and the old rider strode past them.

"Leave the dead as they are," Brode said. "We can't afford the smoke."

# 36

# THE CHASM

Night descended as they hurried north. Even if the moon and stars could help him, Holt couldn't see them down at the true dark of the forest floor. He felt like he had entered a trance-like state of exhaustion. Mouth parched, belly rumbling, eyes dry, and head sore, he shuffled more than walked. All he carried was his pack with the recipe book and some cooking utensils he couldn't bear to part with. The others carried the rest of the load.

Talia was upfront and held her rider's blade overhead. A constant swirl of fire encircled the sword, creating a torch for them to see by. Pyra stepped heavily and seemed unable or unwilling to keep her head held to its usual lofty height. Ash padded loyally beside Holt, although the dragon was quiet. Burning out the cultists' poison took its toll on the dragons.

A few hundred paces seemed like a league or more. Yet march they did, until a lurid green light flickered ahead.

They approached cautiously, but Ash assured them he could hear no heartbeats. The trees thinned as they passed – chopped to stumps or rotted away – until they came upon a sprawling campsite. A ring of wooden stakes marked out the perimeter. The cultists had been close to them then. Yet what lay beyond the campsite stole Holt's last strength away.

The forest floor dropped into a jagged ravine, its sheer opposite side half a mile away. He approached the precipice to peer down. A thick fog cloaked the depths of the gorge, through which only gray-green light filtered out as if through a poisonous mist. The air reeked of death and felt so close it could be cut with a knife. Yet it was more than that. Holt felt the place press upon his heart, threatening to turn his blood cold and even suck the warmth out of his bond with Ash.

"Search the camp," Brode said. He went off on some mission of his own. Talia began rifling through the base as instructed.

Too weak, Holt stayed put. He wasn't sure he could have taken another step and instead found himself transfixed by the canyon. Above all else, it looked crooked, unnatural.

*"Holt, there's food here. Holt!"* Ash's voice was like a lighthouse in this nightmare.

"W-what?" Holt said groggily.

He'd half turned when a small loaf of bread was pushed into his chest.

"Food," Talia said. "Eat this before you pass out." She tore a chunk out of her own loaf.

Holt took a bite and his jaw tingled as the muscles worked back to life. The bread was a chewy rye and tasted luxurious to his starving mouth. Good condition too.

"They must have been resupplied recently," he said through a mouthful.

"What makes you say that?"

"If the bread were stale, it would be hard to say when it arrived." He swallowed. "But as it's not, it must have arrived within the last four to five days."

"Mm," Talia said. She gave him that intense studying look again.

Holt ravenously tore off another large chunk of his bread and chewed fiercely. "What?" he asked of her.

She shrugged. "I couldn't have gleaned that from bread."

He swallowed a little too hard and nearly choked. "You don't know when bread goes stale?"

"Never needed to know, pot boy." She took a bite, and it was clear she found it distasteful. "I admit, I don't know how people of your rank put up with this stuff. It's so... *mealy*."

"It tastes of something," Holt said, taking another great mouthful. "That white stuff nobles and riders eat is way too sweet."

Talia shook her head and continued chewing.

They ate quietly for a while. As Holt's energy and wits began to return to him, he found eating near this green trench entirely unpleasant. Judging from the eerie light, the sickly stench, it could only be related to one thing.

"This is a scourge chasm, isn't it?" he said. He'd heard of them in passing before. Although he'd never had a clear picture of them.

"It's not too big," Talia admitted. "Could be why we never found it."

"Not big?" Holt said, astonished.

"You've heard of the Great Chasm, right? And the Northern Tear?"

Holt nodded, though he couldn't have said where the Northern Tear was beyond the obvious geographical direction.

"Those chasms were the openings to the largest incursions in history," Talia said. "The Great Chasm destroyed the Aldunei Republic in a single stroke. Ripped the ancient city in two. I've seen it." She spoke as though the mere memory was frightening. "Saw it from Falcaer Fortress when I went to forge my blade."

"And this is small compared to that?" Holt asked.

"It looks endless when you're there," Talia said. "I can't speak for the Northern Tear, but it must be huge. They say it shook the foundations of one of the Storm Peaks until the mountain collapsed."

Holt gulped. "So... the scourge attacking Feorlen came from here?"

"A lot of them," Talia said. "The biggest bugs, for sure. It's unpredictable where a chasm will erupt, but if the Order catches them quick enough then the waves of scourge can be better controlled."

"I suppose the forest hid it."

"Maybe," Talia mused. "During the day, the green mist wouldn't be so noticeable from high above." She turned away from the chasm, looking back toward the cultist camp. "I fear we know why no hunters or jacks ever reported it."

Holt followed her gaze. Brode had returned and was standing in the middle of the cultist camp holding a woodcutter's axe. There was something unsettling in the way he stood there with his head and shoulders hunched. Even the dragons stopped eating to pay attention.

"There's a pit." Brode's usual gruff voice had fallen to darker depths. "A few hundred yards west of the camp... I couldn't count the bodies in the dark..."

He seemed to want to say more but couldn't. He slammed the axe into the ground and balled his fists.

Holt stood stunned. It wasn't like Brode to lose his demeanor like this. The old rider breathed hard, his chest rising and falling as though he were struggling for air. How quickly had he moved between the camp and the pit? Or was even Brode reaching the end of his Champion's strength?

"We can't even burn the bodies," Brode ended darkly.

Holt looked to Talia for some indication of what they should do or say. Seeing Brode like this, almost defeated, made him more afraid than the chasm. Talia gave Holt a worried look, then approached Brode as though going to his sickbed.

"Master Brode, are you okay?"

Slowly, as though in pain, Brode raised his head. He looked to her, then to Holt, then leaned his head back as if seeking answers in the stars.

"Spending a lifetime in an endless fight against the scourge could seem futile," he said. "Even when I lost Erdra, I clung to my duties. The fight had meaning, and I still had a purpose. How fate conspires to show you how naïve you are."

Both Talia and Holt said nothing. What could you say when your mentor and guide seemed lost?

"These tents are military quality too," Brode said. "Well supplied. This is no rabble."

"I can't piece it together," Talia said. "Why would Harroway work with the Wyrm Cloaks?"

"You said he dislikes the Order," Holt said.

"His faction doesn't want the riders wiped out," Talia said. "Just to take less in tax, or ideally take none. Pay for their own upkeep. That sort of thing. Everyone knows we need the riders because of the scourge." It seemed like she was trying to convince herself it wasn't true, but it was impossible to escape reality in this grim place. "Let's say he did recruit the Wyrm Cloaks. Why then would they be defending the location of the scourge chasm like this? Why would anyone want to hinder our efforts against the scourge?"

"Silas would want that," said Brode.

Holt continued picking at his loaf. He agreed with Talia that it didn't add up, couldn't add up. "We went over this before and couldn't make sense of it. Why would an anti-rider cabal work with Silas of all people? Harroway can't have condoned Silas driving the scourge into the kingdom."

"And why would the Wyrm Cloaks take orders from a rider?" Talia said.

"There has to be some explanation," Brode said fiercely. "I won't believe that Silas turning traitor, your brother's death, his implications of Harroway's cabal, and heavily armored Wyrm Cloaks defending a scourge chasm is all mere coincidence. Someone sent these cultists here."

Holt's thoughts still circled around the puzzle of the cultists. He remembered now what their leader had said and the question it raised.

"The cultist leader spoke of someone called Sovereign," Holt said.

Brode frowned. "I don't recall that..."

"Holt's right," Talia said. "Only I can't remember the cultist's exact words. It's not a term I remember from reading about the Wyrm Cloaks. They've rarely had a united leadership, and when they do, it's a Grand Master."

"Maybe the name has changed," Holt said.

"Maybe..." Talia said, but she didn't sound convinced.

Pyra joined the debate then, rumbling deeply to let them know she was about to speak. Then her voice entered Holt's mind.

*"I recall everything that wretch said. He told me that there was 'still time for me to take my place at Sovereign's side.' But I'd sooner die disgracefully than stand side by side with whichever fool of a human leads them."*

As Pyra finished speaking, Talia's expression turned from despondent to ecstatic.

"That's it," she said. "Whichever fool of a *human* leads them."

Holt blinked, still unsure. He finished off his loaf in the hopes that his brain might work better.

Talia barreled on regardless, more animated than she'd been in some time. "Who would the Wyrm Cloaks follow above all? Not some human. They want dragon rule. This Sovereign – whoever they are – must be a dragon."

Silence reigned as the idea sunk in.

"A dragon, you say," Brode said. "It's... possible."

He seemed to be warming to the idea, but Holt wasn't so sure. The notion of an evil dragon struck him as wrong somehow. They protected humans. They were the whole reason the riders existed and could beat back the scourge. Then again, Clesh had gone along with Silas's betrayal.

Brode seemed to sense his dilemma. "Dragons aren't all that different from us, Holt. Anyone is capable of evil."

*Not Ash,* Holt thought. He sent a pulse of his own across the bond, which the dragon returned.

"Even if it is true," Talia said, sounding weary again, "I'm not sure how this helps us... *wait.*" She pointed to the sky and drew her sword. Above them, dark clouds raced to blot out the stars, clouds that had suddenly appeared in a clear sky.

Lightning flashed to the west. Holt started counting. The thunder struck in less than three seconds. Silas was less than a mile away.

"Drop everything," Brode said, drawing his own rider's blade. "We'll run."

# 37

# THE STORM LORD

Fresh lightning forked across black clouds and the thunder drowned out Brode's words of flight.

With a heavy heart, Holt emptied his pack of what utensils and pans remained from the Crag to lighten his load. He kept the recipe book though. That he would not throw away.

Even performing such simple motions left him dizzy. He might have gotten something to eat, but his lack of proper sleep was starting to make him feel delirious.

*"You aren't strong enough to run, boy,"* Ash said.

"What choice do I have?"

It wasn't like Brode or Talia could realistically carry him. But how would he keep up? He blinked, grinding knuckles against the corner of his eyes. Shook his head. Just staying awake was an effort.

Just then, Pyra smashed through the campsite toward him. She knelt on all fours and snaked her purple head around to face him. He met her glowing amber eyes.

*"Get on, little one."*

Before he could think, someone grabbed him by the waist and hoisted him up onto Pyra's back. It turned out to be Talia. Princess Talia was lifting him bodily into the air. Too tired to think any more of it, Holt scrambled into position between two of Pyra's spinal ridges and clung on for dear life.

"Move," Brode called.

And they were off, heading east at haste through the remainder of the forest. Talia's blazing sword lit the way. Pyra no longer cared about stealth and crashed through the undergrowth, likely drawing on her magic to smash obstacles aside. On occasion she and Talia burned a path for them. And all the while, claps of thunder hounded them.

A part of Holt, the servant in him, thought their effort folly. A servant might run from their master's whip, but they'd be caught in time. They might outrun Silas for a while, they might even make it out of the forest, but if Silas had their trail, he'd catch them in the end.

But who was he fighting? Why was he calling on magic which would, and had, alerted them to his presence?

His addled mind fumbled considering it. It was about all he could do to stay seated on Pyra as she wove between the trees. Time meant nothing to him now. He only stayed awake by drawing on morsels of magic across his strained bond.

In his mind's eye, Ash's core flickered dangerously, like a candle at the end of its wick. Yet the beating remained. Always there. Beating fast now as Ash ran and fear held them in its grasp.

Holt couldn't see Ash, but he could feel him close by, following Pyra as she carved out a path with brute force. The beat of the bond became frantic, and Holt feared the effort of keeping pace with Pyra would be too much for Ash.

*"You ran for me,"* Ash told him. A memory of smoke, of fire, of screaming flitted across the bond. *"I'll run for you."*

They ran for hours and the world began to lighten, both from the approach of dawn and the thinning of the trees. Until, in what seemed a sudden burst from darkness, the endless trees dropped away, and the party emerged from the Withering Woods.

Brode and Talia came to a skidding halt. Pyra attempted the same but required a longer distance, gouging deep wells of earth as her talons dug into the ground.

Holt hadn't a clue where they were. He wanted to ask the others, but he could barely open his parched mouth.

"I think we lost him," Talia said jubilantly. She bent over, clearly exhausted and at the breaking point of her Ascendant's body.

Yet even as she spoke, the storm clouds gathered. What little pale light of dawn there had been was snuffed out, and a dragon roared. A roar of fury, of deep rage.

Brode raised his sword. Talia moaned and drew herself upright. Holt attempted the same out of solidarity, even knowing it was futile.

Silas had caught them.

Clesh swooped down from the clouds, landing with a monstrous thud, roaring all the while. Holt had not appreciated Clesh's size before now. Four war horses could have stood side by side within his great frame. His tail was as long as his body, his wings great enough to sweep a company off their feet. His granite-gray scales looked as impenetrable as stone, and his eyes lit with a fierce blue power. Holt had thought of Clesh as a venerable old dragon at first, but now, gripped in his full fury and power, Clesh looked more of a force of nature, a savage yet calculating beast.

Silver-blue sparks hissed in the air. A tingling ran over Holt's body, causing the hair on his arms to stand up.

Holt crested out with his burgeoning magical senses and felt a power so dense, so pure, it caused everything around it to seem dim. He hadn't felt this when Silas arrived at the Crag, because he'd been blind to it then. This was the power of a Lord, and it was not something to contend with.

Great gobs of spittle sprayed from Clesh's mouth as he roared one final time, subsiding into a satisfied growl. He'd cornered his prey. He folded his wings, and Silas leaped from his back. Silverstrike near flew himself as he crossed an inhuman distance in one jump to land before them.

Silas hadn't drawn his sword. The jagged, sparking blade remained on his back. He regarded them coolly, although Holt had the uncanny impression that Silas was taking a moment to catch his breath. His white wind-wild hair was matted and dirty, his breastplate scratched in thick lines. Somehow, he was as worn out as they were. Despite his toil, Silas smiled at Brode.

"I hoped it was you."

"If you're here to kill us," Brode said, "be done with it."

"Save yourself, Brode," Silas said. His voice sounded sad and tired, the musical lilt in his voice now strained. "I only need the girl."

"To kill me like you killed my brother?" Talia spat. A plume of fire blew back from her shoulders like a phoenix. "Blight take you." Then she launched a jet of flames at Silas. He deflected it with a lazy wave of his hand.

"Lay your brother at my feet if you will," Silas said, clenching a fist. Talia fell to her knees, caged and bound by lightning she could not push free from. "One more hardly matters now."

At once, Pyra reared back and rushed forward. In answer, Clesh stomped closer, making Pyra's footsteps seem like a child's. A wave of his power hit Holt, and the sheer force of it nearly knocked him out cold. For a second, he blacked out, knew how Ash saw the world, then came back to reality. Pyra had halted. Trembling, her neck was bent low to the ground.

Ash left the relative safety behind Pyra to come out and stand between her and their enemies. He flexed his talons, spread his wings and stood defiantly as if to defend Pyra.

"Who is this?" Silas asked.

Holt felt the Storm Lord bear into him, not with his gaze but through magic. An unwelcome touch raked over his soul. Holt winced.

"A Novice and a sick hatchling," Silas said. He looked at Brode and nodded gently. "Of course, you would spare them. You always had a soft spot for the downtrodden."

Clesh snarled and snapped his jaws. Lightning coursed around his dagger-sized teeth.

Silas threw his dragon a glance. "Really? Must the hatchling die too?"

"*The whelp is weak.*" Clesh's voice sounded like a raging storm. "*Broken. An insult to our race. Sovereign will not tolerate it.*"

Clesh spoke of Ash as though he were a 'thing'. Despite his fatigue, anger burned in Holt's chest, anger enough to push the hateful presence of Clesh away.

He'd spoken of this 'Sovereign' as well. Talia's theory may well be true. Though they weren't going to live long enough to do anything with that information.

"Fine," Silas said, his tone both harsh and resigned. Of the pair, it seemed the dragon was the dominant one. Was he forcing Silas to do this?

"Why do this, Silas?" Brode asked. "What's in it for you?"

"I hope it ends the scourge, or else it will all have been for nothing. A waste." Clesh snorted, roared, clawed at the ground, and the sky rumbled. Silas gave them a grave look. "Also, I'm afraid I don't have a choice."

"End the scourge?" Brode said. "You're working with them, controlling them!"

Silas shook his head. "Sovereign commands. My role was to remove all riders in the land." He looked imploringly at Brode. "You're not a rider anymore, not really. My offer stands. Leave while you still can. Don't make the same mistake twice."

Brode ran one finger up his blade. "Running is your way. Not mine."

Silas snorted. "You *chose* to stay behind that day."

Brode remained surprisingly calm. "Our oath is to protect the innocent and fight the scourge. We'd never run before."

Silas's fury turned his face gruesome. A bolt of lightning struck the ground beside him, though whether on purpose or out of anger, Holt didn't know.

"Our oath is to *defeat* the scourge. We can't do that if we're dead. Clesh and I stopped the incursion at Athra. And for what?" He spat those last words. "So that years later we fight them all over again. Now that is a waste."

Holt could hardly believe what he was hearing. Silas spoke of fighting the scourge, yet he worked with them now; he'd killed so many of the Order. The smoking bodies of Mirk and Biter were all too clear in his mind. And then he saw his father's face, the moment when he'd thought Holt was speeding off to safety.

His anger boiled over. He jumped down from Pyra's back and staggered forward. Reaching Ash, he placed a hand on the dragon and felt stronger for it.

"The real waste was ever respecting you."

Silas frowned. "I don't recognize you, boy."

Without warning, Ash jerked his head to the side. *"Someone is coming. From the forest. I hear their... heart?"*

*"Cultists?"* Holt asked, finding telepathy easier now their bond had grown a little.

"His name," Brode said loudly in answer to Silas, "is Holt Cook."

*"It's not human,"* Ash said. *"But it's not dragon either."*

"He worked in the Crag kitchens," Brode continued, "and he's more a rider in his fool heart than you've ever been."

Clesh bellowed in fury at that and began gathering power at his mouth.

*"There's no time. End them!"*

Silas unsheathed his sword.

Brode looked at them all. "Goodbye," he said, then he started running, right at the Storm Lord. Talia's scream was muffled by her lightning cage. Silas's magic kept her encased, and Pyra was still cowed by Clesh. Desperately, Holt tried to summon power for a Lunar Shock – anything at all to help.

But he should have learned by now, like Brode had told him, that things were not going to just work out.

Brode screamed Erdra's name as he charged. He may have had the body of a Champion, but he lacked a bond and access to magic. He reached Silas, attacked, and met only air. Silas side-stepped – making Brode look as clumsy as Holt at swordcraft – and in one fluid motion ran his blade up Brode's back. Blood spurted, and Brode's black traveling cloak fell, cut clean away.

Before Brode could even fall to the ground, Silas caged him with silver lightning as he'd done to Talia, lifted him high, and threw him aside. Holt watched in horror as Brode's prone form flew as far back as the tree line of the forest.

Talia cried out again. Pyra let loose a chilling growl. Ash wailed.

Holt was too stunned to do anything. He couldn't take his eyes away from Brode's smoking body, even though Silas was seconds away from killing them all.

Suddenly Ash went quiet. *"It's here."* He spoke with the same reverence as Holt had once held for Silverstrike. And then Holt saw it.

He wanted to say someone, for the figure that emerged from the Withering Woods wore a cloak with the hood drawn. Yet it wasn't a cultist cloak, and judging by its sheer size – at least seven foot tall – it could not be truly human. Still, it had a human frame, and its cloak was so dark that it reminded Holt of the harvester of souls from children's tales. Instead of a scythe, the figure held a tall spear with a glassy orange blade that looked like a rider's sword attached at its tip. Its hands were covered in what Holt took to be scaled auburn plate armor.

Stranger than the mysterious figure was the reaction of Silas and Clesh. Both stepped back as though in fear before Clesh unleashed the full might of his gathered breath at the new arrival.

The creature in black spun its polearm and a hazy, transparent veil formed in front of it. Clesh's lightning bolt crashed into the swirling veil and dissipated. Clesh attacked again, but the figure kept moving, pushing back against Clesh's might. Silas raised his sword and lightning struck from above, over the creature's magical shield, yet the creature rolled to evade at blinding speed. Then, in what seemed the blink of an eye, the creature closed the distance in a single blurred step. One moment it was thirty feet away, the next it was right before Silas and bringing its polearm down. Silas blocked it. The boom when those strikes met was a thunderclap all of its own.

With Clesh and Silas distracted, Talia's cage dissipated. She scrambled upright, half choking as she fought to regain her breath. Together, she and Pyra eyed the fight, but Holt thought they ought to stay well back. Whoever or whatever the creature in black was, it was going toe to toe with Silas and Clesh at the same time.

It may even be winning.

"We need to go," he called to her. Talia looked between him and the titanic fight and nodded.

Holt called for Ash and ran to check on Brode, stumbling on legs as stable as jelly. Pyra could carry Brode's body. They could get away.

Stray lightning struck in Holt's path and sprayed him with dirt.

He ran on. He made it.

Brode was lying face down, his back a bloody, torn mess.

Holt dropped to his knees. "Master Brode?" He turned the old rider over. Brode's eyes were closed, but he still drew shallow rattling breaths.

"Help!" Holt called as Talia joined him. "Get him onto Pyra."

Talia dropped down to join him. She took Brode in her arms but didn't stand.

"What are you waiting for?" Holt said.

"It won't help."

"He's not dead!" But Holt's words were lost amidst a crack of thunder.

*"His heart barely beats,"* Ash said.

"What then?"

No one had an answer for him.

A howl of pain from Clesh brought Holt's attention back to the duel. The creature in black had pierced Clesh's side. It pulled the orange blade free and spun aside to avoid Silas's counterattack. The creature's cloak lifted as it moved – revealing a reptilian tail.

It slid back and readied itself in a guarded stance, but Silas did not advance. He ran to Clesh instead and jumped onto his dragon's back. The Storm Lord then took off, dispensing a storm of lightning at the figure on the ground to cover himself.

This at last seemed to make the creature sweat. It wove deftly but was struck, grounded by the power of the strike. Recovering, it stood, raising and aiming its polearm as if intending to throw it after Silas. But as Clesh shrank into the distance, the creature thought better of it and lowered its weapon.

The clouds parted, revealing the beautiful morning they'd been hiding. Light stung at Holt's tired eyes, and he raised an arm against it. Something slick ran off his forearm onto his head. Blood.

Brode's blood was on his hands.

That thought he couldn't escape. If he and Ash hadn't been with the group, Brode and Talia might have flown to Sidastra long ago. If he'd never stolen the egg, Brode and Talia would at least be safe and well. He, Holt, would have fled with his father from the Crag and been with him right now.

Ash sensed his turmoil and sent him comfort through the bond. The beat was steadying now Silas had gone, although the mysterious creature might just as quickly turn on them. It remained in place, as though guarding against Silas's return.

Holt felt Brode stir. The old rider reached out a hand, and Holt took it in his own. He didn't know why he did that. It just seemed the only thing to do. Talia mirrored him, taking Brode's other hand. She had blood on her too.

With a great effort, Brode half-opened his eyes.

Holt seized his chance. "I'm sorry," he sniffed. He wanted to cry, but his drained body couldn't muster the tears. "I'm sorry."

Brode shook his head. "You two have a job to do."

"Master Brode," Talia managed to say through falling tears.

"Get to Sidastra. Warn the others. Save the kingdom."

They nodded, although the task was insurmountable.

Holt felt Brode's grip slipping. Brode struggled to speak now, each breath wet and choking.

"You can't die," Holt said.

"I died once already," Brode rasped. "Everything since has been borrowed time. It's been too long."

"We need you," Holt said.

"We're not ready," Talia said.

Something dropped to the grass nearby. Ash stood over Brode's sword and nudged it toward them with his snout. Brode struggled to speak, but his smile conveyed it all. Holt tried to pass it over the bond so Ash could understand, but it was too hard to focus.

"He says thank you," Holt said.

Ash started a sad rumble in his throat, and Pyra joined him.

Talia reached for Brode's blade and placed the hilt into his hand. Holt brought Brode's other hand to the hilt as well. With the last of his strength, Brode grasped his sword, and then his fingers fell limp. He let out a shuddering sigh and closed his eyes.

# 38

# THE EMERALD FLIGHT

Holt couldn't think straight. Brode lay limp between him and Talia.

"Brode?" Talia said, as though he'd only dozed off. "Brode?" Her voice cracked like a breaking branch.

A shadow loomed over them, and Pyra and Ash growled. The creature in black planted the butt of its polearm into the ground and lowered its head.

"I would step away, if I were you," the creature said. Its voice sounded like a human nobleman but contained an edge of something dragonish, something larger than himself.

Holt did not.

"It's for his own good, you know," the creature insisted.

Talia got up first. She trembled but stepped away as the creature instructed.

Holt remained. He couldn't move. Brode had been the only rider who'd ever treated him like a person rather than with irreverence. A bastard who had become a rider.

Beneath the creature's hood, two huge blue eyes flashed like sapphires. Holt felt a presence cresting toward his soul again, but unlike Silas's clawing reach, this one was gentle.

"How curious," the creature said. It offered out a hand to Holt. Up close, the true nature of the creature became plain. It wore no plate armor. Those burnt orange scales were real and covered the whole back of the creature's hand. Morphed human-like fingers, equally scaled, ended in blue fingernails thick as talons.

Ash came over and pushed on Holt. With that, Holt got up, but he did not take the creature's hand.

"I see manners are still lost on youth."

Holt ignored him. It felt wrong to leave Brode to die on the ground. Even as he thought this, roots sprouted from the earth. Huge perfect leaves blossomed and enveloped Brode, covering his face. They tightened.

*He'll suffocate*, Holt thought. He tried to move, but a swirling barrier of power blocked him.

"It's helping him," the creature said. "Be humble and respectful and he may live. The Emerald Flight has arrived."

As soon as the creature announced this, dragons in all shades of green glided over the edge of the Withering Wood. Holt stopped counting after a dozen. They maintained a tight formation like a flock of birds until suddenly they scattered and landed to encircle Holt and the others.

No dragon had a rider, and they were all the same type. Emeralds empowered by nature magic. Holt had somehow found himself in the middle of one of the reclusive Wild Flights.

"Fear not," the creature said.

"Are you with them?" Talia asked. "Who are you?"

"I'm not *with* anyone." He lowered his hood to reveal a face caught somewhere between human and dragon. The human had won out, but there was a serpentine nature to his nose. Scales in shades of autumn leaves covered him like skin. Instead of hair he had sinewy blue flares and small ridges running down to the nape of his neck. When he spoke, it was clear his teeth were largely human except for two small fangs that hinted toward the dragon.

"My name," he said with a flourish, "is Rake."

Talia's jaw dropped and Holt ground his knuckles into the corner of his eyes, unable to fully believe what he was looking at.

"I know," Rake said. "Do try to contain yourselves at my magnificence. I suggest you remain calm. The West Warden does not favor vivaciousness."

Rake faced the center of the newly formed ring and took a knee.

No one protested. Even Pyra lowered her head without a fight.

A pair of great wings beat in the air, and a final emerald dragon appeared. This one was as large as Clesh and dark as pine needles. It landed remarkably gently in the center of the circle of lesser emeralds.

Rake spread his arms. "Hail the West Warden," he began loudly. "It is my great privilege to have fulfilled the burden set by your Elder."

The West Warden's tail flicked much like Pyra's did when she was annoyed.

*"The Elder would have desired fewer losses."* The scorn in the Warden's voice reminded Holt of riders speaking to subordinates when in a foul mood. *"A good thing you sped so far ahead of the flight to see your task complete."*

"An excellent thing," Rake insisted, without missing a beat. "And your timely arrival saves me having to find you in turn. A fine end to the *days* I spent hunting him."

*"Very well, soul-cursed. Your actions did prevent further harm to my flight. For that, I judge your bargain with the Elder fulfilled. You have earned our favor."*

Rake bowed theatrically. "Your fairness is matched only by your knowledge of birds." Then he got up and seemed ready to leave Holt and Talia to their fates when the Warden called him back.

*"Stay, Rake. We are not done here."*

Rake bowed graciously again.

*"What of the younglings?"*

"Oh them," Rake said as though he'd forgotten. "Yes. They had the pleasure of watching me save their lives, honored Warden."

Green smoke puffed out of the Warden's snout. *"They are lower members of the Storm Lord's Order. They must have been assisting him."*

"Not unless Lords train their juniors by attacking them with full force," Rake said. "Then again, it has been a long time since I trained there myself."

The Warden was not amused by this. He turned his attention to the group. A second later, his eyes narrowed onto Ash.

*"Blindness..."*

Two emeralds bared their teeth and advanced upon Ash. Ash backed away and the bond began to thrum.

"Hey," Holt cried. Throwing respect to the wind, he got up and ran to Ash's side. "Keep away from him."

Desperate, Holt looked imploringly to Rake. Their would-be savior gave him a look as if to say, 'you're on your own.' Even so, Holt swore that Rake tightened his grip upon his polearm.

It was Pyra who acted. She ran in between Ash and the two emeralds, snarling and gathering fire.

*"Back with you,"* she cried, her burning power evident in her voice. It must have been draining the last of her core to do so. *"Back with you or face me. I who have inherited verses from the Fire Elder himself, he who bent the searing mountains to his will. This hatchling is under my protection."*

She ended by snapping at the air.

Despite the danger, Holt beamed.

*"You'd give your life for the hatchling?"* the Warden asked. *"Never have I known a daughter of fire to tolerate the weak."*

*"He is the greatest weapon in the fight against the scourge,"* Pyra said.

The Warden gave a hearty rumble of laughter. *"I doubt that."* He lingered upon Ash. *"Hmm... a song I do not recognize."* Next, his full gaze fell upon Holt. Once more, Holt had the sensation that someone was observing his soul. *"And your connection... so pure..."* This seemed to trouble him. *"Prove what you claim."*

Another emerald from the circle came forward. This one had several packages hanging from vines around its neck. Each was a bundle of the same type of large leaves covering Brode. One of the vine straps snapped free and then slithered through the grass to lie before Ash. Finally, it unwrapped, revealing a cut of bramble bush. The bramble was more thorn than fruit, and what blackberries remained were turning green and oozy.

"Are you strong enough?" Holt asked.

*"I think so,"* Ash said. *"For something small."* White light – its core so bright that its edges appeared dark – gathered at his snout before he

gently pressed it onto the bramble. As expected, the bush was cured. Its thorns shrank then fell off, and its fruit swelled in size and ripened.

Every emerald in the vicinity began growling or rumbling in surprise.

The Warden's eyes widened in shock. He inclined his head. *"I have judged too hastily. Settle now,"* he added with a look to the emeralds advancing on Ash, but they were already backing away, their heads also inclined.

Holt sighed in relief, as did Talia. Rake nodded and lowered his weapon.

*"Excuse the actions of my flight,"* the Warden said flatly. It was crystal clear he didn't mean it.

"No," Holt said. "I won't."

Rake winced.

"Holt…" Talia moaned.

It wasn't smart, he knew. Brode would cuff him and tell him he was thinking with his heart again, but he couldn't help it. If Pyra could change her attitude, so could these wild dragons.

"You shouldn't just kill dragons like Ash. Admit it, you wouldn't have stopped your dragons if he couldn't cure the blight."

He felt the Warden's magic press against his soul again, more forcefully this time, like a healer conducting an examination.

*"Perhaps you are right, child,"* the Warden said, sounding almost sad. He recovered and continued. *"These discoveries will be of great interest to my Elder. No emerald before has been born with such gifts. We sensed his power distantly in the woods. A fragment of the blight cleansed away. We believed only a Lord of your Order would have such power."*

*"I am no emerald,"* Ash said. *"I am a son of the moon. My song is written at night."*

Every emerald present reacted to that revelation. If dragons could exchange shocked whispers, these emeralds were doing so. They growled lowly, rumbled in their throats, and twisted their heads from side to side to look at one another.

*"Lunar?"* the Warden mused. *"A magic of light. Yes… that may explain it. Step forward, Ash."*

Tentatively, Ash did so. His oversized blue eyes were fixed on a point somewhere far past the Warden's right wing. The Warden then lowered his head, as though he might glean information from proximity.

*"Ah, yes, I can hear notes akin to the moon and stars. Immature, yet there as the songbird chirrups his first melody. Yes, you are a son of night."*

"Now that is quite something," Rake said. He looked at Holt again with great interest. It reminded Holt of his father scrutinizing a new and exotic recipe, and he didn't feel entirely comfortable about it.

*"A new flight is born, and the world grows,"* said the Warden. He threw back his head and roared; roared as though the whole world had just bent before him. For a dragon, this was joy unbounded. His latent power became tangible around them. Petals bloomed from thin air; rock and stone burst from the ground, rising as though untethered to the world; and tremors ran through the earth.

As quickly as it began, it ended. The Warden regained his composure, although he too had a hearty rumble in his throat now.

*"My Elder spoke wisely. I should not have lost faith in the natural world to grow a solution."*

"If I may ask, honored... Warden," Talia began carefully, "why were you in the Withering Woods?"

*"The blight affects all, child. This troubles my Elder deeply. Yet centuries of attempting to undo its rot have been in vain. The power of the Life Elder can reverse the corruption of the scourge, but it takes a great deal of his strength to do so, and then only in a small way."*

Holt gasped. This Elder was surely one of the most powerful beings in the world, attuned to the natural world, and even he struggled to do what Ash could.

*"Harmonizing our collective songs can achieve more than one of us alone, yet even if we spent eternity doing so, the spread of the blight would win."*

"You mean, it's constantly spreading?" Talia asked.

*"Piece by piece it conquers the land. The woods first, which are our home. But the truth is worse. The blight burrows, its grasping roots run deep. Poison leaks at the ocean floor, and in the cellar of the world, dark things move unseen. When news reached us of a new presence in this land, we were sent to see if the corruption is abolished easier when fresh. Alas, not by enough. It gladdened my heart when I felt a portion of the horror in the woods vanish in an instant."*

"It was just one tree," Holt said.

*"A drop of water during a drought is gratefully received."*

"But why Ash?" Talia asked. "Why his powers rather than fire or the healing possessed by some emerald or mystic dragons? We don't understand."

The Warden snorted, drew his head back, seeming to look at the horizon. At last he seemed to decide upon something.

*"What do you know of the origins of the scourge?"*

"Very little," Talia said. "Only when the first incursion attacked the world and the riders formed. That's over a thousand years ago now."

*"I remember it well."*

"You were there?" Talia said in awe. "But of course, you were, mighty Warden," she added hurriedly. She even curtsied.

Rake smirked.

Talia's face went bright red, but she soldiered on. "Do you know something of how the scourge began? Some reason why lunar magic would be so effective?"

The Warden looked at Talia, then at each of the others in turn, ending with Holt, and quickly looked away. *"Much of the scourge remains a mystery."*

Holt thought that a lie. The Warden had clearly hesitated. It was a common enough thing Holt had noticed in his time. Powerful people, important people, were less subtle around their subordinates than they thought they were.

*"However,"* the Warden continued, *"the scourge is not natural. We should know. Foul powers took an existing race of insects and turned them into the bane of the world. Do you know of which race I speak?"*

Talia and Holt exchanged a look.

*"Their venom rots their victims, for that's what they desire to feed upon. They prefer darkness below ground."*

Talia had the tell-tale face of trying to rack her brain for an answer. Holt hadn't a clue. There were probably loads of insects he'd never heard of.

*"The vethrax."*

Realization crashed into Holt. "Omens of death. They tried to take our rotting meat in the forest. Brode... Brode said they hate daylight."

*"All light."*

"But the scourge can move by day or night," Talia said. "They favor the night, in fact. It doesn't hinder them."

*"The powers which enhanced the vethrax made their poison strong. Strong enough to negate the effect of the sun or moon that their lesser brethren cannot bear—"*

"But a magical light would even out the power difference," Talia finished. "Just as it takes an Ascendant to equal an Ascendant in physical strength."

*"Ash throws much into question,"* the Warden said. *"I must inform the Life Elder at once."* As he spoke, the leafy case containing Brode rose and floated over to land before him. *"This one carries an echo of our flight. Distant. Notes of sorrow. Yet from afar I assumed him to be the one we sought. Alas, soon those notes will pass forever."*

A lump formed in Holt's throat.

It was Talia who managed to speak, "The man you speak of is our tutor." She fell to one knee again. "He was gravely wounded by Silas the Storm Lord. Will you not help him?"

*"Only my Elder has such power."*

"There must be something you can do," Talia said. "Your servant, Rake—"

Rake threw up his hands. "I made no such guarantees."

*"I should hope not,"* said the Warden. An edge had returned to his voice again. *"Nor would any such promise bind me or my Elder. Rake, soul-cursed, is no member of our flight."*

Holt dropped to his knees too and clasped his hands like a beggar. "Please, we need him."

*"To claw life back from death disrupts nature. It is a desecration. Even were it in my power, I would not do this."*

Talia sobbed and hid her face. Holt desperately wanted to cry but nothing would come. Only painful heaves of breath. His eyes felt raw while his nerves *were* raw.

The emeralds began taking off one by one.

"Help *us* at least," Holt said hoarsely. "Help us fight back against the scourge and Silas."

*"We do not interfere in human lands. That was the pact made when your Order formed."*

Holt failed to see what some agreement made that long ago had to do with anything. He was about to say more – he had nothing to lose in trying – when the Warden spread his wings.

*"I am sorry for your loss,"* he said. *"As a parting gift, my flight banishes your weariness and heals that which would heal in time."*

A fresh wave of power emanated from the Warden. Holt felt it vibrate through the air. When it struck him, it banished all the aches in his body, his hungry stomach became full, and he felt as refreshed as if he'd woken from a deep, dreamless sleep. The dragon bond too felt whole again, but Ash's core wasn't replenished – the Life Elder could not simply transfer him lunar motes, after all. Holt could hardly complain. He hadn't felt this good since Ash had hatched.

Pyra was especially pleased. Her wounds from Midbell and battling the Wyrm Cloaks healed over, leaving no scars. She stretched her now mended wings, flexing them with a nervous energy.

*"Go forth and do your duty as I must do mine."* The leaves around Brode began to unwrap. *"As for you, Rake, come in your time and seek an audience with the Life Elder."*

"Actually," Rake said, thumbing his polearm as though this were all causal, "I'd like you to grant me my favor now."

One emerald dragon actually stopped mid-take off at those words.

The Warden narrowed his eyes. *"I cannot give you what you have asked for."*

"Well then, it's a good thing I'm changing what I'm asking for." Rake smiled, threw Holt a wink, and then nodded toward Brode's body. "I'd like the old man there to be healed."

The Warden snorted green smoke, and the grass beneath his talons grew then shrank at an alarming rate. *"You waste your favor on this?"*

"You said your Elder had the power, after all."

*"He will not do this thing."*

"Ask him anyway. My mind is made up." Rake bowed again, too theatrically to be entirely respectful.

*"So be it."* At once the leaves regrew around Brode's pale body. The West Warden growled at one of his subordinates, and the emerald

picked up Brode in its talons before joining the others as they climbed higher into the sky.

With that, the Warden took off without another word.

Rake turned his back on the flight, smiling mischievously at Holt and the others.

"Finally, we're alone."

# 39

# AN IMPOSSIBLE TASK

Rake continued grinning at them even when no one responded with enthusiasm in turn.

"Where are they taking Master Brode?" Talia demanded. With her strength back, she'd regained her royal tone. Either that or she didn't think Rake worthy of the same reverence as the Warden.

"They're taking him to the Life Elder," Rake said slowly, as if Talia were a slow child.

"And where is he?" Talia asked.

Rake shrugged. "Don't give me that look. The Emerald Flight likes to move around. But I'm sure one as learned in lore as yourself knows that."

"I'm just trying to—" She calmed herself. "Can it really be done?"

"He wasn't fully dead," Rake said. "There was still a fluttering of brain activity. The leaves of the Emerald Flight will keep him stable for a long time."

"He was still alive?" Holt asked.

"Gracious no," Rake said. "His heart stopped, but the mind continues a little longer. The things you discover as a mystic! No, I'm afraid he's a corpse, but as fresh a corpse as the Life Elder could hope to receive."

Holt wondered whether the Life Elder frequently received corpses but reckoned Rake was being dramatic. Despite his misgivings, Holt found himself drawn to the orange half-dragon.

"So," Holt started tentatively, "this Life Elder can actually bring him back?"

Rake shrugged again. "If anyone can, it's him."

"The Warden said the Elder would refuse," Talia said.

"The Elder can't make a decision on a request that isn't presented to him," said Rake. "Besides, there may be other benefits to sending your mentor to the Elder."

"What does that mean?" Holt said sharply.

"It means I hope I haven't entirely wasted my favor with the Elder. Do you know how hard such things are to come by?"

"Why do it then?" Talia asked.

"I've taken a liking to you."

Despite Talia's ire, Rake couldn't remove his permanent curling smile. It wasn't as if Rake had to fear either of them, even combined. He'd driven off Silas Silverstrike, and from reading between the lines, it sounded like Rake had been skirmishing with the Storm Lord for days. Rake's insistence on helping Brode also made him trustworthy in Holt's estimation.

Now Holt's bond with Ash had been patched up by the Warden's magic, he decided to try checking Rake's core. Rake was unique to say the least, and Holt wanted to understand more about him. Moreover, the constant checks from other people and dragons made the intrusion seem commonplace, and he felt left out.

Gingerly, he pulled on a thread of magic from Ash's core and crested his mind outward, slithering to inspect the dragon – or whatever he was. As he did so, he found something strange. Rake's core was there but also not there, as though a transparent box hid something invisible inside of it.

Holt risked drawing on a little more power and focused harder. Straining, he didn't get a glimpse of Rake's core, but he managed to hear a few notes of his song. Or was it songs? There were two strands to the music, almost in harmony with each other but just slightly off, as though one strand echoed the other seconds later.

What little Holt heard spoke of a rich power but also discord written in long ago.

Not wanting to drain Ash's depleted core dry, Holt stopped and opened his eyes.

"Have a good look, did you?" Rake asked.

"I don't understand," Holt said.

"You're veiling your core... somehow," Talia said.

"I value privacy."

Talia ignored him. "The emerald Warden was stronger than Silas. Not by much, although it's still amazing that he is at all. How do you compare to him?"

"About equal," Rake said. "But the Warden is at least thrice my age," he added proudly. His smile dropped then, and he became serious. "I was once a human and rider like you. And yes, I am more powerful than a Lord, and in other ways not as powerful. My journey – our journey – ended in this half-life."

Talia bit her lip, her brow creased. "There are no ranks beyond Lord."

"What about Paragon?" Holt asked.

"Paragons are the most powerful of the Lords," Talia said. "You can't possibly gain more power than, well, one hundred percent of your dragon's core."

"How then do you account for the Warden's strength or his Elder's?"

"A dragon's core still grows," Talia said. "Paragons are the eldest surviving Lords, those who have had the time to Forge their dragon's core to incredible heights. Old wild dragons might reach such power in time, but it would take them much longer."

"Centuries," Rake said. "Millennia for some."

"But you're not a dragon, are you?"

"What am I?" Rake began. "A pertinent question for a keen mind. Not even I am sure. And I cannot be more than a Lord, you say, and yet I tell you I am. However, I think these are questions for more peaceful times. In any case, you two have me at a loss. We've not been properly introduced." Rake seemed cheerful at the idea of something so banal.

Talia introduced herself first.

"An Agravain?" Rake said. "I think I met your great-grandmother once, or was it your great-great-grandmother? Charming woman, whichever ancestor it was. And a relentless tease." Talia was spared a reply as Rake dipped into another theatrical bow. "Your Highness. A shame I hadn't known ahead of time. Securing the promised favor of a royal is nothing to be sniffed at."

"Come to Sidastra with us then," Talia said. "Help us defend it against the scourge and I'll ensure that my uncle rewards you, if that's what you want."

"Tempting, but I only want *one* thing, and it's not in the power of any human, whether monarch or pauper, to give."

"Won't you help us anyway?" Holt asked.

Rake ignored the question. He instead crossed the distance between himself and Holt in that same, rapid, blink of an eye movement he'd used when fighting Silas. He dropped his polearm and got down on one knee. Even then he was still a towering figure.

"And you, Holt, who is your family?"

A sudden nervousness came over Holt. What if Rake dismissed him for his birth? After all, he'd been a rider once and a nobleman. Telling off the emerald Warden had felt instinctual to Holt. He'd been defending Ash, and he hadn't cared for the Warden's approval.

"My family are Cooks," Holt said. "I am Holt Cook. Son of Jonah Cook. We worked in the Crag's kitchens."

"A servant?" Rake's blue ridges flared. "It's good that you are used to toil. Your hard work is just beginning, Master Cook."

"You don't care?"

Rake extended a scaled finger and gently lifted Holt's head so that he looked the half-dragon in the eye. Rake did the same to Ash and looked between the two of them.

"Once I would have," he said, "but now, I know what it's like to be different. An outsider."

*"Did it get easier for you?"* Ash asked. It was one of the only times Holt had heard Ash speak in a truly sad tone. It caused an ache in his chest.

"No," Rake said, "but I decided to stop defending what I was and merely present it forthrightly. No apologies. It didn't stop the scorn, but I didn't care so much after that."

Ash inclined his head. *"I will think on this, Master Rake."*

Rake smiled, genuinely this time. "So how did a commoner join the Order?"

"He stole Ash's egg," Talia said.

"Really?"

Holt folded his arms. "I like to think of it as *saving* Ash's egg."

"Well, you have spirit, that's clear. And were it not for you, we would not have Ash, so I applaud your madness."

"Master Brode called it foolish."

"There's a fine line between a fool and genius. Clearly a genius in this case as you joined the Order."

"They never found out," Holt said. "I haven't taken the oath yet."

Rake's eyes widened at that. Holt got the uncanny impression he was being sized up again.

"It's a long story," Talia said.

"I'd like to hear it," said Rake. "The Warden may not care about human affairs, but I do."

They explained to Rake everything that had occurred since the attack on the Crag, up to the battle they fought at Midbell and the Wyrm Cloaks guarding the chasm in the woods. When they finished, Rake ran one hand up and down the shaft of his polearm, deep in thought.

Pyra stamped and belched flames into the air. *"We should not tarry here with idle chatter."*

"Idle chatter?" Rake said. "But it is all rather exciting... with some minor distresses thrown in, to be sure. Silas Silverstrike. Hero of Athra. Leading the scourge, working with Wyrm Cloaks and attacking wild dragons... although I suspect he came to the woods hunting you two and became... distracted. On their own, none of these things connect, but they must. We're missing something."

"That's what Brode thought," Holt said.

"Then he was a wise man," Rake said. "I fear these events are not isolated to Feorlen or Silas alone."

"No incursions have been reported elsewhere," Talia said. "Not from the Skarl Empire, Risalia, Brenin, or any of the Free Cities."

"True enough," Rake said. "I roam widely, and scourge activity has been low. Too low, I'd say. Unnaturally so for years now. And Silas isn't the only rogue rider I've heard of."

"What?" Holt gasped.

"Don't be so shocked," Rake said. "Riders have turned off the... moral path before now."

"Who else apart from Silas do you know about?" Talia asked eagerly.

"In the here and now?" Rake asked. "There are no names. Only vague stories. But the Wild Flights are angry. Each has lost members of late – drakes are disappearing or turning up dead. They move in groups now like the emeralds you just met. They're afraid – yes," he added when Pyra snorted smoke, "even dragons can be afraid."

Holt looked at Ash, remembering the attack on the Crag. "I know they can."

"And the emeralds were afraid enough to ask for your protection," Talia said. "Better you risk yourself than send more of those Wardens."

"Spoken like a pragmatic leader," said Rake. "And yes, something like that. Honestly, the Life Elder may have just wanted to get rid of me. I've been entreating for his aid for years and, I think, under pressure to improve safety for the group heading west, he saw an opportunity."

Holt knew Rake wasn't telling him the whole story. Had he really been working for years to secure something from the Life Elder only to drop it the moment he ran into Talia, Pyra, Ash and himself?

"But why would Silas or any other rogue rider attack wild dragons?" Talia asked.

Holt's head started to hurt from all of this. Nothing added up. Everything seemed backward. Cultists famed for killing dragons of the Order were trying to recruit them, while rogue members of the Order were killing wild ones.

"I don't think attacking is their first priority," Rake said. "I managed to arrive in time to save one group of emeralds from the Storm Lord. They told me that his dragon – gray fellow, what's his name?"

"Clesh," Talia hastened to answer.

"Well, apparently Clesh had urged the emeralds to join a cause for all dragon kind."

"Sovereign." Both Holt and Talia said the name together.

"The cultists mentioned him," Holt said.

"And Silas did too…" Talia said. "Something about Sovereign commanding him."

"Yes," Rake said. "The emeralds under my care said the same. Slowly the curtain lifts. Too slowly, I fear. This puppet master has long been at work. He has powerful servants and been hitherto unnoticed. To refuse the invitation to join him is to die." He scoffed. "I'm offended I haven't been asked yet."

"This person," Talia began hesitantly. "I mean, well, it cannot be a person, can it? The cultists wish for dragons to rule. Wild dragons would not follow a human either."

"Talia thinks a dragon is behind this," Holt said.

"It makes the most sense," Talia said. "Doesn't it, Rake?"

"Don't go seeking my higher authority. If you're sure, then stand by it."

"Okay," Talia said, a little hesitantly. "Then, yes, I do think a dragon must be behind all of this."

"I agree," Rake said with a wink. "Not that this helps us understand their motives, or anything about them, or what their goal is in all this. Quite the mystery!"

"Do the Wild Flights think another dragon works against them?" Holt asked.

"Your guess is as good as mine," Rake said.

"Seems like the emeralds should have stayed to help," Holt said. There was a mountain of chores to get on with, so to speak, and many hands make light work.

"It's not their place," Rake said.

"And what does that mean?" Holt said. "Sounds like they are trying to get out of the job just because it isn't strictly theirs to do. The stablehands and maids would pitch in to help us with the extra work during a feast." He felt a heat rise to his cheeks. Old frustrations with the rigidity of the system he'd grown up in had sprung up with renewed vigor. Dragons were meant to be better than this. "What does it matter whether the Order are supposed to deal with the scourge alone – it affects the wild dragons too, doesn't it? We need help. Now."

Ash puffed his chest out and roared in agreement.

"They can't just act as they've always done," Holt said, "if it means everything burns."

He saw the ruins of the Crag, the ash falling, the burned town and the bodies. The same would happen everywhere if nothing changed.

"What would you do about it?" Rake asked.

"I… I don't know," Holt said, his outburst fizzling to a halt.

"In my time," Rake said, "I've discovered that change must be hard-earned. No rider of the Order can progress in rank just because it would make sense to do so. They must fight for it. And you must fight for it."

"I just don't understand," Holt said. "Dragons are part of the Order. They know how important this is."

"Chaos spreads now," Rake said. "And when chaos comes, people cling more desperately to what order they do have. Dragons too. This Sovereign threatens to destabilize everything. I must go and find out what I can."

"You're leaving too?" Holt said. He couldn't believe it. Not after all of that.

"An enemy unseen cannot be struck."

"Please, Rake," Talia said. "I know we are the ones who owe you our lives, but the lives of all the people of Feorlen are at stake."

With a sudden movement, Rake lowered his polearm and lunged at Talia. She had no chance to defend herself, but Rake held back his strike.

"It has been a frightfully long time since I left the Order, but I wasn't aware their teachings had softened. What have we just discussed? Will it make you stronger if I fight your battles for you?"

"There are tests by combat, and then there is suicide," Talia said, not taking her eyes off the pale orange shard inches from her face.

"All the more impressive should you survive," said Rake. "And all the greater your strength will be for it."

"If I wasn't a rider, it would be my kingdom – my people."

"Your kingdom?" Rake purred. "Your people? Hm. That sounds like a reason to fight as hard as you can." He withdrew his weapon, straightened, and tightened his cloak about himself. "Besides, I am hardly welcome in polite society. And you'll reach Sidastra quicker without me. I can't fly." He looked seriously at Holt. "I gambled away a chance to get the one thing I want on you. I need you strong if it's to pay off. Fight hard. We will meet again."

And with that, Rake left them, running east at a pace that would shame a horse.

Holt, Talia, Pyra and Ash were on their own.

At length, Talia spoke. "Fine then, we'll go on alone." She spun on the spot as though to gauge their bearings. "I can't say where we are for sure, but we're somewhere on the eastern edge of the woods. Sidastra lies to the south, but by flying it shouldn't take us more than two days." Pyra growled eagerly and spread her wings, ready to take to the skies she yearned for.

Holt hesitated. He and Ash had only taken short flights up to collect lunar motes. They were hardly ready for a journey.

"It's like Rake said," Talia began. "We'll grow faster if we push ourselves."

"What if we crash?" Holt said.

Talia shrugged. "Then you crash, pot boy. What's the alternative? Stay out in the open for Silas or the scourge to get you?"

"Brode said you couldn't outfly Silas if he did find you."

She gave him a hard look and said again, "What's the alternative?"

She was right. Holt drew a deep breath and readied himself. "Okay. Okay."

"Stay close to Pyra, and if you're in trouble, have Ash reach out to us."

As Talia mounted Pyra and prepared herself, Holt looked for Ash, only to find he had slinked off. However, the dragon was already returning from across the meadow, carrying a dark, dirty bundle between his teeth. It turned out to be Brode's traveling cloak that had been ripped off in his brief encounter with Silas.

"Good idea," Holt said. "It will be nice to have some reminder of him."

*"I had something else in mind,"* Ash said, dropping the cloak at Holt's feet. *"I wish to cover my eyes."*

"What for?"

*"They call me weak,"* he said. *"I was not supposed to hatch—"*

The knot of guilt twisted horribly in Holt. "Don't say that—"

*"I will say it. I won't forget it. Other dragons never will. They sense my blindness and wish me gone. You were right not to accept the Warden's false apology. Were we not of value against the scourge, they would not care. Rake is different too, but he does not cower or beg. Nor shall I. Cover my eyes so that everyone who looks at me will know, and I will show them I am just as capable."*

Holt understood the strength of Ash's conviction on this. It crossed the bond and made him stand straighter and pull his shoulders back. Taking the knife from his belt, Holt cut a strip of black cloth from Brode's cloak. It was frayed and uneven at the edges but thick enough to cover Ash's eyes. He was about to wrap them when he stopped.

Although he understood why Ash wanted this, Holt found it a shame that those icy blue eyes would be covered; the eyes he'd seen when Ash could still fit in the crook of his arm. The eyes that had taken his heart.

*"What are you waiting for?"*

"Just... getting my bearings. Lower your head right down. That'll be easier."

Ash did. Holt stepped behind the dragon's head, placed the strip over Ash's eyes and secured it. Ash raised his head, and Holt took a step back to admire the effect. He had to admit it worked. Before, Ash's off-center focus or looking entirely in the wrong direction had made him seem submissive, very much a young hatchling in an over-sized body. The black blindfold fixed that. Not being able to see the dragon's eyes made it harder to read him. And it was unusual, the unknown. People feared the unknown. Ash had turned his weakness into an asset.

"I think you look more intimidating."

Ash bared his teeth and growled in mock menace.

"Ready to fly for real this time?"

*"I've dreamed of flying since before I hatched. I'm ready."*

# 40

# A BELATED BIRTHDAY

"If either you or Ash needs to rest on the journey, just say so," Talia said. "It will be no good if one of you drops out of the sky."

"I will," Holt said.

*"Me too,"* Ash told her, although his voice was set. Holt reckoned of the two of them, it would be himself who gave in first.

"And," Talia said seriously, "if Silas finds us, go on without me."

Holt pressed his lips together. He wanted to say 'no' but felt it would only lead to an argument, and this wasn't the time. He just hoped it wouldn't come to that.

"Time to sense-share," Holt said to Ash, patting down the dragon's neck. He bent to pick a tuft of long grass, stood and then reached for the bond. Keeping the connection open, he brought the grass close under his nose and sniffed deeply. Ash padded closer. He picked up on what Holt was doing and also focused on the smell of the grass, on the hints of hay and spring heat contained within it.

As their senses began to blend – easier now than the first time they had tried this – Holt began to speak the words Brode had taught them.

"My eyes for your eyes."

Ash reached out and pressed his snout against the fist Holt held closed around the grass. *"Your skin for my skin."*

"My world for your world," they said together.

At once, Holt's senses altered. He saw farther than mere human sight could cope with, heard bird calls from distant nests, and found his nose bombarded with new smells, among them the earthiness of the dirt and the potent odor of his sweaty, bedraggled clothes. Within his chest, he felt the dragon bond grow taut as the connection steadied.

Sharing their senses wouldn't draw on magic from Ash's core, but it would strain the bond over time. A rest would be required if he didn't want the bond to fray before reaching the capital.

Holt climbed onto Ash's back and braced himself. "We're ready," he said and found his voice contained a faint rumble to it while connected to Ash like this.

Pyra let loose a bellowing roar that took Holt aback with its ferocity. His now sensitive ears rang, and he clasped his hands over them even as Ash roared as well.

Then, with a great lurch, Ash sprang into the air and began climbing toward the clouds. Holt clung on madly, squeezing tight with his legs as his hands scrambled for purchase on Ash's neck. Once they leveled out, Holt breathed easier and they fell in behind Pyra and Talia, following them south.

Holt found the experience overwhelming. Unused to all the extra sensory input, he resorted to closing his eyes for a moment.

*"Keep your eyes open!"*

Holt berated himself. *Idiot.* This was the whole point of sense-sharing. He opened his eyes at once.

*"Sorry, boy."* It was effortless to speak mentally to Ash while sense-sharing.

Holt made a point of keeping his attention faced forward and on Pyra so Ash could follow. It was an odd thing to do, as flashes in his peripheral vision kept tempting him to look around, but he had to stay focused for Ash. The dragon for his part kept his neck and head low to give Holt a clear line of sight.

*"This is so fun!"* Ash said.

Joy passed through the bond, and the tension in Holt eased

because of it. Soon he was enjoying himself too, as much as when they'd first flown.

The world below was small, so small and fragile. Little farmhouses dotted the verdant green-yellow landscape, and even whole villages looked like they'd fit into the palm of his hand.

Yet after the sun had passed the point of midday, Holt thought he could be doing more than merely holding onto Ash. They'd been flying for hours and would be flying for hours more. He should be making the most of every moment to prepare for the fights ahead, just as any good Cook would prepare in the morning for the work of the evening.

First, he checked on his dragon bond. Its edges rippled, but it was far from in trouble. Confident that the bond would hold, he drew as much magic into his soul as he dared and began to Cleanse.

The process was difficult enough under normal circumstances. When he was sitting cross-legged on solid ground, eyes shut, calm, and often next to a nice warm fire. Now, he was beset by the rushing wind, gripping onto Ash lest he topple to his death, and keeping his eyes open so Ash could see where they were going.

But he tried anyway.

Of course, the hardest part of all was that he couldn't hear any crackles in the magic above the din of the wind and the beating of wings. He had to rely on feeling them instead, a much more delicate business. Still, with great concentration and effort, he managed to Cleanse some impurities that had built up since before their fight with the Wyrm Cloaks. Arduous and inefficient though it was, he felt all the better for doing something.

Riders were supposed to push themselves to advance, after all. Rake claimed to have pushed beyond the boundaries of Lord. Who knew what else might be possible?

As daylight slipped into the first dull rays of twilight, the world below began to change and not entirely due to the light. Streaks of land scarred black and sickly green could only mean one thing. The scourge had passed through here. Soon the blighted areas of land grew larger. What farmhouses or villages had once been here now burned with the same dark magic that had taken the Crag. Holt hoped the people had made it to Sidastra. The Summons had gone out long ago. Surely, they had.

His worries turned again to his father. Even now he was somewhere far below, and far south, perhaps sheltering behind the walls of the city, wondering what would happen to him and where Holt was.

*I'm coming, Father,* Holt thought. *As fast as I can.*

Cleansing became difficult with so much fighting for attention in his mind, and the dragon bond began to shake. Though just a warning sign, he didn't want to take any chances.

*"We need to rest,"* Holt told Ash. *"Well, our bond could use a rest."*

Ash reached out to Pyra in turn, and soon they began to descend. Talia had them drop low over a river, following its course south before branching off down a lesser stream. She allowed them to land in a secluded clearing under a rocky hill. A cave granted them some shelter.

"No fire," Talia said as she dismounted.

Holt nodded. "Do you think they're close?"

"The scourge?" Talia said. "I don't think so. It looks like every bug has moved south for the city. We might see the swarm tomorrow as we fly over it."

Holt gulped. Talia thumped a hand down on his shoulder on her way past.

"It's always a lot worse before it starts," she said. "Or so they tell me." She stalked off toward the cave entrance, drawing her sword for good measure.

Feeling suddenly dizzy, Holt shook his head. It was quite disconcerting to return to normal after sense-sharing with Ash for so long. He felt lesser, shrunken somehow, as though he were now looking and hearing everything through water. Tilting his head back, he saw the very first star of the evening twinkle back at him.

"We should sit out in the open as long as we can, boy," Holt said. "Let you soak up as much moonlight as you can."

Talia returned to confirm the nearby cave was safe. Sadly, they had no meat for the dragons. Pyra declared she would go without food rather than risk bringing the scourge or, worse, Silas down upon them. Ash agreed he would follow suit, although Holt could feel his hunger pangs across the bond. The dragon's rapid growth both in size and magic hadn't stopped demanding fuel.

With little else to do, Pyra took refuge inside the cave. Talia followed her inside to Cleanse and Forge while Holt and Ash awaited the moonrise outside. Silver light shone down from the waxing moon and Ash spread his wings as far as he could, exposing every inch of his body to it. The moon was almost full, and Holt wondered what would happen when it was. Would he and Ash feel a power boost from it? And conversely, would they be weaker once the moon waned to a sliver in the night's sky?

For now, Holt checked upon Ash's core. A foggy haze still surrounded the central ball of light. Even so, there were now so many lunar motes flooding in that the whole space was near blinding again. Deciding the daytime was for Cleansing, he began to Forge as many of the motes into Ash's core that he could, knowing he couldn't Forge them all, but each he did was another small victory, another tiny step toward strengthening them for the battle to come.

Losing track of time, Holt only opened his eyes when Talia called, "That's enough."

He blinked and looked at her with a puzzled expression. She was still sitting cross-legged and clearly still Cleansing herself.

"But we must advance," Holt said. "Ash's core needs to be as strong as possible."

"Yes, but if you don't get real rest too, it won't mean much. The Warden's magic was helpful but it's no substitute for proper sleep."

"You're not resting," he said pointedly.

"Someone has to keep watch," she said, fighting back a yawn. "Besides, I can sleep once we're both safe behind Sidastra's walls."

"Safe until a huge scourge army starts assaulting it."

"We'll have a day or two at least," she said. "I hope," she added. Closing her eyes again, Talia returned to her meditations, and that was seemingly her last word on the issue.

Sensing she wouldn't relent, and feeling quite exhausted at any rate, Holt got up and retreated inside the cave. Ash followed, curling up by Pyra at the back of the cavern. Pyra for her part looked frustrated by the confines of the cave, flicking her tail, but she raised no fuss.

Holt sat beside Talia, bringing his knees up to his chest. A wave of weariness overtook him again, one deeper than his bones.

"There is a chance for us, right?" he asked.

Talia opened one eye. "I thought I told you to go to sleep."

"Aren't you worried too? About defending the capital. Facing Silas at some point?" He did his best to remain optimistic, but the future looked grim.

"Doesn't matter," Talia said. "We go anyway. That's what riders do."

"I'm not going to run away," Holt hastened to add. "There's no way I'm abandoning my father. Not after all this."

"Good," Talia said. She closed her eye again. "We'll stand a chance against Silas with an army at our backs."

"What can soldiers do against him?" Holt said, remembering the might of Clesh and Silas as the sky broke and their very power pressed upon his soul.

Talia sighed and opened both eyes this time. She gave him a weary look but softened as she spoke. "You saw the Wyrm Cloaks do damage to Ash and Pyra. We'll have thousands of archers and spearmen and great ballistae all along the walls and atop every tower in the city. Silas and Clesh are powerful, but even a Dragon Lord can't take on an army alone. But," she continued sadly, "I doubt they'll be so foolish as to leave themselves exposed long enough for ballistae to turn and fire on them."

"But... there is a chance?"

"There's a chance."

Talia didn't return to her meditation, but instead played with a stone at her feet. They sat in silence until Holt shivered.

"You're cold," Talia said.

"It's fine," he said, though his teeth betrayed him by chattering.

"Don't be a martyr." She cast a hand around him, and the air grew warmer. His shivering ceased.

"Thanks," Holt said.

"I sometimes forget what it's like not to have an Ascendant's body."

Silence fell again. To Holt's surprise, he didn't find it uncomfortable. Talia too seemed content just to sit quietly, gazing out at the night and listening to the owls hooting. Their first rather tense night after they had left the Crag felt like a lifetime ago.

"It's not the same without... without Brode," Holt said.

Talia sniffed. "Not at all."

Holt mustered his courage to ask his next question. "Do you think he'll come back?"

Talia pressed her lips together, apparently steeling herself as well. "I'm not getting my hopes up."

"Rake wouldn't have asked the Warden to take him if there was no hope... surely?"

"We don't know what Rake would or wouldn't do," Talia said. There was an edge to her voice.

"Do you not trust him?"

"I don't know. He did save our lives, so there's that."

"He's not working with Silas. That much is certain."

"Yes, but all the same, I think we should be careful around him. At least until we know more."

"If he wanted to harm us, he would have," Holt said. He wasn't sure why he was defending Rake. Perhaps it was the way Rake had encouraged Ash. In any case, the orange half-dragon didn't strike Holt as 'evil'.

"He seemed obsessed with the two of you," Talia said. "He didn't take his eyes off you the whole time the emeralds were present unless the Warden spoke to him directly. And I swear he was about to jump in and help you when those drakes were advancing on Ash. Just... just be careful around him, is all."

"If he comes back," Holt said. "I hope he does."

Talia nodded but said no more on the subject. At length, she changed topics.

"This will be your first time visiting the city, won't it?" She seemed to be forcing a more upbeat tone into her voice.

"It will. I have always wondered what the City of a Hundred Isles looks like."

"Well, it's not quite a hundred islands," Talia said. "But it is beautiful. The bridges, the cool wind, the way the lake sometimes sits like glass."

"Do you miss it?"

Talia shrugged. "Sometimes. The Crag can be a harsh place."

"Makes for tough people though," Holt said, puffing his chest.

Talia sniggered. "Makes for rough people."

"Mr. Hunter always said it was better to be rough and capable than a city dandy."

"Cities have their own rough edges," Talia said more seriously.

"Will I... will I be accepted there, given what I am?"

"You're a Novice rider. You'll be with me. If people want to talk, they can do so quietly and behind our backs... like they always do." She faced him. "But it might be prudent to not shout about the fact you're a Cook. If you can help it."

Holt nodded. He'd assumed as much, yet hearing her confirm it still stung.

"They'll find out eventually." By 'they' he meant everyone. The rest of the Order, the nobles of Feorlen, everyone. "I can't keep it a secret forever."

"No," Talia said. She smiled. "But we'll just deal with it when it happens."

Holt smiled back. It was so strange, he thought, that just a few weeks ago he would have included Talia as a part of the amorphous 'they' but now he no longer did. She didn't seem like part of the system. She was more like him, a broken spoke on the otherwise perfect wheel. One a royal who should never have been a rider, and one a commoner who should never have dared to dream.

"Do you think it's fair?" he found himself asking. "How we're born and raised and die in a role we don't get to choose?"

"I've never thought much about it, truth be told. Is that why you stole Ash's egg?"

"I took Ash's egg because it felt so wrong to leave it there to be destroyed. I know I was only saving one, but something sort of snapped in me. I think... I think learning about the choosing soured the riders for me." He shrugged. "Like I've said, I didn't really think it through."

Talia didn't respond at once. She played with a flicker of fire between her fingers, as though flipping a coin across her knuckles.

"Order defeats chaos," she said. "It's why things are the way they are."

"And it's worked so far," Holt said, hoping he hadn't come across as bitter or resentful. "The scourge have never won outright. Order works."

Talia raised her eyebrows.

"You don't think so?" Holt asked, a little confused.

"Order, such as we've made it, has worked. The scourge have never won completely. But we've never fully defeated them either. I know Brode was angry at first, but I think he's right. A little bit of chaos might be just what we need. I'm glad you're not a Cook's apprentice anymore."

Holt laughed lightly. "I hadn't even started my proper apprenticeship. Father was going to start early with my birthday coming up soo —" Then it hit him. He'd not even realized with so much going on, but his birthday had passed already, hadn't it? "What day is it?" he asked, but he started the mental calculation before Talia even answered. When he reached his conclusion, he rushed on in astonishment, "I turned sixteen two days ago. The day before we fought those Wyrm Cloaks."

At the back of the cave, the dragons stirred.

*"Your hatching day has already been?"* Ash said. *"If I'd known I'd have let you eat my portion of the tasty meat."*

"Don't worry about it," Holt said. For the first time in his life, he didn't care that his birthday had passed without remark. Such things seemed so trivial now.

Pyra spoke next. *"May the year ahead be full of strong enemies to slay and test yourself against."*

"Erm, thanks, Pyra."

The purple dragon puffed smoke toward him affectionately. Spluttering, Holt emerged from the cloud to find Talia stifling a laugh of her own.

"Happy belated birthday, Holt," she said. "If only I had something to give you... hang on," she added, and she ferreted around in her own traveling knapsack before pulling out two small linen-wrapped bundles. She handed them to him, and he discovered they were the jerky and hard biscuits soldiers received as rations. "It was all I could grab at the last minute from the cultist camp," Talia said. "Last of our food. You can have it."

Holt stared at her, so grateful that she'd had the wit to grab something when he hadn't and amazed she would let him take it all. Rider body or not, she still had to eat.

Perhaps the look on his face gave his thoughts away, for Talia hastened to add, "It's fine. Honestly. I'll manage."

"Talia..." Holt began, his voice rather dry. "We'll share it." She'd already opened her mouth when he raised a hand and cut in, "I insist."

She smiled. "Thank you, Holt."

They ate their meager meal, and then neither of them could fight back deep yawns. Pyra's aura sent out waves of warmth, and Holt couldn't resist the slow blinking of his eyes. When had they last slept? Must have been days ago.

*"I will keep watch,"* Pyra said, in as soothing a voice as she was capable of. *"Sleep, humans."*

Talia seemed to have been waiting for this. Without another word, she slid to the cave floor and curled up. Holt thanked Pyra, thinking dimly that she too had mellowed a lot since their first night at camp. Perhaps rough living was good for dragons.

He lay on the hard stone, but the discomfort didn't matter. Within seconds, he fell asleep.

# 41

# THE HORSE AND THE HOUNDS

Bird song woke him in the early morning. Blearily, Holt looked around the little cave. It took him a moment to remember where he was.

Red hair fanned out before him, the tips of it nearly tickling his nose. Talia was still asleep and showed no signs of stirring. Even Pyra had succumbed to sleep in the end. Both she and Ash's great breaths rang within the cave.

With a small groan, Holt managed to sit upright. With a further effort, he got to his feet and shuffled out into the dawn, blinking against the light as he headed for the nearby stream. He cupped his hands, dipped them into the water, gasped from the chill, then splashed it onto his face. Gasping again, he at least felt awake and alert.

The singing chaffinch was perched on a branch of a birch tree with its back to him. Holt looked at it for a moment, marveling that something so small and innocent had evaded the gathering scourge. It hopped along its branch, then turned to face him.

And Holt's gut squirmed.

The bird was missing an eye. Its remaining eye was bulbous and green, its feathers slick from a dark slime, and chunks of its plumage were missing. It chirruped as though nothing were wrong.

Before Holt could react, the chaffinch swooped down upon him. Holt waved his arms frantically to drive the bird away, slipped on the damp grass and fell by the water's edge. The bird's flapping wings grew quieter as it flew off. Suddenly breathless and feeling none too ashamed of himself, Holt scrambled to his feet.

Clearly the influence of the scourge was still present in the area. He'd have to wake the others quickly and—

Rustling from the undergrowth made him spin to face it. This time he didn't hesitate to draw his sword.

A horse with a half-rotting face and dead black eyes stepped silently into the little clearing. Still without uttering a sound, it pulled back its lips to reveal bloody, sharpened teeth. It would have been less terrifying if it had been screeching.

Holt's breath caught in his throat. If it charged and caught him, he'd be trampled under its hooves. He didn't dare call for the others in case this triggered an attack from the blighted horse. He tried to take a step back, but more movement behind the horse made him freeze.

A pair of blight-infected hounds came swiftly and silently in the horse's wake. Across the stream, on the opposite bank, a wolf emerged, baring its own teeth and drooling a green ooze, which hissed as it fell upon the grass.

Desperate now, Holt fought to steady his breath. He'd been caught off guard, but his Lunar Shocks could handle these poor creatures. Turning his focus inward, he found the dragon bond had recovered during the night. Ash's core was full of light.

Carefully, Holt began gathering lunar energy in his free palm and was reassured by the heat of it. Still, he couldn't help his heart hammering nor the fear racing up his spine. Something of it must have passed through the bond for he felt Ash stir, but then the horse sprang forward.

Instinct took over. One blast wouldn't be enough. Holt dropped his sword and brought his hands together for a combined attack. The dragon bond shook; power burned down both arms. A thick beam of white light blew a hole through the horse. Momentum carried the horse on before it toppled over. Holt dove aside, but the hounds were on him. He yelled and kicked out, striking one dog on its nose.

"Ash! Talia!"

His legs and arms flailed as he tried to right himself and keep the dogs off. A Lunar Shock required concentration and while sprawled on the earth with his hands occupied, he couldn't summon one. He pulled on magic for extra strength just in time to catch a slathering mouth as it snapped at his throat. Yet the other hound was free.

Pain seared in his leg. He fought back an overwhelming desire to vomit as teeth sunk deeper into his thigh. Tears boiled and fell. Only magic prevented him from passing out from the pain of it. Screaming, he threw the hound he'd caught aside, sat up and punched the one at his leg. Both hounds squealed and retreated but continued to circle him, sensing weakness.

The wound on his leg sizzled from the toxins of the blight, and the veins around it turned green as it spread. He collapsed.

Desperate, Holt looked for his sword, but it was out of reach. And then the wolf came bounding over the stream onto his side of the bank. The hounds fell in beside it like two thugs.

Holt could not move his leg now. His vision blurred and it was all he could do to raise his hands for Lunar Shocks, but even if he managed two of them, one of the three enemies would make it.

A scream of defiance bellowed from his left. Talia landed between Holt, the wolf and the hounds. Power radiated from her, lifting her hair like a billowing cloak. The blighted animals charged just as Talia stepped forward, driving her heel into the earth. A cone of fire erupted in front of her.

*Her Flamewave ability,* Holt thought.

The flames fanned out low along the ground, burning the grass and then the blighted animals. Only the wolf staggered through it and Talia met it, slicing down with her great rider's blade, cleaving its head off in one smooth strike.

She spun, sheathing her sword upon her back in one movement.

"Idiot!" she declared. "I shouldn't have fallen asleep. Why didn't you wake me up at once? What did you—"

She cut off. She'd seen his wound. In a blur of speed she was kneeling by his side, cradling his head.

"What happened?"

"Got bit," Holt said through clenched teeth.

"It shouldn't be spreading that fast or at all. You're not sick or old or too young."

Holt gave her an exasperated look. He didn't think this the time for being curious.

Ash came galloping up, already gathering his lunar magic on the end of his snout.

*"I'll get rid of that."*

"Wait!" Talia said, throwing out an arm.

Ash growled but halted a few feet away.

"He can get rid of it," Holt said. There wasn't much time. He could feel cold sweat over his entire body.

"You have access to Ash's lunar magic yourself," she said. "Push the power down to the wound."

Holt gulped, not sure whether he'd manage it. A general boost of magic to his whole body to increase his strength or speed had been easy, and until now he'd only channeled significant power through his arms for Lunar Shocks.

"Try it," Talia urged. "You'll thank me later."

Gritting his teeth, Holt drew energy into his soul and then tried feeding it toward his injured leg. It wasn't a smooth process. The magic required a pathway, and he was carving out the river as he went. Initially he reached the outer spread of the blight before he lost focus, which at least halted it.

"Where's that emerald Warden when you need him, huh?" Holt said, grunting back against the pain.

"Keep going," Talia said. "Ash is right there if you need him."

Huffing and puffing, wishing it would just end, Holt tried again. And again. Each time he carved the river out a little more but faced resistance every inch of the way, though whether from his own body or the blight, he did not know.

Near giving up, he directed magic to his palm and raised his hand, intending to slam the lunar energy directly into the wound.

Talia grabbed his wrist and held it in an iron grip.

Holt screamed. Ash growled and seemed ready to knock Talia aside, but Pyra blocked him.

Holt blinked; lights popped in his vision. He looked up at Talia, but she was coming in and out of focus. Only her voice was solid.

"Pain and trials. That's how we advance."

Though his head felt like lead, he nodded. Only deep trust in Talia kept him going, not that he could do anything else with her holding him down. And fearing his cries of anguish might alert every scourge beast within miles, he pushed on. Through the pain. Through the terrible effort.

At last, with a gasp of air as though he'd been choking, Holt forged a clear pathway for concentrated magic toward his leg. The blight was expelled, the toxin burned away as thoroughly as when they had cured the blacksmith's daughter. And like her, Holt now sported a silver-purple coloring over the previously infected area. Yet the bleeding entry points of the hound's teeth remained.

"Lie down," Talia said, even as she pushed him flat on his back. She ran off, returning seconds later in another blur of speed carrying her cloak. Ripping a large strip off with sheer strength, she pressed the material down on his leg with an alarming pressure. Holt groaned again but fought against the urge to squirm. Talia tied off the wound. "Luckily for you, I don't need to cauterize these."

She sighed and sat down, her eyes returning to their regular green as she let the excess magic return to Pyra's core.

Ash continued to keep his gathered magic prepared. He patrolled back and forth along the riverbank, his tail flicking dangerously, daring any other scourge creature to try its luck. Pyra stood vigilant beside them, her amber eyes narrow.

"You okay?" Talia asked. She helped Holt upright, and he winced.

"I think so," he said hoarsely. "Why... why did you make me do that?"

"For one, in case it happens again and Ash is far away on a battle-field, you know you can cure yourself without wasting a full Shock. Second, your next ability involves channeling magic through your legs. Now you have at least one of the pathways open."

"Couldn't I have done that, you know, when I wasn't in danger?"

"It's not easy to do," Talia said. "Master Brode never had time to explain mote channels to you. Most new riders drag the process of opening new ones out. I thought the urgency would spur you on. And it did."

"Must riders always be in peril to advance?"

"No," Talia said gently, "but you heard Rake. Only by pushing ourselves to the limits will we reach our potential."

"Thank you then, I think." Having seen Talia display her second main ability got him thinking. "Now I've opened up that pathway, can I send out magic like you just did?"

"You'll need to reach Ascendant first to make it safe," Talia said. "It pulls on a lot more power to use than your single target attack and your bond needs to be strong enough to hold up when using it."

"I hope that's soon. Being able to blast a wave of power would have been useful there."

Talia gave him a piercing look and Holt felt her presence brush up against his soul, inspecting the bond.

"Rock solid," she said, only now she sounded impressed rather than frustrated by it. "You and Ash have something special. And you've been through hell compared to most Novices. Might advance sooner than you think."

"Here's hoping," Holt said. He couldn't help but feel a rush of excitement at the idea.

"Just remember what Brode tried to teach you," Talia said. "You shouldn't rely on magic for everything in battle." She picked up his sword. "What happened to this?"

"Dropped it," Holt said, not meeting her eye. She gave him a look so reminiscent of Brode that he almost did a double-take. "Thought I ought to blast the horse with double the power."

"Hm," she said, handing him back his sword. "Skilled blade work and weaving in single Lunar Shocks would have done just as well there as an area ability. You must conserve your magic for when it's needed most. It's no good if your bond frays mid-combat."

"I know," he groaned. "I'm not... well, I'm not used to this yet."

"Nor am I. Not really."

"And I don't think I'll be doing much sword work until this is better." He tried moving his leg and white-hot pain shot through it.

By the riverbank, Ash suddenly froze, his whole body growing taut as it had done when he'd heard the Wyrm Cloaks approaching.

*"I hear the buzzing of great wings. All over. Some coming closer."*

Talia cursed. "Stingers."

Pyra clawed at the earth and her tail stiffened. *"We need to move. Can you still fly, Holt?"*

"If I can sit, then I'll manage."

*"There will be a great deal of pain."*

"I'll manage," he insisted, meeting her great amber eyes. Pyra rumbled approvingly.

Talia hoisted him up with one arm as though he weighed nothing, and he threw an arm over her shoulder.

"Ash, come here," Holt called.

He bounded over and lowered himself so Holt could be more easily pushed up and onto his back. With a pang, he realized this was the second time in almost as many days that Talia had helped him onto a dragon's back. Inwardly he vowed never to let it happen again.

She needed him to be stronger. His father would need him to be strong too.

With another powerful jolt in his stomach, he remembered the recipe book.

"My bag," he began in a panic. "My father's book—"

Talia ran off and back in another blurred flash. He hoped she hadn't strained her bond too much already today.

"Thank you," Holt said when she returned. He took the bag and strapped it safely over his shoulder. He sagged, partly from the relief of remembering the recipe book, partly from his leg.

*"I'm worried for you,"* Ash told him privately.

Holt replied mentally. *"You just fly as fast as you can, boy. I'll hold on."*

Ash sniffed, probably sensing Holt's pain over their bond, but they had little choice.

*"They are closer now,"* Ash told the group. *"Many to the south."*

*"The swarm gathers,"* Pyra said sagely as though she'd witnessed the great swarms of a dozen incursions. Maybe she had, from the memories passed down to her through her dragon lineage. *"Their bodies are tough, but their wings are frail."*

Ash unleashed a burst of lunar light. *"We shall see how strong their hide truly is."*

Holt rubbed down Ash's neck, then began the sense-sharing process. This time, along with the usual increase in his sight and hearing, Holt found the pain from his leg dulled. It seemed to have been shared as well.

"We don't stop now until we reach Sidastra," Talia called.

And with that, they took off. Everything else had been left behind. All they had left was themselves, their weapons, and one old family cookbook.

# 42

# FLIGHT

They didn't make it far untroubled.

A group of stingers began tailing them just after takeoff. With his senses heightened, Holt heard the buzzing gathering behind them, but he didn't dare glance around – he had to keep facing forward so Ash could see.

Talia and Pyra were ahead by a good arrow shot, too far for Talia to shout any instructions. On they flew, Pyra pulling even farther away, which forced Ash to beat his wings furiously to keep up.

Holt held on. Held on and kept his gaze straight. What more could he do?

But no matter how fast they went, the buzzing followed, gaining on them, until Holt could almost feel the creatures by his ears. It made his skin crawl, and he swatted at his head as though they were small flies. Monstrous bats said to inhabit distant lands would have been preferable. Why did they have to buzz like that?

Despite himself, Holt couldn't help but turn his head by a fraction. He wished he hadn't. A stinger flew so close on their right that its frothing mouth gnashed at the air, trying to bite Ash's leg. A second later it shrieked and fell back.

*"Got it with my tail."*

Holt let his appreciation wash across the bond but there wasn't time to celebrate. Ash was barely staying ahead. Did Talia even know? She and Pyra seemed to be gaining fresh height now as though they were about to leave him and Ash behind.

*"We can't outrun them,"* Holt said. *"Tell Talia."*

*"She knows. Pyra says to hold on."*

Holt gritted his teeth. It was well the dragons could communicate over the distance and elements between them.

*"We're to turn on Talia's signal and attack,"* Ash said.

*"Signal?"* But even as Holt asked, he saw Talia draw her sword and knew instinctively what it meant. A jet of fire swirled up her rider's blade and Pyra turned, tucked her wings into her sides and hurtled down.

Ash banked left. Holt tightened what grip he had of Ash with his legs. Fresh pain surged from his injury, but he kept squeezing.

Pyra roared, stingers screamed, heat from the flames kissed the back of Holt's neck.

Ash turned to face the skirmish. One charred stinger was already falling. Four remained. They had scattered and were now encircling Pyra.

Holt didn't have to speak. His desire to help passed effortlessly through the bond, and Ash climbed toward the battle.

As wearing as sense-sharing was on the bond, and as cumbersome as it was, it did have its advantages. Holt and Ash were like one mind, homing in on the closest stinger, their decision made in a split second where words would have taken longer.

Holt let go of Ash with one hand to charge a Lunar Shock. Ash came up behind the unsuspecting stinger and, with a jerking stop, the dragon halted to allow Holt better aim. The Shock of light took the creature in its bulbous abdomen even as Ash sent his own beam-like breath at another stinger. Ash missed, and Holt became briefly gripped by the dragon's frustration.

He let Ash know it was okay, that it must be hard to aim while seeing from a perspective that wasn't his own. Their bond began to burn and beat furiously.

Holt's target howled, writhed in midair but did not fall from its injury – until Pyra flew by and Talia opened its side with her blade.

Three stingers remained.

One zipped by so fast Holt barely registered it. Ash twisted to chase it with such force Holt almost lost his grip. He clung on with both arms again – wondering how on earth he was supposed to fight properly and stay on Ash's back at the same time – right as another unseen enemy collided with them.

It had come in sting first, clearly meaning to pierce Ash. But Ash's spin had thwarted the angle of its attack and brought them into a blunt embrace instead. The bug had little hooks of green carapace along its legs which swung down, mining for purchase. Many glanced off Ash's scales, but a few sunk in. Ash roared, then snapped furiously at the creature's neck, but he couldn't clamp down hard enough to break through its armored exoskeleton.

They thrashed in midair. Holt cried out as enormous mandibles sought him. A smell like warm rotting fish sickened him, and he saw his own terrified reflection in one of the stinger's many onyx-orbed eyes.

Then inspiration and Talia's recent lesson came into one. He could have blasted the stinger, and maybe he ought to have. But the bond was already growing hot and they had a long journey and who knew how many enemies ahead of them. He had to be sparing with magic where he could.

So, he drew his sword, swiped at the stinger's antennae, then rammed the blade into the eye of the beast. Its scream was worse than its smell, but it did let go, giving Ash free reign to rake his talons through its wings. Down it went, shrieking the whole way.

Ash swooped down then up, weaving so as not to be caught again. They saw Pyra and Talia dispatch another foe. The final stinger fled.

Holt desired to hunt it down. His blood was hot – both from the heat of battle and the burn of the bond – but Ash's thoughts collided with his own.

*"Talia says we go. We shouldn't chase it into a trap."*

*"Fine,"* Holt said. And Ash changed course again, heading south in Pyra's wake.

While the world they'd left behind had enjoyed the light of dawn, the world ahead suffered in darkness. Heavy clouds covered the skies. Given what they now knew of the origins of the scourge, it made sense that the bugs and ghouls would seek cover where they could.

Holt wondered whether this always happened when the true swarm gathered or whether Silas's mastery over storms granted the enemy additional benefits.

More stingers harried them on their journey south, never more than a handful at a time, but their buzzing never seemed far away.

Until, in the distance, they saw it. The swarm.

It could only have been the edge of the scourge forces, for the dark mass came together in a jagged edge but stretched off west as far as Holt could see. And he could see for a long way this high up. A veritable cloud of stingers swirled far off too, gathering in a writhing spiral above a small hill.

The hill moved. Holt blinked. His eyes had deceived him. The small 'hill' sprouted wings of its own. A giant bug. It had to be the Queen of the swarm.

Pyra and Talia banked to the southeast and climbed higher. Ash followed.

*"We've to go through the clouds."*

Holt held on, watching as Pyra disappeared as though into smoke. Soon he and Ash passed through the clouds too. Holt expected to emerge wet or at least damp, but not a drop of water touched him. He did breathe in, without thinking, and nearly choked on the noxious air. Whatever these clouds were, they were not natural.

Yet once through the heavy clouds, the air was clean and the sun bright. It may have been too bright had the sunlight reflected off the clouds below, but these dark masses seemed to ensnare the light instead.

Pyra settled into a gentler, gliding flight and Ash followed suit. They fell in beside each other, close enough that Talia could shout over to him.

"With any luck they won't find us up here, at least until we have to descend."

"That swarm—" Holt began.

"Is enormous, I know," Talia said. "All the more reason we can't stop now. Sidastra needs to be warned the attack is imminent."

"How will we find the city up here?" Holt asked. The black clouds seemed to stretch on forever.

"I'm assuming those clouds have been conjured to cover the approach of the swarm," Talia said. "By following them south we can't go far wrong. Once we see the end of them, the city will be close, but I don't want to risk dipping down below often to check. Better to over-shoot and then circle back around in any case. Less chance of running into scourge that way."

Holt nodded, feeling surprisingly comforted. Whatever Talia might think about her readiness, she could lead well and decisively when required. Her plan made sense in any case. He dearly hoped they wouldn't run into any more scourge on their way, and yet Rake's words, and Talia's reminder this morning, made him feel guilty for thinking it. Guilty for being afraid. Well, he'd have to face more and worse soon.

Even now, Holt could feel the bond beat like a fiery drum. Its edges seared outward, growing painfully inside his soul. The whole bond trembled as he looked inward to it. A worrying sign.

*"Hey, boy, think you can keep straight without seeing? With the fight this morning and then the stingers, I think it might be wise to stop sense-sharing for a while, if you can manage."*

*"I can. If only I could aim 'straight',"* Ash added in a rare moment of sourness. He growled and rallied at once, shaking his head from side to side. *"I will train. I shall conquer this just like Master Rake."*

*"You will,"* Holt said, and then he let the connection fade.

The world lost some of its luster as his senses returned to those of a human, yet his head swam less from the intensity of it. There truly were benefits and curses with every aspect of being a rider. He'd been starry-eyed indeed to think otherwise.

Still, now he could fly.

Unfortunately, the pain in his leg returned in full force too. He checked on the rudimentary bandaging. Talia's work had held up well so far, but he tightened the knot all the same. Out of habit, he checked to ensure the recipe book was still there in his satchel and felt it there, reassuringly solid.

Sighing, he settled into their journey, his thoughts turning from everything from his father to the best place to hit a stinger with his Lunar Shock. He supposed he'd find his father soon enough in the capital or else he might see him on the battlefield as a ghoul, beyond the help of even Ash's magic. One or the other, it seemed. Neither prospect excited nor horrified him – they were both so distant, even now. And it would not fully hit him until he knew.

As for stingers, it seemed the best place to hit one – beyond its head – would be the pinched waist between its upper body and the fatter abdomen. That must sever easier. The abdomen on the stinger he'd hit earlier had taken damage, but it had withstood his blast. As he ranked up, that would change, but even lunar magic wouldn't help him if he wasn't skilled and capable with it.

He wondered when he'd be able to empower his sword with magic, as Talia frequently did. Would he need a special rider's blade like her? New Ascendants journeyed to Falcaer Fortress for their weapons. He would craft one himself in time, once he ranked up and took the oath.

Yet that thought only brought him more anxiety. Why? Why did that decision feel like another looming battle? He'd been so eager to swear it to Brode, yet now, now he wasn't so sure.

The day wore on. At length, the blue imprint of mountains arose on the eastern horizon. They had to be the edge of the Red Range, which bordered and separated the three kingdoms of Feorlen, Risalia and Brenin. Only last year another war had been fought there, Holt knew, as so many had been before. The war that claimed King Godric's life.

Holt looked to Talia. She too faced the mountains and did so for a long time. He couldn't see her face, and he reckoned that was on purpose.

When he had heard that King Godric had fallen in the final battle for the Toll Pass, the news had washed over him as though a kitchen-hand had dumped more dishes into his basin. Now, he felt quite differently about it. Talia was his friend. She'd lost a lot in those faint blue mountains and even more since.

Brode had been right yet again. Who had it harder between the two of them?

The afternoon sun turned dark orange before Talia called to him again.

"The clouds aren't breaking."

Holt checked the horizon directly ahead. He felt he could see, very dimly, the dusky sky beyond the black and gray edge of the clouds.

"You sure?" he called back.

"Those mountains mean we've crossed over Lake Luriel. We're probably flying over the middle of the city right now, but those clouds look like they go all the way over to the banks of the East Weald." She craned her neck as though to get a better look at the endless weather. Sitting back down, she shook her head. "We'll need to descend."

"Can't we fly farther east and get away from the clouds?" Holt asked. "Then come back in under them with the city in sight?"

"I won't have us take another day," Talia said. "I want us in the city before nightfall, and we don't have much time now."

Holt nodded, and patted Ash on his neck. They had already started the sense-sharing incantation when Talia called out,

"I'll go first."

She drew her sword, and Pyra slid gracefully down through the clouds and out of sight.

The moment the sense-sharing started, Holt felt the dragon bond quiver. That could not be good. And he'd only just adjusted to the sensory information when Pyra's voice screamed into his mind.

*"They're everywhere – dive now. Don't stop!"*

Holt clasped at his head from the intensity of it and had barely registered Pyra's warning when stingers emerged through the black clouds. More than stingers came this time. Great hulking beetle-like bugs that looked as armored as knights; countless infected birds – seagulls chief among them – all buzzing and squalling.

Worst of all, there came a scourge risen dragon.

What type the dragon had been in life, Holt couldn't say. Its scales were gray-green and discolored now; its body so thin that its ribcage could be seen through its hide. Bile ran from its dead eyes and a ghostly power gathered at its open mouth.

Ash dove.

Holt sucked in a breath before they broke the clouds. His world became darkness. Enemies pursued on all sides.

They emerged to worse. Hundreds upon hundreds of dark figures flew toward them. Below, Pyra and Talia blazed a fiery trail, seeking the safety of the white city walls. Ash followed through. Holt cried out as a heat wave struck his face. He ducked as low as he dared, but the smoke made his eyes stream and sting.

Ash poured lunar energy out, twisting his head from side to side, but whether he hit anything in the mad rush Holt never saw. He himself raised both hands and began blasting out Lunar Shocks as fast as he could and pressed his legs so tight into Ash that his right leg might have fallen off from the pain of it. Fresh blood wet the bindings on his wound.

He lost the ability to think. Everything was pain, shrieking, roaring, light, fire and burning – not just from Talia's magic but from his bond too. His soul was on fire. The bond beat so hard this time it really did crack a rib. Holt gasped, unable to breathe.

And still they dove – down, down, down, hurtling with ever greater speed until a roar cut above all else. Holt recognized that dragon.

Clesh. Clesh and Silas were on them now.

And just as all seemed lost, great thwacking sounds joined the cacophony. Long bolts with glinting steel heads blasted from the city, rapid as arrow fire.

Scourge scattered.

Their path cleared.

Sheer white walls rose as though up from the dark waters of the lake. Torches flickered through the crenellations and helmets reflected the firelight like so many candles. Large ballistae dotted the battlements, more powerful than those at Fort Kennet had been, each launching a thick bolt to cover their descent.

In seconds, the space between them and the walls closed. Clesh roared louder.

Holt clung on with all his might and then they reached the walls, passed over them, pulled up hard and missed the buildings on the other side by a hair.

Pyra carried on and Ash followed, leaving this island outpost behind to glide low over the lake and land hard on a grassy bank. Holt was thrown violently from Ash. He hit the grass and rolled badly – crunching bones and muscle as he went.

At last he stopped. Lying on his back, he stared at the chaos of the blackened sky. His sense-sharing with Ash had ended, but he could just discern dark outlines soaring in all directions, growing fainter as they escaped the range of Sidastra's defenses.

A final roar from Clesh carried across the lake. Silver-blue lightning struck somewhere out of his sight. A flicker of red and orange rose. A fire. Holt thought the Storm Lord would swoop down, sweeping all defenses aside in his hunt of them. But one strike was all the retribution he carried out.

Once Holt realized they had made it, he also realized he wasn't breathing. He tried to shout for Talia, but his voice had abandoned him. His limbs were numb to his will. He felt nothing. With the last of his strength, he reached out for Ash.

*"Help."*

But Ash did not answer.

Panic took him. Ash would never ignore him. Never leave him. That could only mean – no, no, it could not mean that.

He twitched, then his body started undulating there on the grass. His skin sizzled, a smell like burning wood engulfed him. Was he burning? It felt like it. His soul was still ablaze, and now the rest of him must be too.

Voices called. Boots thumped nearby. Another roar. Then Ash was beside him, baring his teeth at people Holt could not see.

Ash was here. That much he knew for sure, even as all else spun out into haze and blackness. All the fear in Holt vanished. Ash was here.

*"I'm with you. Hold on."*

And with his words came a memory, a memory of breaking through a tough shell, feeling cool air for the first time and smelling damp straw. Only all was dark and frightening. Stumbling, lost, meaty smells he loved but could not find. Then there came a voice – Holt's own voice – light and echoing as though in a dream.

"It will be all right. Come here. Follow my voice. It will be all right."

The voice was everything, and when the owner of the voice ran a warm hand down his back, he knew he would be okay.

Ash's comfort overwhelmed the pain, and the memory kept looping, his own words mixed with Ash's.

"It will be all right..."

*"I'm with you..."*

"It will be all right..."

"Holt! Holt!"

That voice was sharper than the others. Closer.

"Wake up, Holt!"

His eyes burst open. Dull gray light greeted him with all the delicacy of a heavy pan crashing to the floor. He gasped, caught his breath, and found Talia slumped in a chair in the corner of the room. She had changed her clothes, and great dark bags hung under her eyes, but otherwise she looked unhurt.

She beamed at him. "Thought we might have lost you there in the transition. You looked broken like a rag doll and had lost so much blood."

"Trans—what?" Holt rasped, still trying to get a grip on where he was. Just like after Midbell, he seemed to have passed out and now found himself on a plush bed. He made another personal vow to never let that happen again either. "Where's Ash? What happened?"

"Ash is fine. Pyra is too. They're getting food. We made it. For now."

She continued to beam at him, and he didn't have the faintest idea why.

"How does it feel?" she asked.

"What feel? Huh?"

A gentle presence ran over his soul. Flushing as though caught naked, he quickly looked inward to inspect himself. To his relief, he discovered his soul was no longer on fire. In fact, it felt incredible. The dragon bond beat. Slow. Assured. Powerful.

Talia leaned forward, still grinning. "Welcome to the rank of Ascendant, Holt."

# 43

# THE HERO OF FEORLEN

Holt could hardly believe his ears. An Ascendant? A true dragon rider? Him?

Then purest joy thundered through the dragon bond.

*"You're awake!"* Ash said. Roaring came from somewhere outside; a roar of triumph, much lighter and less guttural than when Ash was angry. Pyra started roaring herself, which Holt appreciated.

*"I can sense you much easier now too,"* Ash said. *"Come outside!"*

*"Just a moment, boy. I've just woken up. I need to catch my breath and talk with Talia."*

Communicating telepathically to Ash felt a lot easier. He stared at his own hands as though they would provide answers for him. He didn't *feel* all that different. Then he realized his previously injured leg no longer ached. He moved it and found to his surprise that he could not only lift it but that he could do so higher and quicker than before, throwing the bedsheets off in the process. He'd never been half so flexible before.

"It's like watching a kitten taking its first steps into snow," Talia said, still grinning from the corner of the room. She sat as relaxed as Holt had ever seen her, garbed in fresh clothes. A moss-green quilted doublet by the looks of it, over which she wore a chainmail hauberk under a final layer of fine leather armor. Links of the mail were visible at the nape of her neck and at her shoulders. Her trousers matched the moss color of her doublet and dived into knee-high leather boots.

"You've changed," he said unnecessarily.

"Nothing gets past you," she teased. "I don't know about you, but my clothes from the road were not in a good way. I've had the same brought for you." She pointed toward a cabinet at the far wall where a neatly folded pile sat topped with shiny new leather boots. To the side stood an armor stand, holding up a pristine chainmail hauberk. A tray of food had been set out as well. Bread, butter, ham and apples. Yet Holt's gaze landed upon something much better. His satchel lay there too, bloodied and battered but miraculously still with him.

He let out an exasperated laugh and wiggled his leg again. "It's healed."

"Slow today?" she said, fighting back a laugh. "Your whole body will be stronger. You'll never be sick again, not unless you're pushing yourself to extremes."

Holt sat bolt upright and inspected himself. Someone had clothed him in fine white sleeping silks. He pulled the shirt out and stared down at his torso. To his disappointment he didn't discover fine cut muscles. In fact, he didn't see much alteration to his physical appearance at all; he was as lean and wiry as ever. Still a skinny youngster on the cusp of manhood. And yet he could *feel* the extra strength in his muscles, latent and ready at a moment's notice.

"But, there's a catch, right?" Holt understood how this worked now.

"Were you a member of the Order, the drawback is you'd now be considered fit for combat in the event of an incursion."

A familiar rush of excitement pulsed in his chest as the news sunk in, yet his heartbeat remained steady. Although he felt as though it should be beating faster, like a phantom trace of the frailer body he had left behind.

He took in his surroundings. The linens on his bed were of high quality – he could feel each thread weaved through the material in a way he never could before – but the bedframe was merely functional. This applied to the room at large. A little extra than the basics, but other than the patterned curtains and a solid writing desk, there were no luxuries.

Eager to test his new body, he leaped out of bed only to crash against the wall and crumple. In an instant he was back up, balancing on the balls of his feet and ready to jump again if needed. Not even a bit of pain. He smirked, then saw Talia in such a state of suppressed mirth his face felt scalded from embarrassment.

"Oh please, please do that again," she said. "Maybe my uncle will keep you on as a jester."

Holt was too thrilled to be annoyed. His memories of their entry to Sidastra were hazy, however.

"You might have warned me that ranking up was that... that—"

"Awful?"

"Exactly."

"Well, normally it's not quite as bad as that. But you lost a lot of blood from your leg, were weak from lack of food and sleep, and broke half the bones in your body when you were thrown from Ash's back."

"Rake said to push ourselves."

"I'm not sure even Rake envisioned that. I'm sorry I didn't warn you, but the point is you made it."

Holt took a moment to consider how close he must have come to the brink of death. Then again, perhaps it would be better not to dwell on it. Plus, he was starving.

"Have you eaten?" he asked.

"I could eat again," she said.

Holt raced to the food, pulled it all toward him and began applying lashings of butter onto a torn chunk of bread and stuffed the lot into his mouth. As he chewed, he noticed his taste had not enhanced with the rest of his body. That was well. He wouldn't want this white noble fare tasting any sweeter. He cut a wedge of ham, began eating it before even swallowing the bread and reached for an apple.

"May I take a piece?" Talia asked. "Or am I in danger of having my hand bitten off?"

"Sorry," Holt said with his mouth full. He ripped the loaf in half and passed it to her. "I forget my manners when I'm hungry."

"Me too," she said, tearing unceremoniously into the loaf. "Especially when you don't need to impress anyone."

Once the tray had been picked clean and Holt's stomach felt satisfied for the first time in weeks, he sat on the edge of the bed and sighed.

"We made it then," he said.

"Barely."

"That was Silas chasing us near the end, wasn't it?"

"I didn't see him, but Pyra recognized Clesh's roar."

There was a nervous silence as the intensity of their close shave impressed itself upon them.

"I thought he might follow us anyway," Holt said. "Finish the job."

"Like I said, he's powerful, but he can hardly take on an army alone. Clesh is strong and can probably take a shot to the thickest parts of his hide but if a ballista bolt ran through his neck, or shredded his wing, he'd go down."

Outside, their two dragons roared in fresh delight.

Talia glanced to the window. Her smile faltered a little and she bit her lip. "We often forget, even in the Order, that dragons are still flesh and bone like us. They're strong, terrifying at times, but they bleed too. They die if you strike their heart or the blight takes hold – like poor Erdra."

"I know," Holt said. "Wasn't so long ago that I could cradle Ash in my arms. Still, I can't imagine Clesh being defeated."

"Lords have fallen in battle before. Many will fall before the scourge finally does."

"Well, we have a long way to go until we reach Lord."

"That's optimistic."

"We're alive, aren't we?" Holt said. His brush with death and the insanity of that dive through hordes of screeching stingers had bolstered him. Things seemed somehow less bleak when he felt this strong, had food in his belly, and had a friendly army surrounding them as opposed to being lost in the wilderness.

Today, he'd find out what happened to his father too. That was a pang of anticipation, but he had hope now. Much more than he had the day before at any rate.

Thinking on the day before, his mind turned to another benefit of his rank up to Ascendant.

"I'll have access to a new ability now," Holt said.

"If there's time later I'll try to teach you," Talia said. "Although there's so much we need to—"

An audible voice rang from just outside the room. A commanding voice. Guards shifted aside, and then the door opened.

In stepped a man Holt had never met, and yet he knew him at once. This man captured the concept of broad and made it his own; his leather and mail armor clung as naturally as a second skin. His true skin seemed as weathered and coarse as the armor he was so comfortable in. A handsome man in truth but old before his time, with close-cut brown hair mottled with gray. At his waist hung a pair of thick bladed axes, and his movements mimicked the brutish straightforward techniques that wielding them demanded. Strangely his eyes were softer, pale and distant: the thousand-yard stare of a soldier who'd seen his share of horror. Yet when he focused on Holt, his eyes turned piercing – almost threatening.

Holt fell to one knee. Only Commander Denna had inspired such a natural and unquestioning reaction from him. Yes, he must bow to those of higher station, kneel even if they asked, but few people – either rider or noble – had truly *earned* that response from him.

"Your Majesty," Holt said to the floor.

Osric Agravain's boots came into view.

"Uncle," Talia said. Chair legs scraped across stone as Talia rose to greet him. She also stopped just short of the regent. Holt imagined her bowing too before stepping in to embrace him. "You came?"

"Of course," Osric said. "It is good to see you, niece. When word of the Crag reached us, I feared the worst."

Those words alone sent another quiver of excitement through Holt. If word from the Crag had reached the city, then its refugees must have made it.

"You were right to fear," Talia said. "The worst has happened. We do not fully understand ourselves, but Silas Silverstrike has turned traitor and allied with the scourge."

"Silverstrike? I assumed my men spoke of scourge sorcery when they mentioned lightning last night."

"There's more," Talia said, "Much more, far more. It's about Leofric. He—"

"Not here," Osric said. "And not in front of your manservant, girl. Is your tongue so loose or is the boy a mute?"

Holt's face burned. He could feel Osric looking down at the back of his head, judging. It had been the rush to kneel that had given Holt away. Riders knelt for no one.

"And he's not appropriately dressed besides," Osric said.

"What?" Talia said. "Oh. Oh no, Uncle, you are mistaken. Holt is a dragon rider too."

"A rider?" Osric said with no hint that he believed it. "Look at me, boy."

Holt lifted his head, straining to look up while still kneeling. He should have stood, looked the war hero in the eye, but something about Osric kept him rooted there; some aura of Osric's – almost a magic of his own – that reminded Holt of what he had been born as.

"There is a strength in his eyes," Osric said as though Holt were not there. "Your name, boy?"

Osric would want to know which family he hailed from and whether that family was hostile to the Agravains or allies. The king's penetrating stare bored into Holt and he found it suffocating. He even struggled to breathe.

"Cook, Your Majesty. My name is Holt Cook."

"Cook..."

Osric's piercing eyes flicked to Talia and Holt breathed easier again. He'd never reacted to a superior like this before. Then again, Osric was not heralded as Feorlen's greatest warrior without reason.

"A Cook?" Osric said again. "Much to tell and more, niece. But not here. A barrack gatehouse on the outer isles is no fit place for two riders." A painful beat passed in which no one said or did anything. Holt looked at Talia, then back at Osric. Then, with a look of part confusion and part irritation, Osric offered his right hand to Holt. "You may rise, Holt Cook."

Holt's insides turned to ice. He had hesitated to even stand of his own will. Just as riders shouldn't kneel, they shouldn't be offered such a demeaning invitation to stand. Osric would have expected him to get to his feet.

Now the regent had offered him a hand. Should he take the hand or dismiss it? Which would save face more?

To excuse himself, Holt pretended to admire the back of Osric's hand. For there was another famous tale of this man made real. Inked upon his skin was a symbol from the Skarl Empire, three interlocking horns: a sign of their most elite warriors. And they had given it to Osric, a foreigner. An iron band encased his wrist, it too embossed with weaving patterns of that frigid land.

Osric may not be a rider, but he seemed as formidable.

Holt decided he would take the hero's hand and squeeze it. He did so, perhaps too firmly.

Osric grunted but returned the gesture with a bear-like grip of his own. "A rider indeed. I advise you change, Holt Cook, lest you wander through the streets in your small clothes. We shall await you outside." He swept out an arm and beckoned at Talia to follow him. She did so, and just like that, Holt was alone.

Wasting no time, he hurried to the pile of folded clothes and stripped off his bed silks. He examined his leg. Though it had miraculously healed, a scar remained from the bite. The flesh around it bore the same purple-silver bruising that Ceilia Smith's forearm had after lunar power drove the blight from her.

Quickly he pulled on the clothes and armor. Luckily, none of it required a squire to strap into place. Each item also fit him near perfectly. They must have taken his measurements as he lay passed out and supplied him with similar garb as Talia. His doublet was a different color, as navy as the backdrop of Ash's core, and it felt heavier than expected. More of an arming doublet in truth, with padding to absorb blows and protect his body from his own chainmail. His new woolen trousers were a navy to match the doublet and they tucked tight into his new knee-high leather boots. Over his doublet he pulled on the mail hauberk, finding such mail weighed nothing at all to him now. Finally, there was the burnt-red leather breastplate trimmed with yellow runic letters of Feorlen's ancient tongue, from the time when the Skarls had first ruled this land.

After strapping on his sword and swinging his bloodstained satchel over his shoulder, Holt stopped and glanced at himself in the mirror above the cabinet.

He hardly recognized himself. Oh, it was him to be sure – his father's thick, wild black hair was unmistakable – and yet he saw something of the past weeks in his eyes. So plain and boring and brown they had always been, and though still brown, they had hardened like aging oak. A thin nose and his smooth skin still showed his true age, although some of the puppy fat had been stripped from his cheeks.

Holt lingered for a moment and tried to strike a threatening pose. That only showed his age more. Still, he was sixteen now. Eligible for formal apprenticeships. Ready to inherit his father's role if the blight took him early. In truth, he was a man grown now. He ought to remember that. He doubted Osric, Talia, or any rider he met from here on out would let him forget it.

# 44

# THE CITY OF A HUNDRED ISLES

Having readied himself, Holt descended down through the gatehouse and outside. Ash roared at once, and a company of guards leaped aside as the dragon bounded to meet him.

Ash bowled Holt right over and licked his face. Holt rolled from side to side, trying playfully to avoid Ash until he managed to catch one of the dragon's talons and hold him in place.

*"You're not as squishy as before!"*

Half-gasping, half-laughing, Holt said, "This squishy human has made it through a lot already!"

After a few more rolls, Ash settled and the bond glowed warm. Holt gave him a hug around the neck and caught Osric giving them a disapproving look. Holt ignored him and checked on the black strip of Brode's cloak wrapped around Ash's eyes. It too had survived the carnage, but he tightened it to be safe. It was good to have this small piece of Brode with them, even if it would have to be replaced one day when Ash grew.

For now, Ash's growth spurt had slowed. Pyra was about half the size of Clesh, and Ash smaller and weedier than her. Holt and Ash shared that wiriness to them. Holt expected to fill out in time, and

Ash should as well, although he couldn't help but worry still for the dragon. Such worries were unlikely to ever leave him.

Holt ran his hand up and down Ash's neck. "You were amazing yesterday. Flew just as we needed."

*"Down is hard to get wrong. It pleases me more that I scorched many bugs along the way."*

"There will be plenty more to come."

*"They'll regret meeting us on the battlefield."*

"Until our bond frays or your core runs dry."

Holt looked inward to check the state of Ash's core. Now his bond was greater, more secure, his window into Ash's soul was larger and clearer. It was easier to pick out the lunar motes from the confusion of other mote types. The core itself had been brought into sharper relief. At its heart, Holt thought he saw something white and dense spinning.

Brode had spoken on the core changing its appearance to his human understanding as it matured and gathered power. His bond's status was separate to that, but his better insight into Ash's soul was granting him more clarity already. Given Ash's magic type, Holt had a strong suspicion as to what that white orb forming in the heart of Ash's soul would become.

And as he focused solely upon it, he heard the music playing. The tinny quality to it had smoothed out, its rhythm calmer, stronger, yet a sadness echoed in it, as though a lone voice drifted across an endless night. Ash was the only one of his kind, and blind, and something of that had seeped into the music, yet without a note of pity. Stoic. Resolute. Sad, yes, but not pitiful.

Holt ran his hand up the dragon's neck again. "We'll fight them to the end."

With that he parted from Ash, and as Osric spoke with his guard and Talia, he took in his surroundings. The island they had landed on was large enough for two fortified gatehouses guarding its bridges and little more. A narrow stretch of grassland curved south into the lake. Holt reckoned they had landed there as to their east was a greater island with walls and rooftops poking above ramparts.

With the looming clouds it was impossible to tell the time of day, although it was definitely daytime. Barely any lunar motes passed through the orbit of Ash's core. Yet such was the dimness of the gray light that poked through the heavy clouds, torches were already being lit along the walls of the many isles of Sidastra. Torch fires flickered into life along the bridges and atop the siege platforms as well. Down at ground level Holt couldn't get a clear sense of the scale of the place, but one island and the building at its heart did stand out.

In fact, it took his breath away.

In the center of the city sat what might have been a smooth white-walled mountain with red slated peaks. Even at this distance, its size crushed upon his imagination. Numerous towers were set in and around it, topped with ballistae and catapult platforms. Surely it was impregnable from an aerial attack.

How many people lived and worked there? He let out a low whistle at the thought of the size of those kitchens, envisioning an endless sprawl of steaming pots, hot fires and worktables stretching into the distance. The clatter of hundreds of servants in such a cavernous space would surely be deafening.

Talia called him over then and they set off with the king's guard, through the northern gatehouse to cross the bridge there. Ash stayed on the ground while Pyra took to the skies, keeping low and circling overhead. Another populated island lay before them, and it seemed the palace crossing was still another four bridges away.

Holt kept pace just behind Talia. He didn't feel like being too close to Osric if he could help it.

"Reports of the swarm toppling Fort Ord arrived five days ago. I sense the attack is imminent."

"How great is the swarm?" Talia asked.

"As a dragon rider, I'd hoped you'd tell me."

"This is my first real incursion, Uncle."

"Might be your last. Inspect the defenses. That is what the Order does, is it not?"

"I don't—" Talia started, but she cut herself off. She turned to Holt, looking determined. "Come on."

Pyra swooped down, and Talia jumped from the bridge onto her back. Despite all he'd seen, Holt was impressed. Osric walked on. His royal guards, however, looked to Holt as though expecting he equal Talia's feat. He swung himself up onto Ash without giving them a second glance.

*"Something troubles you."*

"It's nothing," Holt muttered. Only it wasn't. "Being away from other people for a while... just with Brode and Talia... it was easier to forget what things are like. Let's not fall behind now."

They both focused their hearing upon the lapping water beneath the bridge as they began the sense-sharing technique. Once done, Ash took off after Pyra.

Islands stretched out to each point on the compass and in every size and shape. The majority clustered to the west, but three 'rings' of islands could be discerned. The outer ring, the inner and the central. At the heart of the central ring was the palace isle itself.

Between each major ring were smaller pieces of land used as bridge supports, gatehouses or jetties. Certain isles between the outer and inner rings had been given over entirely to trebuchets, enormous siege engines that could hurl rocks far onto an army gathering on either bank.

The scale of the defenses was visible everywhere. Platforms and towers for ballistae were densely packed throughout the city; rooftops adapted for everything from siege equipment to archery work. Yet there was beauty also. Wide boulevards seemed common in the central ring, with trimmed trees lining the walkways. Private gardens, their blooming colors faded in the gray light but nonetheless there, orchards too, hedge mazes and grand statues of nobles and riders alike.

*A place worth saving,* Holt thought. *Even were the people not here.*

Evidence of the Summons could be seen in the countless trickles of smoke and steam rising across the islands. Tens of thousands had traveled to the city, temporarily swelling its population to draw the swarm. Sidastra was supposed to be their haven.

Holt faced west. Out there, far beyond the city's white walls, the swarm gathered. How close would it be now? A day or so by flight, but the ghouls and other land-based bugs might take longer.

A background buzz filtered down from the dark skies. Their

pursuers had clearly hung around out of sight in those unnatural clouds where their most powerful enemy most likely concealed himself.

If this was to be their end, then Holt had to find his father today. Right now.

There was a lonesome-looking island to the south of the west quarter, connected by a bridge much longer than the others. A great plume of smoke rose from a corner of that island, suggesting a controlled bonfire. Unlike any other isle save for the great western and eastern entrances to the city, this one was also connected to the shore. To Holt it seemed darker than the rest of the city, with an aura about it that made his blood run cold.

*"I sense the blight there,"* Ash said.

*"Maybe we can help?"*

Before Holt and Ash could decide upon that, Talia and Pyra had moved off to patrol the city. He and Ash followed, and after a couple of loops of Sidastra they made toward the great red-tiled palace.

They landed inside the island's walls, and Osric and his entourage soon caught up with them.

"Well?" he demanded.

Talia dismounted. "Everything looks well-manned on an initial sweep, but we might be better served to place more men in the west quarter. A besieging swarm is supposed to attack over days, some-times weeks, hitting the walls in waves. But this one seems to be biding its time. Perhaps gathering its full strength before attacking. I fear we won't repel it if it comes at once."

Osric gave nothing away. He waved a hand toward the palace. "Further discussion of strategy should take place inside."

Holt found his voice then. Talia could discuss strategy and the business of Harroway with Osric quietly herself, but he had his own pressing concerns.

"Your Majesty," Holt began, "by your leave I wish to search for my father. He will have arrived with refugees from the Crag. If he made it."

Once more, Osric's attention fell fully onto Holt, and that piercing stare seemed to root him to the spot. "It's my understanding that riders swear away familial bonds. The defense of this city is more important than one man."

Holt looked to Talia, but she only looked guilty herself.

"Your Majesty is correct that such oaths are sworn by riders of the Order." Conjuring the right words to speak in this manner was careful work, taking attention and thus slowing his speech. Better than Osric finding his manner too common. "Yet I have not had the opportunity to take my oath."

Osric frowned.

Afraid the king was weighing up whether to arrest him on the spot, Holt continued. "Though riders do not partake in the wars between realms or aid their family in any other way, surely affection cannot be wholly withheld. Oath or no. You yourself, Your Majesty, greeted your own niece warmly today."

"I did," Osric admitted.

"Then you surely understand my desire to know of my father's fate even if I one day swear to cut ties from him. Should I discover that he has... died... my position will only be clearer for it and I can return here in haste."

Osric's expression was impassive. "Had you taken your oath, you would be under the command of one of your own superiors. I defer to my niece on this issue, though I see you are your own man, Holt Cook. I cannot command it, but I advise you heed her authority. The measure of a man is not in willfulness but in doing his duty."

Talia licked her lips. Holt gave her an imploring look. Surely she wouldn't ask him to stay just to appease her uncle?

"Go, Holt," she said.

"Thank you." He inclined his head awkwardly to her as though a month's worth of friendship had been undone in an instant.

"Very well," said Osric. "Although I would not get your hopes up. Civilians from the far west were placed in quarantine upon arrival. Many were infected with the blight, and few have been deemed symptom-free long enough to be allowed to cross."

Holt's insides froze over. If he was too late...

"My men can escort you," Osric said.

"There is no need," Holt said, thinking of that lonesome, sad island.

"As you will." The king swept away without another word, his guard following in his wake. Talia held back, then came over to Holt.

"I'm sorry about all that," she said in an undertone. Holt shrugged. Now wasn't the time to discuss it. "I hope you find him. I hope he's... I hope it's not too late."

Holt smiled but struggled to find his voice again. Now the time had come to learn of his father's fate, the weight of the worst case felt unbearable.

"Listen," Talia said, "don't draw too much attention if you can help it." She checked again for any eavesdroppers before continuing. "Harroway's men could be anywhere. Once I tell my uncle, he'll want to move quickly. We'll need your help in case things get violent."

"Of course," Holt croaked through his dry throat. "We're in this together." Thinking on the evidence her brother Leofric claimed to have hidden for her, he added, "I hope you find what you're looking for."

"You too." With that, she ran off after her uncle.

Pyra puffed smoke in his direction, said, *"Good luck, little one,"* and followed Talia.

Ash braced himself, clearly preparing to fly again.

"No, Ash," Holt said. "Stay here with Pyra. Get some food. I can tell how hungry you are, remember?"

Ash rumbled and beat his tail. *"I'm always hungry! And this is far more important."*

"Thank you," Holt said softly. He needed Ash to come more than the dragon knew. Or maybe Ash did know. Sometimes it felt as though they didn't need words, even when not sense-sharing.

He climbed onto Ash's back, ready for the final leg of his journey.

# 45

# THE LAST OF THE AGRAVAINS

Talia turned her back on Holt with a mixture of apprehension and guilt. Doubt swirled in her. She ought to have gone with him. The only two riders left to defend Sidastra – her home – shouldn't be taking risks, even inside the safety of the city walls. If something happened to him and she wasn't there...

No, she couldn't think about that. Her nightmares were bad enough already.

She turned inward to warm herself and her soul on Pyra's embers of affection, drawing on more comfort from the dragon than she dare let others know.

*"A hatchling must learn to stretch his wings alone,"* Pyra said. *"And you have a rat to smoke out."* A flare of Pyra's anger traveled across the bond.

Talia weathered it. Pyra's fire hadn't overpowered her since they'd returned to the Crag. To think she'd reached for a blade against Ash, directed more by Pyra's emotions than her own sense.

She loved Pyra, and Pyra loved her, but dragons were dragons. Mirk had been cold from Biter's influence, and Commander Denna so strong-willed from Ysera's might she often ignored counsel. All riders had to contend with an aspect of their dragon's nature. Power flows only one way through the bond, after all. The dragon seeps into the human, not the other way around.

Not Ash though. Yet another curiosity about the white drake. Holt hadn't shown any sign that Ash was overpowering his personality; if anything, the pair of them were in sync more often than not. It couldn't just be because Ash was a lunar drake. Lunar couldn't be so different. Something else made the pair of them special.

She only noticed then that Pyra was watching them fly off as well.

"It's nice you care, girl," Talia said.

Pyra snorted. *"I'm happy the baby is gone. He's always squawking about food and following me like a duckling."*

"And there was me thinking you liked admiration from others."

*"If he just remained calm some of the time…"*

Talia directed her next words over their bond. *"You like that he looks up to you. And you care. Can't hide it from me."*

Pyra ruffled as though shaking off water. Talia smiled, stepped closer and reached up. Pyra obliged and lowered her head, allowing Talia to press her own forehead against the ridge of the dragon's purple snout.

"There are nesting areas and plenty of space for dragons in the sheltered courtyard behind the kitchens. I'll tell them how you like your beef." She ran a hand down Pyra's face and their bond glowed.

Parting from Pyra, Talia noticed that Osric and his men had almost made it to the palace doors.

"Go on, now. I need to attend to that rat."

*"I won't be far,"* Pyra said before she took off.

Talia had slipped the all-important letter from Leofric down the front opening of her doublet. The grainy paper lay against her breast. She reached a hand up absentmindedly to check it was still there. It was. A splash of ink had survived all these ordeals while her brother had not. Resolved, Talia drew power from Pyra's core before she flew out of range and sent the magic to drive her legs. Within seconds she had caught up to her uncle, stopping right in front of him to arrest his own advance.

"We must speak privately."

"And we shall. Inside."

"No. Out in the grounds. Just the two of us."

"If you insist." He barked an order to his guards.

Talia called after them, "Send word to the kitchens that my dragon prefers her beef with medium spices."

Osric had already strode off toward the gardens. She followed. Even this colorful place appeared lifeless with the threat hanging over them. Talia sought out a fountain so its running waters might further conceal their words from any prying ears.

"You're nervous for a dragon rider," Osric said. He scratched at the stubble on his chin, which, combined with the severe close cut of his hair, gave him the look of being enveloped in shadow.

"It's not my own safety I fear for."

"This city is defended well enough."

"Well enough? Are you expecting reinforcements? Did you send word to Brenin?"

"Leofric may have sent messengers," Osric said. "Some time ago. If they reached the court there, they haven't replied."

That was most worrying news. Her mother was sister to the King of Brenin. He was Talia's and Leofric's uncle by marriage. Surely he would not abandon his own family to the scourge, not least because no kingdom could be allowed to fall. Risalia would not send aid unless out of the utmost necessity, of course. But for the King of Brenin to refuse his nephew's pleas for assistance was unthinkable.

Osric grunted. "If only more of your Order had survived the attack."

She found the sudden change of topic strange. Osric was rarely evasive on anything. Blunt and to the point, that was his nature. Was it pride then? Pride in seeing off the foe alone, and to prove that Feorlen was more than just a small country at the edge of the world? That had been her father's vision after all, and it had got him killed.

It was too late now to seek help in any case, either from Brenin or the other Order Halls. They were on their own.

"Only Holt truly survived," Talia said. "Had I not been away from the Crag at the time—"

"You were not there?" Osric interjected.

"No... I went to meet Mother. Didn't she tell you?"

"I haven't heard from Felice since she left for the northern estate. Took her whole household guard with her. Could have used them in the fight to come but so be it. What happened at the Crag?" he asked suddenly. "We've heard only conflicting tales from overwrought refugees."

Talia explained as best she knew from speaking with Holt. The end result was clear enough to convey.

"Makes sense," Osric said. "It's what I'd do if I were on their side. I'm amazed the scourge haven't struck at Order Halls prior to an incursion before."

"The enemy hasn't had the guidance of a traitor rider before."

"He was here not two months ago. As charming and arrogant as any puffed-up Lord of your Order ever is."

His response took her by surprise. She'd always thought her uncle to be a great admirer of the riders; he'd even fought alongside them against the scourge in his travels. Then again, she'd not had many occasions to speak with him since she was a young girl. Had she made a false image of her adventuring uncle? Or had Harroway gotten his ideas into him? Was that why her mother had not confided in him either?

"What I want to know," Osric continued, his gaze becoming – if possible – more piercing, "is why and how? Do you have any theories?"

Talia wasn't sure how much she should burden him with on this matter. Rake's theory of a powerful puppet master, the mention of a 'Sovereign' from the Wyrm Cloaks and Clesh that aligned with that theory. Osric was tough and cunning, but he dealt with men and steel, not dragons and magic.

"Some," she began, "but these are matters for my Order to deal with. But that's not why I had to speak with you. There is another threat closer to home."

He nodded, and she got straight to the point.

"It's Harroway. He needs to be summoned before the court and questioned immediately."

"Not this infighting again. Is this your mother's doing? Political grievances can wait."

"Grievances? Uncle, he ordered the western garrisons not to march to Sidastra."

Osric's eyes appeared to drift into space for a moment. The pupils shifted strangely, he glanced away, then looked back with a piercing intensity.

"He did what?"

"We discovered much on our journey from the Crag. The Knight Captain at Fort Kennet told us quite plainly of his orders from Harroway."

"Are you quite sure?"

"Why would the Knight Captain lie about such a thing?"

"I do not know. Yet for Harroway to weaken the city's defenses as the swarm gathers does him no favors. None at all. He's performed commendably as Master of War, far better than that sop Burken your brother put in at your mother's request."

Another rift between Osric and her mother then. Things weren't as united as she'd hoped for.

"There's more—"

"To prefer him over Harroway, who has actual military experience, on the grounds of ideological differences was foolish. Your father wouldn't have done it."

Talia's next words died half-formed in her throat. That had stung. Finding her strength, she said, "Father would have wanted the two of you to work together."

"Godric wanted many things. He wanted you to wed that baby-faced weasel prince of Risalia. He wanted me to stand idly by his side rather than forge my own place in the world. And he wanted the Toll Pass too. He didn't get the things he wanted most."

That stung worse. Osric had slipped a dagger of ice into her heart. Why bring up old traumas? And suddenly she was warding off fresh tears of rage and guilt as a voice in her head told her she should have just married that boy, then her father wouldn't have gone to war, then Leofric would be alive, then none of this would be happening.

Her hands shook. She balled them into fists and flames danced across her knuckles.

"Will you not even hear what I have to say?"

"I don't have time for petty infighting," he said, perhaps harsher than he'd intended. His shoulders slumped, and he gave her a pitying smile. "Forgive me. I'd hoped you would have been spared this truth, but your brother was a sick young man. He became wild of thought in his final days. Shouting at his councilors, mistrusting everyone, holing himself up in his room and inspiring little confidence in his ealdors that he would see us through this crisis."

Talia thought that strange. "He had the wherewithal enough to send out the Summons."

"The king's seal might have adorned the orders, but I assure you he did not issue them," Osric said. "His last true act was to pay ludicrous sums of money to get prisoners back from Risalia despite my winning that war – we shouldn't have had to pay a damn copper for them. Sentiment for his old tutor, no doubt."

He groaned, then carried on. "Meeting them when they returned only excited wilder stories from him. I'm sorry, Talia. Whatever sickness long plagued him must have struck at his mind. When he finally passed, I was glad he found some peace."

Talia choked back the grief threatening to consume her. Was it true? Had she been chasing ghosts? No. No, too much on the road had pointed to a conspiracy in the palace. Brode had agreed. Nibo had not given any indication that Leofric had been sick with anything other than worry.

She extinguished the flames around her knuckles and brought her hand to her chest, aiming to draw out the letter. As she did so, she met her uncle's eyes. They had a chill certainty to them. It was then she realized the letter would mean nothing to him. He had already decided her brother was unwell. Only hard proof might sway him, and even then she wasn't sure. Something wasn't quite right, either with Osric or the situation between him and her mother. What if Osric told Harroway of the contents of the letter? What if she was prevented from getting to the evidence first?

Talia raised her hand to run it through her hair to excuse the sudden motion to her chest.

"Are you listening?" Osric asked.

"Yes, Uncle."

Osric grumped. ""We have a battle to plan. The court has already been summoned to discuss these urgent matters. I urge you not to cause divisions now. Do it after, if you must. If we live."

He left her alone in the gardens.

He left her but one option. If it would take hard proof – and it would always have come to this in the end – then she'd go in search of the promised evidence Leofric left for her. If she found none, so be it. Harroway had been falsely accused. She'd deal with the pain of her brother's madness in her own time.

But if she found proof, well, it would take more strength than even her uncle had to stop her from burning the traitor herself. Oaths be damned.

Resolved, she stormed off for the palace. She knew just where to go.

# 46

## CHAOS

It didn't take long to soar across the city. When they reached the lonely island, Ash landed atop the dilapidated walls. There was a distinct lack of aerial defenses and no patrolling soldiers here.

Before Holt could think about descending, a worried voice shouted from the gate below.

"Honored Rider!" A guard waved up at him. "Beggin' your pardon, but you ought not to go in there."

Ash flew down, and Holt jumped off to meet the guard. He landed hard on the stone bridge – his stronger legs absorbing the shock without pain – and righted himself in a graceful movement.

"There is something inside I must search for," he said in his best impression of a nobleman's tongue.

The few men posted there turned to each other. Some bit their lips.

"Far be it from us to question the will of a rider," the bolder of the guards said. "But it wouldn't be wise to enter the quarantine zone now."

Holt waved a hand. "The blight does not concern me."

The guard gulped. "Honored Rider, the disease is more potent than ever. Almost no one on the island has been symptom-free for the required three days to be allowed into the city."

Osric had said as much. A lump formed in Holt's throat. If his father was inside, he'd be infected now. Given the increased ferocity of the illness, holding refugees on the quarantine island had become a recipe for disaster.

"I notice there are no defenses," Holt said. "Are these people simply to die when the fighting starts?"

"They're dead already, Honored Rider." The guard's tone was perfectly level, matter of fact.

"I'm going in anyway. I can help."

The guards gave him a final imploring look, then stepped aside. The portcullis rose, and Holt walked through. Ash followed in his wake, and the gate clanged shut behind them.

A scene of misery rushed to meet him. Too many people were crammed onto too small an island. They sat on the streets, hung limp and lifeless out of windows, sat in dark doorways with blank expressions. The draining grooves in the cobbled streets flowed with bile, vomit and yellow puss. Holt's stomach turned thrice over at the smell. Children cried unseen, grown men wept through bloodied, grime-covered hands. On a distant corner of the island, a column of smoke carried the memories of the dead up with it.

Ash mewled sadly. *"I can hear their hearts beat slowly, but there is little life here."*

Holt stepped forward lightly, his own heart hammering despite his Ascendant body. Through the dragon bond, he and Ash tried to find solace in one another. Yet surrounded by this evil, it had all the comfort of drinking cold tea.

He recognized no one and kept walking. A woman collapsed ahead of him. Before Holt could arrive, a group of men carried her body away. He didn't follow.

People stared at him now. His frame was too upright, his skin unmarked, his eyes too bright. Health stood out here. They pointed to Ash, woke sleeping companions to point out the dragon and rider who had arrived.

A shaking old man fell before him. "Have ye come to end our misery, sir?"

Holt trudged past in a daze, only realizing later what the man had asked for. Soon others gathered around them, pressed upon them. Their voices became one lost wail of despair.

"I'll try to... try to help." His voice shook with every word. "Father?" He couldn't see him. "Father!"

Ash beat his wings and growled just enough to ward people away.

*"We could try curing them."*

Holt's mouth went dry. There were just so many people. He and Ash alone couldn't help them all, could they?

"I need to find him, boy," Holt said. "Father!" he called out. "Father!"

He pushed through the crowd, his strength and their weakness making it easy but terrible, like wading through a river in which reeds tried to pull him down.

This wasn't how things were supposed to be. Sidastra was the refuge, the haven for an incursion – all subjects were to come here, be sheltered, and draw the swarm, and before the city walls it would be smashed. Laid to waste. Lyrics he had known since childhood echoed again in his mind.

*Hear the call and answer swift, Take only what you'd surely miss, Husband, wife, child and kin, Gather now for life to win.*

"Father!" he cried again. And again. And again. Until, at last, he recognized a man in the doorway of what looked to be a tavern.

"Mr. Weaver," he called with near jubilation. Someone from the Crag. He fought his way over.

Mr. Weaver was not well. A pale green crust had formed over his throat. He squinted, rubbed at one eye, and croaked, "Holt Cook?"

"Yes. Yes, it's me—"

"We thought you was dead."

"My father," Holt hurried on. "Please tell me—"

"Ah now, he's inside, but—"

"Ash, wait here."

Holt darted around the weaver and entered the tavern door without a second thought. Inside he found many more faces he knew. Mr. Monger was there, the Potters, old Mr. Cobbler, Mr. and Mrs. and Miss Carpenter, the Tanners, even the Oysterers, and countless others besides. It seemed those who had not stayed at Fort Kennet had made it to the city, or the bulk of them had.

Yet signs of infection were plain. Green veins roved up necks and faces, people scratched at skin already hardening into bug-like shells. The air was thick, as thick as the Withering Woods. Dead eyes stared at him.

"Who's that?" someone asked.

"Have they sent us food?"

"It's Holt Cook." Gasps of shock followed but were drowned out by frightful fits of coughing on all sides.

It was all Holt could do to be heard. "Where's my father?"

A few managed to raise their hands and point toward a door behind the bar. Holt groaned with realization. Yes, of course his father would be back there. He leaped over the bar and burst through the kitchen door.

Several faces, both familiar and strangers at once, turned to face him. Kitchenhands, a maid or two, and their families, their faces slick with sweat, clinging to one another for support. Someone lay face down on a worktable. And on a chair by the hearth, sitting limp, taking in ragged breaths, was Jonah Cook.

Holt's own breath stuck in his throat. No. His very worst fear.

"Holt?" Jonah said, barely able to utter the word. He tried to rise, stumbled, clasped a hand to his chest and fell.

Holt came to his senses and bounded forward in time to catch his father, then sank gently with him to the floor. His father's pallid head landed in his lap, and wavering eyes tried to focus on his son.

"Father—" Holt choked. Jonah was thin. Painfully thin, now, and bald where his hair had been thick.

Frantic, unable to do more than act on instinct, Holt unfastened his father's baggy, filthy shirt, the better to see how bad the infection was. Of course, he knew how bad it was already. He knew. Gangrenous skin only confirmed it.

Tears blurred his vision. He wanted to say something, anything that might express his regret at leaving, at causing his father so much pain and worry. Yet the words – if any could have expressed it all – eluded him. And what could he say now to make it right?

"I brought your book," he said thickly. He fumbled with his satchel and withdrew the recipe book. It had suffered on their journey. The corners were bashed, the leather scratched here and there, and blood – possibly his own – had stained a page or two. "I brought it with me."

Jonah's lips twitched up, trying to smile.

Nobody else moved, nor said a word. Had the illness already rotted their minds?

"And I can help," Holt said hurriedly, hating himself for not just doing this straight away. He dropped the book, reached for Ash's core, drew on the light, gathered it at his palm.

This had to work. This. Had. To. Work.

Holt pressed his hand onto his father's chest. He pushed the magic out gently, broadly, just as he and Ash had done with the old oak in the forest. He pushed the magic into his father.

Jonah gasped, seized up. Lunar light lent a new spark to his struggling eyes, and for a wonderous moment, Holt thought he had done it. But the light faded. As did the last signs of strength in Jonah's eyes.

"Magic?" Jonah wheezed.

Holt nodded. "I... I'm a rider now. I saved a dragon." How could he sum it up any better?

"Did you?" Jonah said, his voice soft, and growing fainter with every word. "Proud of you," he managed. "Such a kind heart... Proud of you."

Holt pulled him up and held him close. "Father, I'm sorry. I'm sorry. I'm—" His words broke down into incoherence as he sobbed and pressed his face into his father's bony shoulder, just as he'd done with Brode in the forest. First Brode, now this.

"I'm sorry I left you," he managed at last.

Jonah let out a rasp of air by way of accepting the apology.

"But I'm here now," Holt said. "Maybe with proper rest and help you—"

Jonah shook his head, barely a tilt to either side, but it was plain to see. "Too late... held on to... had to see... you..."

Holt shook his head fiercely. He was barely sixteen. This was not supposed to be happening. The Crag should not have fallen. They should all have been safe there. And why hadn't his magic worked? It was the old oak in the woods but a thousand times worse.

"I'm not strong enough," he said aloud. "Hold on. Hold on and I'll For—"

"Help the others," his father whispered. He mumbled more, but Holt could no longer register the words. He placed his ear right over his father's mouth so that he might hear him.

"I love y—" His father's last word rolled into one long, final sigh.

Holt's world stopped. He held his father close, refusing to let go, and mumbling "no" over and over until the word made no sense anymore.

Misery sank into his soul.

Ash's wails could be heard from outside, a wounded animal, making the sounds Holt wished he could make, but he had not the breath nor wits to do anything but rock, rock, and cradle his father's body.

Burning would be preferable. Cold steel ripping flesh held nothing on this. Pain. Purest, truest, deepest, that which leaves invisible scars never to heal. The pain which makes death seem preferable.

Holt did not know how long he sat there. Only that after enough time had passed, a few of the braver people in the room crept over to him. They made hushed sounds and tried to pry his father away.

He found his voice then. "No," he said, light flashing on his palm in warning. They would take his father away and burn him. To that giant smoke pillar on this island without ceremony. "Back," he warned, and they scuttled away to their corners.

He slumped again. Not knowing what to do.

"*Holt.*" Ash's voice was the one balm to his wounds. "*Holt, you did all you could.*"

"*I was too late.*"

"*We were too late.*"

"*I… I wasn't strong enough.*"

"*We weren't strong enough. This is not your fault.*"

"*I left him.*"

"*To save me…*" Ash said, guilt weighing down his voice as much as it did Holt's heart. "*We have to make it worth it.*"

*"How?"*

*"We should cure all those we can."*

His father had told him as much as well. "Help the others," he had said.

"What if I can't save any?" Holt said aloud, too loud, and too suddenly. Those scared people in the corner hunched and curled up further.

Ash must have heard Holt shout through two walls, for he insisted, *"We save any that we can."*

Holt raised his shaking hands.

*"Even if we can, how do we choose who lives and dies?"* His heart began hammering again. What if Brode had handed him some other egg and Ash had never lived? The sheer randomness of it all was overwhelming.

Chaos. All of it chaos.

A darker thought arose. Perhaps the rigid order of things was the right way after all. No thinking. No thought. Do as has been done, do as is expected. To question is to open doorways leading to more doorways. Questioning was chaos.

Holt had brought chaos, and he had been punished for it.

*"Get up, Holt,"* Ash said. *"'You're my boy, and I am yours. Get up and keep fighting. I'll fight with you."*

A bolstering surge of courage passed over the bond. Holt gritted his teeth. Nodded. Got up. He cast his gaze around the cramped kitchen of this run-down inn, finding it hard to recognize the sick faces looking back at him in fear.

"I have magic now. It can help if the blight hasn't taken too strong a hold. Follow me."

He picked up his father's body, steadied himself, breathed deep, then took his first step. He took another.

As he passed the people of the Crag, they pressed toward him, but he told them to be patient and follow him outside.

Emerging out onto the street, he found it almost deserted. Some brave onlookers had gathered and a small group of children examined Ash at a safe distance. Most looked too ill to do anything more than sit and gaze at him. A bolder girl reached out until a sickly parent hobbled up and pulled her back.

*"They won't let me help."*

"They're afraid," Holt said. The girl did not look so sick, just a green tinge in one eye. Then, still carrying his father between his arms, he said aloud, "It's okay. Ash here can help."

The mother looked uncertain, but she took in his clean clothes, his armor and fine cloth, looked at Ash, then let go of her daughter.

"Raise your hand," Holt guided her. The little girl did, and Ash gently pressed his snout against her palm, as he'd done with Ceilia Smith.

A flash of light. A shriek from the mother. And the girl was cured. Her infected eye turned violet flecked with silver.

Onlookers began to murmur and whisper in excitement.

*"You see,"* Ash said, *"we can help."*

Holt nodded. He wanted to help, but he also didn't want to let his father go.

"Give him here, son," a voice said. Holt turned. It was Mr. Monger. He and a handful of other able-bodied hands from the Crag looked upon him pityingly. "We'll take care of him."

Holt sniffed. "You keep him here. You keep him here so I can take him with me."

"That's right," Mr. Monger said. "We will."

Ash padded closer and nuzzled into Holt's side. Holt looked at his father one last time, drew a final shuddering breath, then handed him over. He turned away at once, the better to get on with what he had to do.

In one hand he gathered lunar power; with the other he patted Ash.

"We've got work to do, boy."

# 47

## GHOSTS

Talia blazed through the palace with a singular purpose. Courtiers, household members, guards and sycophants alike bowed or acknowledged her as she went – their methods as varied as the people greeting her. No one was quite sure how to treat her as a princess dragon rider. Only when she reached the royal apartments did she pause, checking the coast was clear.

The evidence Leofric promised was the key to all of it. It would convince Osric and the court. With luck, the threat from inside the city might be removed in time.

She had known exactly what Leofric had meant when she'd read his final words to her.

*Should something happen to me, you can find what you need where even the scourge cannot reach.*

Leofric had chosen those words carefully. Should the letter be intercepted as he feared, it would be indecipherable to anyone else. The words only had real meaning to her. She clung to that thought, for she didn't think it spoke of a man delirious from illness. He knew what he was writing. And he'd been scared.

He'd been afraid, and he'd needed her.

*And I couldn't be there.*

Her eyes prickled as she fought back tears.

*No. Not until I know for sure.*

Talia found herself at the door to her old bedchamber. Her old-old bedchamber, for she had moved to a larger room down the hall two years before joining the Order. She twisted the handle, pushed, and the well-maintained door swung in without a creak.

She recognized the space but not the room. Since leaving for the Order, her mother had turned the place into a nursery. There had been talk of more children. Not anymore. The empty crib seemed a sad reminder of that reality; the fact it had been left untouched for over a year was even worse. The ghost of her father haunted every inch of it.

Talia would not have entered unless she had to. It wasn't even her final destination, for there was an attic space above this turret room. In the old days, she'd had to reach up with a long pole to open the attic door and bring the stairs down. Now she could just jump and grab it. She did so, landing back on the floor with a thud, and the stairs banged down after her.

She climbed. The dusty attic had been left untouched longer than the nursery.

Time had stood still here. Not much but a timber floor, cold air and rafters. A lone telescope still stood by the narrow window. Toys lay scattered and forgotten: Leofric's soldiers and her own wooden dragon lay on a lost make-believe battlefield. She picked up the dragon, blew off the dust.

It was bright red with yellow wings, and she'd given it the inventive name of 'Scorcher' as a little girl. Even then, she had been destined for fire. Even then, she had wanted to fight the scourge.

Yet like all children, she had also been afraid. A toddler's memory had never left her: of crying inconsolably as screeching monsters flew over the city and dead men rose from the lake. Years later, while playing in the attic with her brother, she had confided fear of those horrors to him. He'd comforted her and dubbed this room to be so high that even the scourge could not reach it. Up here, they were safe.

She dropped the hand holding Scorcher to her side and examined the room again for some sign of Leofric's evidence. Nothing obvious sprang to her attention. No package had been left out, but that would have been foolish of him. No trail through the dust now time had passed since his visit – if indeed he had come.

Perhaps under the floorboards? She moved around, hoping to hear some sound or find a loose plank but found none. Tapping Scorcher against her head, she tried to think it through.

Doubt crept up her spine. She pulled the letter out and re-read it for the thousandth time. The key information came in the opening:

*Evidence has reached me of a conspiracy so terrible it is hard to fathom. Yet it is undeniable to those in our family. A rot which has burrowed to the very heart of our kingdom. Given how deep it runs I dare not move without you by my side. As powerful as our opponents are, they cannot hope to stand against a dragon rider when the time comes.*

*I have told no one else. I cannot. I know even my conversations with Mother are overheard by prying ears in the palace, and I have long suspected that my letters to councilors are opened and read before they arrive.*

The letter was vague on what the conspiracy entailed, only that it was deep and that Leofric had felt in danger. Talia assumed this to be an attempt on his life and seizure of the throne. All the more reason Osric should listen to her. His life might still be in danger.

His conversations were being listened to, his letters opened before reaching their destination, other than letters given to loyal Nibo. Whatever was going on was happening right in the heart of the palace.

But what sort of evidence had come to Leofric's attention? Letters? If he had come by letters between Harroway and other conspirators, then surely Leofric would have been able to act without her. The evidence, in his words, was absolute. Undeniable.

Undeniable to those in the family. She chewed on his choice of words.

Leofric had specifically told her to come to their old play den. No one else would have known that. Each part had been crafted to implore her to come to his aid without giving much away in case Nibo had been captured.

She dismissed the idea that the evidence was in letters. Anything in ink would be undeniable to anyone who read it, not just their family.

The answer came to her, but it raised more questions.

Ghost orbs. The memories within those devices could only be experienced by the person who made them or those who shared their blood. But, if she was correct, then the orb and its memories could only have come from their father.

The implications were dizzying. When would this orb have been created? Why had it only resurfaced recently? What had Harroway been doing in the meantime if their father had known of the betrayal before he died? Her father couldn't have known before going to war with Risalia, she decided. Godric Agravain had been a proud man, an impatient man, but not a mad man. He would not have marched while his house stood divided.

Once more she scoured the room to no avail. Ghost orbs weren't large. They could fit comfortably in the palm of your hand.

She fixated on the telescope. No... could it be?

The journey across the attic seemed to take an age. If it wasn't in here, it wasn't anywhere. She had to bend right down to press her eye against the glass. Only darkness met her, which made sense given the black clouds outside.

But it wasn't pure darkness. There was a purple hue to the dull light.

Heart hammering, she approached the other side of the telescope. She checked on the lens. It would have been imperceptible at a distance, but the lens looked just out of place. Twisting it, she found it loose. Inside, wedged within the widest part of the brass tube, was a ghost orb.

With haste, she upended the telescope, shook it, and caught the orb as it fell out. She'd always thought they were otherworldly in hand. Though made of glass, the orb had a distinct weightlessness to it, like trying to hold onto the very smoke that would rise from it when shattered.

She wanted to yell in triumph but calmed herself, steadied her breath. A rider remained in control. She reached out to Pyra.

*"I found it, girl!"*

Pyra's purr of satisfaction bloomed from Talia's soul into her whole body.

*"You're my rider, of course you did. What does it reveal?"*

"*It's a ghost orb. I haven't looked into it yet.*"

"*I am ready to do what is necessary,*" Pyra said, her voice cold.

"*Pyra,*" Talia began, unsure how to phrase her concern, "*if it comes to swords, it will mean harming humans. Me breaking my oath to get involved at all is bad enough. You don't have to as well.*"

"*An unstable kingdom will make easy prey for the scourge. My oath, our oath, was to fight the scourge at any cost. I mark this task as fighting the scourge.*"

"*That's clever, but you know the Order won't see it that way.*"

"*We are daughters of fire and we shall do what we must!*"

The bond beat reassuringly hard, which she was grateful for. Watching this memory would not be easy.

Ready, she looked upon the orb and saw her own eyes reflected on its surface. That stare stretched on until the smoky innards of the ball swirled and an image took shape. Not a hazy impression as shattering the orb would produce, but as clear and perfect as though she witnessed it herself.

Her eyes rolled back, and the memory took over.

She was in what appeared to be a castle keep, with maps and half-eaten dishes scattered over a great table. It was hot, close and stank of sweat. Guards lined the walls and stood at the doors in force, while robed advisors leaned over the maps with their eyebrows raised or else were deep in whispered conversation.

She stepped forward – that is to say, her father stepped forward, for it was his memory after all. She was revisiting events from his perspective, and so she could smell what he had smelled, feel what he had touched. As a member of his bloodline, even an echo of his thoughts and emotions reached her too.

"How long until the Risalians reach the valley?" Godric Agravain asked.

Talia found it a strange sensation: to feel as though the speech came from her own mouth.

Several of the king's stewards looked up and then to each other. One at last spoke, and it was a man Talia had known well.

"Before week's end," Deorwin Steward said. Plump, balding with a horseshoe ring of white hair, Deorwin had been her father's eldest advisor, hailing from a long line of Stewards who tended Feorlen's monarchs. Talia felt a pang just hearing his voice again. As far as she knew, he had perished in the Toll Pass along with her father.

For this must be where they were. In the fortress that sat at the gateway between Risalia, Brenin and Feorlen. The site of eternal disagreement between the three kingdoms. The place her father had died to take.

She was forced to look away from Deorwin then as her father's gaze shifted down to the maps of the terrain. He fixated on a group of Feorlen flags pinned some way south of the Toll Pass.

"I shouldn't have let Harroway go," Godric said, tapping near those pins.

"Based on what we knew at the time, it was the right decision, Your Royal Highness," Deorwin said. "Osric was in need."

"Our need is greater now." Godric pressed upon the map with his hands as though staring at his brother's symbolized regiments might summon them forth. "Recall them both at once."

The memory began to fade, swirling again, until a new scene formed. Her father had left a series of memories for them – mere snippets of each as the orbs could only hold so much.

What hit her was noise she hadn't been ready for. The cacophony of battle; two nations clashing in a narrow valley. The ringing of steel, the death screams, the great bangs of stones crashing against walls.

Godric Agravain stood on the balcony of the keep, peering over the balustrade. Talia could feel an echo of her father's emotions. Dismay. Fear. Where had Osric gotten to? He should have been here by now.

The black and white Risalian flag continued to gain ground. Their troops poured out from siege towers onto the walls.

Someone called to him, pointing toward the southern ridge. The Feorlen side.

There at last he saw Osric's banner, two crossed gray axes. His heart leaped. He and his men were saved.

Godric gripped the balustrade, willing his brother to charge. Together they'd make such an end as to elevate Feorlen to greatness and enter their names into song.

Yet Osric did not descend into the valley. Godric gulped and caught sight of more banners speeding along the ridge. At their head was the crowned black eagle on a white field, one talon gripping a sword and the other a scepter. The flag of Risalia.

Talia felt her father's heart sink then, through the memory and all the time since she felt his pain. There was no clash upon the ridge. No skirmish at the flanks of the forces. Those banners stood together.

Godric had been betrayed.

The memory swam again, the world blurred as though moving at a speed Talia could not comprehend. When it righted, Godric stood before a group of knights and stewards. Deorwin was amongst them. Upon the table where the maps had been laid before were now a number of small, open lockboxes. A purple orb sat inside each one.

"You must ride hard and fast," Godric said, his every word breathless and desperate. "Each take a different route once out the western gate. There will be forces laid against you even in our country, but you must not fail. Make it to Sidastra and warn my son."

The knights and stewards nodded. The warriors were prepared, the stewards not so. Deorwin's bald head shone with sweat, but he hid his fear. Grim-faced, he bowed and nodded like the rest, ready to serve and fulfill his role until the end.

"I do not think we will meet again," Godric said.

He began imparting memories into the orbs. Servants followed behind, placing each filled orb into a box and then passing that to one of the knights or stewards. Before Godric reached the final orb, a door burst open and a soldier rushed in.

"Horses are assembled in the west courtyard, your majesty."

"Go then," Godric barked. "Break through. For Feorlen!"

The men hurried off, except for Deorwin, who had yet to receive his lockbox. For the older steward, Godric spared a moment for one parting embrace. Then he reached for the final orb, and the memories ended.

⁓

Colors shimmered into nothingness, then reformed as the attic space above Talia's old bedroom – where even the scourge could not reach.

She'd fallen to her knees. Tears streamed down her face, running hot and salty into her mouth as she choked out breaths. Her grip on the ghost orb turned limp. The orb ran down her fingers, hit the floor and rolled through the dust.

Talia let it roll. Her mind was far away still. She could envision the last moments of her father's life unfold. She pictured Godric's slumped shoulders as Deorwin left, all the fight drained out of him. He would have lost himself in turmoil as to why Osric had done this: not just the personal betrayal but allowing Feorlen to lose the war.

*No*, she thought grimly, savagely. Hatred struck Talia as no rage of Pyra's ever had. *Uncle Osric would never lose a fight.*

And, of course, he had not lost the Toll Pass. She saw it now, in her mind's eye, her father lost and bewildered atop the keep, watching as his men were slaughtered and the Risalians over-committed themselves. He had probably seen Osric's full force arrive on the ridge, seen the confused shuffle up there as the Risalian standard bearers were struck down. The traitor betraying his conspirators. Perhaps hope had kindled in her father then; perhaps he'd even felt bad for distrusting his brother as Osric's charge shattered the Risalian flank and cleaved through their army like so many dragon riders through ghouls.

Perhaps Godric had welcomed his brother atop the keep in the Toll Pass with open arms. Perhaps Osric had planted the axes in him himself.

She couldn't keep it back any longer. Fire blazed from her shoulders like a red cloak as grief and fury took over. Pyra's fire was her fire. The bond pumped as though her life depended on it. Talia was a dragon now, and she would burn this whole twisted place to cinders, leaving less than ash and nothing for even the worms to feast upon.

Panting, she got a hold of herself. Falling forward onto her hands, the fire in her and on her guttered out. The grief she had held at bay all day, holding back all year, broke through her defenses. She wept. Curled up in the dust of the attic floor, she wept.

Outside, Pyra wailed like a maimed animal. The dragon didn't know the details, but Talia had sent the pain across the bond, both so Pyra could understand and so it wouldn't consume her completely. It might have otherwise.

Osric had killed her father. Osric had killed her brother. For what? The throne? Osric always said he never wanted it. And that was the worst part. She did not understand why.

Her father's knights and stewards could not have made it far. Osric's men must have caught them, or they perished on the road in some other way. Yet one had made it over a year later.

The prisoners. Osric himself had just told her that Leofric paid far too much to get prisoners from the war back. He had put Leofric's charity down to "sentiment for his old tutor," and perhaps that had been right. Unknown to Osric, Deorwin had been taken by the Risalians and kept hostage. The last orb bearer had fulfilled his final mission to Godric upon returning. She wondered where Deorwin was now. Maybe Osric had killed him too.

Time had passed, and what light there had been through the small window was now fading. At last she heaved a final sobbing breath, then sat up. This was the wrong time for such horrors to come to light, but she couldn't stand her uncle sitting in her brother's chair a moment longer. The court would already be assembled. The time to act was now.

She snatched up the ghost orb and jumped down through the attic door.

*"It will come to swords, Pyra. Be ready."*

*"I'm always ready."*

For the first time in what felt like years, Talia was too. She didn't know what would come of it. She didn't know if this was the smart course, the right course. She didn't care. For once, she wasn't plagued by doubt and knew what needed to be done.

# 48

# THE TWINBLADES

A bead of sweat ran from Holt's temple into his eye. He blinked, then rubbed it away. Another pale, sickly hand touched his own. Light flashed from his palm, and he gasped as the dragon bond gave its first tremble.

A sea of the infected had pressed into the street. All sense of cohesion had long been abandoned. And Holt's strength waned. Even Ash staggered away from his latest patient.

Holt took stock. They hadn't yet managed to cure all those from the Crag that they could, never mind the countless others in sight. Ash's core had dimmed in his inner vision. It would make better sense to leave, rest, eat, Cleanse and Forge and return later. He'd keep at it, night and day, until they were all cured if he had to. Get as many as he could out into the main city before the swarm arrived.

"Ash and I must go now," he called out. "We'll return, I promise—" But he broke off as a clamor of protest arose. It was no use trying to make himself heard now.

Those capable of walking rushed or shambled toward him, bearing a resemblance to the ghouls they might become if not cured.

Ash backed up, and through the bond he felt the dragon's sensory assault and confusion.

Holt gritted his teeth. Even coming back fresh wouldn't help with the greatest problem, the sheer volume of people. Curing them one by one was too slow.

What he needed was a way to spread the lunar magic out. What he needed was to learn his new ability that the rank of Ascendant allowed. Yet Talia had her own battles to attend to.

He *could* try to do it himself.

Brode's voice reasserted itself. *You think with your heart over your mind.*

Trying out new magic on his own was not wise, but the situation was desperate. And he had to try. Had to.

His father's voice replaced Brode's. *Help the others.*

Whether wise or not, those words drove him now. If he did not follow them, then all he'd done would be for nothing. His father's death would be for nothing. Besides, Talia had helpfully forced him to torture himself in order to set up the mote channels to one leg already.

Ash roared, and the crowd took a cautious step or two back.

"Let me try something," he said to Ash.

Then he drew upon the dragon core and guided the magic down to his leg, through the wider channel he had carved out. Now he tried this, he understood at least in part why this ability worked through the legs. Just as more blood flowed to those larger limbs, so too was this mote channel larger. He could push more magic down to his lower body than through his arms. The bond grew taut as he drew on Ash's light, a sign he was pushing himself.

He only had the technique used to form a Lunar Shock to base this on, so he began gathering lunar power loosely at his heel and sole. He struggled to maintain it, felt the heat begin to rise to uncomfortable levels as the power threatened to burst out of him.

*No,* he thought in alarm. *Not like that.*

Letting the magic rush out in force would cause damage. Charged Lunar Shocks had blown the Wyrm Cloaks clean off their feet. His magic wasn't gentle enough to heal unless he made it so. But with so much magic rushing down to his leg, he had a much harder time controlling it.

It took everything he had not to let it blast out. His leg began to shake, and he had a sudden horrifying image of blasting scores of innocent people high into the air.

Folk at the front of the crowd started to sense something was wrong. They tried to back away but couldn't get far while those behind were still keen to push forward.

"Ash, I can't hold it!"

Ash maneuvered himself in front of Holt, shielding the people. Lunar magic boiled in his leg, eager to break free. At last, he had an idea. When Talia had sent out her Flamewave against the blighted hounds she had stamped her foot, which likely aided in blasting the power outward. He couldn't control the power well enough to make it gentle and healing, but he could at least direct it. What if he pushed it into the ground instead? Or as much of it as he could. That was how it worked from his hand, not a blast but a push. That might blunt its effect and spare the people from his foolishness.

He could not hold on a second longer. Holt pressed his foot hard into the cobblestones and kept pressing. The magic left slower at his behest instead of blasting outward. Holt gasped, both from letting the magic go and thinking he'd averted a crisis. But that wasn't the end of it. He stared bug-eyed at the ground as jagged white lines criss-crossed the street, radiating out from his foot. They sped out, creating a shining web underfoot until they stretched for ten feet in all directions.

Ash took up a great deal of space in front of him, but his botched magic slithered under the feet of refugees to his left, right and behind.

People cried, yelped as though burned. Holt's heart stopped, then skipped a beat. He couldn't breathe. What had he done?

"Am... am cured! Cured me he has!"

Holt twisted around so quickly in search of the voice that his neck cricked.

"Same," squealed a woman. "Oh same, Honored Rider."

"The blight's gone from my arm."

"Mine too!"

Stunned, hardly able to take it in, Holt found his breath again as every person standing on the lunar-infused stone claimed the blight had been lifted. They all tried to show him their healed skin.

Beneath their feet, the white web of lines still glowed.

"Move off," Holt called. "Let others take your place."

There was a great deal of shoving and jostling, but he picked an infected old man out from the crowd to watch and study the effect. The man stumbled in his haste and fell onto the street. As his hands touched the shining stone, white-purple wisps of flame – they weren't quite flames, but it was as best he could conceive them – licked up, and within seconds the green scaled skin on the old man's cheek healed.

Just as Holt started to feel excited, the lunar magic in the ground winked out. The temporary power of the magic vanished, yet the stones retained a white scarring.

Holt checked on his bond. It had taken a hit from that ability – Talia had been quite right that these wider area techniques put far more strain upon the bond. As a fresh Ascendant, his bond strength would be on the lower end to boot. Still, he ought to push it. Not quite to the point of fraying, but this would mean hundreds more lives could be saved.

Ash got himself out of the way, continuing to help individuals while Holt gathered magic and pressed his foot into the street for a second time. As before, the same white light scratched its way over the cobbles, curing the blight as it went.

*The ground must blunt the power enough to allow it to heal,* Holt thought.

The refugees shuffled again, and he performed the magic for a third time.

"*I'll need a name for this,*" he said to Ash. "*How about Lunar Quake?*"

"*I don't like it.*"

"*How come?*"

"*It sounds… uninspired.*"

"*You were fine with Lunar Shock.*"

"*That has a ring to it.*"

Holt frowned. "*How about Lunar Web?*"

"*That's even worse!*"

"*Fine. I'll think on it,*" Holt said.

Despite himself, despite his failure of hours ago, a smile tugged at the corner of his lips. Seeing dozens of people cured did not banish the pain of his father's death, but it did help to numb it.

He was just about to repeat the process when Ash growled. The dragon faced back down the street in the direction he and Holt had come. His ears pricked.

*"Men in steel cages are coming,"* Ash said. *"They are calling for you."*

Holt broke off and faced down the street himself. He couldn't see anything over the sea of people, but a ripple of unease wound its way through the crowd, silencing them, until those at the back began to part. A coarse voice could then be heard.

"Master Cook! Present yourself."

Holt did not like the tone of the summons but couldn't see what harm there would be. Likely the envoys had been sent to track him down and drag him back for some war council. As if he had any idea of battle preparations.

Ash stood beside him, his head low to the ground. *"I don't like the smell of them."*

As the crowd parted, the group came into clearer view. They were largely regular guards, although there were a lot of them. About twenty men in all and leading them was a duo in stronger plate mail. Over their plate they wore charcoal gray tabards emblazoned with a blue falcon.

"Rider!" one of the duo called.

"There's his dragon," the other cried, pointing to Ash.

Holt moved to meet them. Ash followed by his side, planting his front claws hard into the ground. They stopped twenty paces from each other, the refugees giving them all a wide berth.

Holt looked the leading men up and down. He could see little of them, for bandannas covered their nose and mouth to ward off infection. Both had the same dirty blonde hair, one in a lush mane, the other short and wild.

The rest of the guards wore bandannas too. They carried crossbows and spears, like the Wyrm Cloaks had, only less specialized.

Holt's hand twitched for his sword. He couldn't imagine them wanting to pick a fight with a rider, but why else bring the crossbows?

"Here I am," Holt said.

The duo both cocked their heads.

"By order of His Majesty, Osric Agravain—" the first began.

"—you are under arrest," finished the second.

Holt looked between them, then to the guards. The duo didn't blink; the guards were less assured but seemed resolved to follow their orders.

"I think there has been some mistake."

"Your true name is known," one said.

"Your rank too, commoner," said the other.

"And I do not know yours," Holt said.

"I am Eadwulf," said the first. "My brother is Eadwald."

"The Twinblades of House Harroway," they said together.

"Harroway..." Holt muttered. Now their aggression made more sense.

Holt considered his options. If he went quietly, perhaps this would all be sorted out at the palace, and if they tried to ambush him on the way, well, they'd regret it.

"Am I to know the reason for my arrest?"

"Thievery, fraud, and breach of rank."

Holt clenched his jaw. "I'm a dragon rider."

"You are not," Eadwulf said.

"You've sworn no oath," said Eadwald.

"An outlaw," Eadwulf carried on. "Let it be known," he raised his voice for the crowd, "this boy is a commoner of the westerlands, who stole a dragon. He is to be brought before the king's justice."

"The regent, you mean," a brave voice said from the crowd. "No true king would leave us here to starve!"

"This boy's been helping us," called another.

Still others were not as friendly.

"He refused to cure me but did for others!"

"If the blight is too strong, there is nothing I can do," Holt called out, hoping they would hear him.

"Cures my daughter but not me," a woman shrieked. "How is she to live on her own?"

A cold feeling sank through Holt's stomach. How was the girl indeed? He hadn't known, but he'd only been trying to help.

"Chaos bringer!" someone shouted. Others joined in.

Holt's heart picked up. He heard his father's last rasping breath again and again in his mind.

"Deceiver!"

The crowd had split into two sections now. Those in favor of Holt and those not.

Ash growled and bared his teeth.

*"How can they hate you when you've tried to save them?"* Ash asked.

*"Because it's all they know."*

Talia said Harroway disliked the Order. Yet here were his men ardently defending its honor. Brode had been right yet again. Nobles like Harroway feared those more powerful, but what they feared above all was people below them gaining it.

"Your name," Eadwulf demanded.

Holt stepped forward. "Cook," he said defiantly. "Holt Cook."

The Twinblades stepped forward as one.

"You admit to your crimes?" Eadwulf asked.

"If saving a life is a crime, then yes."

Ash braced himself and *thunked* his tail threateningly upon the street.

The guards with crossbows raised their weapons.

"You don't want to fight," Holt said. Although a part of him sought it. A part that wanted to break the world for robbing him of his father. Cleansing techniques helped in more ways than one, and Holt steadied his breath, remaining as calm as he could be. "I may not legally be a rider, but I have the powers of one."

Holt's words may as well have fallen on deaf ears, as the second brother, Eadwald, said, "Surrender your sword, Cook. One of your rank does not have permission to carry arms in public."

Several people from the Crag ran out in front of Holt then. People he had cured. Mr. Monger, Mrs. Baker, Miss Furrier, Master Tanner, two kitchenhands, and even old Mr. Cobbler stepped forward to shield him.

Eadwulf and Eadwuld both drew throwing knives from their belts.

"Part," said Eadwulf.

"To shield the outlaw is to be guilty yourselves," said Eadwald.

"We ain't going nowhere," Mr. Monger said bravely.

"Don't," Holt pleaded, "I'll go to the palace if I must. But not with you," he added to the Twinblades.

"You will come with us, Master Cook."

"Or we shall punish them for your crimes."

Holt found it harder to maintain his cool. "If you hurt him, hurt any of them, I'll—"

"Surrender your sword," the Twinblades said as one.

Holt checked on the bond. It wasn't in a good state, but it was good enough to take this lot.

*"Ready when you are,"* Ash said.

Holt very nearly attacked. Then he sighed and unstrapped his sword belt. He and Ash may well win, but how would killing a score of guards look? And it would only take one thrown knife, one stray bolt, and innocents would be dead. Enough people had suffered for his actions already.

Holt stepped between the people of the Crag, nodding to let them know it was okay, and threw his belt and scabbard at the feet of the Twinblades.

The Twinblades looked at each other, nodded, and once again stepped closer until they were only an arm's length from Holt. Their eyes flashed in triumph. Eadwulf picked up Holt's sword while Eadwald spoke.

"Kneel, criminal."

"I won't."

"Kneel, or have others pay your price."

"Holt…" Mr. Monger said weakly.

"It's okay," Holt said, getting down on his knees. "Keep my father safe for me. Talia will set things right." He looked up at the Twinblades. "You're making a mistake."

Eadwulf rose, Holt's belt and scabbard in one hand. "Say your name."

"Holt."

"Your role?" Eadwald asked.

"Dragon rider."

Eadwulf struck Holt's face with a backhanded blow.

Holt rolled with the strike, finding it didn't hurt much.

"Your name," Eadwulf demanded.

"Holt Cook," he said louder.

"Your role?" Eadwald asked.

"Dragon rider," Holt said, louder still.

Another backhanded blow from Eadwulf.

"Do that again and I'll break your hand," Holt said.

The Twinblades laughed.

"The pup barks," Eadwulf said.

"Do we believe him?"

"Nay, brother."

"Your name?" Eadwulf asked.

"Holt—" Eadwulf struck before Holt finished.

The Twinblade raised his fist again. "Your name?"

"Holt Cook!" Holt bellowed. This time he caught Eadwulf's fist inches from his face.

He held the man at bay with ease, able to squeeze, pull and twist hard if he wished. But he wouldn't risk more lives. The Twinblades had the measure of him. He was about to let go when he noticed Eadwald pull out a small vial of dark red liquid and drain it.

Before Holt could react, Eadwald's fist met the side of his head. He imagined this was what being hit by a frying pan must feel like. Colors flashed, and his vision swam as he collapsed.

Ash roared, scraped his talons off the stone, and Holt felt the bond pick up its beat. He had just enough wit left to communicate to the dragon,

*"Don't do anything, boy. We must keep the others safe."*

*"Holt…"*

*"It's okay—"*

But his thought was broken by a blow to his stomach. All his breath rushed out of him, and his ribs and head ached. Pain exploded in his back next, and the offending foot drove in for a second time. Holt rolled over, taking more blows. He spat blood.

Through the pain, he turned all his focus to the bond and to Ash. As long as Ash was there, he could weather any storm.

When the Twinblades were finished, they heaved him upright.

"Take that bag off him."

His satchel with the recipe book was wrested from him and dropped onto the cobblestones. The final insult made, they began dragging him through the streets.

# 49

# THE GREAT SHOW

The Twinblades of House Harroway dragged Holt through Sidastra. Ash prowled behind, growling low. More crossbowmen and spearmen had met them in the west quarter to act as escorts and keep Ash in check.

Much of the city passed in a daze, both because Holt's head still rang from Eadwald's empowered fist and from the dizzying link between the Wyrm Cloaks in the woods and men under Harroway's command.

Eadwald had drunk dragon blood.

It confirmed Brode's fears that someone high up in the Feorlen military had supplied the cultists. But to adopt their vile tactics in turn? This anti-rider cabal had delved to a sickening low.

They dragged him all the way to the palace.

"The dragon stays outside," Eadwulf instructed the guards.

"Take him around the back to the other one," said Eadwald.

Ash bellowed.

"*Be good,*" Holt told him.

"*I won't leave you.*"

The Twinblades were already hauling Holt off again.

"*Stick with Pyra,*" Holt said. "*Keep yourself safe.*"

"*They'll be sorry if they try pointing those sharp little trees at her,*" Ash said.

"*Talia will sort things out,*" Holt said. "*Don't worry.*"

"*We were just trying to help... tell them that.*"

Holt said nothing. Poor Ash didn't quite understand how this worked.

Ash stomped through one of the hedgerows, and then Holt lost sight of him as he passed through the palace gates. He entered a cool stone hall with tall columns on either side. The place was packed with well-dressed nobles, ealdors perhaps or their envoys at court, stewards, coteries like Nibo, and countless soldiers, many standing in the wings while others sat or stood in the galleries. At the far end towered a tiered series of high-backed chairs, leading up to the throne.

Osric sat upon the throne, looming over everyone.

The Twinblades walked Holt out onto the floor as though it were a stage and he the leading player.

"Kneel before your king," the Twinblades said together.

Holt got down on both knees as a murmuring rose from the onlookers.

He looked at Osric, wondering when this would start, wondering why he had allowed Harroway and his thugs to treat him like this.

"*Little one,*" Pyra spoke to him. "*There is more danger here than we realized. Talia is coming, but her allies in the palace are few – she will unmask her uncle but be ready to fight.*"

*Her uncle? The traitor? Fight?*

His mind reeled from the news, but he wrestled himself back into a state of calm, mastering his breath. His ear still smarted from where Eadwald had struck him, but otherwise he was unharmed. Fearing the fight would come soon, he checked to make sure he could still pull on magic from Ash's core. He had never tried it this far apart.

His bond beat as firm as ever, but the core appeared distant. Its light was just out of reach. That might be a problem. Without magic, he would have to rely on his strength and skill. Strength he had, but he would be the first to admit he lacked skill with a sword, and he imagined the Twinblades were named so for good reason.

Behind the throne, a large portion of the wall was ornate stained glass. He focused and sent a mental image of it across the bond to Ash.

*"If you need to break in..."*

A middle-aged man crossed the floor to meet Holt. Dressed for battle, his plate suit fitted over a round belly, complete with the same blue hawk tabard that Eadwulf and Eadwald wore. The tabard of House Harroway. The man's eyebrows and mustache were so thick that it looked like three hairy caterpillars clung to his face.

The Twinblades inclined their heads to him.

*So*, Holt thought. *This is Ealdor Harroway.*

Considering how long he and Talia had pictured him as the mastermind of events, Holt was disappointed. For one of the most powerful men in Feorlen – and currently the Master of War – he wasn't imposing. He had nothing on the otherworldliness of Silas Silverstrike or the stature of Osric Agravain.

Without rising from his chair, Osric made a gesture for the hall to quieten.

Nothing further happened. Where was Talia? He found he didn't want to wait. They would expect him to be silent and cowed as one who had breached rank so severely should be when caught. He wouldn't give them that.

"Am I to know the meaning of this?" Holt asked, his voice ringing through the throne room.

"The court has been summoned to discuss the impending attack upon this city," Osric said.

"That isn't what I asked."

The court broke out in fierce whispering at that.

Osric rapped his fingers on the arm of his throne three times. "We can begin early if that is your wish?"

As though waiting for this cue, the doors to the hall were shut and heavy bolts slammed into place.

"Begin," Osric commanded.

Lord Harroway cleared his throat and, to Holt's astonishment, wiped his glistening brow. "Your Majesty, are you sure now is the best time for this? The swarm will be upon us soon after all, and a dragon rider – however the boy has become one – would be invalu—"

"Is the hair in your ears as thick as your brow?" Osric said. "I said, begin."

Harroway swallowed his words. "Yes, Your Majesty." His mustache twitched, and he wiped his face again. "I call upon the Steward of Names to bring forth the census records."

A surprisingly young, pockmarked man bustled out, nearly tripping over his robes in his haste. He carried the largest book Holt had ever seen.

"Ealdors of Feorlen," Harroway continued, "eminent members of Sidastra, before you kneels a young man who claims himself to be a rider. He is a fraud."

A great deal of muttering followed these words. People stood up from their seats to get a better look at him.

"I am bonded to a dragon," Holt said.

Another blow to the back of his head, though this one barely hurt. At least the buff from the dragon's blood had worn off Eadwald.

"His name is Ash," Holt said. "And he's right outside. You can all come to meet him."

This time, Holt was ready for the strike. He bent back to dodge the blow and, rather than hitting him, the brother's momentum carried him forward to stumble. Holt righted himself, focusing on his breathing, not giving them the satisfaction of seeing him beg or even bristle at the injustice.

"I am a dragon rider."

He was also playing for time. Reaching out to Ash, he asked, *Where is Talia?*

Harroway took the book from the young steward and opened it at the marked page. "Your name is Holt Cook. You were born at the Crag sixteen springs ago. Your father was a Cook."

Holt's insides turned to ice. It was all he could do to fight back fresh tears. The wound was still too fresh.

"Your grandfather was a Cook," Harroway continued. "Thus, you have acquired the powers of the *noble* Order through theft and fraud, preventing a trueborn son or daughter of the deserved ealdors from taking their rightful place in defense of our country."

"Do I get a chance to speak?"

"You fully admitted your name and rank to the king himself," Harroway said. "Do you deny it?"

"No," Holt said.

"You admitted to His Majesty that you did not swear an oath to the Order?"

"Not yet, but—"

"Then you are—" Harroway raised his voice even louder, "—hereby charged with breach of role and with instigating chaos during an incursion."

The audience began shouting then. What they shouted at him and to each other was incoherent noise. Holt ignored Harroway and stared dumbfounded at Osric.

Punishment for the latter charge was death.

"Given the unique circumstances," Harroway called, "the usual sentencing cannot be dispensed. You are neither fully under the jurisdiction of the king nor the Order. You will be held prisoner until such time as members of the Order arrive to advise upon the matter. But henceforth, Holt Cook, you are stripped of name and role, and are banished from Feorlen."

The impact of this didn't fully register. Holt wondered whether he was in shock or whether he simply did not care. Let Osric and Harroway have their show. Once Talia ousted them, it would not matter.

Yet now the baying of the nobles became focused and clear. They cheered the decision, jeered at him, called him a chaos bringer and scourge friend. They didn't know what he'd been doing out on the quarantine isle. And they did not want to know.

Let them strip him of his name and send him away. He had lost everything else.

A booming sound cut over the crowd. Before the guards could react, a door to the far right of the throne broke open. At the head of the group pouring in, her sword drawn, fire blazing on the steel and in her eyes, was Talia. Behind her came knights and other soldiers of the family household Osric had not yet had the time to replace. Compared to the number of troops and Harroway's men in the throne room, they were outnumbered, but a dragon rider in full fury counted for a lot.

"This sham ends here," she cried, and Holt thought he heard a trace of Pyra in her speech. She was angrier than he'd ever seen her.

"Not now," Osric said.

Talia's arm shook as she pointed her blade up to him. "Get down off that throne, Uncle. You're not fit to sit on it."

For the first time in the proceedings, Osric sat up straight and took notice.

"I am unfit?" he called, with all the authority of a man who'd never lost a battle. "Why? Because I wouldn't entertain your fanciful notions about a trusted ealdor of the realm? Settle, niece."

"You are unfit," Talia carried on, her voice shaking with rage. "You are unfit because you are a traitor. And not just to your family and the kingdom but to all of us – all of the living too, if I'm right."

Dead silence met her words. Holt tried desperately to catch Talia's eye, but she didn't take her gaze off her uncle.

At length, Osric rallied. "The former princess is clearly stricken with grief for her brother. Forgive her outbursts."

"Don't you dare," Talia screamed. "Don't you dare mention them – murderer!"

"This is most irregular," Harroway declared. "Princess, please consider who you're talking to."

Talia rounded on the fat ealdor and, for a split second, Holt thought she might leap across the room and gut him. Then she returned her gaze to Osric.

"Tell your lapdog to be quiet or I'll cut out his tongue. Get down from the throne, Uncle. I won't ask you again."

"I believe she means it, Ealdor Harroway," Osric said. "Fine then, let's have it out. Tell the court of your theories and let them decide. I tried to warn you."

Talia did not lower her weapon, but she did turn to address the hall.

"The crimes of my uncle are long. I believe he poisoned my brother, that he consorts with Wyrm Cloaks, and that he is in league with the traitorous rider Silas Silverstrike and so, worst of all, the very scourge which threaten this land."

"Nonsense!" someone barked from the stands.

"Base lunacy!"

"Really, princess," Harroway said. "What wild tales are these?"

"But you, Ealdor Harroway," Talia said, walking dangerously toward him. "You are part of this, aren't you? I admit I cannot see what you have to gain from it. Yet we can cut to the heart of it all right now. Why, Ealdor Harroway, as Master of War, did you order the western garrisons not to march to Sidastra in our time of need?"

That quieted the court.

"Not march?" Harroway boomed. "Of course I did!"

"Then where are they?" Talia spoke to the galleries again. "Why is it that almost a quarter of our forces have not come to join the city's defense?"

"They have been waylaid," Harroway spluttered. "Attacked or slowed on the road. Or so our last intelligence reports—"

"Don't lie," Talia said. "The Knight Commander of Fort Kennet himself told me of your troubling orders. Tell the truth, or it shall be revealed by one of the commanders once the swarm is defeated."

"Prince...Lord Ride... Talia," Harroway blustered. "I would never... why would I do such a thing?"

Talia twitched. She lowered her sword by a fraction

"Believe me," Harroway said. "Why would I seek to weaken my own home?"

And Holt believed him. It was too good a performance otherwise. Harroway had not sent those orders.

Some of the fire in Talia's eyes burned out. "You... you didn't know?"

Harroway shook his head.

She rounded again on her uncle.

"There is no proof for these wild claims," Osric said. "I fear my niece is suffering from the same delusions her brother succumbed to."

"My brother was not mad!"

"You are testing the patience of this court," Osric said. "As a dragon rider, your input and service will be valued in the coming days, but you parade your magic and your temper in this throne room as though you have a right to it. You sacrificed that right years ago. You swore away your family and your title. As far as this court is concerned, you have no right to speak unless I grant it. I take it away."

Holt thought him to be remarkably calm himself under the circumstances. If Talia really did lose it, he'd be dead within seconds, no matter how many guards he had. Yet he goaded and pushed her as though he had all the power.

Talia did the last thing Holt expected. She started to laugh.

"Oh, Uncle, you think this will go away just by silencing me? You think you can convince everyone because there is no proof?" She produced, as though from thin air, a small sphere of purple glass.

*A ghost orb! Leofric did leave her something after all.*

Talia held it high, and the court drew a collective breath.

For the first time, Osric stiffened. "What is that?"

"This?" Talia said, her voice high as she struggled to keep herself under control. "This ghost orb contains the last memories left to me by my father. Your brother, who you betrayed."

Harroway bustled over to her. "Tali—Honored Rider, are you certain?"

"I am. You were there as well, were you not, Ealdor?"

Harroway blustered incoherently, his jowls quivering as he sought words.

"We all know the events of last year's war, don't we?" Talia said to the court at large. "What happened at the Battle of the Toll Pass. My uncle won that battle, and so it is his version we hear. That he hastened to help my father, arrived too late to prevent the Risalians taking the fortress but descended with brotherly fury into the valley, vanquishing their tired host to avenge our king."

Osric flicked a hand in some command, and the guards at the base of the tiered chairs readied themselves. Holt felt the Twinblades shift beside him. They looked to Harroway, but the Master of War stayed them. The soldiers who had entered with Talia gripped their own hilts, lifted shields, and tightened ranks.

"The truth is my uncle conspired with the Risalians before he betrayed them in turn. In one move he stole both the crown and victory for himself."

"Seize her!" Osric cried. Too few guards advanced to make a difference.

"Let them see!" Talia screamed, and she smashed the ghost orb upon the floor.

Up from the fragments of glass rose more smoke than should have fit inside it. It spun itself out into a room's worth of people, their voices echoing within the hall.

Everyone was gripped by the memory weaving before them, but Holt kept an eye on the soldiers and the Twinblades. If anyone started a fight, he would spring up in an instant.

The smokey scene flattened then rose anew to show a raging battle and many banners upon a distant ridge. Mutterings around the hall rose into shocked gasps. The banners meant little to Holt, although he guessed the one with the two axes on it belonged to Osric.

Harroway spoke up as the scene played out. "We understood it that the king had not sent up the signal." He pointed at Osric. "What was the meaning of the meeting with the Risalians?"

Osric said nothing. He had become unnaturally still.

Below him, upon the tiered seats, the stewards and other nobles of high office began to clamber down. The soldiers wearing the Harroway colors began to close in toward their ealdor. Those guarding the throne moved away to join Talia's men.

Holt let out a sigh of relief. Perhaps no fight would come after all.

The smoke faded. King Godric Agravain's last words died with it.

"Come down, Uncle," Talia said. "It's over."

# 50

## AN AUDIENCE WITH SOVEREIGN

At last, Osric got off the throne and stood. He moved languidly, as though wearied by some nuisance he now had to deal with. Everyone looked at him.

"Friends, nobles, countrymen," he began. "My time here has ended."

Before anyone could react, he raised his hands and his eyes warped into two black voids. When next Osric spoke, it was with a ringing, commanding boom.

"Be still," he said, and underneath his human voice was something greater, something ancient.

Holt was halfway through getting to his feet when he heard the sweet voice at the back of his mind. It was quite convincing, and so he slowed himself down until his limbs barely moved. Everyone else suffered from the same effect. Talia raised her blade a sliver at a time. Harroway's expression remained stuck in a silent gasp of surprise.

The sweet voice at the back of Holt's mind told him again to *"be still."* Holt froze in place, stuck in a half-squat. He could only blink and shift his gaze. He tried to shout but couldn't, tried to summon magic but couldn't.

Osric had just used magic. That meant he had become a dragon rider. And, like Rake, he had somehow cloaked his soul to prevent either Talia or himself sensing his presence. Not that either of them had thought to inspect him for a bond. The pair of them were outclassed once again.

"*Stay still,*" the sweet voice said.

Holt fought it.

"*Stay still,*" it said. "*There's no need to move.*"

"*You can't make me,*" Holt told it. He pushed with all his might and his legs rose by another inch.

Gripped by his magic, Osric's black eyes had lost their pupils, but Holt knew he was now looking straight at him. The piercing stare had become literal. Lances of pain cut into Holt's head like iron rods, and Osric's voice entered his mind like a dragon's.

"*You are not like the others.*"

A harsh presence swept over his soul. Nothing gentle about it.

"*Impressive for a bond to be so strong in one so young. And what is this song?*"

Once again, stabs of blinding pain coursed through his head. Memories flashed before him, though he had not summoned them. They whisked through everything relating to Ash, lingering on the emerald Warden's pleasure at discovering lunar magic. All the while, Holt continued his slow rise, pushing back against the power trying to keep him in place.

"*Yes. You are the solution I've been waiting for.*"

"*Get out of my head, Osric.*"

The voice laughed, and as it laughed it lost all its humanity. Only the ancient, powerful, hateful part remained.

"*Submit, Holt Cook. Know your place.*"

No sweet voice this time. This time the need to stay still overwhelmed him. His knees buckled, and he hit the stone hard.

Why? Why did everyone want him to bend? He was his own man. He made his own choices, and he had faced the worst consequences already. For a lifetime he would feel the pain of those consequences. Once again, Holt fought back. Tears streamed from the effort and he worried his face would explode from concentration, but he lifted one leg to plant a foot firmly on the floor.

"*Impressive,*" the voice said. "*You and Ash should join me, Holt. With your powers, my plans will be complete.*"

Join him? Holt knew at once who this was now.

"*I won't join you, Sovereign.*"

"*You will be mine.*"

Holt's head seared again. With dawning horror, he realized this must be how Silas Silverstrike had been turned. He wasn't really a traitor after all.

"*Oh, but I'm afraid he is, child,*" Sovereign said. "*Clesh is the true believer in my cause. Silas is a begrudging pawn but understands he must submit if he is to live. There will be space for you and Ash in my new world, if only you'll join me freely.*"

"*Never,*" Holt said, his inner voice trembling under the strain of Sovereign's will. "*You killed Talia's brother. You killed Brode. Your scourge killed my father. It's all because of you.*"

Out of the corner of his eye, he saw movement. Talia had started to defrost. Fire gathered in slow motion in her hand. Others were beginning to break free too, though much slower. Harroway backed away one glacial step at a time. Enough of Sovereign's will must have been focused on Holt for the others to gain a chance.

"*I see them moving too, child,*" Sovereign said.

Several things happened at once.

Holt gasped as the presence of the dragon left his mind and he collapsed. The magic holding Talia and everyone else broke. Talia released her Fireball at Osric. And from outside came shrill shrieks.

Osric – his eyes still black and possessed by Sovereign – flicked Talia's magic away as easily as Silas had. He drew his axes and cleaved through the guards attempting to subdue him with horrific efficiency. Talia ran toward the fight.

Holt had only just picked himself off the ground when Ash cried out to him, "*Scourge coming!*"

Even as Ash spoke, the huge stained-glass wall behind the throne shattered into a rainbow of glistening shards. Stingers poured in alongside the heavier, beetle-like bugs.

Holt spun around. "My sword!" he yelled to Eadwulf.

To the credit of the Twinblades, they didn't hesitate. Eadwulf tossed Holt his sword, and the pair of them drew theirs. Holt snatched his scabbard and belt out of the air, unsheathed his weapon and strode forward. The Twinblades flanked him like an honor guard.

Talia reached the steps to the throne just as the heavy beetles landed in the middle of the hall, cutting off Holt's view of her. Their hardened backs lifted and out jumped, fell, or crawled dozens of ghouls that had been packed inside.

*"Ash, we need you and Pyra in here now!"*

*"We know!"*

No more time to think. A ghoul swung a two-handed sword at his right side, but Holt's new body allowed him to twist and turn the strike away with ease. The dragon bond began to thrum, but weakened from the day's efforts it wouldn't last for long. Ash was still too far away for Holt to draw upon the core.

Courtiers screamed. Everyone who wasn't trained for combat ran for the exits to the upper or lower floors. Soldiers rushed to the center of the throne room where the carriers were unloading their ghoulish payloads, but stingers picked individuals off.

Ash and Pyra roared their way in through the breach in the stained glass. Ash followed close behind Pyra as though she were a mother duck but dived for Holt upon entering. The dragon stumbled his landing, smacking into the back of a grounded carrier before toppling onto Holt's side of the room. Ash scrambled up, sweeping his tail to knock ghouls over as he rose.

Holt darted to him. "We need to help Talia."

As he spoke, she screamed out of sight and Pyra's tail fell with a stone-cracking thud.

Two more carriers entered, landed, and opened their backs. Ghouls shuffled at speed to join the melee in the center of the hall.

Holt didn't have the luxury of cutting his way through. He summoned Ash's light, channeled it to his leg, ran into the midst of the scourge and drove his foot down. Light cut across the floor, creating white veins as though the stone had turned to marble.

The ghouls did not react at once. Whereas a Lunar Shock blasted holes clean through the creatures, this light weaving along the floor did not do instant damage. Holt cursed, worried he'd ruined his chances at an effective area attack. Purple-white light did curl up at the feet of the ghouls, and though they howled from it, they kept fighting.

Holt felt a rush through his own body, perhaps a second wind. He struck quick and hard at the nearest enemies, who seemed to slow with each passing second. Lunar magic began to lick up at the feet of the ghouls who stood upon light-crossed ground. They howled in pain.

His ability, whatever he had created, appeared to damage the scourge over time. Not ideal, but it was something. And those ghouls on the lunar ground were less dexterous than before, while he and the human guards were unaffected.

Enough ghouls fell to create a path through to their carrier.

*"Come on,"* Holt said to Ash. Holt softened the shell of the carrier with a Lunar Shock, and once they got so close that Ash could not miss, the dragon bathed the bug in his breath. Sizzling, the carrier slumped. Holt jumped, high enough to carry clean over the fallen insect, and landed hard on the other side.

Talia and Pyra were both directing jets of fire at Osric, who held them back with a spinning technique similar to how Rake had reflected Clesh's magic.

Ash landed beside Holt with a beat of his wings and the pair of them started forward. Osric turned his black eyes upon them. Once more, Holt felt lancing pain in his head and the total compulsion to stop moving. He dropped his sword.

*"Do not waste your breath on this doomed city. They would not even defend you. They would have had you strung up for—"* And just as suddenly as it had started, the voice of Sovereign broke off, replaced as though from far away by a human voice.

Osric's voice. *"Tell Talia I'm sorry. Tell her for me…"*

His words trailed off into nothingness, and Sovereign returned.

*"Think on my offer, Holt Cook."*

With that, Osric swept both Pyra and Talia aside in an explosion of dark energy. Talia flew back, landing badly, and rolled. Pyra reared her long neck back, growling in pain.

Mixed with Pyra's groans came a new ragged roar. The last panes of glass shook from the wall and a scourge risen dragon entered the fray. It moved unnaturally, scuttling quite unlike a dragon. Its milky greens eyes were fixed on Osric.

"It begins in your wretched land," Osric announced in his dragonish voice. "You rodents will be purged. The scourge shall fulfill its purpose!"

Osric sheathed his axes, turned and leaped onto the back of the scourge dragon. They took off through the breach, and what stingers remained in the hall buzzed out after them.

Holt sent a Lunar Shock after one but missed. His soul burned, so he checked on the dragon bond. A flaw had appeared at the edge like glass beginning to crack under pressure. Time to stop.

Pyra looked, ready to chase after Osric, but Talia called her back.

"Let him go."

As the last ghoul sputtered to its death, Holt moved to stand by Talia's side. He said nothing, and she said nothing.

The enemy had struck at the heart of the kingdom. If there was even a kingdom left, after this.

# 51

# LESSON ONE

Corpses littered the throne room. More ghouls and bugs had fallen than men, but the scourge had bodies to spare. This attack had had only one objective: to extract Osric.

Talia said nothing, and Holt took his cue from her. And, if Holt was honest with himself, he didn't feel like talking either. He would have to retell what had befallen him earlier that day. Have to tell her of Osric's – the real Osric's – plea for forgiveness; that some vestige of her uncle remained. At least they could at last put the puzzle pieces together, although Holt still could not figure out one thing.

Why was Sovereign doing all of this? Why take control of the scourge? Speaking through Osric, the dragon had announced that "the scourge shall fulfill its purpose." What purpose could that possibly be? It almost sounded as though the scourge had been created like a common utensil.

Turning his attention back to his immediate situation, Holt knelt and wiped his sword on a dead guard's cloak. Sheathing it, he went to meet Ash and they touched brows. He wrapped an arm around Ash's neck. A soothing heat passed over the bond.

*"We should have known Talia's uncle was false."*

That took Holt aback. "How could we? I never thought to reach out and see if he had a bond... but nor did I sense any magical presence about him at all. Did you?"

"No."

"Then how could we have known? Talia and Pyra noticed nothing. Rake can hide his core, and this Sovereign seems more than powerful enough to do so."

*"Nothing in his voice spoke of treachery. He spoke with conviction, with a truth. His heart beat steady."*

"Sovereign seems to think what he's doing is right. He spoke to me. And if he's the one controlling Osric, then it may never have really been Osric speaking."

*"Sovereign spoke to me too."*

Holt dropped his voice. "What did he say?"

*"That I shouldn't rely on you for strength... that I shouldn't weaken myself to serve you... that you'll cause me pain in the end."*

Holt wrapped his other arm around Ash and pressed his head harder against the white scales. "That sounds like a mouthful."

*"I wanted to tell him he was wrong, but it was so... so hard to speak against him."*

"He's extremely powerful."

*"And,"* Ash carried on, a low rumble awakening in his throat, *"he said he would help me break our bond, once we were finished with you."*

"He does realize we talk to each other?"

*"I found it hard to speak back,"* Ash said again. *"But I could think of you and showed him what you meant to me, and that's when he said he'd let you live in his new world if I joined him. The only way you would live."*

"Your magic counters his forces. Of course he'd want you on his side."

Ash lowered his head and twisted away.

"What's the matter?"

*"When he asked me again, after threatening you... I didn't know what to say."*

Holt tried to pull Ash closer, but the dragon squirmed away.

*"If... if it was the only way to save you—"*

"It won't come to that," Holt said. "We won't let it."

Ash growled but said nothing. Holt let the matter slide. Truth was, he felt as powerless against Sovereign as he had been as a pot boy facing Ysera.

"You're wounded," Holt said, noticing the bleeding cut on Ash's side.

*"It's nothing."*

Holt checked it anyway and decided it was minor enough to shrug off. Bits of glass had also lodged into Ash's thick scales, likely from when he'd scrambled through the shattered window.

He had just finished picking the glass out when some of the nobles cautiously returned to the throne room. Many retched at the sight of the dead, or it might have been the smell: the death stink of the scourge and the coppery tang of blood. It was amazing how fast he had become accustomed to such things.

The plump figure of Ealdor Harroway caught his eye. He was making straight for Talia, the Twinblades moving to flank him like loyal hounds. Pyra snarled and bared her teeth at the man. He gulped, raised both palms and stopped dead in his tracks.

Talia gave him a scathing look, up and down, before allowing him to approach.

Holt hurried over too. He had his own grievances to settle.

"Speak," Talia said.

When Harroway at last managed to form words, they were half choked. "I did not know. I swear—"

"Know of what?" Talia said. "That you betrayed my father? That you unwittingly allowed the kingdom to come to the brink of destruction? You're either as duplicitous as my uncle or you're a fool, Harroway. Decide."

"Then I am a fool."

Talia shook her head, unable to even look at him anymore. "Did you not for one moment suspect?"

"I was blind. Blinded by my frustration with your father's pointless war, his placating of your Order – the realm was suffering for his ego. I... I thought it for the best when he fell in the battle..." He trailed off meekly but rallied to say, "But I would never knowingly weaken this kingdom with an incursion brewing, especially so close after the war. No one in their right mind would."

"What about your men using dragon blood?" Holt asked.

"What?" Talia said hoarsely.

"Dragon blood," Holt said, "Eadwald here drank some before he tried to knock me out. Just like the Wyrm Cloaks."

Pyra's snarl deepened and she dragged a single talon along the stone floor, causing an awful screech. Harroway shuddered, perhaps from realizing he had been caught on some other charge, perhaps from Pyra's talon.

"The king, ah, that is to say, your uncle, told us it was a potent elixir he'd discovered the recipe for on his travels beyond the Jade Jungle."

Talia took a step closer. "Stop lying or I swear, oath or no, I'll burn off your tongue."

"That is the truth. It's what he told us. I saw it as a way we could prove the Order was no longer necessary. I was blinded again, but I... well I did wonder as to the nature of—"

"How much of it is left?" Talia cut over him. She directed her question at the Twinblades.

The brothers had remained so still throughout the exchange, Holt wondered if they weren't entirely human themselves. They glanced at each other after Talia's question, then back at her.

"At least one crate," Eadwulf said.

"Enough for one company," said Eadwald.

Harroway fell to his knees before Talia. "We will destroy them. We'll throw them into the lake or burn them – yes, burn them. Please, Honored Rider, princess—"

Talia raised a fist wreathed in fire. There was a manic glint in her eye, and again Holt wondered whether she would take his head then and there. Also, again, he heard that part of himself that felt it justified. He and Talia had lost so much. Why should this fat noble escape pain?

"Call me by my name," Talia said. "I cannot be half a rider and half a princess at once. As for the blood, as much as it sickens me to say so, you will not destroy it. This city will be attacked within days. Your men will need it." Her voice was grim.

Holt glanced at Pyra, sure the dragon would not abide this. Her fury was contained for now, although the air became sweltering as her aura flared.

Harroway's head and hair were slick with sweat. "Forgive me."

"I don't think I can, but my uncle was right on this much: by law I am no longer your princess, only a dragon rider. It's not up to me to decide your fate." She lowered her fist, and the fire on it and in her eyes went out. "Do your duty, Master of War. Defend this city and you'll earn a shred of redemption." She backed away, and Harroway got unsteadily to his feet.

"Thank you."

"Don't thank me," she said with disgust. "Go and prepare for the siege."

"We'd welcome your counsel, as a dragon rider."

"If you're willing to listen to a green girl who has not survived her first incursion? I know your feelings on the Order are not—"

"I'd be grateful for your input," Harroway interrupted. "In my hopes to prove a human army alone can defeat the swarm... I never accounted for such a swarm to be so well controlled, with our western forces absent and without a monarch—"

"It's a time for generals," Talia said. "Leofric would have relied on others to prepare the city."

"We were all relying on Osric, but a monarch is more than the person. With the throne empty and with no clear successor, I fear for the stability of Feorlen. Order defeats chaos..." Harroway pursed his lips and glanced at his plush shoes. He breathed heavily and looked back up with a determined frown. "And laws... can be changed, Talia."

She looked away. Her face could have been cold stone.

Onlookers had gathered by now, lurking behind the columns or by what remained of the seating in the galleries. Many seemed to be holding their breath. Harroway had all but offered Talia the throne.

"I'll inspect the western isles soon," she said. "First I must make sure the dragons are fed and have strength for the fight to come."

Harroway took the evasion well. He inclined his head – not so low as to be a bow – and repeated this for Holt. "I would of course value your own input, Honored Rider."

"I thought I was banished. A chaos bringer worthy only of the dungeons?"

As Harroway blustered on, Holt ignored him and paid closer attention to the gathered courtiers. Most of them had bayed for his blood within this very hour. Had Osric not been unmasked, Holt would have been thrown in a cell or forced to fight his way out and flee.

He'd long had dreams of being a dragon rider; in none of them had he been beaten, stripped of his name, and cursed for his service. In none of them had he cradled his dying father and been unable to summon the power to help.

"It's not my role," Holt said, cutting over Harroway. The ealdor gulped. His mustache quivered. Holt gave him a mocking smile. "I could arrange you a feast, but not a battle. And there are more important things for me to do in this city than listen to your two-faced lies."

Time to go. He had to retrieve his father. And there were too many people on the quarantine isle who needed his help. He was just about to climb up onto Ash's back when Talia called,

"You can't go back."

He ignored her, got onto Ash, then felt a strong hand around his ankle. He twisted around, finding Talia below him.

"You can't," she said softly.

"I found my father." His voice cracked. "I couldn't save him."

Talia appeared to feel the blow as much as he had. Her grip on him fell slack, and for a moment she had nothing but pity in her eyes.

"But I can save others," Holt insisted. "There are thousands there."

Talia's grip on his ankle returned with renewed force. She gave him a look that offered no rebuke, a commanding look. "There are hundreds of thousands in the whole city. I'm sorry, but I need you and Ash to be fighting fit when the swarm comes."

"Talia—"

"You can't save them all, Holt. That's lesson one, remember?"

"I'm not in the damned Order," Holt said, finding it harder than ever not to scream. Talia of all people should understand this. "I haven't sworn your oath or learned your lessons."

"One day, you will," Talia said. "And you'll have to follow orders. Even ones you don't like. Get used to it."

The strangest thing about her words was how numb he felt at hearing them. Had he been waiting, perhaps hoping, to hear them? A reason to stop. He was tired. Not so much physically but in every other way. His mote channels ached like muscles in need of a hot bath. His will had drained more and more after each terrible revelation, each awful thing.

Talia softened. "You may collect your father's body but do no more. We'll burn him properly. We never got the chance with Brode..."

Holt slumped, felt all the breath and fight go out of him. She was right. Maybe, just maybe, Brode's wish for him to think and not leap had sunk in. He and Ash weren't strong enough. Not yet.

"I know we can't save them all," he said. "But I wish we could."

She couldn't quite meet his eye but let go of his ankle. "Cleanse and Forge once you return," she said. "Night and day until the battle. Your body will handle the lack of sleep for now."

Holt nodded again, wishing now to just be alone. Just he and Ash. The pair of them sniffed deeply at the metallic blood upon the air, listened closely to the ringing wind as it blew in through the shattered window. They spoke the words and their senses blended. They took off out through the window, over the corpses of stingers and carriers, over garden hedgerows, turned southeast, and headed for the grim quarantine isle where smoke still billowed.

# 52

# NO SUCH THING AS PARTING

Holt knew he ought to Cleanse and Forge every minute they had left until the swarm arrived. With Osric's departure, that would surely be soon. He knew fine well that if he and Talia failed, then the city, the whole kingdom, would fall. And that if Feorlen fell to the scourge, the swarm that would rise in its wake might be too great for Brenin or Risalia to handle. One by one, they would fall, and then the Free Cities too. The whole world could fall.

But he had something more important to do first.

He and Ash made it back to the quarantine isle in good time. They found the Crag's people. Mr. Monger and the others had kept his father away from those who would take him to the pyres. Not only that, he had retrieved Holt's satchel and the recipe book inside it. Holt thanked him, thanked them all, slung his bag back over his shoulder, and then, arms trembling, took his father's body. He had decided upon his short flight from the palace that he would carry his father's body out of that wretched place himself.

No shortcuts. No flight. No magic. Not that his father's frail, limp form weighed much now.

Holt carried him through the streets as easily as a babe. He wept the whole way. Ash walked by his side, lending him support and encouragement over their bond when he needed it most.

He led the cured people of the Crag with him as well, and a grimmer procession he could not conceive of. Husbands parted from wives, brothers from brothers, sisters from dearest friends, children from parents. Holt had hated explaining he could not help more of them. Either they were too sick, or he had to conserve his strength. He would never forget their faces. Nor the silence that consumed their long march off the quarantine isle.

Talia met them in the west quarter and hurriedly gave him directions to one of the smallest islands between the outer and inner rings. One of the isles they used for burning bodies after an incursion ended. It had already been prepared.

Yet once they had made it to that sad small isle, Holt found it hard to finish the job. He stood with Ash, holding a torch before the small pyre, his father a dark figure on its top. Black waters lapped all around them. The night was pitch black and close. And he could not summon the right words. Something had to be said.

What was left of the people of the Crag were behind them. He could feel their collective stares. They had their own respects to pay.

He turned. "I know this isn't my fault," he began, "but I might have been able to help... if I were stronger. I swear, I will never let weakness hold me back again. I'll train. We'll train. Harder than anyone has before, and I won't let people die just because I wasn't strong enough..."

He trailed off into a sniff. Not as heroic as he would have liked. Not the conviction of Commander Denna, not the presence of Osric, not the undeniable power of Silas Silverstrike. But Denna was dead. Osric enslaved. And Silas a traitor. There was only Holt and Talia now. Two children left where the heroes had fallen or lost their way.

Just as he was about to set his torch to the wood, Talia and Pyra swooped down to join the funeral. For years, she too had called the Crag her home. Holt nodded to her, glad she had come, and she came to place a reassuring hand upon his back.

"A servant completely out of his depth once told me that if you love with your eyes, death is forever. If you love with your heart, there is no such thing as parting."

Holt sniffed, heaved a deep breath, and at last he set fire to the pyre. Pyra's amber eyes glowed bright, and the fire roared to life. He stepped back and leaned into Ash, watching as the flames took his father away from the cold dark world.

One by one, the people of the Crag stepped up to the pyre and threw on tokens of their own. Shoes from loved ones; a sobbing father threw on a doll of his daughter's; an elderly woman parted with pairs of gloves she herself had knitted.

A small voice started singing from the crowd.

"Far beyond the Sunset Sea, Where even dragons cannot fly, I know there is a place, Where the living do not die."

Soon the whole congregation began singing. The sad, small, discorded notes of grief.

"Far beyond the endless blue, Where every harvest overflows, Where the blight cannot take hold, Far beyond the sea."

Holt and Talia joined in. Half singing, half mumbling as each word cut as deep as any wound.

"Yonder cross the Sunset Sea, Where winter cannot bite, I know, I know there is a place, Where dreams may come to light. Out there, far beyond the sea..."

As the last words faded away, Talia approached the pyre. She pulled out the letter from her brother, the last piece of him she had, and placed it gently into the flames, her skin naked to the fire. A few onlookers inhaled in shock, but the heat did not bother her. She held the letter there until it caught, then, with what seemed a great effort, she at last pulled away and returned to Holt's side.

"I can't stay much longer," she said.

Holt nodded.

"There is so much to prepare," Talia said, "and every hour is precious. Hard to tell even when dawn will come under these storm clouds."

Holt checked on Ash's core. A handful of lunar motes still raced across the navy night around the ball of light. If the dawn were approaching, he reckoned even these few would disappear.

"Dawn is still a while off," Holt said mechanically. "Ash and I should go. Cleanse. Forge." He wished he could speak to her as they had, but nothing seemed right now. He just wanted Ash. Without Ash, he would have nothing. Nothing other than revenge.

"I've sent word to the kitchens for you," Talia said. "They'll provide you both with regular food and drink. You'll need it to keep up your strength without sleep."

Holt nodded again. He got onto Ash, then found his voice.

"Thank you for letting me do this."

She smiled weakly. "Brode was right. I'd have rather been able to pay my respects to my own brother but was denied that chance. If we don't do these things, what are we fighting for?"

Holt grunted. "Train night and day until they come," he said aloud. "I'll be ready."

And with that, he and Ash took off, making once more for the palace isle at the heart of the city.

# 53

# PREPARATIONS

Talia spotted Ash with ease. His white scales sparkled like water under even this drab light. At least he would be easy to find during the fight ahead.

Pyra glided down to join them. Ash appeared to be asleep as he didn't stir on their arrival. Such a skinny dragon in truth, the likes of which she hadn't seen before. Holt sat on the grass, his legs so tightly crossed it looked like he hadn't moved for the past day or night. Plates and drained mugs beside him spoke otherwise.

"Get some rest, girl," she said to Pyra. "The kitchens know you're to be fed again."

Pyra gave a hearty rumble and padded down a patch of grass before curling up.

Holt didn't open his eyes. Light burst from his shoulders in a wave that trailed off into glistening dust.

Talia checked on Pyra's core and winced. A thick veil of smoke obscured the bonfire. She would be hacking and spluttering her way through that for hours. No rest for her then. No meditation room, and no pre-built area for fire drakes to nestle around great braziers and drink the motes in. Hardly the preparation that was needed, but then the city was barely prepared either.

"Where are the people from the Crag now?" Holt asked, still with his eyes shut.

"They've been taken to an eastern barracks in the central ring," Talia said. "That's as safe as can be when the time comes."

Holt sniffed and said no more. She knew what was on his mind; her order not to aid the rest of the infected refugees. Did he think she found it any easier?

*No, he doesn't,* she decided. *That's just the hunger and tiredness talking.*

"There isn't much game in the kitchens," Holt said. "Ash has eaten a little of it, and then I suggested he have chicken until closer to the battle. That way we can make the most of the boost to his power."

"A good idea," Talia said.

Holt at last opened his eyes. "Are you going to join me?"

She realized then how awkward she was, standing on ceremony. She took up a space on the grass in front of Holt and felt the tiredness weigh upon her. Not on her body. That should last through the battle, assuming the swarm arrived that evening, but she was exhausted to her bones, nevertheless. Too much to process too quickly. Too much uncertainty and pressure before survival had even been achieved.

"I think I'll wait until after I eat to Cleanse," she said. There must have been something in her voice, for Holt pressed his lips together, clearly concerned.

"The staff here have been excellent," he said. "They've brought me nairn-root tea and molten cakes on the hour."

"We're not the first riders they've catered to." *Although we might be the last.*

"If you aren't about to Cleanse, I have some questions for you. Rider questions."

Talia sat up straighter. At least this was an area she had experience in.

"When Ash eats venison," Holt began, "we find the swell from his core hard to control. The first time was the worst, you remember?"

Oh, she remembered – remembered it fondly in fact. Their time in the woods, desperate though it had been, seemed quaint to where they were now.

She nodded, and Holt carried on.

"I wondered if I might help?"

"You could try pulling the raw motes into yourself," she said. "Your enhanced body should soak them in easily enough. Though as they are only raw, I'm not sure what good they would do you."

"I see... I shall think on this."

Talia supposed as the senior of the two she should have insisted on him calling her Master; that he should incline his head when wisdom had been imparted. But Holt wasn't in the Order, and she didn't see the need for it.

*A couple of months out of the ordinary and I let protocol and etiquette slip. What's next?*

She pulled at a clump of grass in a vain attempt to distract herself.

"I have another question," Holt said.

"Go on."

"If our dragons benefit so much from their meat type, shouldn't we eat it too?"

"Ah," Talia began. She had asked this same question years ago. "When dragons eat their preferred meat, it doesn't create more motes per se. I doubt beef contains motes of fire, or at least no more than is naturally in the world. But after eating their preferred meat, the pull of their core becomes stronger, drawing in more ambient motes than usual."

"Seems there might be some advantage if the rider eats the same meal – more motes might be attracted over should they be close together."

"Motes are drawn to dragons, not us. We have no cores of our own."

Holt frowned now. "Well, it sounds like I should be Forging while Ash eats."

"I suppose in an ideal world," Talia said. "It was rarely something we did at the Crag. A handful of extra motes might make a difference to a hatchling's core, but as the dragon and core mature, the gains from such small intakes diminish."

"But if you could do everything, if Ash ate his food at night under the stars while I Forged—"

"You'd get better results for the time, sure, but that can't always be arranged. Steady work over time will still increase your rank."

"Why not rank as fast as possible?"

She had wondered that herself. Indeed, she'd pushed as hard as she'd been allowed at the Crag but was ever told to be patient, calm and mindful. Yet Rake – that powerhouse with his mysterious veiled core – had been anything but patient. Perhaps Holt had a point. On the other hand, Brode, in his rare moments of openness, had also made good points.

"It's a long life, Holt," she said, recalling what Brode had once told her. "Do you wish to slave away at this all day, perhaps for a hundred years or more? You're not wrong, but the differences you're speaking of would be marginal at best per day."

"Shouldn't we be aiming for the best?"

There was an edge in his voice Talia found worrying.

"Don't berate yourself," she said. "You've only just begun—" She broke off as his eyes drifted off beyond her, a hurt and longing plain in his wistful stare.

*Well*, she thought. *I can't blame him. It comes to us all in the end. The guilt of not being strong enough. Of not helping enough. The shame of letting others down, whether justified or not. It just got to him fast. And hard.*

"Commander Ysera told me of an interesting technique," she said in a hurry, hoping to distract Holt and herself. "Lords – or some Lords at least – have such control over their mote channels that they can keep magic circulating around their body without using it. Takes an absurd amount of concentration or else it will erupt from them like any of us, but if they maintain it, they have a store of energy ready to use in a split second or even if separated from their dragon... What?"

"You were smiling," Holt said. He shrugged and made a mild attempt at a smile of his own. "Was good to see that."

"Enjoy it while it lasts, pot boy. Any more questions?"

"Many," Holt said. "I thought about pushing myself to carve a mote channel to my other leg. I feel my second rank ability would benefit from using both legs at once."

"It would, but like always you'll have to weigh up the cost on the bond and the drain on Ash's core with having extra power in the ability. When I've tried it, it doesn't double the power of the ability as you'd expect but still costs twice as much magic. So no, I wouldn't torture yourself to open the channel right now."

Holt looked relieved, then sheepish.

"And... can your abilities be altered?"

Talia frowned. Her weary mind had only just caught up with his meaning. He'd already tried out his Ascendant rank ability without her – the idiot. She was just about to open her mouth when he stood up.

"I'll show you."

Light began to pulse beneath his foot.

Talia jumped up then backward to get out of range. "What do you think you're doing?"

Rather than stop he kept going, and rather than stamping his foot, he pressed hard into the grass. The soft ground sunk under his strength and jagged lines of shining white power cut across the ground.

What had he done? It should have come out in a blast of energy. Stranger still was the way the light lingered in the ground, pulsing as though it had a heartbeat.

"Why didn't you wait for me before trying this?"

"I needed a way to cure multiple people at once," Holt said. "It worked, Talia."

"But..." She didn't know quite what to say.

"Well, it healed those with a mild infection, whereas blasting the power out would probably just have knocked them over."

"And you're worried it won't be effective in combat?"

"It does hurt the scourge," Holt hastened to add. "I tested it in the throne room. It seems to slow and weaken them, as well as inflict a light burn. It should make it easier for me to work with my sword."

"Hm," Talia mused. Riders liked instantaneous effects, raw damage to clear an area or root enemies to the spot with ice or earth. Yet if it gave Holt an advantage over the bugs and ghouls with his blade without drawing on extra magic to do so, then the benefits might work out. He needed that help. And the effect seemed to last a long time for the magic he had put into it. Only just now had the lunar power winked out. Where the light had been, the grass was now stark white, purple or silver.

"I say you keep it," she said.

"You're sure?" Holt asked. "I... worried I might have done something wrong and broken it."

"Our abilities are not set in stone," Talia said. "Lords can manipulate their magic in ways we never could. The reason we focus on perfecting several key abilities is to make them more efficient. Our mote channels adapt to how we use them, you see. The more you perform a technique, the more proficient you'll become in it."

"What does that mean?"

"It means over time you'll need less magic to generate the effect and cause less strain on your bond. You could force the mote channels in your arms and legs to work in other ways, but it would be costly. And if you wished to change the style of a frequently used technique forever, then the channels would sort of reset. You'd go back to square one. Paragons are said to have such robust channels it does not matter, but for everyone else—"

"I understand," Holt said. "I'll keep it then. Aside from hurting the scourge in battle, I also think I get a boost when I'm standing on the Lunar Quake."

Talia blinked. "What did you say?"

"When I stand on the ground, I gain a slight edge whereas the scourge are weakened—"

"No, no – the name you said. Lunar Quake? Is that what you're calling it?"

Holt flushed.

From beneath her wing, Pyra snorted, then spoke privately to Talia, *"Well, he couldn't be remarkable in every way."*

"What would you call it?" Holt asked, only a little defensively.

She considered. "How about Consecration?"

He looked blankly at her.

"Trust me, it sounds like a real ability now."

Further discussion was halted by the arrival of a group of kitchen staff. As Holt had foretold, there was nairn-root tea and molten cakes for the riders, as well as chicken and beef for the dragons. The spices from Pyra's dish would once have made Talia choke, but she inhaled them deeply now. Ash awoke with his nose sniffing at the air and stalked over while Pyra waited for the servants to come to her.

Talia realized how hungry she was after taking her first bite. Steaming cheese oozed from the center of the meaty scone. Holt blew on his and picked at the edges while she devoured two in quick succession.

She took a hearty swig of the steaming tea and wrinkled her nose in distaste. They had added extra sugar to it to suppress the spice. Many did prefer it that way, in fact she had once preferred it that way. Had they remembered her order? Well, she had taken on some of Pyra's preferences since then.

The remainder of the meal passed in an amicable silence. And as the warmth of the food and tea mixed with the renewed glow of her dragon bond, Talia almost felt relaxed. Perhaps she would get some sleep after Cleansing. It would be wise to do so. But there was so much to do, and so little time to do it in. Would such exertion on her part even help in the end?

"We're not well prepared," she said, as though Holt had asked her to explain the situation. "Turns out Osric wasn't doing a good job at overseeing the defenses." She snorted. "Probably just killing time, going through the motions until the full swarm gathered to hit the city hard. My brother did send messengers to Brenin for aid, but I imagine Osric ensured they never made it. There aren't enough troops, thanks to his ploy with the western garrisons, and an unacceptable amount of the ballistae need repairing. Those who migrated to the city as per our incursion strategy have been erratically sheltered. Almost none of the civilians on the western isles have been moved east for their own safety, so we're rushing that now. And too many of the soldiers are inexperienced – the cream of the standing army fell in the Toll Pass year. That was Osric's doing too..."

Just how long had this been planned for?

As bleak as things looked, it felt better just to admit it. To everyone else, she had to present a brave face. With Holt, she could be honest.

"Won't the Order send more riders to help?" Holt asked.

"How would they know we're in danger?" Talia said. "They already sent us help, remember, or they thought they did. Silas was supposed to be our aid. The swarm seemed a small thing for the longest time. One Lord should have been enough with the Crag's riders at his back. Falcaer will assume no news is good news."

"How long until no news becomes bad news?" Holt asked.

Talia shrugged. "Too long for us, I know that much."

She could fly to Falcaer herself, but it was out of the question. She'd return to find Sidastra a ruin and all her people turned to ghouls or worse.

"Well," Holt began, as optimistically as he could, "the defenses around the palace did a good job. Just look at how many stingers and carriers got shot down trying to get Osric out."

"There's a difference between a strike force and the whole swarm – you saw how many bugs chased us on our way in. From all I've read about the sieges at the peak of incursions, the battle comes down to commanding the sky. With only two riders, and no Champions or Lords to help us, I don't see how we'll manage it. Truth is, if the bugs want to take an area by brute force, we can't stop them."

"Then we focus our attention," said Holt, as though it were the easiest thing in the world. "You can't boil an egg and fry it at the same time."

"Do you always think in terms of food?"

"What I mean is, if we can't cover enough ground we shouldn't try to."

Talia smiled wryly. "Where do you think I've suggested the civilians be moved to?"

Holt's eyes widened. "What, here? To the palace grounds?"

"The palace grounds, and as much of the central ring as we can. I didn't just give the Crag folk special treatment."

"And the nobles are okay with commoners cramming into their space?"

"Some protested. There are whole outer islands largely left empty to accommodate people during a Summons, but we have other plans for those. Harroway didn't protest, actually. I think he still fears I'll take his head."

"The commoners are always pushed to the fringes of siege cities,"

Holt said. "The first to fall to the blight or a ghoul's teeth. Talia, I'm..." He seemed genuinely lost for words.

"It's the right thing to do. I'm only sad it took strategic necessity and dire circumstances to bring it about. Even so, we'll still have a lot of ground to cover. I think we should stick together and shore up the weakest points where we can. Their stingers can only do so much. The real threat is when they hold an area without resistance and so their carriers can begin landing ghouls unchecked, bypassing walls altogether."

"And the water," Holt added.

"Sidastra's main advantage is also its weakness. All the islands and bridges create choke points for our troops to make the enemy's numbers count for less, but it makes it equally hard to retake positions that are lost. Still, the city can lose its fingers long before a limb or the body becomes endangered."

Holt nodded, though his eyes looked distant.

"Are you following this?" she asked. "I need you to know in case I—"

"Don't say it."

"Then answer me."

"Yes, I follow," though he looked miserable at the thought of being the last one standing.

Talia rolled her shoulders and carried on. "Ballista points are crucial. Even those guarded with stone roofs will be vulnerable to Silas's lightning if he unleashes a full attack on them."

"Silas..." Holt said. "If he comes at us head-on—"

"I can't see him risking himself needlessly," Talia said. She said it to convince herself as much as Holt, but she'd thought on it for the better part of two days. "Why bother attacking if the swarm will handle it all? With any luck, he'll sit out most of the fight." She looked at the black clouds that pressed upon the city. "I've never heard of such a covering for a swarm. If it's all Silas and Clesh's work, then a lot of their power will be going into it. If they do attack, they'll be weakened, I'm sur—"

"You should have let me finish. I was going to say I hope we kill him. He needs to pay for Brode. For everything," he ended in a tone most unlike himself, deep and sinister.

She hadn't been expecting that.

*"You should stoke that fire in his belly,"* Pyra purred. *"Burn away his fears with it."*

"Yes," she said, an edge to her own voice. "If he comes, and we can, we'll kill him. For Brode."

"For my father too."

They shared a look of fury.

"Are you not afraid?" she asked.

"Of course. But not in the paralyzing way I was when things turned sour at Midbell. There's a whole army at our backs here. So, there is a chance... unless Sovereign himself turns up."

"If he wanted to do that he'd have done so already," Talia said. "Seems he likes to stay afar and keep his puppets on long strings."

"He has a long reach indeed if he could control Osric from, well, wherever he is."

She sensed his worry and shared it. Sovereign's power was unlike anything she had experienced. Enough distance between rider and dragon should nullify a bond. Proximity was needed to channel magic efficiently. Therefore, Sovereign was either close enough to Osric that he may well enter the battle himself, or he was so vastly powerful that the thought of resisting him really did seem futile.

Back in the throne room, she had tried in vain to fight back against his will. Yet the voice in her mind telling her to stay put, so light and so sweet, and so compelling, had rooted her. Pyra had fared worse, for he'd spoken to her directly.

"Did he speak to you?" she asked.

"To me and Ash," Holt said. He explained what Sovereign had demanded.

"He demanded the same of Pyra."

"It adds up with what Rake said. About Clesh trying to recruit members of the Emerald Flight to Sovereign's cause. He wants dragons, not us, but he'll accept riders too if that's what it takes. He especially wants Ash."

Talia watched as Ash blasted a few moonbeam breaths at the

corpse of a large carrier at the base of the island wall. His aim was fine on a stationary target, at least.

"Ash represents a threat to the scourge," she said. "It only seems natural that Sovereign would want Ash on his side instead of fighting against him."

"I suppose," Holt said, though he didn't sound wholly convinced.

Talia sighed and rubbed fiercely at her eyes. It was all so much.

"I think we're only cracking the surface of this, you know," she said. "If Osric is this dragon's rider and he's as powerful as a Lord, then they must have been partnered for years, although I have no idea how it was kept a secret for so long."

"I don't think Sovereign bonds in the usual way," Holt said. "Osric is as much a tool as anyone else."

Talia gulped. Even a morsel of hope that all had not turned to rot was enough for her to seize on. "Don't say that just to make me feel bette—"

"I heard him, Talia. Osric. The real Osric. For a moment, just before he left, I think he took back some control and spoke to me. He told me... he told me to tell you that he's sorry. He's sorry for everything."

It was too much. Heat prickled at her nose, and a single tear fell before she could help herself. She sniffed, tasted the salty tear and then wiped her face. If true, he might be saved. A third chance for her.

"What's the point of it all?" she said. "Why is he doing this?"

"Something about the scourge fulfilling their purpose," Holt said. "Do you remember him bellowing that at the end?"

"The scourge have no purpose."

"Other than to kill everything," Holt said.

"If Sovereign killed everything and everyone, he'd be king of only ashes."

"Perhaps he's mad," Holt said.

"Maybe the Order will know more. When we tell them. After the battle. If we win."

*If we win, now there is a mad thought.*

"I thought," Holt continued, "that we might return to the Withering Woods for a time. If we make it. I know you hoped to work with your brother to stem the blight in those woods, and though he's gone, that dream doesn't have to die with him."

"I'd like that. I'd like that very much." Then, catching up with his words, she added hastily, "What do you mean, 'for a time'?"

"Before Ash and I… move on."

"Don't be cryptic."

"Leave." His voice deepened again, losing much of the naïve upbeat flair she'd found so irritating at first. "I am banished, after all. Nameless."

*He isn't worried about that, is he?*

"That proclamation wasn't properly sealed by Osric, and even if it had been, Holt, who in the world would abide by it?"

"The sentiment was clear," he said, still with that harsher tone. "I am a chaos bringer, a rank breacher. I'm as bad as the scourge in their eyes."

"No one has asked you to leave sinc—"

"Because they need me," Holt said. "Need us. Funny how the rules apply until people get desperate. I understand it. I agreed with all of it. Even while I picked up Ash's egg and carried it down the steps of the Crag, I understood it. But let's be honest. If Osric hadn't fled I'd be in a dungeon right now."

Talia bit her lip. The truth of it was the worst part. She'd known it from the moment she'd learned what Holt had done.

"Who cares what they think?" she said. "You can still join the Order. Then it won't matter."

But Holt shook his head. "Ash and I need hard training. His powers offer hope, but we're so fragile right now."

"The Order will protect and train you!"

"Not fast enough," Holt said. "Not nearly enough. They have their own rules and pace, and they can't push beyond the boundaries of Lord – we know that's possible now!"

"Holt—"

"I can't sit reading scrolls or practice sword stances while people die of the blight. I can't let it happen again. I can't bear it. Every time I close my eyes, I see his gaunt face staring back at me."

A lump formed in her throat. She understood, better than anyone. "But where else will you go if not to the Order?"

"I don't... I don't know. Just somewhere else. Far away from here."

He looked sheepish. She knew then exactly what he had in mind. "I don't trust Rake."

"He saved our lives," he said. "And he all but offered to train Ash and me."

"Exactly," Talia said. "Very quick of him to do so. What does he have to gain from it? He's... he's—"

"Different?"

"A rogue element," she said, happy with her phrasing. "He clearly defected from the Order."

"Or they kicked him out."

*"Master Rake had great power,"* Pyra chimed in. *"He would have much knowledge and skill to impart."*

Talia rounded on Pyra, annoyed that her own dragon wasn't supporting her. "You were just besotted with him."

Pyra flicked her tail and curled up with a snort.

Having seen off the challenge from that quarter, Talia returned to Holt. He seemed defiant. She gave him a stern look. There was being honest, and then there was being stubborn.

"You should join the Order. It's what should be done."

"Is that what you'll do if we win? There is no Order in Feorlen anymore. You'd be forced to fly off to Athra, Coedhen, maybe Fornheim, and leave your home behind – could you do that? After everything that's happened?"

Talia sat straighter, stiffened. Had he meant to prod this most tender spot, the decision she had blissfully thought out of the question and out of mind until a day ago?

She'd sworn her oath, that bound her to the Order. She was as nameless as Holt would have been if the sentence had held. Her duty would be to rejoin the Order, be dispatched to her new post, and serve in defending that country.

All while her homeland bled.

If she left, Feorlen might survive the incursion only to descend into civil war. Her mother would return to Brenin, and the great families would vie for succession, and if no unanimous decision could be reached then swords would be drawn. By adhering to order, she might leave more chaos behind her. Brode had been right yet again. Royals were not supposed to be riders for a reason.

"I know my duty," she said at last.

"That isn't an answer."

"That *is* my answer," Talia said.

"Why are you trying to pretend you don't care?" Holt said. "Brode cared. We're still human, whatever the oaths say."

That was all well and good for him to say. He hadn't sworn them yet. He didn't have to choose between honor and chaos, between the right thing and the easy thing, and she wasn't even sure which option was right or easy anymore.

When she didn't respond, he carried on, a cold edge to his voice. "Maybe we're different, but I can't just turn away like you can."

A fire rose in Talia, this time of her own making, as did a great desire to slap the stupid pot boy. She understood the pain he must be in right now, better than most, but that did not give him an excuse.

"If that's how you feel, you don't need me here."

At least Holt looked ashamed of himself, but he didn't bring himself to offer an apology either. Talia pushed her anger down and decided it would be better to let it slide for now. There was a battle coming up, after all.

"None of this will matter unless we win," she said. "So, we Cleanse and Forge. And rest."

With that, she got up and stormed off.

"Talia," Holt called out.

"Cleanse and Forge *alone*," she called back without turning.

There was a scuffling sound as Holt got to his feet. Pyra stirred then. A wave of hot air rippled out from the purple dragon, and she kneaded the ground menacingly with her talons.

*"Careful, little one."*

Judging by the lack of a follow-up, Holt must have remained where he was. Good. Talia stopped on the other side of Pyra, so she was out of sight of Holt, then sat down, crossed her legs, jammed her eyes shut and began to Cleanse.

Before she could even begin to calm herself down, Pyra reached out to her.

*"He may need less to stoke the fire than I thought."*

*"Thinking with his heart alone will get him killed. Brode was right on that front."*

*"My worry is for you, child. You can't look out for everyone."*

*"Child? I'm twelve years older than you are!"*

Pyra tittered across their bond as though dealing with an amusing infant. *"There are notes in my song—"*

*"—since the fires of creation, I know. Ash doesn't act so high and mighty. You could learn from him."*

*"The hatchling is the first of his kind,"* Pyra said. *"He writes his flight's first song even now."*

A pang of unexpected and intense pity welled in her for the white dragon. She had lost most of her family, but Ash had none. Only Holt.

*"I'm right to worry about them going off on their own,"* Talia said.

*"Hm,"* Pyra hummed. *"For now, let us concern ourselves with the battle ahead. Matters will brighten when we triumph."*

*"You know what else you are, girl? You're too confident."*

*"I know, child. I know."*

# 54

# THE BATTLE FOR SIDASTRA

**Holt**

Three days since arriving in Sidastra, two days since he burned his father's body upon the pyre, hours at most until the swarm arrived. Even with all the activity surrounding him, Holt had stayed put, Cleansing every impurity and Forging every drop of magic into Ash's core, standing now because there was nothing more he could do.

Ash's core shone diamond bright, more silver-white than ever before. Holt thought it had become denser too, a result of his fastidious Forging over the last thirty-six hours. Especially at night.

If only the clouds would part to allow the moonlight to rain down, then there would really be a difference. No matter. For now, Holt had done all he could. He and Ash were as prepared for a war – magically speaking – as they could be under the circumstances.

Ash stirred from his nap. *"Finally, you're up."*

"It's for your benefit, you know," Holt said. "Come. We need to pick up your food."

After speaking with Talia, he'd decided to wait until battle was upon them for Ash to eat his venison. He appreciated what she'd said about marginal gains, but he thought, given the circumstances, they should take every edge that they could.

She had taken her leave sometime around supper to continue preparations with Ealdor Harroway. Holt had feigned deep concentration at the time, still raw and a little ashamed from their heated conversation. He had not explained himself well.

As painful as her choice would be, she'd be welcomed by the party she chose to commit to. Whereas Ash and himself would be outcasts wherever they went. Still, he didn't like how they had parted, especially before a battle. He'd try to find her and make things right before it began.

He and Ash walked across the palace grounds together, heading for the kitchens. Soldiers called to each other along the walls. Torches and braziers attempted to relieve the gathering night. A smell of potato and leek soup lingered in the clammy air. Holt told Ash to wait in the yard then entered, weaving through the staff as naturally as one of them. Most had their heads down and didn't notice him; those who did betrayed the fear in their eyes. Had he looked that afraid when the scourge burned the Crag? He must have.

The kitchens were as vast as he'd envisioned: red brick arches held up a high ceiling, allowing air to breathe despite the great charcoal fires and ovens running down both walls. Every type of pot, pan and utensil hung above the long oak tables, their pristine copper reflecting a warm glow of their own.

And he had thought working in the Crag's kitchens had been hectic.

The head Cook caught wind of Holt's arrival and rushed to greet him. "Honored Rider—"

"Please just call me Holt. I'm a Cook, like you."

"Forgive me, yer honor, but old habits." He bobbed on the spot and snapped his fingers at a group of kitchenhands. They brought a black roasting dish over and the Cook pulled off the lid, letting loose a strong, gamy smell tinted with licorice.

"This type of dragon is new to me," said the Cook, "but I thought roasting the haunch with aniseed would be a nice starting point."

*That explains the smell*, Holt thought. He'd have to remember to note down Ash's reaction to it, if he got the chance.

"It's been left to rest so it should be tender," the Cook said.

"So long as it gives my dragon more power, he'll wolf it down however it tastes," Holt said. "We can't be picky. Wrap it in linen and I'll take it with me."

Once he had the meat in hand, he found it awkward to leave. The other servants bowed to him, repeatedly, likely wondering why he hadn't swept from the hot, noisy area yet. They must have heard of his story by now, or a rumor of it. Perhaps they admired him, one of their own who had elevated himself. Or did they too secretly curse him as a chaos bringer while smiling to his face? It was impossible to know, and whatever their feelings, Holt didn't think knowing would bring him much comfort nor cause further distress. He was an outsider now, even inside a kitchen, which should have been his domain.

By the time he made it out to the yard, horns were blowing.

*"They have come,"* Ash said. *"Their stench is thick in the air; their shrieks pierce the night."*

Holt clambered onto Ash's back, placing the meat in his lap. They weren't going to waste a single mote from it.

"Time to show them what a lunar dragon can do."

### Talia

Pyra heard them first. A quiver ran across their bond. Talia heard them a few seconds later and leaned on the ramparts, squinting to get a glimpse of the enemy. The black clouds over the city might be thick, but miles beyond the boundaries of Sidastra, a glimmer of the true night sky remained. A sliver of starlight lit the swarm as it closed in, and even under Silas's storm, the wet sheen of the bugs gleamed.

Talia checked Pyra's core. The bonfire raged clearer than it had that morning, although she hadn't had the time to Cleanse all the smoke away. It would have to do. Pyra's core was more mature and denser than Ash's, and fire still hit the blighted filth hard, if not as well as lunar magic.

They would burn many before falling.

And while Holt and Ash were powerful, they were limited in the ground they might cover. Ash needed Holt to fly, whereas she and Pyra could be apart and remain effective: Pyra covering the air, and she on the wall.

She drew back from the rampart and took a deep breath. Beside her, Ealdor Harroway sighed. It seemed a sigh of relief, and Talia too released the breath she'd been holding. There was something calming about the battle beginning, after all. Worse than the fight was the agonizing wait.

"I trust every siege team knows to shoot a gray dragon on sight?"

"They have been briefed," said Harroway. "Have hope, Talia. We are not so reliant on the riders as many say."

"Let us hope you are right." She looked this great Ealdor of the realm up and down. She did not recall him from her youth; his father had held the title in those days. "You must have defended Sidastra during Feorlen's last incursion."

"I did."

"I was only a young girl. I hid in the tower above my room."

"As children do."

His gaze was all on the swarm. The clacking, shrieking, and buzzing grew ever louder.

"Are you ready to die, Ealdor Harroway?" Her tone was level.

He finally looked at her – right at her. "Yes." He gulped, and his jaw quivered. "I am. For what's left of my honor. For you."

She turned away. *Already he treats me like his queen.*

"Fight for our home instead," she said. "No matter what they make me swear, this is still my home."

"For *our* home. My only fear is rising again to be part of its destruction."

Over on the shore, the front ranks of the swarm enveloped the waypoint beacons. They were in range.

"It begins, Master of War."

She reached behind her head, grasped the ever-warm hilt of her rider's blade, and drew it with purpose.

Harroway moved off, passing orders. Signal fires were lit, repeated back across the islands. Before long, the first flaming payloads from the trebuchets soared into the writhing darkness. The swarm passed another beacon; they were close enough now for catapults and to be seen.

Flayers sped ahead of the horde, their blade arms scything before them; huge hammer-headed beetles, the juggernauts, stampeded like bulls; swollen carriers and fast-moving stingers filled the skies. And of course, masses of ghouls.

The swarm passed the final beacon and met a hail of arrows. Ghouls fell. But more ghouls just ran over them while the juggernauts passed through unscathed.

The noise was incredible. That was something they never prepared you for: just how easy it is to lose sense of things when you can barely hear the person screaming next to you.

Talia focused inward. *"Stingers are the priority,"* she said to Pyra. *"The carriers are easier targets for the ballistae."*

*"With pleasure."*

Pyra answered the swarm's bellows with a roar of her own, loud enough and defiant enough that it caused the soldiers on the western wall to cheer.

*"And where is Holt?"* Talia demanded.

*"Ash says they're on their way."*

"They better be," Talia said aloud. She gathered a Fireball and aimed for a flayer on the banks of the shore. Too fast for her, the flayer avoided the attack on its determined surge toward the bridge. A group of juggernauts led the scourge charge, their armored skulls lowered to ram against the gate. A ballista bolt hit the leading juggernaut, but even that did not slow it down. Flayers followed close behind. They would attempt to scale the walls – their uncanny agility and spiky bodies allowed for this, but while climbing they would be easy prey for the defenders.

Yet this was no ordinary incursion, and this no ordinary swarm.

Talia watched in horror as the first flayer leaped, right into the path of a second bolt heading for the lead juggernaut. It fell dead into the water, and the juggernaut slammed into the gate at full tilt. More flayers did the same.

All the usual strategies and expectations could not be relied upon.

Before Talia could think of a solution, the buzzing of wings rose to dominance. Low flying stingers raced above. *Why are they flying so low?* She drew from Pyra's core, empowered her legs, and launched herself straight up, keeping her blade held high. She impaled one bug, ripped her sword free, plunged it into another on the way down, and kicked the corpse free of the wall so it wouldn't crush soldiers beneath. She hit the battlements in a crouch, rose and ran for the gatehouse.

The gates had to hold. As long as possible. Retreat was inevitable, but this would be too quick a defeat if the gates fell so soon.

Orders rang along the wall.

"Swords!"

"Carriers inbound!"

Now the low flight path of the stingers made more sense. They were covering for the carriers. But carriers were supposed to fly high over the defenses as well, to land at weaker points within a city.

*"Talia, they're making straight for the walls."*

Pyra's words had barely registered when sheer instinct brought Talia skidding to a halt. A fat carrier crashed down, crushing soldiers beneath and throwing others aside. Arrows had ruined its wings already, but the impact alone must have broken its body. Yet even as its death throes gurgled, ghouls loped out from under the raising carapace of its back.

*The carriers too are being suicidal. All to take the walls quicker.*

It was unlike anything Talia had heard of. But it made a grim sense. When the swarm won, many of the dead would rise to join the swarm. Sovereign could sacrifice a large portion of his existing swarm to ensure victory and swell his ranks afterward.

Soldiers nearby looked as shocked as Talia felt, but the time for despair was still a long way off. She channeled fire into her blade, igniting the red metal.

"With me!" she cried, running to meet the enemy.

**Holt**

*"We have to make for the walls,"* Ash said.

*"We will,"* Holt said. *"I just need to see this with my own eyes first."*

He willed Ash to head to the southern tip of the western quarter, where the quarantine zone could be glimpsed as a black shadow on the lake. Ash perched on the roof of a townhouse just behind the wall. Soldiers gawked and called to him, wishing his blessing. Holt only had eyes for the isle to the south.

*"Pyra says we are needed now!"*

*"Tell her we're on our way. I need to know."*

*"What do you need to know?"* Ash stiffened his neck, pointing forward like the needle on a compass. *"There is more death than life there already."*

Holt looked down at Ash, which given they were sense-sharing meant Ash was also looking down on Ash. Thinking it through just made him feel dizzy.

*"Why do you linger on this?"* Ash asked, sounding impatient for the first time. A reasoned explanation was clearly demanded of Holt.

Yet that was it. Holt's feelings weren't wholly reasonable. It was all in his gut, his guilt-ridden squirmy gut. A philosopher might explain it, perhaps someone old and wise.

From his right, he heard the swarm close in on the city. From his left came the swish and thrum of the trebuchets.

"I just..." Holt began, "wish things could have turned out differently."

*"I do too. One day we'll make things right."*

A sudden thought entered Holt's mind, one he had to get off his chest before the night was over. "I'm not sure I ever said I'm sorry to you, did I? I'm not sorry I saved you, but I am sorry for your blindness and how other dragons treat you."

*"Never worry about my eyes – I'm glad to experience the world as I do rather than not at all. And as for others of my kind, they can accept me or not as they choose. I will not allow my own worth to be determined by them."*

"You might be the bravest person I know," Holt said.

Just then Ash's ears pricked. Holt heard it too – lighter over their shared senses but still there. Screaming from the quarantine isle, and many buzzing wings to the south. The squirming in Holt's stomach boiled into cold fury. Ash roared so loud it caused the soldiers nearby to duck and clap their hands to their ears.

Holt started unwrapping the haunch of meat.

"Whatever happens, I'm glad you're my dragon."

*"I'm glad you're my boy."*

The dragon bond burned fiercely. Stingers whizzed overhead. Ballista bolts sailed into the night with great *thunks* and *thwacks*.

And Holt tossed the venison in a high arc.

Ash raised his long neck and snapped the meat out of the air. He munched greedily. The taste echoed on Holt's own tongue from sense-sharing; the dragon's pleasure flitted across the bond. Raw lunar motes poured into the orbit of Ash's core.

"Pull them into a breath attack," Holt said as they took off for the western wall. "Hold it as long as you can!"

## Talia

She entered the tower on her side of the gatehouse and took the stairs. Bodies clogged the stairwell; blood and bile flowed down the spiraling steps. She took the first exit onto the wall directly over the gate, leaped over fallen soldiers, and blocked the strike of a ghoul hoping to make a corpse of another. Dispatching the ghoul, she pivoted and raced for the parapet.

From her right came the sound of breaking wood and screaming. She skidded to a halt and looked up to find another fat carrier where a ballista and its crew had been moments before. What soldiers remained on the gatehouse rushed to the stairwell of that tower, ready to engage the ghouls as they descended.

*"Stay close to the remaining tower at the gate,"* she said to Pyra before continuing to the parapet.

As she reached it, the gate shook. Below, the juggernauts withdrew from their latest assault. Another two were charging down the bridge. Other than the stingers and carriers, the full might of the swarm sat with chilling ease on the opposite bank, allowing the juggernauts and flayers to bring down the gate for them.

And Talia had hoped to hold here for hours at least.

Sheathing her blade, she brought both palms together and pulled power from Pyra's core. Fire lashed forth in a searing, twisting line toward the closest juggernaut, striking it on its thick forehead. Talia poured power in, too much for one bug, but she didn't see another option. Her target fell.

She wrung her hands and took aim again. Fire lashed, and a flayer jumped into its path. She cut the attack and aimed again. A flock of squawking seagulls descended, soaking her flames. They swerved up and around, engulfing her in a storm of pecking and flapping wings. As a few sharpened beaks jabbed into her face and neck, Talia howled in rage, and she slammed a foot into the hard stone. Her Flamewave ran low over the gatehouse, burning few of the birds but driving the rest away.

She rose and made it to the rampart's edge just in time to see a flash of writhing purple-black power. She ducked as the shadowy bolt of dark magic shattered against the battlements. Even their casters were providing cover from afar.

*No regular swarm indeed.*

Talia unsheathed her sword and rose again, ready this time. More bolts of black magic hissed from the shore. She dodged one and blocked another with her blade. Steel forged at Falcaer Fortress could handle the punishment. Now with just one hand she tried again to weaken the assaulting juggernauts, but it wasn't enough.

*We're going to lose the gate.*

"Look out!"

The call came from behind.

Talia spun only to be thrown back by the impact of another swollen carrier. Bony fists punched their way through the carapace shell, sending the carrier itself into fits of pain as whatever it bore ripped free.

Three giant skeletons emerged. The bones of these blight victims had mutated, growing larger but leaving the rest of their bodies behind. Muscle, sinew and ragged clothes hung from exposed yellowed bones. Oversized skulls swiveled on vertebrae the size of fists. Hollow sockets scanned for prey. Each bore a great two-handed weapon that looked small against their frames. Dark magic fueled them where nature could not.

Abominations. Talia had feared meeting these the most.

*"Pyra, I need help here!"*

*"Coming!"*

Breathing hard, Talia raised her blade and rocked on the balls of her feet. As large as they were, they were surely lumbering and slow. That would be her chance.

Every soldier left upon the gatehouse had rightly backed away. The abominations opened their wide jaws in rattling cries, raised their weapons—

Then a blinding beam of white light hit the carrier. Another shock wave rushed out from the epicenter of the strike, cutting through the abominations like scythes through a meadow. And a white dragon came hurtling down.

Ash landed on the stone scorched by his lunar magic, roaring in triumph. Silver vapor spilled from his mouth like steam. Talia ran to him as Holt jumped down.

She shoved him roughly. "Where have you been?" Before he even opened his mouth, she carried on. "Never mind. What was that?"

"Marginal gains."

She snorted, beamed at him, then started dragging him back to the ramparts. "Ash, keep those ears trained above us. If anything even thinks about landing, I want you to blast it into oblivion."

*"Pyra, help Ash out. We'll need the sky above us clear if we're going to have a chance."*

*"Many are getting past,"* Pyra said.

*"Much of the outer ring is empty. Let them waste their time there. If we don't hold the gate now, we'll be lost before we get a chance to fall back properly."*

The gatehouse shook again. More juggernauts had completed a run.

"Come on," she yelled at Holt, throwing him forward. To his credit he didn't protest, and he pre-charged one of his Lunar Shocks. They reached the edge of the wall.

"Take the juggernauts," she said. "I'll keep the rest from interfering."

Holt unleashed his Shock. It did a lot more damage to the armored juggernauts than her fire, but it still took him a good two or three blasts to kill one.

Talia scorched stingers as they flew in, just enough to chase them off; staggered flayers with fully charged Fireballs; cleared the way enough that a ballista bolt landed a clean strike into the softer side of a juggernaut while Holt took down another.

When the last juggernaut fell, she pulled Holt back from the edge. The slightest tremor shook the edges of her bond.

"Well done," she gasped, more from nerves than exhaustion.

She watched as Ash aimed one of his beams of light at a carrier overhead. He missed initially but drew the beam after his victim and seared a hole through its bulbous body. Maintaining the attack like that was no small feat. Maybe they could buy more time than she thought.

"We should get ready for the next wave," Holt said.

She caught his arm. "We can't hold this spot on our own forever. Our bonds will fray."

"We killed them—"

"We've bought time, that's all. I want you and Ash to head down into the streets and find the choke point Harroway set up by the east gate – we need to get the troops off this island, and you can hold the scourge at ground level better than me. Tell him to start the retreat to the inner ring. Go on," she added, waving a hand. "Go before more juggernauts come."

He looked like he had something to say but bit his lip and nodded. Then he ran to Ash, got on his back, and together they descended into the west quarter.

She called Pyra down and got onto her back. Soldiers appealed to her, and she told them the same thing she cried to everyone as they flew circuits around the walls.

"To the inner ring! Fall back!"

# 55

# RETREAT

**Holt**

"To the rider!"

"Shield wall!"

Holt backpedaled as a fresh group of soldiers in the blue hawk colors of House Harroway formed a shield wall in front of him. He checked on Ash – the dragon had many small cuts, but it could have been much worse. An abomination had broken through the last shield wall and the barricade had almost been lost because of it. Only a dual Lunar Shock to the creature's head had toppled it.

Holt's palms stung. A shiver ran through the dragon bond.

"We'll have to fight smarter."

Ash, who still had one of the abomination's bones between his teeth, spat the bone free and stamped on it. *"Cleave off their legs next time. Then their heads shall be easy."*

"Not sure my sword can handle that. It isn't like Talia's."

*"We must conserve our power somehow. This is not yet the final hour."*

Holt thought it might as well have been.

The street Harroway had tasked them to defend was well designed. It was a narrow funnel that led all traffic from the island toward the eastern gate. All scourge forces on foot would have to pass this way, and here their numbers counted for less. Barricades created a zigzag run to further slow the enemy. Their carriers could not simply fall here as they had upon the wall, for they needed the street clear to move their own forces through once the defenders fell back.

Yet even a thousand men could not have held this forever. Bodies from both sides were piling up now. It was all some of the soldiers could do to clear a space for the shield wall to work effectively. The bloated corpse of a blighted boar lay where a spear had finally sunk in, too heavy to be moved.

As the last of the reinforcements joined the shield wall, two men hung back. Holt didn't recognize the Twinblades at first; they wore plate armor splattered in gore, and their blonde hair was lost under more grime.

"Our ealdor requires more time," Eadwulf said.

"We must hold longer," said Eadwald.

"Time for what?" Holt asked. "Soldiers stopped coming this way ages ago."

"Many move by the walls," said Eadwulf.

"The last of the barrels must be laid."

"The what?"

More squads of soldiers hauling carts of small wooden barrels answered that question for him. They took the barrels and placed them seemingly at random, but especially beside the stakes and upturned wagons of the barricades.

"*More ghouls,*" Ash announced. Sure enough, a fresh wave of scourge forces rounded the street toward them.

"Fine," Holt said. Talia had told him to hold the choke point as long as Harroway needed. If the Master of War wanted more time, then he and Ash would give it to him.

"Hold!" men from the shield wall cried as ghouls and flayers hurtled toward them.

"Hold fast!"

The Twinblades drew their weapons. "Our swords are at your command," they said together.

"I trust you still have your vials?"

They nodded.

"Don't hesitate if things get desperate." He faced the back of the shield wall, deciding how best to help them. Without a shield of his own, he couldn't function as part of the wall, and even if he picked one up, he didn't have the experience. Until now he and Ash had stood just behind the wall, plugging gaps and cutting down anything that managed to scramble or leap over the formation.

He had a better idea now.

"Stay behind the lines and help Ash," he told them.

*"I don't like them,"* Ash said.

*"I know, but they're good fighters. I'm going to shore up the front."*

Holt pushed his way through the ranks until he was just behind the front row of soldiers. This would be a better use of his power rather than single Shocks. He drew light from Ash's core and channeled the motes down to his foot.

The Consecration slipped under the shield wall, running out to burn and weaken the scourge on the other side without compromising the formation. In practicing the ability, Holt had learned when the pulses of power released from the ground. Every two seconds, the lunar fire wreaked damage on the enemies standing upon it. When the light faded, the scourge at the front were left dead or weakened.

"Break!" an officer cried. And, as one, the soldiers of the shield wall opened to stab or hack at the enemy. They reformed and took a step back. Stepping forward to gain ground was not their aim, nor would holding steady help in the long run. The scourge, unlike men, would be happy to climb a mound of their fallen to continue. So, they stepped back, forcing the scourge that rushed forward to trip or fall over their own dead.

Holt marveled at the training and discipline of Harroway's men. There was a benefit to training troops like these for life. Yet the ferocity with which the ghouls hurled themselves at the shield wall was terrible. Bones crunched, flesh squelched and ripped as they tried to brute force their way through. A stronger flayer hammered its long arms upon the topmost shields.

Holt lay down another Consecration and peered through a gap between two shields to admire the effect. The flayer shrieked and trembled as the magic took effect, allowing a soldier to stab through its torso.

Another flayer leaped off the flames and landed behind the shield wall. A roar followed by a satisfied glow over the bond let Holt know the problem had been dealt with.

Holt aided the shield wall three more times before almost falling to his knees from the effort. He backed out of the formation, stumbled on his shaking leg, and drew ragged breaths. The dragon bond was still intact, but the first cracks at the edges were showing. Ash's core was about one quarter drained in total. Holt could only draw up to around one half before his bond would fray.

Eadwulf steadied him. "Time to go."

"The last barrels are being laid," Eadwald said.

Holt nodded. There were indeed a lot more of those little barrels stacked along the street – all the way back to the gatehouse itself.

"Order your men back then," Holt said. "Ash and I will cover their retreat."

He was about to run to Ash's side when cries of panic rose from the soldiers.

"Abominations!"

A few soldiers at the back of the wall broke and fled. Holt found it hard to blame them. Holding against those monsters was about as likely as holding back a juggernaut at full tilt. Most shocking was how many stayed and held, each one braver than any rider in the face of such foes.

Before Holt could consider options, two abominations broke through the shield wall with sheer force.

One of the skeletons lacked weapons. It didn't need any. It kicked, crushed and knocked men aside. Soldiers flew, crunched against building walls and crumpled. The other held a great sword in one hand and a scavenged pike in the other, stabbing with a monstrous reach.

Out of the corner of his eye, Holt saw the Twinblades tip small vials to their mouths.

Ash bounded toward the closest abomination – the one without weapons – gathering light between his teeth. The dragon sent a beam against it, and the abomination brought its bony hands together, conjuring dark power of its own – the same black magic the smaller casters wielded. The abomination cast its own spell to clash with Ash's power, and the channels of magic battled for dominance in the air.

Holt would have helped, but the second skeleton was bearing down upon them and he had to keep it off Ash. He sent a Lunar Shock which glanced off its shoulder. That got its attention at least.

Holt dodged the pike thrust at him and rolled to avoid the sword. He placed a half-charged Consecration before pirouetting away. It was better than nothing. The abomination howled as the ground it stood upon became infused with lunar magic. Despite being weakened, it raised its sword and struck down with such speed Holt could only dodge again. Forms, guards, stances and craft were nothing against this thing.

The next attack came too quickly. Out of instinct, Holt raised his own sword to block the strike, knowing as he did so he would be crushed. Then two more blades raised in time to aid his own. Eadwulf, Eadwald and Holt's combined and enhanced strength managed to block the blow, catching the abomination's sword in a bind with all three of theirs.

Holt had a split second to decide what he did next. He saw Ash's magic push his opponent back, felt the dragon's core drain at an alarming rate, but Ash couldn't just drop his attack or else he'd be struck by the skeleton's magic. Holt decided. Still on his Consecrated ground, he already felt a slight boost. Why not amplify that? He pulled on magic, sending it out to his muscles, especially to his shoulders and arms. His Ascendant's body drank the power in, demanding more than before to feel the benefit now. But the difference, well, it was indescribable.

With a light push, he threw off the abomination's sword stuck in the bind. In a single leap, he crossed the distance between himself and the giant's leg. With all the force he could muster, he swung his sword at its knee. All in what seemed an eye blink.

Holt landed in a crouch and ceased the flow of magic. Ash's core dipped well under half its total strength.

Reality came back to him in a jolt. The light of his Consecration winked out. His legs ached from the jump, his shoulders burned from the effort of his swing, and the blade of his sword had broken. Yet the abomination's lower leg lay broken beside him too.

He turned and ran out from under the giant as it fell, heading to Ash and yelling. "Use what you need, boy – take it down!"

Holt felt the quake through his soul as Ash's core flickered. The beam emanating from his mouth swelled, blasted the abomination's magic aside, and burned a hole through its midriff.

It was a Pyrrhic victory. With the shield wall broken, their retreat was in disarray. Ghouls swarmed toward the barricades at a frightening speed. Even above, Holt saw smaller animals scurrying up walls and along rooftops; squirrels with shining green eyes, cats with bile running from their mouths. Everything was being thrown against the defenders.

"Fall back!" Eadwulf cried.

"To the gate!" his brother yelled.

Holt jumped on Ash's back. "We need to do what we can to cover them."

And they did their best, turning every so often so Ash could rake with his talons, breathe his lunar breath, turn again, and tail swipe some more before running on. They were the last to make it through before the portcullis of the eastern gate banged shut.

They kept running. Over the bridge. To the first outpost of the inner ring, narrowly avoiding attacks from swooping stingers that made it through the crossfire. They only stopped with the others once they were through the next gatehouse.

"Rider," Eadwulf called to him.

His brother waved him over too. "Our ealdor would see you."

Ash growled. *"Can't we get a moment?"* People hastened to step aside as Ash made a beeline for the Twinblades.

"I hope holding that long and losing those men was worth it," Holt said.

"It will be," Eadwulf said.

"When the princess has her way."

Just then, Pyra's voice entered Holt's mind. *"Get well clear, little one."*

She roared and Holt craned his neck to see her fly low over their outpost, straight for the island they had just abandoned. Every ballista in range fired to cover her.

Once Pyra and Talia were at the walls of the west quarter, they began bathing the island in fire. A few swooping turns belching flames and an inferno began. Pyra emerged unharmed and without any stingers on her tail.

"What was in those barrels?" Holt asked.

"Pitch, resin, pig fat," said Eadwulf.

"Poured onto the streets and thrown against walls as we fled," said Eadwald.

Holt was speechless. The blaze spread as it hungered for thatched roofs and wood.

*"The scourge burn,"* Ash said in awe.

A quiet fell over the outpost. Rattling armor ceased as soldiers stood still. The endless buzzing in the air even dropped, and the ballistae too fell silent.

"The Master of War knows his trade," said Eadwulf.

Eadwald held up a new sword and scabbard. "To replace what you lost."

"Thank you," Holt said, taking the spare blade and discarding his broken one. "Where is Harroway?"

"Follow us, rider," Eadwulf said.

Holt got down from Ash and followed the Twinblades. They entered a fortified tower, climbing several floors to a small command room. Through a narrow window, Holt saw the fires of the west quarter dance upon the surface of the lake, reflecting enough light to stave off the darkness on this side of the city.

Inside the war room, stewards and other non-combatants repositioned blocks of colored wood upon a great map of Sidastra. Breathless messengers relayed news to them or passed scrunched notes before dashing off. A purple block and a white block sat by a small isle on the inner ring. Holt reckoned those represented himself and Talia.

Lord Harroway stood at the center of things, studying the map, gesticulating, and barking orders. When he caught sight of the Twinblades he stopped and stomped around the table to greet them.

"Holt," he said roughly, clearly deciding to follow Talia's suggested protocol. "Fine work out there. How is your dragon?"

Some choice words sprang to Holt's mind, but he refrained from speaking them. Now wasn't the time to let grudges influence him. "I'm afraid it cost us a lot to hold that choke point. Ash's core is running low already."

Harroway frowned. "I see," he said, though it was plain he didn't much understand the mechanics of magic.

"Your men deserve more praise," Holt said. "They fought like riders themselves."

Harroway beamed at the Twinblades like a proud father. "I only pick the best. But let us save further self-congratulatory statements until we win the night."

"You think we'll win?" Holt asked.

"The swarm has backed off, has it not?"

Just then Talia burst into the room, her face dirty and glistening with sweat and her eyes burning. "This is just a respite," she said. "It won't end until the queen dies. We need to force her into the fight."

"I would think burning half her swarm would force her out," said Harroway.

"This isn't a usual swarm," Talia said. She steadied herself. "Good idea on rigging the island. It was hard but the right move in the circumstances."

Harroway inclined his head. "I've reports that our other outer ring traps are filled with bugs too."

"Then Pyra and I will go while the skies are clear." She only seemed to notice Holt at that moment. "You're alive!"

Holt patted himself down. "Seem to be. Ash's core won't last much longer."

She bit her lip. "We do what we can. That's all. Stay alive, please." With that she dashed off.

Holt clenched his jaw, feeling they ought to have said more.

Harroway entered a low conversation with the Twinblades, so Holt took a few moments for himself. He moved to glance at the map of the city again. Red crosses had been placed upon the western quarter and on other locations on the outer ring. More islands had fallen then or were about to be set ablaze. Even if they pulled through the night, Sidastra would suffer for it.

Although Holt could not see them making it to dawn. Just how would they even begin to kill the queen when it took Champions and Lords to bring one down?

And they hadn't even considered Silas yet.

His heart began hammering; the dragon bond picked up with it. He was spared spiraling in his own thoughts by Harroway calling him again.

"The brothers tell me your magic is of benefit to a shield wall. Slowing the wretched bugs as we fall back will be invaluable."

"Ash and I will do what we can," Holt said. "But eventually our magic will run out."

Harroway harrumphed. "As will our arrows and bolts before the queen emerges, at this rate. You're dismissed for now."

Happy to leave, Holt descended back to the courtyard and to Ash. He pressed into the dragon and Ash wrapped his neck around him, and they enjoyed a quiet moment together.

Around them, troops began moving again. The remaining trebuchets continued to whistle and thump, ballista teams called to one another, and siege equipment groaned as they repositioned.

Not wanting to waste any time, Holt got on Ash's back to sit in peace and opened the bond to look on the core. Some lunar motes swirled freely, so he got to Forging. If they were lucky, he might hammer enough of them in for one extra Shock or Consecration.

Talia

The skies were clear, but it would not last for long. Pyra flew fast to the north while Talia gleaned as much information on the state of the battle across the city as she could.

Though the bulk of both their forces and the scourge were concentrated in the west, carriers had landed ghouls wherever else they could. But Talia, Harroway and their war council had anticipated that. And in this regard, the scourge at least seemed to be acting as expected. Perhaps Silas, or Sovereign, or whatever dark power drove the scourge now, had not anticipated the living changing tactics too?

Harroway had done the work, and damn him, he'd done good work. Strategic outer islands had been cleared of ballista teams to make those islands appear weak and easy pickings. Talia and Pyra were en route to the most northern one now.

"I sense them," Pyra said. "Crawling all over the island."

Talia smiled. The ghouls and bugs would have hoped to kill the people there, infect them and raise them as more drones for the swarm. But the island was empty and was as rigged to ignite as the west quarter had been. And with the sky briefly clear, Pyra had free reign.

Their bond burned in satisfaction as the scourge below burned. Homes could be rebuilt. Walls repaired. Yet whether ghoul, juggernaut or abomination, it didn't matter; all were consumed by such a blaze. Pyra's pleasure became her own, and for once Talia did not resist it.

After torching the island, Pyra turned east. Talia bid her fly low to the lake so the troops at far-flung outposts might see them at work. Let them know a dragon rider was with them.

Yet their domination of the sky ended there. Shrill shrieks came from the west. Talia twisted her head around to see distant stingers and carriers reemerge from the cover of the storm clouds, descending near vertically like a shower of putrid stars. The swarm had regrouped and now focused all its efforts in one direction. Since the west quarter had been torched, the defenders had no more traps to spring.

"We should go back," Pyra said.

"We can't," Talia insisted. "There aren't enough men to defend the south, east and north because of this plan. We light the traps and then head back."

Pyra roared and pushed herself on even harder. After torching one of the rigged islands in the east, Talia feared their cunning plan was now being used against them. While she and Pyra flew around the city, the scourge pushed in the west with only Holt and Ash for any magical aid, and he'd said Ash's core was low already.

When they lit the eastern isle without encountering resistance, she knew they had been played. The swarm was happily sacrificing pockets of its numbers to keep the fire rider occupied – yet she couldn't have left those scourge forces alone, or else the beleaguered defenders would face a fight on all fronts.

At least with the west quarter impassable by foot, the scourge ground forces would have a harder time pushing in.

Pyra turned south. On their way, Talia saw just how tenacious the scourge could be.

Ghouls crawled up from the lake onto the embankments of lesser islands, connecting islands, any scrap of land that lacked walls. They wouldn't make it through gatehouses on their own, but they were cutting off escape routes, forcing battalions to fight their way through even as they retreated.

Talia and Pyra were halfway to the southern islands when the western sky streaked with silver.

"No!" Talia cried.

"*Clesh...*" Pyra said, her voice betraying fear. That Pyra was afraid turned Talia's blood cold.

"*Hurry, Ash and Holt are alone!*"

They were so far away that Pyra couldn't hope to communicate with Ash. Speed was everything now.

When they burned the southern island, there was no pleasure left in the purge. Pyra bathed the bugs in fire and they circled back, flying with all their might to the western front. The fighting had pushed deep into the inner ring now.

A storm of silver lightning tracked Silas and Clesh's progress. The Storm Lord flew toward the central ring, then toward the palace itself. Then up and up, until the black sky itself lowered to engulf the roof of the palace and Talia lost sight of their foe.

Stingers buzzed on every side. Pyra tucked her wings in and dove, pulling up just above the lake's surface where the heat of the burning west kept the stingers at bay. The surface of the lake shone like a pool of blood, blood that boiled and churned as ghouls climbed out onto the embankments.

The swarm only slowed as it tried to cross the final bridge between the inner and central rings. There, beyond the ruined gates, the blue hawk banner of Harroway still flew. Assailed on all sides, the battalion fought the last desperate fight as divisions of troops fled in disorder to the palace grounds. Swords fell like thrashing claws, spearmen thrust against oncoming juggernauts and did not waiver.

Talia wished to aid them, but the palace was still lost in darkness. As they began their ascent, a screaming roar rent the night – enough to sap the last of the heat from Talia's heart.

A dragon had died.

# 56

# A FINAL INVITATION

**Holt**

The swarm returned with such fury that the living had been forced to retreat at once. The inner ring was taken with hardly a fight. There were too many stingers in the air. Even if Talia and Pyra had been here, it wouldn't have helped.

Here, at the gatehouse to the central ring with its portcullis shattered, Harroway had demanded his best men make a stand. Clad in plate armor, armed to the teeth, the cream of Sidastra's soldiers drank vials of dragon blood and stand they did.

With their strength, the choke point of the ruined gateway, and Holt's sparing Consecrations, not even abominations threatened the line. Just as it seemed they might hold, the air grew thick. Still at the front of the shield wall, Holt waited with bated breath. He cast out with his magical senses, but the storm clouds above distorted everything.

Then came the flash. The boom hit a split second later, drowning out the battle. Holt dashed out of the formation to see one of the ballistae on the gatehouse reduced to splinters. A second flash and silver lightning blasted another crew from their nest. Thunder deafened their screams.

After a third lance of lightning, the Storm Lord and Clesh followed in its wake.

So, Silas had chosen to enter the fray after all. Holt gritted his teeth, not afraid, just resolute. It had been inevitable really. He checked his bond. It shook as though gripped by a fever. Well, that had been inevitable too.

"We have to do something," Holt said. "Or they'll blast every siege engine we have."

*"We can't do anything on the ground,"* Ash said.

"You have an idea?"

*"Yes. Let's go!"*

Holt would have questioned anyone else. Focusing their senses felt easier than before. Perhaps because their blood was up, their bond so open and raw, or because the noise of war and the stench of blood and death was all they could hear or smell. Holt climbed on Ash's back. They said the words and their senses blended.

At once, Clesh's roars reverberated worse in Holt's head. And now the dragon had dropped below the cloud line, his magical presence was as stark as a lone mountain upon a grassy plain.

Ash took off, veering right to skirt the edge of the burning island, which the stingers avoided. They banked a hard left, bearing around to approach Clesh from behind. Lightning fell all around the gray beast.

*"I don't think an ambush will work,"* Holt said. *"They'll sense us."*

*"Exactly. I'm counting on it."*

Ash shot a beam at Clesh's back. It missed, but the dragon did turn.

*"Do not tempt me,"* Clesh said. *"How I would like to wipe your broken notes from our race's song."*

Ash had continued flying toward Clesh and now veered past, fast as he could, heading back to the central ring.

*"Feel free to try,"* Ash called back. *"Unless you fear a blind hatchling will outfly you."*

Clesh laughed aloud, a hoarse roar that made Holt's skin crawl. He glanced over his shoulder and, sure enough, Clesh and Silas followed them.

*"Want to let me in on the plan?"* Holt asked.

"*I just thought this would distract them,*" Ash said. "*Now I'm not sure.*"

They crossed over the central ring of islands where the battle now raged. Corpses of stingers and carriers piled up due to heavy air defenses.

A fork of lightning struck ahead of them, removing a ballista platform from their flight path. Holt grimaced. Silas would take out any obstacle in his path one by one unless they somehow got him surrounded.

"*Make for the palace,*" Holt said. "*The aerial defenses are heavy there. One team might get a shot off before Silas can destroy them all.*"

Ash beat his wings furiously.

"*Come back, whelp,*" Clesh called.

Another fork of lightning, this one so close that static shocked Holt's limbs. Clesh and Silas surely wouldn't miss them. They were playing with them.

"*Sovereign extends a final invitation.*"

Ash came within range of the palace's outer defenses.

"*You must be special, weakling, to command his attention even with your impure blood.*"

Holt felt Clesh's hot breath on his back, then, in an instant, it left, and he sensed Clesh's presence rising. Bolts shot out. Ash flew in low under them while Clesh appeared to continue ever higher.

"*Climb,*" Holt said. Many civilians had been packed inside the palace. "*He'll start attacking the palace unless we're on it. Seems like he needs you alive.*"

Ash roared from the effort of pulling up so suddenly, then they climbed, higher and higher. Holt clung on as tight as his enhanced body would allow and then Ash reached out with his talons, hit the red-tiled roof of the palace, and began scrambling up it. Part crawling, part leaping, part flying, Ash kept climbing until they reached the peak. Even up here, there were ballista teams at every point of the compass.

Soldiers called out to him, trying to ask what was happening. Holt faced the team to the east, but a silver bolt shattered the engine and threw men from the walls.

"Attack us!" Holt bellowed. He looked for a sign of Clesh, but the clouds seemed to close in on the palace, as though the sky was falling. A black fog engulfed the rooftop. Holt lost sight of even the ballista teams.

"We're the ones you want," he yelled.

Another flash even through the thick haze of fog; another boom, dampening the splintering wood and screams of the dragon's latest victims.

*"Leave with us."*

A second warning shot, this one so close that the force blew Holt from Ash's back. Ash howled, but Holt was gone. He rolled down the steep incline of the roof, flailing, fearing he too had gone blind from the flash before he landed with a crash.

Holt groaned. Even with an enhanced body, that had hurt. His senses were once again his own – the impact must have severed his sense-sharing connection with Ash. Forcing himself to his feet, he discovered he had fallen onto a flat piece of connecting roof between two turrets. Ornate outcrops and windowsills protruded from the red tiles. He could climb and get back to Ash.

*"Holt!"*

Panic surged across their bond.

*"I'm all right."* He squinted through the fog. A ballista platform was nearby. *"We need to get a shot."*

*"Come, for your rider's sake,"* Clesh said.

Holt started to climb. At least the black fog made it impossible to look down.

*"Your threat has no teeth,"* Ash said. *"If you kill him, I'll never come with you."*

Holt leaped from the head of a statue to an arched window frame.

*"Of course not,"* Clesh said. *"But if you care for your human at all, you'll come with us and bring him. It will be the only way to keep him safe."*

*"S-safe?"* Ash said, his defiance slipping.

*"Don't listen to him,"* Holt said, before making another jump. He landed at his destination but lost sight of Ash in the fog. Just one more effort and he'd be at the ballista.

Clesh must have sensed Ash's hesitation as well, for his voice become silky. *"Safe. Protected. A new world is coming, Ash, whether you help*

us or not. It cannot be stopped. A world for dragons. But our master is reasonable. He understands."

"He's lying," Holt said. But, to his horror, he felt a quiver of doubt
flit over their bond.

Ash was listening.

Holt made his final leap. His grip faltered as he half-pulled himself
up and soldiers rushed to help him.

Clesh pressed his advantage. *"He is like us, youngling. A dragon raised
in captivity. A dragon raised in servitude to humans. He understands what the
bonds do to us. How they trap us. He lost his rider long ago and wishes no
dragon to feel that pain."*

*"If... if I come with you... Holt will live?"*

*"Yesss,"* Clesh hissed. Fresh lightning struck in the dragon's
excitement.

Holt couldn't believe what was happening. This insanity had to
end right now.

"Shoot him," he pleaded with the crew.

"Can't see anything, sir," the soldier in control of the ballista said
in a high voice. "Nuthin' but darkness."

Holt shoved the man aside, taking hold of the trigger as though for
all the world he could see any better through the fog. He couldn't even
see Ash, and they were far enough apart now that even the dragon's
core seemed distant and small. Panicked, Holt struggled to communicate telepathically.

"Ash!" Holt called, hearing his own voice falter. "Don't listen to
him. Don't. They're evil. They killed Brode!"

*"I know,"* Ash said, his superb hearing picking up Holt's words.
*"But you felt Sovereign's power. We can't fight him, Holt. I... I don't want you
to get hurt."*

"If we go, Talia and Pyra will die. We didn't come all this way just
to abandon them!"

*"You see,"* Clesh said, *"you see how the human guilts and controls you. Our
master knows all too well. Sovereign, mightiest of the mystics, greater than the
Elders – he shall free all our kind!"*

Heavy wings beat on the air. Holt scanned ahead, desperate to see movement in the fog, anything to suggest where Clesh might be. Yet the thick smoggy clouds did not betray their summoner.

*"You are right, Master Clesh,"* Ash said. *"I will come, if Holt will be spared. I do not wish the pain of it."*

*"You choose wisely..."* Clesh hissed again before celebrating with more of his twisted laughter that rattled the night as he beat his wings heavily. Holt felt the wind blown by them brush his face, but the fog remained impenetrable.

Holt's breath caught in his throat. With a great effort, he reached out telepathically and said lowly, *"Ash, no..."*

In reply, Ash sent him a memory – the same one he had sent when he'd lay half-dying, half-transitioning to Ascendant. Breaking through a tough shell, feeling cool air, smelling damp straw. All was dark. Frightening. There came a voice – Holt's own voice – light and dreamlike.

*"It will be all right."*

Ash's voice followed up, quiet but strong. Only for Holt to hear. *"My eyes for your eyes."*

Holt's jaw dropped. He wanted to sense-share? Would it even work? Brode said it would strain the bond greatly, even over a short distance.

But that memory said it all. Ash trusted him in a way that was beyond words. Holt did too.

*"My skin for your skin,"* he said.

*"My world for your world,"* they said together.

Holt gasped, ready for his world to change. The dragon bond soared painfully under the effects. Cracks at the edges began fracturing. It would fray quickly. Worst of all, nothing came of it. His eyes could not pierce the fog.

*"I don't need eyes to see him,"* Ash said. *"Aim to the left."*

With dawning, wonderous realization, Holt shifted the position of the ballista as Ash guided his aim.

*"Come then,"* Clesh boomed. *"Find your rider and—"*

*"Now!"* Ash said.

Holt pulled hard on the trigger. The bolt sang.

Clesh screamed. A scream to shake the foundations of the palace.

A beam of white light burst from the fog. Ash's core flickered and sputtered out. Empty.

The sense-sharing broke. Their bond held by a hair.

And Clesh continued wailing. He hit the roof somewhere out of sight, smashing and scraping along the tiles. He roared and roared, his cries growing distant with each second until suddenly he roared no more.

~

**Talia**

They crossed into the palace grounds. Then froze mid-flight. Clesh was falling. His wing torn, he thrashed as he descended. More bolts found their mark, piercing his stony hide. Clesh fell and crashed into the gardens before the palace gates, his limbs collapsing beneath him.

He howled, writhed, failed to rise, then slumped over. Dead.

A void appeared in her magical senses where a giant had been moments before.

Talia almost fell from Pyra in shock. There wasn't a moment to take it in. Stingers were on them. Pyra hurled fire while Talia swiped at the bugs with her blade.

*"Land, girl,"* she said.

Pyra weaved through their attackers and found a clear spot on the palace wall to perch on. The battle raged on, but they needed a moment.

Talia's heart hammered. *"Can you reach Ash? Are they—"*

*"They live!"* Pyra said.

A high triumphant roar rang, and Ash descended from the storm clouds of the palace. Pyra greeted him with a roaring chorus of her own, waving her tail with such glee as to cause the soldiers nearby to scarper.

Ash landed beside Pyra, and Talia jumped off her dragon as Holt did his.

"How did you...? What did you...?"

"It was all Ash," Holt said. He ran back to give the white dragon a bear hug. "He tricked Clesh so we could get a shot. Had me going for a second there too, the sneak! When did you get so cunning?" he said, more to Ash than the others.

*"I've heard how you talk to those who think themselves your superior,"* Ash said.

"I still can't believe one shot did it," Holt said.

"You hit his wing," Talia said. "Once out of control he was an easier target for more bolts, but I think the fall alone would have got him. I'd say I can't believe it, but with your luck..." She broke off, too high on adrenaline and euphoria for words.

*"There is still a swarm to deal with,"* Pyra said. *"And unless I am mistaken, Silas as well."*

Talia's high dimmed. She rubbed at her eyes. "What?"

*"There, by Clesh's body,"* Pyra said, pointing her long neck down toward the center of the grounds.

Sure enough, a lone figure now stood before the body of the fallen dragon. He bore a jagged blade of cold gray steel, although it sparked no longer, and he trudged forward, one pained step at a time, heading for troops scrambling to reform in the wake of the retreat. He started cutting the soldiers down.

"Come on," Talia yelled. She'd just jumped on Pyra's back when a screech rang from behind.

So loud, so painful, Talia pressed her hands against her ears to little avail. Ash wailed, an animal howl from the pain of it. A screech to mark the death of the world.

It ended a moment later, although Talia feared she'd hear that screech even in death. Her hands shook, and even the heat of Pyra's core seemed snuffed out as though the screech had brought a frozen gale from the north.

Knowing what she'd find, dreading having to turn, she did.

The queen of the swarm had arrived. Huge did not suffice for this creature. To her, Pyra was but an insect. The queen flew, passing over the raging fire of the west quarter, summoning all her stingers to her side. It descended to an island on the inner ring, and what Talia took to be a lower abdomen unfurled into four mighty legs upon which the queen landed. She – it – was unlike anything else of the scourge. There was a disturbing human quality to the way it stood upright, with the hardened carapace of a juggernaut draped over its frame like a traveling cloak. It even had a cowl of that same armor, casting its face in darkness, other than where two pools of malicious red energy swirled for eyes.

"Ash's core is spent," Holt said mechanically.

Talia checked Pyra's. Maybe ten percent of the total power remained. Their bond shook from the night's work.

Silas slaughtered men before the palace. The queen rallied her swarm for the final push. Talia almost laughed – stuck between a quick death and an instant death. Given that, her choice became easy.

She tightened her grip on her blade. Sidastra was lost. Feorlen was lost. She'd known that in her heart since she'd returned to the Crag to find the Order gone. Sidastra was lost, but Talia would go down fighting.

# 57

# TO THE DEATH

**Holt**

People still fought. That amazed him the most. Despite the world-breaker of a monster that had risen, people still fought.

Talia too looked ready to fight to the death. Sword in hand, she leaped onto Pyra's back as though the certainty of their fate had released her last reserves of strength. No need to hold back for the morrow.

"I'm going to stop Silas," she said.

*"Allow me to bathe him in flames,"* Pyra snarled.

"No, girl," Talia said. "He's a Lord. His skin is near as tough as dragon hide." She raised her rider's blade; crimson steel forged at Falcaer Fortress under the magic of the Order. "I need to do it."

"I'll help," Holt said.

"No, you won't. You just said Ash's core was dry—"

Whatever else she said was lost within another howl from the queen.

"You can't fight him alone," Holt protested. His heart wrenched in agony as he watched the so-called Hero of Athra slice through panicked troops in the palace grounds.

"He's lost his dragon. It's a fight of swords, not magic."

Holt understood. He'd be cut to red ribbons fighting Silas. Yet with Ash's core dry and their bond shaking, he wasn't sure what they could still do.

"We'll cover you from above," he said. "We can do that much before the end. For Brode."

"For Brode," she said.

The dragons roared together.

Holt got back onto Ash, and they readied for flight. Now they were this close again, the difference in the strain on the bond while sense-sharing was remarkable. Talia and Pyra took off first, Pyra gliding low so Talia could jump from Pyra's back to land by Silas. Holt kept his gaze straight for Ash to see. Pyra rose again, and Ash took off to fall in behind her as stingers swarmed into the palace grounds.

Magicless, with only a standard steel blade to hand, Holt could only stab or swipe at passing scourge. While Pyra still had some fire in her belly, Ash resorted to crashing talons-first into the creatures, raking and biting. A rotting taste flitted over their flickering bond each time Ash sunk his teeth in. It was brutal – desperate.

Bolts sailed. Carriers landed in the palace gardens, and beyond the crest of the walls the defenders on the central ring lost ground with each passing heartbeat. The living were surrounded. The living were done.

And then, the clouds began to part.

*Clesh is dead*, Holt thought. *His magic has died with him.*

Holt risked a glance up, hoping that he and Ash might see the stars one last time. At least they might die under a velvet sky rather than a dead one. Light from the raging fires of the city polluted the night, but a few bright spots twinkled.

"*They're beautiful,*" Ash said.

Holt looked through the bond. Lunar motes drifted down, drawn toward the dragon's core. A few more whooshed by like shooting stars. Then more. Even more. Above, Clesh's storm dissipated like smoke on the wind, revealing a full moon. An argent orb with a white halo, gleaming so bright it seemed pearl smooth. The moon had come to the battle flanked by countless stars.

As it shone down on Sidastra, the lunar motes pouring into the orbit of Ash's core became a cascade.

Holt looked straight again to keep them on course and found the scourge staggering for a moment under the soft moonlight.

Ash gave a mighty roar as his scales began glowing.

*"I can feel it,"* Ash said. He weaved between two stingers with ease, then bathed a third in his silver breath.

Holt didn't dare pull any of it into himself. The bond would surely break if he pulled magic, even raw magic, across it now. But they had dealt with this earlier when Ash had eaten his venison. This was just greater.

Ash had barely opened his mouth when a beam of lunar power shot out. It scattered carriers ahead of them, scorching one, though not killing it outright. It made sense to Holt, as much as he understood these things.

Raw motes of magic were unrefined and lacked the density of those integrated into the dragon's core. Now, Ash's beam was powered only by the raw stuff. It was weak. But there was an endless supply of it.

*"Breathe out every drop you can,"* Holt said. *"Let's do some damage."*

They flew back out over the palace walls to the battle for the central ring. On the bridges and islands of the inner ring, flayers, ghouls and juggernauts surged onward in tightly packed ranks. That was a mistake.

Ash swept over them, bathing them in lunar magic with each pass. Stingers shrieked and shied away from them as though afraid of Ash's aura.

Holt almost laughed. As fast as Ash could pull upon the raw motes, more poured in. Ghouls fell after a pass or two. The bigger bugs only howled as though stung, but for the first time the tenacity of the scourge wavered. Their mindless meat grinding forward momentum slowed, and on the bridges it reversed.

Flayers turned, running at impressive speed away from the danger. Juggernauts knocked ghouls aside as they too attempted to flee Ash's flight path. Only the abominations held. Those skeletons with magic of their own threw dark bolts up at them.

The queen bellowed in anger. Her cries snapped the retreating bugs back into line. That done, the queen of the swarm began advancing herself.

"*I think we got its attention,*" Holt said.

"*Now that's a big target,*" Ash said.

"*You can't miss this one,*" Holt said. "*Better move fast. One hit from that thing and we'll be dust.*"

Ash turned and fired beam after beam at the queen's great body as she rose. Each one struck her; each one fizzled like water in a hot pan. The cloak of armored carapace rippled and pulled back as two arms rose from beneath it; one ended in a giant pincer, the other in a crude hand of razor-fine fingers.

The queen snapped her pincer and thrust at an alarming speed. She cast a flurry of chaotic bolts of magic at them from her long-fingered hand. The unnatural red pools that were her eyes tracked their every movement.

Ash swooped dexterously, but they were like a fly to her. A team of Champions and Lords fought together to stand a chance against these terrors. All Holt and Ash could do was annoy her.

The queen kept moving forward between her attempts to kill them. She stood upon the bridge to the central ring now, ready to sweep aside all remaining resistance to her swarm. Ready to end this battle that had already dragged on for too long. She howled her longest, greatest shriek yet, and a chorus of roars answered her.

Distant roars, all from the north and east.

Holt could hardly envision that any more could be brought against the people of Sidastra, but it sounded like a score or more of scourge risen dragons. Perhaps Sovereign had sent them to ensure the job was done.

Whatever it was, Holt didn't have the heart to look at what was coming. He focused on the queen.

"*One last push, Ash. Aim for its head.*"

**Talia**

She landed in the mud. Stampeding feet had churned the once

pristine ground of the palace gardens. Not far away lay Clesh's body, lying sprawled like some monstrous boulder. The dragon had flattened a small tree and two hedges and shattered a fountain. Closer still, attacking pleading soldiers, was Silas.

"Lord Silverstrike," she called. "Have you no shred of honor left?"

He gutted a huddled soldier, then turned to face her. Dirt and leaves had tangled in his long white hair, and his sun-kissed skin had turned ragged and leathery. But it was his eyes that made her pause. Madness. That was all she saw in him.

"Mindless killing won't bring Clesh back."

"I don't want him back," Silas said, his every word laced with guilt, fear and heartbreak. It chilled Talia.

"You could still atone," she said. "There's still—"

"There's no atonement for what I've done." As though to prove it, he cut down another wounded soldier begging at his feet.

Talia winced and felt her own anger rise. Fighting to cool herself, she said, "I know what it's like to have the dragon take over."

"No, you don't," he said, stepping closer. "Not yet. You will, one day. And you'll learn that the love we have for them makes us do terrible things. *He* knows our greatest weakness all too well."

Silas readied himself into an advanced guard position. Talia did the same, stepping forward with care.

"They made you do it—" she started.

"No, girl. No one made me. I did it because Clesh insisted upon joining Sovereign. I did it because I'd be killed otherwise, and I'd have gladly died, but even now... even now I wouldn't want Clesh to feel the pain of this... ripped in two. I did it because I loved him, even though I'm also glad he's gone." His voice cracked horribly. "I have nothing now."

He struck. Talia judged his feint, blocked, countered, danced aside. It was just enough. Silas had lost his dragon; he had no access to magic, but his body was that of a Lord – not such a leap from a human to Ascendant but a leap nonetheless.

"Very good, very good," Silas said, spittle flying. He wiped his mouth and came at her again.

Quick and fluid, that was her chance, using momentum in her favor. Be fast and skilled, and you need not be strong.

Their swords met hard in the bind; both fought for control. The odds tilted to Silas. Talia's sword point was not aligned with her body, meaning Silas could cut down at her. She had a split second. Her dragon bond trembled like a crippled leg with too much weight upon it. Pyra's core was a guttering wick in a cold cavern. She pulled as much fire into her as she could. Her bond frayed, but her muscles blazed with a final effort and she cut around. Even still, Silas's reactions were like the lightning he once produced. The tip of her blade cut into his shoulder as he dragged himself backward.

She had drawn blood. He didn't wear armor because a Lord's skin turned hard as scales, but she wielded steel forged at Falcaer Fortress.

They were a good distance apart now, circling each other. All noise of the battle, the stench of the scourge and the tang of blood forgotten. Her whole world was the fight: crossing blades with a Storm Lord in the mud and the blood while her home fell to ruin.

The fight seemed to mean little to Silas though. He broke off, glanced away, looked to the bellowing queen, then back to Talia.

"You've lost."

"I know."

"You're all going to die."

"I know."

"So why fight?"

Pyra roared in pain from above. Talia's heart skipped a beat.

"I've lost a lot too," she said. "But I haven't forgotten why I became a rider."

He grunted and twitched. A spasm ran down his arm from his injured shoulder.

"Brode never forgot," she said. "No matter the pain he felt, he never forgot!"

Silas's face contorted – shame, fury, loathing all pulled at him. When he opened his eyes, tears fell.

"Kill me," he said.

"Then don't fight me."

He laughed a wicked laugh. "No, Ascendant. You must earn your kill of a Lord." He drew himself straight, for a moment a proud member of the Order once again. Then the madness engulfed him.

His strikes were wild, his stance too wide. Perhaps it was the rage he was in; perhaps he had grown so used to commanding Clesh's power he'd forgotten what a real fight felt like. But Talia found her opening as he overreached.

"Kill me!"

She parried, sidestepped, and thrust forward into his torso. Her rider's blade pierced him with ease. His weight carried him down the metal, all the way to the crossguard. Dark blood flowed over red steel.

Silas grunted, then let out a long, tired sigh. His mouth sagged, his eyes drooped.

"That's for Brode," she said.

"Thank you," he rasped.

She stepped back. Silas Silverstrike, Storm Lord, Hero of Athra, a living legend, fell dead at her feet.

Talia collapsed to her knees, fighting for breath. Her chest burned and not just from her soul. She'd avenged Master Brode, Commander Denna – everyone who had been murdered at the Crag. It wasn't revenge for her father, for her brother, or even for her uncle trapped under Sovereign's will, but it was a blow to his cause. Yet nothing about it felt sweet. Not even bitter. Such a waste, such a waste to fall so far. And he'd done it for love?

She wouldn't be capable of that, would she? No matter the price?

*"It is done,"* Pyra said.

Talia started as though rudely woken.

*"The song of fire triumphs,"* Pyra continued, although her rapture faltered in pain. Now their bond had frayed, Talia couldn't see her core anymore, but the hurt in her voice suggested it was all but spent. *"Ash and Holt are taking on the queen. We must join them."*

Talia almost laughed. That was nonsense. Holt couldn't be standing up to the queen alone. Only then did it dawn on her that there was moonlight now.

*More luck than they know what to do with,* she thought.

The earth shook as the queen stamped closer to the palace isle. It looked like it stood upon the last bridge. Sure enough, a streak of gleaming white raced through the night, blasting beams of light at the queen. Holt and Ash were fighting.

Somehow, Talia found the strength to stand just as Pyra landed. Her beautiful purple drake bled from cuts on her chest and neck.

*"Come on,"* Pyra urged.

Talia sheathed her sword, then half-staggered, half-limped to Pyra's side, paused for breath, then hauled herself up. She righted herself with a groan.

The queen shrieked again, as deafening as when she'd first arrived. Almost in answer, a fury of roars rang from the east. From the north. From the south.

*More scourge risen dragons?* The last ember of fight in Talia burned out. She slumped on Pyra's back, wishing to cry if she had the strength left. *Let it be quick,* she thought. *Let it just end.*

Pyra growled. Her ears pricked.

"I know," Talia said. "Daughters of fire do not die on the earth. Let's fly then. Fly to our doom."

Pyra didn't move. The roaring grew closer.

"Come on then, girl."

*"Talia, those aren't scourge calls."*

"What?" she said, unable to process anything other than that Pyra was just standing there.

*"Those roars are not of the scourge, not even their blighted dragons."*

"But—"

Talia was spared the difficulty of thinking by fresh roaring over-head. She craned her neck back and could not believe what she saw.

Dragons. More dragons than she had seen outside of Falcaer Fortress. All were green, but not the sickly, rotting green of the scourge. They were every shade of spring grass, of summer leaf, apple, and lime, lit by the soft silver glow of the moon. Emerald dragons.

Talia struggled to speak. "How many are there?"

*"A flight's worth!"*

Talia could not have said how many that was at a glance. Over a hundred at least. Maybe hundreds. The emeralds descended upon the scourge, filling the sky with green gales of power. Earth in the palace grounds rose to clamp abominations in place. Trees from the gardens uprooted themselves and swiped at ghouls with long branches. Vortexes of wind caught stingers mid-air. Members of the flight landed to fight side by side with the defenders of the city.

Pyra bellowed a greeting to them, and Talia felt the dragon's body grow hot. The will to fight sparked back to life with a vengeance as a voice she recognized called out to her.

*"Riders!"* the West Warden cried. *"Fall in by the Life Elder. The queen must fall!"*

~

## Holt

Tears of joy streamed down his face. At the Warden's summons, they turned away from the queen to find a massive emerald approaching from the north. The aura of the Elder was as bright as the sun in Holt's sixth sense.

Nor could he believe it when he saw the purple dragon flying up to meet them.

"They made it?"

*"Silas is dead,"* Ash said as they flew in close beside Pyra.

*"Little ones,"* Pyra said wryly, as if she'd known all along that one of the Wild Flights would save them.

"Talia!" Holt called, unsure if his voice would carry over the roars and howls and wind.

She seemed to sense he was reaching out to her and waved back.

By then the great dragon Holt took to be the Life Elder was below them. It dwarfed the other dragons and would not have been comfortable inside the hatchery at the Crag.

*"The honored Elder requests you take shelter behind him,"* the West Warden instructed. *"He has the privilege of the first strike."*

Holt decided not to mention he and Ash had been striking the queen repeatedly to no effect. Somehow, he didn't think the Elder would have the same trouble. They fell in at the Elder's flank, beside the West Warden.

The Life Elder spoke to them. *"That four hatchlings should fight my battles deepens my shame to new depths."* His voice was pleasant as honey yet as ancient and solid as a mountain. He spoke louder next, as if to his whole flight. *"Tonight we fly for the living, as we should have long ago. Tonight, life prevails!"*

The queen bellowed her defiance. She plucked an emerald out of the air with her pincers and squeezed slowly, almost as though inviting the challenge. All stingers were directed toward the Elder, and she launched volleys of magic.

A clover of green light burst before the Elder, deflecting the black magic with ease. His own roar drowned the others as he gathered his power. Even from behind, Holt shielded his eyes from the brightness of it, a breath attack with all the might of nature behind it.

The queen raised her own magical defenses, but the clash was so bright she was lost behind it. There came an enormous splash and a torrent of water. As the light faded, Holt saw the queen had been pushed off the bridge into the lake.

It thrashed in the shallow waters, as helpless as a beetle on its back.

*How did that not kill her?* Holt thought.

Yet it was over. Even the scourge knew it.

Stingers began to flee. Emeralds gave chase.

The honor guard of the Life Elder arrived over the fallen queen and encircled it.

No further orders were needed. The Life Elder and his guard, including the West Warden, Pyra, Ash and Holt attacked the queen together. Holt felt his bond tear as he sent his weak Lunar Shock down into the bombardment. He didn't care. It was worth it.

The queen ceased thrashing. Smoke rose from its body to join the plume from the west quarter. The battle was not yet over, but the living had won.

## 58

## AFTERMATH

**Holt**

Holt spent the rest of the night helping to mop up the bugs and ghouls scattered across the city. They relieved the barracks and strongholds on the central ring first, where civilians were held up. Without a guiding presence, the scourge became manageable. Numerous and vicious they still were, but also lacking in that single-minded purpose that had driven them forward without caution. They could be cornered and killed.

Many more of the ghouls and bugs fled entirely, scattering east and west. They would have to be hunted down in time. Yet the rising dawn marked the end of the incursion of Feorlen.

Holt and Ash found themselves in the palace grounds, helping to find the injured and carry them off the battlefield for treatment. As the morning light caressed Holt's face, he spotted the Twinblades walking silently. Between them they carried a stretcher with a blue hawk banner draped over the body.

Admiration stirred in Holt despite his feelings toward the late Master of War. Harroway might have made mistakes, he might have been duped, he might have thrown Holt in jail given half a chance, but deeds spoke volumes. Harroway had been a true defender of Feorlen through and through. Until his dying breath.

Ash had wandered to sit before Clesh's body. Still as a statue, he just gazed at the fallen dragon.

Holt caught up to him. "You really did have me going for a moment up there."

Ash continued sitting in silence.

"Clesh must have always had a darkness in him."

*"I have no memories of such wickedness. These experiences locked in my blood, the knowledge of my ancestors, none of it contains treachery."*

"Maybe not everything is passed on," Holt said. "Maybe not everything is remembered."

*"It ought to be,"* Ash said.

The West Warden reached out to them then. *"Younglings, the honorable Life Elder requests your presence on the west bank."*

Holt blinked. They should probably find Talia and Pyra and go together. This was surely about Brode. Talia would want to be there.

*"I shall find Talia first,"* Holt said.

"No," said the Warden. *"Only you and the lunar hatchling."*

*"Honored Warden, I think she has a right to—"*

*"You and Ash. Now."*

Holt thought it best not to question or delay. Talia would have troubles enough at the moment. Perhaps the Elder would summon her later.

And so Holt and Ash made for the west bank. They could still sense-share with a frayed bond – it wasn't broken, after all – but the sensations were blurred, more confusing than helpful, and caused them a headache. Thankfully, the flight was short and easy enough without stingers to contend with. When they landed upon the west bank, both boy and dragon groaned from relief.

Once Holt's senses righted themselves, he looked upon the Life Elder and let out an awed breath. He seemed even larger down at ground level. His scales rippled like a meadow under the morning sun, and his eyes shone like spring condensed into two bright wells. The flares and ridges across his back were dark as pine needles.

*"Thank you for coming,"* said the Life Elder. *"Ash, son of night, know you*

*are free to walk among my flight. I have ordered they treat you with the respect of any emerald."*

Ash padded forward and bowed his neck to the ground at once. Holt hastened to follow, getting down on one knee.

*"Rise, young ones. It is I who ought to bow."*

The West Warden snorted at that.

*"I do not jest,"* said the Elder. And he bent his legs and bowed his massive neck, bringing his great snout down to touch the grass. Obediently, the other emeralds present, including the Warden, bowed in turn.

Holt gulped. Ash shifted uneasily.

"Honored Elder," Holt began, his throat dry, "it was your strength and that of your flight that won the night. Ash and I do not seek praise, only word of our tutor whose body was sent to you."

*"The man with the wearied song,"* said the Elder. *"Brode, rider of Erdra who was of my kin."*

"You know his name and his dragon?"

*"There is much in a song for those who understand the notes."*

Holt swallowed hard. He wasn't sure if he was missing something or whether the Life Elder spoke symbolically. "Honored Elder, forgive me, but I do not understand. Master Brode was a human. He could not have had a song as a dragon does."

*"You have souls, do you not?"*

Holt nodded. The fact it was his soul that bonded to Ash was proof of that.

*"All souls sing a song, though human songs are faint. Most of my kind cannot hear them. Yet while a blackbird's song is unheard from afar, still it sings."*

"Yes, honored Elder," Holt said, unsure if he fully understood the Elder's meaning. "Will you tell us what happened to Brode? Rake sent him to you with the wish that he be healed."

The West Warden growled lowly.

*"Members of my flight believe Rake showed great disrespect with such a request."*

Holt struggled to think of a response, but Ash stepped in for him.

*"Master Rake only hoped to save his life. He gave up great reward for himself to do so."*

The Life Elder made a deep rumble in his throat. *"Rake is a troubled one. He is not known to be charitable. I found his request... curious."*

Fresh bursts of green light spun before the Elder's snout, and the giant leaves that had wrapped Brode's body appeared, then gently floated to the ground.

Holt dashed to the leaves, knelt by them. He grasped the edge of a leaf, was about to peel it back, then stopped. It had been hard enough seeing Brode pass the first time. Even worse to cradle his father's sunken, lifeless face. He did not think he had the strength to do it again.

His throat had gone bone dry. "Will you honor Rake's request?"

Somehow, he knew the answer already.

*"Only one force in this world deals in raising the dead."*

Holt sniffed. "So, Rake wasted his favor after all..."

Ash placed the tip of his snout on the leaves and made a low, pining noise.

The Life Elder rumbled again. *"Rake can be slippery, but he has a mind sharp as thorns, and I believe his true intention in sending Brode to me was something else entirely."*

"What was that, honored Elder?" Ash asked.

*"To wake me from my slumber."*

As the Elder spoke, the leaves covering Brode pulled back of their own accord, revealing his weathered old face. He might have been sleeping.

*"When at first my Warden presented Brode's body to me, I almost dismissed him and Rake altogether. A human? What disrespect was this? And then I heard such sad notes, such melancholy tinged with love and defiance I had not heard since the first trees shed their leaves. Since the Pact, I never wished to have dealings with humans again. I have been wrong. For so many long years, as have my brothers and sisters. Isolated and wrong."*

Holt sniffed again, rubbed at his eyes and wiped his nose. When had he last slept?

"I just hoped..." He trailed off. What good would words do now?

*"I understand, child. I wish so much could be undone. From this day forth, I shall no longer act like such a craven and fool."*

Holt didn't understand. "Your Warden told us that you and your flight have been fighting back the blight. None would consider that cowardly."

"*Generations upon generations of toil, and only now do I see we have been working blind. Humans can be so much more than what we believed. And you, Ash, you are the greatest proof of our folly. So much faith has been placed in strength – the influence of my fiery brother on us all.*"

"*Deep roots do not shake, honored Elder,*" Ash said.

The Life Elder rumbled with pleasure. "*Indeed, they do not, young one. Were it that the next hatchings were sooner, you might have begun a flight of your own. How many more powers might we awaken if we weren't so exacting in which eggs hatch.*"

"*Holt is my flight,*" Ash said. "*My brother, my friend.*"

"*My Warden also spoke of the purity of your bond. May I feel it for myself?*"

Holt blinked. No one had ever asked permission before inspecting his soul and bond with Ash. The sheer politeness of it knocked him off balance. Truly, this mighty dragon was making a great attempt to redeem himself for something.

"You may, Honored Elder."

The Elder hummed in satisfaction. Holt felt a magical presence inspect his soul; he would have had all the power to push against it as an infant pushing against their father's hand, yet the presence was just as tender as a father might be.

"*Your songs are woven,*" the Elder crooned, "*but so quiet... ah, you are weary from the battle. Rest, young ones. We shall speak again when you are fit once more.*"

The Elder raised his head. All other emeralds mirrored his movements.

"*My flight shall begin healing what we can of this land. Take what time you need. I shall await you here on the bank.*"

Holt glanced at Ash. The dragon nosed Brode's body affectionately. Why were the two of them so special to this Elder? It wasn't just for Ash's magic.

"We will be grateful to rest," Holt said. "Though I do not know in what way Ash and I can be of service to one of your power."

"*Rest assured that you can. I would know everything of your time together.*"

"Yes, Honored Elder. And we would ask for your wisdom in turn, if you'll give it. About the scourge and about the dragon controlling it."

The emeralds became restless again. Holt feared he had unwittingly struck a nerve.

*"Do you know of this dragon's name?"*

"His followers call him Sovereign."

The Elder's enchanting eyes dimmed, the irises rotating through a season of change. At last he seemed to decide upon something.

*"Rest, child. I swear that all I know, I shall tell."*

Holt bowed again, as did Ash.

"May we take Brode's body with us? He should... he should be buried."

*"Of course,"* said the Elder. The preserving leaves unwound themselves from Brode, leaving him lying on the trampled grass as though sleeping.

Holt picked him up and was taken aback at how light and frail the old rider seemed now. If only Rake had arrived minutes sooner, if only Clesh had not fallen to evil to begin with, if only so many things had gone differently.

**Talia**

She watched Ash return to the palace grounds as if in slow motion. He delicately placed a body on the ground before landing. She moved mechanically toward the pair of them, knowing what she'd find. But knowing didn't help prepare her.

Perhaps the exhaustion and all the horrors of the recent days were to blame, but she hadn't realized just how much she cared for Master Brode until she saw him again. That flicker of hope that he might return had been just that.

Rake had failed. Maybe Holt would be less enamored with him now.

She knelt at Brode's side and bent low to his ear. "I got him back," she whispered fiercely. "Silas. I got him. And Holt and Ash got Clesh."

"We should bury him," Holt said.

Talia shook her head. "He wanted to be with Erdra."

"On a forsaken hill along the road east of Athra," Holt said, recalling Brode's words on where he had been forced to leave Erdra's ashes. "We can't take his body there... we don't even know where exactly—"

"We'll cremate him. Pyra will see to it. We can take the ashes and find it."

"Oh," Holt said, as though with great effort. "Good idea."

"You're tired."

"Aren't you?"

"Think I'm past the point of noticing." She got up, looked him up and down. "Where were you?"

"The Life Elder wished to see us."

"What did he want?"

Holt shrugged. "Just to see us, I think. We're an oddity."

"Hm," she mused. It made sense enough. They were the ones with the special powers to counter the blight. Still, what she wouldn't have given for an audience with such a being.

"Talia," Holt began hesitantly, "about what I said before the battle—"

"It's fine," she said sharply. It wasn't, but she did not have the strength to revisit the topic. Worst of all, Holt had been wrong. It was worse than he'd claimed. He had accused her of not caring enough, but the real problem was she cared far too much. Hiding that fact made Holt think she was cold-hearted, that duty was all she lived for. If only that were the case. If only things were that easy.

To abandon Feorlen now would be as difficult as not flying to her father's aid.

Holt didn't look convinced by her evasion. "You're sure?"

"Yes," she repeated, then tried to change the topic. "I'll take Brode to the palace crypts – you go rest. Use the royal apartments."

"I left my things in a room in the servants' annex," Holt said, not quite meeting her eye. "Behind the kitchens. I'll be more comfortable there. Closer to Ash too."

"Of course," Talia said. She gripped the bridge of her nose and shut her eyes against a flare of head pain. Sleep would absolutely be required after taking Brode somewhere where he could lie in peace. The accursed court could surely keep things together for a while. Although with Harroway dead—

"We'll talk later then," said Holt.

This snapped her back to the moment. "Yes, later," she said. She watched him go, painfully aware that things between them had become awkward again, as though the barriers they had broken down on their journey had been erected again and reinforced.

Maybe she ought to have let him speak just now. Shutting him down had been as harsh as what he'd said to her. Nothing would be resolved without them speaking properly again, whatever path she decided to take.

She was just so tired now.

Talia took a moment before gathering herself for one final task. Then, carrying one of her mentors between her arms, she made her way across the grounds, counting the bows and salutes she received along the way. Somehow, she didn't think it was due to rider respect alone.

Already they had decided for her. When nothing else was left, she was their one tie to the world as they knew it. They clung to it. Already, the choice before her made her wish to return to the battle of the night before. It had been easier to face.

# 59

## DUTY

**Holt**

He awoke to the smell of fresh bread and powerful hunger pangs. He ground his knuckles against his eyes to remove the sleep crust and sat up in his bed. This was no noble's soft bed but a straw-stuffed mattress and coarse blankets like he'd had at home. But home was gone now.

The last piece of it lay on the floor by the bedside. Holt bent to pick up his mud-strewn satchel and pulled his family's recipe book out. He had not taken it out since Mr. Monger had returned it to him. Dirt splatted its spine, but it had dried, and a few gentle scrapes suggested it would clean off. The grime and bloodstained pages were another matter, but they seemed a fitting reminder of what it and he had been through.

He flicked through it aimlessly, skimming over recipes he didn't take in, until he saw a note in his father's hand.

*To please storm drakes best, soak the chicken in brine overnight and take it out to dry in the morning. Once dry, roast low and slow, basting with butter. The meat is most succulent this way.*

Smiling, Holt closed the book. He would take it with him, of course, wherever he might be going. Getting up and dressed, he walked in a daze from the servants' annex at the back of the palace into the great yard of the kitchens. Sun had returned to Sidastra, as warm and pleasant as any late spring morning could be. He had slept for at least a full day then.

Ash lay curled up, his face tucked under his wings, as peaceful as when he could still fit in Holt's arm. He checked their bond. Enough time had passed for it to have healed. And like a muscle recovering from a brutal day's work, it had healed stronger for it. The window to Ash's core was that bit larger, its edges more robust. Clearly a lot of work would be needed to advance from Ascendant to Champion. The days of rapid progress were over for them.

Ash's core had also begun replenishing, though it was still dim compared to the diamond shine it had before the battle. Riders really did make a difference to a core's strength and recovery.

He left the dragon to sleep and followed his nose toward the kitchens. Inside, an enormous if simple breakfast was being prepared. Vats of porridge bubbled to perfection, so large that kitchenhands stirred them with spurtles the size of broomsticks. Trays of loaves with blackened tops were pulled from the great ovens. It was an effort to feed countless thousands, a scale that Holt struggled to wrap his head around. Soldiers and even younger stewards in their smart jackets darted around, helping the kitchenhands and cooks when they would never have done so before.

*A strange thing,* he thought, *that we should all pull together in a crisis in ways we never would otherwise, only for things to return to the way they were as if nothing happened.*

Even a large enough break in the delicate order, such as himself, was excused in the utmost hour of need. Yet how long until they returned to seeing him as dangerous?

He found a spot on one of the long benches to break his fast. Simple though the food was, it was what he was used to and suited his tastes. Butter on warm dark bread and thick cuts of bacon. His first mouthful sent a tingle through his jaw and a glorious sense of contentment throughout his whole body.

There would be dark days ahead for sure, but how much better all things seemed on this side of the siege, when the storm had quite literally broken. How much better after a long sleep, and now a good meal. Holt ate in peace. Others gave him a wide berth.

Until, cutting through even the banging and shouting of the kitchens, a familiar haughty voice entered his mind, *"Good morning, little one. Are you rested?"*

*"Pyra! Yes, I am feeling much better. Is Talia—"*

*"She is well. You should make for the curia chambers on the fourth floor to see her."*

*"Right now?"*

*"If it pleases you."*

*"Is something wrong?"*

*"Talia has been summoned by the court masters."*

Holt only had a vague understanding of what that meant, but her tone sounded ominous.

Pyra continued. *"She is worried they are going to offer her the crown."*

*"What, today?"*

Holt got up, nearly knocking a poor maid over in his haste, and then he was weaving through the kitchen staff.

*"Pyra? Pyra?"*

He could not actively reach out to her like he could to Ash. He could only hope she was listening. She did not answer. He cursed himself, first for getting lost in the bowels of the palace, then for how he had acted toward Talia. Taking out his anger and frustration on her had not been fair, nor had he acted like himself.

*"Pyra?"*

*"Little one,"* the dragon said curtly.

*"Tell Talia to wait,"* he said as he hurtled around into an upstairs corridor, scattering servants and soldiers alike as he ran. *"There's something I need to tell her."*

*"Is there?"*

*"Yes… look, I know I acted weird that night before the battle—"*

*"You were hurtful."*

*"I know."*

No response. Holt hit the stairs to the fourth floor.

*"Pyra?"*

*"A friend is what she needs now. Hurry."*

He burst out onto the fourth floor, twisted left then right, and saw a girl with red hair at the end of the long hallway.

"Talia, wait!"

She took half a step forward toward a pair of great doors and stopped at his words. Up close, her eyes were puffy from lack of sleep.

"Holt, I've been summoned by the curia. I don't have time for—"

"You haven't entered yet because you haven't decided yet, am I right?"

She pursed her lips, but her eyes found the floor.

"Look, come here," he said, and he dragged her out onto a balcony away from any prying ears behind those council room doors. Distant blue mountains and a bright sun signaled they were on the eastern side of the palace. Signs of the battle were still evident in the burnt remains of outer islands. Fresh smoke rose from piles of burning scourge. The city would take time to heal.

Pyra appeared, landing onto a section of roof just above them. Her amber eyes bore into Holt. He gulped but soldiered on with his piece.

"I'm sorry for what I said the other night, before the battle." She remained silent, so he continued. "When I suggested you found it easy to turn away from those in need, as if you were cold. That wasn't fair. I was just... well, I'm sorry."

She smiled. "You were in pain. I understand. And after what we've just been through, it all seems so trivial now... but I appreciate the apology."

"But you shouldn't doubt yourself so much either," he hurried on.

Her brow raised and she seemed ready to counter, so Holt plowed on.

"I know that you keep turning your past over. What if you had flown to save your father? Well, you couldn't have known he would be betrayed or even lose. All you knew for sure was that by leaving you would be breaking your oath. You probably wouldn't have been punished. Commander Denna let you in because she wanted the Order to maintain good relations with the court, but such leniency would only have fueled Harroway's side or caused trouble within the Order itself. You didn't make the wrong choice in not flying to the Toll

Pass. You made the right choice even though it must have killed you to do so."

"Holt..."

"I know you think Ash and I have somehow proved that breaking the rules works out. I let my heart get the better of me and, somehow, we got Ash and his incredible magic out of it, and I advanced quickly due to our unusually strong bond. But the result could have been terrible. Most likely it would have been. I was bound to get caught sooner or later, and then what? Only luck, well, it was more like bad luck, saved us both. Commander Denna may have taken Ash from me, or let the others kill him..." He choked at the very thought of it. How narrowly they had avoided such a fate. "It was foolhardy in the extreme to do what I did – my near banishment is proof of that – and if my father had lived, he might have suffered for it too. And all because I let my heart lead me."

Talia's expression softened. "I hadn't thought of it like that."

"It's funny, in a way," he said. "You've been in anguish over a choice you didn't make, while I've been worried over the one I made. Yet you made the best choice you could at the time. I acted rashly. And that's why – that's why you would make a good queen, I think. Because you can make the hard choices, even awful ones. You've got the stomach for it. So, don't doubt yourself so much."

She smiled. "You're not as dumb as you look, pot boy." She followed up with a punch on the shoulder, only this time his enhanced body could take it. "You realize this is an even harder choice than just leaving to help my father in one battle? Whatever I decide, there will be dire consequences."

"Well, I know whatever you decide, it will be the right call. And I'll support it."

"Thank you, Holt," she said, sounding surprised at herself. "That means a lot."

"We have to stick together, right? We chaos bringers?"

Pyra rumbled happily from above.

Holt thought the presence entering his mind was her, but quickly found the power behind it far different. It was the West Warden who spoke to him.

*"Youngling, if you are rested, the Elder would see you."*

"I have to go," he said.

She caught his arm. "The Elder?"

He nodded.

"You'll tell me what he says?"

He didn't hesitate. "Of course."

Still holding his arm, she pulled him into a fierce hug. "Pyra and I could never have done this without you and Ash. Thank you."

Holt was taken aback but pleased and returned the embrace with equal strength.

"We didn't do so bad," he said. "For two lowly Ascendants."

They parted.

"We must have a funeral for Brode today," Talia said. "Sunset?"

"Sunset." He nodded. "Good luck in there."

With that, he dashed off, eager to wake up Ash, eager to learn all he could from the ancient dragon.

～

## Talia

She watched Holt go, feeling decidedly better. *How did he know where I was?* Then she turned and looked at the purple dragon lounging on the roof, entirely pleased with herself.

Pyra puffed smoke at her.

Talia waved it off and stepped closer. "Did you know what he was going to say?"

*"Not exactly. I suggested he had acted poorly, and then his own mind did the rest."*

"I thought ice dragons were the crafty ones."

Pyra flicked her tail, though playfully so. *"Have you decided then?"*

Talia bit her lip. "What do you think?"

*"It is not my decision to make."*

"Being evasive speaks volumes."

A feeling Talia knew all too well passed across the bond, a feeling of being torn.

*"I am wary of it. The guidance of the ancestors should not be set aside lightly.*

*There are reasons for their teachings and guidance, even if we cannot remember them."*

"Then you aren't in favor."

*"We might be bonded, but this is not my decision to make. Whichever you decide, I too shall stand with you."*

"Even if it makes you uncomfortable. Even if it defies the Order?"

*"Do you know why I chose you? I feel the lineage in my blood, a purer song than others of my kin. I wished to write a song of fire greater than any since the Elder. Many humans were brought before me. None satisfied. And then you came along. Hailing from a strong line of your own, the first royal to enter the Order, and with a grit I sensed in few others, even in the Commander. I knew together we would do great things."*

Talia looked out across the city. What would happen to it, to the kingdom, if she left? She should not trouble herself about it. She had sworn such things away.

"I know my duty."

Pyra hummed low. *"The little one is right. Don't doubt yourself so much."*

Taking a deep breath, Talia left the balcony, went back to the council room doors and pushed with a great sense of purpose. She strode inside.

An oval room well-lit by high windows greeted her. Sitting at the edges of the room was a small army of stewards and coteries, those who served the masters and mistresses of court who sat at the long table in the center. Everyone at the long table reacted differently. The court masters were clearly unsure what level of courtesy they ought to give her. Some stood and bowed, others inclined their heads, some stood but did not bow, and the rest remained seated without ceremony, treating her more like a common rider of her Ascendant rank. Already it spoke of confusion.

Most of the faces she recognized. The Master of Roles and Mistress of Embassy had been in place since her grandfather's day. Yet others must have inherited their mother or father's position since she had left for the Order, and so she could only be sure of their status from their seat at the table. The Mistress of Coin looked barely older than herself. *More like the Lass of Coins,* she thought.

A seat lay empty where Harroway, the Master of War, should have sat.

Being the eldest and most venerable of the gathering, the Master of Roles spoke first. "Talia, may I first thank you on behalf of the curia for your most excellent service in the battle for this city."

"It is my duty to defend against the scourge," Talia said. "You should extend your true thanks to the Life Elder. He did not have to come, and he lost members of his flight to save us."

"A delegation shall be arranged," wheezed the Master of Roles.

He indicated she should move to the end of the table; not the end where the monarch would sit, but the seatless end where stewards, knights, and others would be summoned to make reports, be given orders or be reprimanded. She wondered, as she approached that spot, whether this would turn out differently than she assumed. When she stopped and faced them, the members of the curia took their seats, other than the Master of Roles.

"Despite the victory, this kingdom finds itself in grave circumstances." He clicked his fingers, and a youthful steward carrying an enormous book labored from his chair to deposit his burden before his master. Talia reckoned it could only be one of the census books. The Master of Roles opened it to a pre-selected page. "The sudden death of your brother and the departure of your uncle without an heir leaves the role of the monarch empty. In such times, after agreement of the curia, an ealdor might be raised to the position, and subsequent arrangements made to fill the position left in their wake, and so on and so forth. The vacancy left by the late Ealdor Harroway raises further problems. The curia fears for the stability of the realm."

None of this was unexpected. Still, she owed it to herself, her honor and her oath to seek an alternative if she could.

"Can no such candidate be found by agreement?" she asked.

Their silence said it all.

"Very well," she said. "Forgive my bluntness, but were there any other candidate, any at all, they would be preferable."

It was the wizened Mistress of Embassy who answered. "We quite agree, but we are not in a position to appear disunited and frail after an incursion. Already the Risalian ambassador will be penning letters of our exposure to his archduke."

That was hardly a surprise. Risalia might seek to win back the Toll Pass and its incomes while Feorlen was too weak to resist. Still, Talia thought common fear would stay the Risalians. Few of Archduke Conrad's advisors would wish to risk sending their own people to a land so recently plagued by the blight lest they bring it home with them in great numbers.

"Do you truly fear that Risalia would march against us?" Talia asked.

"It is our role to fear the worst," said the Master of Roles.

Talia frowned. Had they forgotten her mother's brother, King Roland of Brenin?

"Brenin would surely intervene if—"

"King Roland left us to our fates," the Mistress said. "Twice."

Brenin had stayed out of the war last year, much to her father's ire. She doubted they would allow Risalia to sweep what remained of Feorlen aside and so come to dominate the region with ease. But staying out of an incursion was another matter.

"Osric must have ensured our messengers never made it to Brenin," Talia said. "King Roland is my uncle too. He would have not willfully abandoned us or my mother."

*Mother*, she thought. It was her last, desperate play.

"Could Queen Felice act as regent until—"

"She cannot," said the Master of Roles and the Mistress of Embassy together.

"Your mother, Felice, only holds her title by marriage," said the Mistress. "As you well know, princess."

"And even if she were here," said the Master of Roles, rapping his census book as though drawing all his power from it, "she could not affect the judgment of the curia without a seat at this table."

Talia did know it and hadn't expected anything different. Yet despite all that, there was a genuine cause for concern.

"I fear what you're asking will only inflame the voices that the late Ealdor Harroway once spoke for. How will it appear if a dragon rider takes the throne?"

The youngest member of the curia, the Mistress of Coin, cleared her throat. "They would not be entirely opposed."

Talia frowned. Now that *was* unexpected. She examined the young woman. Delicate features, skin like alabaster, and flowing golden hair that spoke of Skarl lineage. Such thoroughbred families of Feorlen often liked to boast that the blood of the first settlers flowed in their veins, from a time before the Alduneis had invaded. This made some of them feel superior. Talia wondered if this Mistress of Coin felt that way herself. She was stunning, Talia had to admit, wearing an immaculate white gown trimmed with gold that fit her snugly and modestly at the same time.

Talia shifted uneasily, feeling suddenly bulky and clumsy in her mail and leather. She cleared her throat and said, "Am I to take it there has been a change of heart on dragon riders since the battle?"

"Princess," the Mistress of Coin said, every word spoken with impeccable clarity, "the moderates amongst us never claimed the riders were not useful. Just expensive." She rubbed a thumb and forefinger together to emphasize the point.

Talia thought that too smoothing over too deep an issue. She held the Mistress' gaze, and to this woman's credit she didn't balk. Young she might be, but she seemed to fit the robes of office like a doeskin glove. Better than Talia would suit them, in all likelihood.

"Besides," the Mistress of Coin continued, "you leaving the Order would represent a victory of sorts for those... *sympathetic* to Ealdor Harroway's concerns."

It seemed they were decided.

"How might this affect our relations with the other powers, beyond Risalia and Brenin?" Talia asked of the Mistress of Embassy.

The old Mistress steepled her fingers and pondered for a long time.

*She has no idea,* Talia thought. *Or if she does, she does not wish to give me a reason to reject the crown.*

"There are many factors to consider," the Mistress said at last. "Yet however the decision is taken in distant lands, we shall weather it. Feorlen has long stood on its own feet," she ended proudly. A general muttering of agreement and much bobbing of heads followed that sentiment.

*More like we have long been ignored,* Talia thought. Feorlen was a much smaller realm than either of their eastern neighbors, Risalia and Brenin. And those latter nations were smaller still compared to the power of some of the Free Cities that had risen from the ashes of the Aldunei Republic. North of Risalia, the Province of Fornheim was small but strong, a land of vast fortresses and elite warriors who had long guarded the Skarls from the south until they had claimed a semi-independence of their own. Finally, to the north, through Risalia and then Fornheim by land or by sailing across the great Bitter Bay, lay the Skarl Empire itself. The Skarls truly did stand on their own feet, keeping the rest of the world at arm's length as much out of pride as it was physically separated by mountains, vast dark forests and snow.

Talia observed the council members one by one. As she did so, Talia knew then there was no getting out of it. They were terrified – chaos had come so close to destroying everything. Further chaos could not be allowed.

She wished dearly that Harroway had lived.

The Master of Roles leaned forward, beseeching her. "If we had any other choice…"

The curia nodded collectively.

*Should I warn them of the true threat? Should I tell them that the worst may lie ahead?*

"Have you decided, princess?" asked the Mistress of Coin.

Talia eyed her, looking for some sign that would betray her inner thoughts, but none rose to the surface. The others, however, showed theirs in their eyes, in the way they tilted toward her, and in the speed with which they had made this offer.

She rocked on the balls of her feet and decided to take Holt's and Pyra's words not to doubt herself so much to heart.

"I know my duty."

# 60

# SONG OF CHAOS

Back on the west bank, Holt found himself face to face again with the Life Elder.

*"Thank you for returning,"* said the Elder. *"May I?"*

Holt nodded. Ash bowed. The Life Elder inspected their soul. He hummed with joy, and suddenly the blighted ground for a dozen feet was scrubbed clean. Flowers burst up from the bare soil and bloomed before their eyes. Holt could only imagine the quantity of magic the Elder had just used.

*"It is as my Warden foretold!"* The Elder's happiness seemed an ill fit for his ancient voice, as though he had long since used it.

"Honored Elder," Holt began, "what is it you see in us?"

*"The purity of your bond is unlike any I have felt before. It is a strength I thought impossible."*

"I do not understand. Talia and Pyra are close, and their bond is more powerful, given their longer training. Those of Champion, Lord and Paragon rank have bonds surely greater than ours."

*"A mound of earth may be grown by adding more soil, but the rain will wash it away. Snowdrifts will gather flakes, but heat will melt them. Your bond is as solid as the base of a mountain."*

*"Are not all bonds created in the same way?"* Ash asked.

The Elder sniffed and ruffled his great wings. *"As with all life, much may be similar, but nothing is exactly the same. Tell me of your first meeting."*

Holt took up the tale. As he described the knot of warmth in his soul forming on the night Ash hatched, the Elder interrupted.

*"As early as that... yes... that would account for it. Neither wishing anything from the other except their presence."*

"I'm afraid I don't understand," said Holt. "Talia and Pyra love each other just as much as Ash and I."

*"Perhaps, child. I have not felt their bond. Yet think again on their foundations. Since the time of the Pact, your Order has presented candidates to dragons when both have already matured. I am sure some join the Order to defend loved ones, to give meaning to their lives, yet even such noble causes carry a desire; that the dragon they bond with will be able to grant them power, even if that is only to defend. Some seek the Order to atone for crimes or avoid bleak lives back home; the dragon is therefore their escape, and they depend on the bond. There are more nefarious reasons besides. They want something from their partner. Such desires, great or small, sully a bond and besmirch one's soul. Dragons also fall into the same temptations. Our greatest fault is the arrogance to believe we are better. A fault I am especially guilty of."*

"You speak harshly of yourself, Honored Elder," Holt said.

*"When you know why, you shall think me too lenient."*

"Well, I am pleased to hear my bond with Ash is pure, but I do not know what that means? I couldn't save my own father. I – we – weren't strong enough."

*"Love and strength are not one and the same, child. One day, you will realize why your bond is so exceptional. For my part, I never believed such a bond was possible. I did not trust in humans, but you two have shown me how wrong my siblings and I have been. Even if your magic were not exceptional, this one aspect would still give me more faith than a hundred Lords of your Order. You have given me hope that humans and dragons may share this world in harmony. As true friends."*

Ash ruffled his wings at that. *"Honored Elder, I am so young, yet all I see in my echoing memories is the bond between us and riders. I sense no discord in those notes."*

The Life Elder's eyes flashed, spinning through a wheel of green until settling on a somber shade of sage. *"The magic of my sister locked* much away. *Such is the art of the mystics. My own power may be enough to reveal a portion to you, Ash. Few other than the eldest of our race now remember. I do this in the hope you can understand the importance of the task I shall lay before you."*

*A task?* Holt thought in alarm. *An Elder dragon requires our help in something?*

Before Holt could think further on the matter, Ash began to squirm, then pine, then he growled and struggled against some invisible horror. As quickly as it started it ended, and Ash took a step back, panting like a dog.

"Elder..."

*"Now you see,"* said the Elder. *"Share what you have learned with Holt. He must know as well."*

Holt braced himself. At least it would be over quickly.

*"Ready?"* Ash said.

"Show me," Holt said.

At once, their bond became taut and flared from activity. Vivid images, dreamlike words, and the thoughts and feelings of all involved overwhelmed him as though he'd developed a new sense altogether.

He was high as the clouds. A younger, brighter world rolled out before him. Music played, a perfect harmony beyond what crude instruments might perform. And then, a jarring sound arose. Those humans, which had for so long loped across the land, were growing in number.

The Elder's voice carried over the foggy memories. *"Long had the world been ours. We thought little of humans. And then they became troublesome. The one species capable of defying us. We fought over flocks and herds; trees from our tranquil glades were cut for fires; their sharp, shiny new weapons cut our wings, their hammers crushed bone, their long wooden talons drove into scales. Rats had grown to lions and proved tenacious."*

Holt saw centuries of conflict flash before him, countless deaths on both sides. Villages burned, nests left with nothing but broken eggs, and all the while Holt heard the beautiful harmony descend into agonizing screeches – closer to the cries of the scourge than any song.

He clapped his hands over his ears, but it made no difference.

*"One day, my brothers and sisters gathered to discuss a solution."*

Five mighty dragons stood in a circle, roaring, gnashing, seething. One a wrathful lava red with scarlet eyes; the second so cold a blue it might have been crystalline, with eyes deep as the ocean; the third a metallic gray, its eyes shining like liquid silver; the fourth the yellow of a wheat field at harvest with violet eyes; and the fifth, the fifth was the one dragon Holt recognized.

The Life Elder continued the story.

*"Each of my brothers and sisters put forth their solution. The Fire Elder demanded their crops be burnt so they could not eat. The Frost Elder wished to freeze the rivers so they could not drink. The Storm Elder sought to drive them with wind beyond the deserts. It was the subtle thinking of the Mystic Elder that united us."*

All else in Holt's vision dimmed as the great yellow dragon took prominence.

*"She suggested another force might destroy the humans on our behalf. And it was I who was the first to agree with her. I, the Elder of Life, so sure these humans would sow discord in the world's song, was the first to assent to such a thing. I even suggested what form that force might take, knowing how suscep-tible your kind is to illness and despair."*

Before the Elders now appeared a flat altar of stone, on which appeared a number of skittering bugs.

*"In the vethrax and their venom, I sought the answer. The Fire Elder imbued his rage; the Frost Elder infused her cunning; the Storm Elder passed on his raw power; the Mystic Elder expanded their minds with arcane energies; and I bid them grow. We did this hastily and in hate. The first of the scourge was born, and by the time we realized the true extent of its dark power, it was too late.'*

Once again, Holt soared high like a dragon, observing a world now growing dark from rot.

*"My punishment has been to fight the millennia-long defeat. Unable to stop the plague I helped to create."*

The visions ceased. Holt felt the dragon bond shudder as Ash retracted the ancient memories of his people. He found he had dropped to his knees, his palms pressed against the grass. Breathing hard, he picked himself up.

The Life Elder cast his gaze to the ground. *"You see now my great shame."*

Holt couldn't speak. Couldn't think. Dragons had created the scourge? The very beings who helped humanity fight against the bugs: dragons, proud and venerable, and—

But he knew better than most the pride of dragons. A lifetime of service had taught him that, and if he had learned one thing in recent months, it was just what the Life Elder had admitted. Even dragons could fall. Clesh fell. And the dragon Sovereign had fallen into a darkness perhaps worse than the Elders who had created the scourge in the first place.

At length, Holt found his voice. "So... if dragons hated humans, why did you join forces?"

*"For years we did nothing. Until it seemed humanity would be wiped clean from the world, leaving an unstoppable horde of the dead which we could not hope to overcome. Dragons too fell to the scourge through sickness and battle. The enemy of our enemy became our begrudging allies. We descended from our high nests to aid the humans in their desperate, failing attempt to push back the swarms. And in the heat of those early victories, the first bonds between our races formed."*

"That's how the riders started?"

*"Even as the advantages of such bonds emerged, such was the animosity between us that those who bonded became pariahs. Dragons suffered worse in this. And so, the Pact was made. Hostilities would cease; neither race would interfere with the other beyond the riders themselves."*

Shame wrinkled across Holt's own dragon bond.

"This has nothing to do with you, Ash," Holt said. He patted Ash down his long neck. A strange turn in fortune indeed, that dragons should create the bane of life and now another dragon arrived who could fight it.

Ash had weaknesses but fierce strengths as well. Kindness. Bravery. He was proof that other dragons worked hard to cover their frailties. Even the Life Elder had his flaws. He too let his heart lead him.

"I forgive you," Holt said.

The Life Elder groaned and shook his great head as though he had misheard. *"Did you not understand what—"*

"I did. And I still forgive you, for what it's worth."

*"It means a great deal to me."*

"More hatred won't get us anywhere. There's already one dragon putting out enough of that on his own. Do you know of Sovereign? You hired Rake to defend your flight from him after all."

*"We knew of a threat preying on the Wild Flights. Rake brought word that others were suffering from attacks. We did not know who or what was behind them. I thought it might have been a rogue member of your Order."*

"Well, it was, to an extent. And perhaps there are others. But this dragon, Sovereign – he has control over the scourge. That's why they are acting so differently."

*"They cannot be controlled. We tried."*

Holt's heart sank. He thought for sure that the Life Elder would know the answer, know how they could defeat Sovereign and the scourge.

"If you didn't know of him, what is it you wanted from Ash and me? Why did you come to help us?"

*"Because in the rider Brode's song, I felt such a love for his dragon, even across decades since their parting, and her love for him. Enough to make me question all our old prejudices. That a distant descendant of my flight could feel so powerfully for this human made me reconsider the nature of the bonds that form between us and the chance for our future. News of your power stirred fresh hope in me too, and I had to see it for myself. Your land was threatened, but no longer would I sit idle and let others make amends for my mistakes. For too long have things remained static. It is time to unite, rid the world of the scourge forever, or die in the attempt."*

"What would you have Ash and I do? As effective as Ash's lunar magic is, we are but one young pair."

*"Seek my brothers and sisters. It might be our creation is too strong, but if we gather the strength of all flights, there is a chance. We shall need their aid, especially if this Sovereign has been recruiting riders and dragons to his cause. The world is sick,"* he added with a shudder. *"The blight runs deep. A time of change is upon us all, and we shall either learn to bend to it, or we shall break."*

Holt breathed hard. Where was he to begin?

"Honored Elder, the Wild Flights are known to be reclusive and secretive. Perhaps some of your flight should accompany us to—"

*"That, I fear, would be unwise. The Fire Elder departed in fury, swearing never to have dealings beyond his flight again. The Frost Elder left, uncaring for*

the havoc we had wrought. *The Storm Elder declared he would gather enough power to deal with the problem alone. And the Mystic Elder vanished quietly with her flight, for reasons known only to her. All blamed me for what we had done. Yet if there is anything that can reunite us, I believe it to be you and Ash. I trust that when they feel the strength of your bond, they will realize their folly as I did."*

It was so much to take in. A long journey for which Holt could not make out the road, never mind the destination. There would doubtless be great challenges, and it would help him and Ash grow strong.

Once more he heard his father's final plea. *Help the others...*

Holt curled a fist. *We must grow stronger.*

This mission, as insurmountable as it seemed, would at least give them a clear goal to pursue.

"What if we fail?" he asked.

*"Whether my brothers and sisters bring their might to bear or no, I, the Elder of Life, vow to aid you in the fight ahead. Even unto death."*

Ash roared in agreement. *"I accept this task, Honored Elder."*

*"May the song of night grow loud and rich within you,"* said the Life Elder.

"I too am ready," said Holt. "Only we do not know where to begin."

*"There is time yet. Rest and recover in full. Seek me here when you may to talk further."*

Holt climbed onto Ash's back, still unsure whether he had fully taken it all in. Perhaps it would settle better as he Cleansed and Forged.

"There is another rider in the city," Holt said. "Her name is Talia. We would not be here without her help. May I tell her of all we have learned from you, Honored Elder?"

The Elder let out a gust of breath through his great nostrils. *"You may."*

"Thank you," Holt said. Before starting the sense-sharing technique, he had one last question. Something he hoped would alleviate Talia's concerns about what he knew he had to do.

"Honored Elder, Rake sought a favor from you. That's why he

agreed to escort your flight. He said he'd been asking you for a long time to help him. What did he want?"

*"It is not my place to tell you. Rake's burden is his alone to share."*

Holt nodded; he had expected as much. With that, he and Ash took off, heading for the palace isle. Their final farewell to Brode lay ahead, but given all they had heard and the task before them, Holt knew it was their farewell to much more. His old life was over.

Yet neither would he become a dragon rider.

# 61

# FORK IN THE ROAD

Over the next week, Holt and Ash attended to the sick and injured who had contracted the blight. Holt made a point of visiting the hospitals by night, led by tired physicians. They cured who they could and left to regain their strength while the moon still shone. When the morning came, those lucky few would awake to find themselves cured.

Holt preferred it that way, at least for now. The quiet of the night made it less terrible to pass by those beyond his aid. As they adapted this habit, he and Ash became creatures of the night, which suited them just fine.

Their duties done, they would fly east to Cleanse and Forge in peace. After Brode's pyre had burnt out, there seemed little left for them to do in the city. Talia had her hands full, and they would only get in the way. The bustle of the kitchens, which had once felt comforting, now only reminded Holt of what he'd lost: his father, his naivety, his childish notions of riders, dragons and war.

They favored sitting atop a small hill some miles inland of the eastern bank, where the land started its gradual rise toward the mountains of the Red Range.

This night was cold and clear, the moon still bright, though waning fast. Over a week since the full moon, the volume of lunar motes swirling past Ash's core was much reduced. In another week's time, Holt imagined it would become a trickle.

Holt gathered that their power would wax and wane with the moon. While they would indeed be stronger at night, Holt would have to take advantage of the most opportune times each month to Forge.

By Cleansing fastidiously each day, the time needed to clear impurities shortened. Holt focused now on Forging, encouraging Ash to sit in peace and regulate his own heart so they might keep better control over the beating of the bond. Of the two techniques, Holt still found Forging to be harder. Controlling his breath was entirely under his will but settling his heartbeat or raising it as needed and maintaining it for a length of time was another matter.

Yet days of work and mote after mote Forged onto Ash's core was starting to bear fruit. The pulsing ball of light had solidified further, taking the shape of a denser orb as the backdrop darkened. It took no great leap of the imagination to know what form Ash's core would develop into given more time and effort.

Holt blinked as the first rays of dawn crept through his eyelids. He opened his eyes for the first time in hours and drank in the crimson sky to the east. Northeast, beyond the Red Range, lay the Kingdom of Risalia. Brenin was to the southeast. Beyond that, Holt had little true knowledge, only that from some maps Talia had had her stewards fetch him. There were the Free Cities: Athra lying in the fertile heartland of the old republic; Mithra controlling the Southern Strait and ruling the seas; Coedhen nestled within the Fae Forest. And further east still an endless grass sea. Or so the maps said.

To the north lay the Province of Fornheim, and beyond that the great Skarl Empire. South across the sea lay the Searing Sands and the Jade Jungle, which Holt imagined to be lands of spice and smoke.

"Which way should we go?"

*"It would make sense to travel to the closest flight first,"* said Ash.

"It would, but which one is closest? The Storm Peaks alone are deep inside the Skarl Empire. He thought the Fire Flight would be in the southern jungles. For the Frost Elder, we'll have to travel north."

*"North and north until the mountains are made of ice,"* Ash said, recalling what the Life Elder had told them.

"It's all a bit vague," Holt said. Their maps would help navigate human realms, but the Wild Flights were not conveniently marked.

*"And who knows where the mystics are?"* said Ash.

"Somewhere east, I think. At least that was the direction Rake said he was heading."

*"I should like to find Master Rake."*

"Me too."

At once, Ash lifted his head, his ears pricked. *"I hear dragons approaching."*

"Probably just some emeralds back from a hunt."

*"They are diving right for us."*

Holt jumped to his feet. He spotted the approaching dragons, diving from the east – one frost blue and one a dark stormy gray. Holt crested out magically and sensed they were far stronger than him or Talia, yet nothing on the power of Silas Silverstrike. They were at Champion rank.

The two Champions circled overheard, then landed, one on either side. One was a slight woman with bronzed skin and long black hair. Her companion was a giant of a man with red hair and beard.

"Hail, Ascendant," said the woman in an accent Holt could not place. "We did not expect to come across one of the Feorlen Order so far from the Crag."

Holt stifled a sigh. "How much do you know of what's happened here?"

"I will have to wash out my ears," said the giant man. His accent was of the far north, perhaps from the Skarl Empire. "The tone of your voice leaves much to be desired, Ascendant. Have the Feorlen riders forgotten how to address their superiors?"

"The Feorlen Order is gone," Holt said. "I can explain to you what happened, or you can fly to find the burnt remains of the Crag for yourself."

The Champions' eyes popped. Their dragons growled low, then their attention turned to Ash and the predictable roars of disgust and gnashing of teeth ensued.

"He is blind?" said the man.

"Who are you?" the woman snapped.

"My name is Holt Cook, and this is my dragon, Ash."

Both dragons loosened their jaws and gathered their breaths with no sign of slowing down. Until a sudden wave of power washed over them all. Holt felt it as a warm breeze, but it seemed to affect the two visiting dragons profoundly. Both canceled their magic and bowed so low so quickly it seemed they wished to flatten themselves like pancakes onto the grass.

Both Champions looked at their dragons in alarm.

"What has gotten—" the man began. "What? Here?"

"This close to a city?" whispered the woman. She rounded on her companion. "Sigfrid, if a Wild Flight has invaded human territory—"

"The Honored Elder of Life and his Emerald Flight saved this city from the scourge incursion," Holt said. "We and everyone here are under his protection. As I said, I can explain all that has happened."

The Champions looked at each other. The woman bit her lip; the man, Sigfrid, gulped.

"We would speak to your Commander Denna, insolent boy," the woman said.

"Commander Denna is dead."

"Lord Silverstrike then," said Sigfrid. "He was sent to oversee your response to the rising, though we lack a report from him too."

"Lord Silverstrike is also dead."

Sigfrid's face turned as red as his hair. "Then whoever is the most senior rider now!"

Holt considered this question and decided it would be better not to push the Champions further. "She is in the city. Currently in the palace. I can take you there—"

"No," said Sigfrid. "We go no further until we understand the situation. Bring her to us by the authority of the Paragons of Falcaer Fortress."

Ash rumbled with laughter. *"They aren't going to like this either."*

"Very well," Holt said. He bowed to each of them in turn, then set off to fetch Talia.

.  .  .

By the time they returned to the hill east of the city, the morning sun dominated the sky and Ash's core had all but dried of free-floating lunar motes. Ash and Pyra landed side by side, and Holt and Talia dismounted to greet their guests. Neither Sigfrid nor his companion approached.

"Another Ascendant?" Sigfrid said. "Maria, let's make a note that the Feorlen branch feels it is suitable to waste Order time."

"There is no need for hostilities," Talia said. "As I'm sure Holt has tried to explain, the Feorlen branch was destroyed by betrayal. I was the only survivor."

"Your name, girl?" Maria asked.

"Talia."

"So, Ascendant Talia, you're telling us that your entire branch fell to scourge forces and no one thought to send word to Falcaer?"

"There were many mitigating circumstances." She told their tale in brief, which Holt regretted did not capture the measure of their toil or suffering, but he doubted the Champions cared. Given their expressions, it would be lucky if they believed it.

Sigfrid blinked rapidly.

Maria recovered first. "You killed Lord Silverstrike?"

"Yes—"

"Impossible," said Sigfrid. "No Ascendant can defeat a Lord."

"That's hardly the point," said Holt. "Didn't you hear? Silas betrayed the Order. And there is far worse out there. That's the news you need to take back to Falcaer and then to every other Order Hall."

"Holt…" Talia moaned, but he pressed on.

"You can sense the wild dragons out there," he said. "You can certainly feel the West Warden nearby, even if the Life Elder is too far out. It sounds incredible, but that's because it is. You'd see the truth of it if you flew to the Crag, but that will only waste time."

Sigfrid pinched the bridge of his nose and turned away.

Maria stepped closer. "Very well, Ascendants. I am prepared to believe your tale – *for now*. There are mystics back at Falcaer who will discern the truth of your words in any case. You will come with us now if your branch has really been destroyed."

Neither Holt nor Talia moved.

"That's an order," Maria said.

"I cannot follow," Talia said, and Holt noted she had dropped any honorific for the rider, as a monarch would. "I am no longer a part of the Order."

"And I never officially joined," said Holt.

Maria focused on Holt first. "Of course. Well, a Champion is here before you now. Swear the oath to me."

"I won't be joining."

It was Talia rather than the Champions who rounded on him first, though her tone was level. "Is this truly what you've decided?"

He nodded. "I told you what the Elder said. This is what Ash and I must do."

Sigfrid found his voice and rushed forward. "You must swear the oath, boy. Bad enough that a thief should go unpunished, but there is no alternative."

"You can let me go," said Holt.

Sigfrid scowled and dropped his voice. "You may think yourself safe here as our dragons will answer to this wild emerald, but my blade bites just as deep as their teeth. If you refuse to join the Order, then you declare yourself a rogue rider, boy, and shall suffer the full justice of Falcaer here and now."

"No, he won't suffer your justice," said Talia. "Not while he is under the protection of the monarch."

"Your King Leofric has no say over rider business," Sigfrid said.

"But this is not rider business," said Talia. "Holt has not taken the oath. That makes him subject still to the laws of the realm, as a regular citizen."

"Foolish girl," Maria said. "Your court will declare him in breach of rank and banish him. He'll be nameless. Your King Leofric will not oppose that."

"My brother may not have," Talia said, "but Holt is not yet banished under my rule."

The Champions' expressions passed from frustration to confusion.

"Speak plainly, girl," Sigfrid said.

"Sigfrid..." Maria said slowly, a look of dawning comprehension bulging her eyes. "Her name sounded familiar to me. Talia... Talia..."

"Agravain," Talia supplied for her.

Sigfrid also caught up to his companion's realization. "The royal that Denna let in?"

"That's right," said Talia. "My brother was murdered during the recent troubles. And my uncle has gone missing. The curia elected me to inherit in his place. So, I say again, as Holt has refused to join the Order, this makes him one of my citizens. And I say he is under my protection. The Order would not wish to act in direct defiance of a monarch, would they? I doubt the courts of Brenin or Risalia or the assemblies of the Free Cities would be pleased to hear that the Order openly defied my rule, especially when frustration with the Order grows in every realm."

It was a fine bit of legalese, and all Sigfrid could do was point a long finger at Talia.

"You are the queen here, now?"

"Well, I am yet to have my coronation, but for all intents and purposes I am the queen."

Sigfrid barked in laughter. "Very well. Very well!" He strode off for his blue dragon.

Maria lingered. "You are correct, Talia Agravain. But I foresee as much trouble from those rulers accepting your ascension to the throne as we have in this boy going free. There are reasons that things are the way that they are."

"We're making some changes here," Talia said.

Maria smiled, though it was not pleasant. "Outside of Feorlen, your friend will still be a rogue rider. No other court shall dare to shelter him as you do." She too turned and marched toward her storm dragon.

"Will you report all you've heard to the Order?" Talia called after them. "About Silas, about the dragon called Sovereign who controls the scourge against us?"

They both laughed.

"We shall report all we've heard and seen to the Paragons," Sigfrid said. "That a thief has got free with a damaged dragon and an oath breaker now sits on Feorlen's throne. And that she killed the great Silas Silverstrike as well."

"Please listen," Talia said, "the incursion we faced was better coordinated than anything the Order has faced before. Worse will come. This was only the beginning."

"Of course," Sigfrid said. "What else was it? An evil dragon leading the scourge, controlling the minds of people from afar. A blind dragon with the power to cure the blight and what else? Flying pigs? Perhaps a goose which lays golden eggs?" He gave them a final, disgusted look, then took off.

Maria did not follow immediately but gave Talia a final withering look. "Good luck to you, Talia Agravain. I hope for your sake and for Feorlen you made the right choice." With that, she too took off.

Holt watched them fly east. So, he would have trouble in other lands. What was unexpected about that?

"Thanks for sticking up for me there," he said. "Good thing everyone forgot about my banishment."

"Yes indeed," she said, not quite meeting his eye. "Well, it's done now. It was inevitable the Order would find out. The only thing left to decide is when you'll go."

Holt considered it. What were they waiting for?

"We can leave tomorrow."

"You can stay as long as you like," she hastened to say.

"Tomorrow," Holt said firmly. "Better just to go, I think."

Talia nodded. "That may be for the best. I'd like to say goodbye properly. Don't you dare slink off in the night."

"I won't. I'll wait for you here tomorrow at dusk."

# 62

# FAREWELLS

Dusk settled over the hill east of Sidastra. For those in the city, the day would be winding down, but for Holt it had just begun.

He stood side by side with Ash, one hand running absentmindedly down the dragon's side. Having had time to observe Ash without running or fighting for their lives, Holt was confident that the dragon's growth had slowed. Given what Brode had theorized about it, that might only be a good thing. Now the extreme danger had passed, Ash could develop normally. Or so Holt hoped.

Ash remained lean and scrappy for a dragon no matter how much they fed him. Not that he could judge. Strong he might be himself now, his clothes still hung from his own wiry frame as they always had. He just wore finer cloth now.

They had packed light: a sleeping roll, a simple whetstone, flint and a supply of tinder, one pot, one pan, and other basic cooking supplies. A special case had been made to bring herbs and spices that might best suit venison or other game he wished to test on Ash – bay leaves, juniper berries, rosemary, aromatic savory, and sweet marjoram. And he had brought extra salt. He was *not* going to be caught cooking without salt. And, of course, he had the recipe book. That he would ensure made it everywhere, even through the flames of the Fire Flight's domain if needed.

He was ready. Only the question of where to go remained.

Shortly after the light began to fade, Pyra circled overhead and landed to join them. Talia got down, holding packages of her own as though she had decided to travel with him. The shape and size of one made its contents clear, but the smaller one was more intriguing. Without a word, she unwrapped the smaller one first, revealing a simple lockbox, and she held it before her with some reverence.

"I can't come with you, but... if you have time on your way to wherever it is..."

"I'll make time," Holt said, realizing what this was. He took Brode's remains as delicately as if he were holding a newborn. Talia handed over the key next, already on a chain, which Holt slung over his neck. "Ash and I will find the place."

She brought over the other sword-like bundle. Sure enough, it was Brode's green blade.

"Take it," she said.

Holt reached out for it, but his fingers fumbled.

"Go on," she urged. "It will serve you better than a normal sword, even if it's not attuned to lunar magic. I don't see how else you'll get a blade of your own without joining the Order."

Holt took it. It was much longer than a normal sword, so he would have to get used to its reach, but Talia was right. He wouldn't have to worry about sharpening this, nor was it likely to break even if he sliced through an abomination.

"He'd probably groan at the thought of me clumsily handling it."

Talia grunted in such a good impersonation of Brode's old bark that he couldn't help but grin.

"Thank you, Talia. I wish I could stay, but this is so important, and we'll visit if we can..." He trailed off as guilt and pity suddenly welled on her face. "What's the matter?"

"I... Holt..." She trailed off as Pyra rumbled, and Holt assumed some words passed between them. Talia breathed hard, then faced him again with a resolved if guilty expression. "You can't come back. Once you leave Feorlen, that's it. At least for now."

An icy feeling crept up his spine. "What do you mean?"

"I had to uphold your banishment," she said. "The curia insisted on it. They didn't want to invite further unrest by having you go unpunished."

"So, what you said to those Champions—"

"Was true," she hastened to say, "when I told them. Once I found out you were leaving, I managed to get the curia to hold off until you left. But once you go—"

He raised a hand. "I understand." And he did. The news did not impact him like it should. Perhaps it was because he was leaving anyway, perhaps it was because his old life was quickly becoming some distant memory, a version of himself he hardly recognized, standing over a basin scrubbing dishes.

The dragon bond thumped in his soul. *"Are you sad, boy?"*

"I'm fine," he said, patting the dragon down. "I suppose I am just Holt, now. But I'll always be a Cook at heart."

"And a rider," Talia said.

He nodded. "A dragon rider and a Cook."

"I'm certain I can have it revoked eventually," she said fiercely. "It will just take time."

"Let's make it through the coming years first. I'm sure you'll be a good queen. And I'll send word of your uncle if I come across anything."

"Thank you."

He gulped. This was turning out to be a lot harder than he had anticipated. "It would be better if you could come with us."

"It would be better if you could stay."

There seemed nothing left to do but hug her, and so the commoner embraced the queen. Both outcasts from the Order. Both bringing chaos in their way, but both knowing they had made the right choices. Neither had regrets.

"Goodbye, princess."

"Goodbye, pot boy."

She sniffed and did something he hadn't been prepared for. She kissed him lightly on the cheek. As she pulled away, Holt felt the spot burn, though that might have been his skin flushing bright red.

Quickly he made for Pyra next.

"Didn't think we'd leave without embarrassing you, did you?" He wrapped his arms around the purple dragon's neck. Pyra's throat rumbled with heat and laughter, and her long neck snaked down around him.

*"Farewell, little one. I shall miss your cooking."*

Ash said his goodbyes next. He allowed Talia to hug him then padded over to Pyra, who nipped him affectionately on the snout. The two dragons then pressed their heads together, rippled their wings, and swept their tails across the grass.

Talia jumped up onto Pyr,a and with a final roar and a wave, they took off west, heading back to their city.

Holt allowed himself a moment before he strapped Brode's sword onto his back, secured the lockbox into his pack, then mounted Ash.

"At least we have somewhere to start."

*"We owe it to Brode to honor his memory."*

Holt recited again the vague details of where Brode had buried Erdra. "A lonely hill on the road east from Athra."

He had no concept of how far that was. East of Athra was a lot of land to cover.

*"So long as we're together, I won't be afraid."*

"Same. You ready?"

*"Ready."*

"My eyes for your eyes."

*"Your skin for my skin."*

"My world for your world," they said together.

And with the dying light behind them, they took off. A pot boy and his dragon with the world before them, with all its dangers and all its wonders. A great weight had been placed on their shoulders, but it was a burden they could carry together.

# AFTERWORD

## Please Review

Thank you for reading *Ascendant*! This was the hardest book I've ever written for a host of reasons, but I'm really pleased with how it turned out. If you enjoyed it, please consider leaving me a review on Amazon or Goodreads. It need not be long, only a couple of lines. Reviews are incredibly helpful in getting Amazon to recommend the book to new readers.

## Keep in touch!

If you'd like to read more about this world you can get a FREE novella about Brode and his mission with Silas that went so terribly wrong by signing up to my mailing list at https://www.michaelrmiller.co.uk/signup

Just pop in your email, and the stories will be sent to you. Once you're on my newsletter, you'll also get updates on future books in the series as well as promotions and giveaways,

Of the social media channels I am most active on Discord and you can join the server here: https://discord.gg/C7zEJXgFSc

Other links below:
Facebook: https://www.facebook.com/michaelrmillerauthor
Reddit: r/MichaelRMiller
Twitter: @MMDragons_Blade

**Signed Hardback Editions**

Signed Hardback Editions of Songs of Chaos are now available from The Broken Binding bookstore.

Once again, thank you for reading Ascendant!
   Michael R. Miller

# ACKNOWLEDGMENTS

This project has taken me longer to complete than any other, 18 months as opposed to 12. This is not the place to discuss in full why that is, but one reason was the book's ever-evolving nature.

When writing my first series – *The Dragon's Blade* – I had the fortune of a lifetime's worth of musings and planning at my fingertips. I knew the world and the characters within it. *Ascendant* was not the first book I wrote after finishing *Dragon's Blade* – that was *Battle Spire* – but it was the first that demanded a similar depth to its world-building. And most important to *Ascendant* was its magic system.

Dragon rider magic systems are notoriously hard, I think. It seems evident that the dragon must be the power of the pair, otherwise humans would not necessarily partner with them, and yet if the dragon is the one with the power, why would they ever need the human rider? My personal preference for magic in fantasy is for it to have hard rules. Before me lay the task of creating a robust magic system that felt natural but also allowed a true partnership between dragon and human to flourish. For whatever reason, this was the most challenging element.

In helping me finesse the system that eventually matured in *Ascendant*, I'd like to thank Taran Matharu (author of the *Summoner* series and *The Chosen*) and Brook Aspden (author of *Gamified*) for their constant feedback and thoughts as the book developed. A very special thank you goes out to Will Wight, author of the *Cradle* series. I'm sure many of you reading this have also read at least some of *Cradle*. By chance, my system of the dragon core and motes of magic was in there half-baked in an early draft, but reading *Cradle* gave me great inspiration on how to refine the system. I had the chance to meet Will in person in the summer of 2019, and he could not have been more supportive of what I was trying to do. Thanks, Will!

That meeting was part of a much larger meet-up of indie fantasy authors hosted by the exceedingly generous Michael J. Sullivan (author of *The Riyria Revelations*) and his wife Robin. There, a group of authors known – for reasons we can't quite remember – as the Terrible Ten met up to discuss books, publishing, writing and splash around in the pool. A huge thank you to the TT10 for all the support that group has given over the years, and here's to many more!

Further thanks go out to the alpha readers who read the first completed draft of the book and offered invaluable feedback. They include my parents Walter and Linda Miller, my sister Rachael, fellow author Alex Knight (author of *Nova Online*), Brook Aspden, and soon-to-be writing superstar Neil Atkinson (just finish something man!). Without your help, the book would not be as polished as it is now.

Thank you to Jonathan Oliver, who battled with my awful consistency and grammar during copy edits. A second major thank you to Anthony Wright who gave the proof a fresh proofread and second set of eyes in 2022. Appreciation is also due to the following advanced readers who caught numerous other typos, inconsistencies, and other small errors prior to first publication: Kebus Maximus, Casie Powers, Dakota Heath, Judith Dickinson, and Lana Turner. A very special thank you in this regard goes out to Adele Leach, who sent me the most comprehensive feedback document I've ever seen from a reader. And then she did another round! Adele, your work ethic was astounding for something supposed to be fun! Finally, thank you to John Bierce (author of the *Mage Errant* series) for catching a rather clumsy mistake regarding lunar motes.

An enormous thank you to Raph Lomotan, who provided the initial cover art and wrap. That first full wrap illustration, a scene of the Battle of Sidastra at night with both Holt and Talia, can be found on my website. The time and effort he spent to get the design of Ash exactly right was exceptional. Raph also provided the art for the Brode novella *The Last Stand of the Stone Fist* and captured the vision I had for rider armor perfectly.

The original artwork was changed in late 2020 as the darkness of the nighttime scene didn't work when shrunk into a smaller image on Amazon. The fault for this lay in my conception of the art and not in the art itself. The current bright cover of *Ascendant* featuring a hazy orange landscape and a much larger image of Ash was drawn by Yigit Koroglu. I cannot praise Yigit enough for taking the courage to take charge of the pose of the characters. He knew what was best and produced a stunning piece of work.

Thank you also to the wonderful Peter Kenny for his awesome narration. In one of those surreal career moments I never anticipated, I went from watching *The Witcher* on Netflix, to listening to the audio-books, to then working with that same narrator and hearing the same voice bring *Ascendant* to life.

Throughout the course of writing this book, I suffered some periods of serious ill health, including hospital stays. This, coupled with COVID and the ever-mounting commitments of my publishing company, might have been overwhelming. Luckily for me, I have people around me who will help if I need it. I'm always grateful – I am, really, even if I don't always show it guys! – for the stalwart support of my parents, friends, and partner Pegah, who is always there to cheer me on and pick me up when I'm down.

And as always, thank *you* for reading. Cheesy as it is to say, without the readers this would not be possible. For fans of *The Drag-on's Blade* who came over to *Ascendant,* I am especially grateful that you've taken the leap of faith to follow me on a new adventure. It's crazy to think that I make stories up about dragons and magic for a living, and it's you all who make this dream job a reality.

9 781913 695323